Edward Kennard

The Right Sort

A romance of the shires

Edward Kennard

The Right Sort
A romance of the shires

ISBN/EAN: 9783337345051

Printed in Europe, USA, Canada, Australia, Japan

Cover: Foto ©Andreas Hilbeck / pixelio.de

More available books at **www.hansebooks.com**

THE RIGHT SORT

A Romance of the Shires

BY

Mrs. EDWARD KENNARD.

ILLUSTRATED BY
EDGAR GIBERNE.

WARD, LOCK & CO.
LONDON: WARWICK HOUSE, SALISBURY SQUARE, E.C.
NEW YORK: BOND STREET.

CONTENTS.

LIST OF ILLUSTRATIONS.

THE RIGHT SORT.

CHAPTER I.

" LISTEN to this, Mary. It's the very thing !" exclaimed a young lady, who, while sipping a cup of tea at the breakfast-table, was engaged in carefully poring over the advertisement sheets of the *Field* with an air of profound interest.

The speaker, without any absolute claim to regular beauty, was a decidedly good-looking girl, with the air of freshness. health, and rosiness that, accompanied by youth, have an unfailing power to please. Her small head was covered by thick glossy brown hair ; the broad, thoughtful brow gave evidence of a considerable amount of natural intelligence ; the eyebrows were dark and delicately arched ; while the eyes which sparkled and flashed beneath them constituted the principal charm of an interesting countenance. They were dark grey, fringed by the longest of lashes, and looked you straight in the face with such a candid, innocent expression, such resolute, fearless honesty, that they seemed to mirror the soul within, sufficing to prepossess the ordinary observer, and to instil a belief in the integrity of their owner. A slim shapely figure completed the sum total of Kate Browser's attractions.

B

"What's the very thing, Kate?" asked her companion, a gentle, fair-haired, low-voiced girl of about eight-and-twenty, roused to display symptoms of lively curiosity by the other's ejaculation. "Have you at length found this celebrated hunting-box we have heard so much about lately, or is your imagination soaring to yet higher flights, and contemplating a deer-forest in the wilds of Scotland for the ensuing autumn?"

"No, no," replied Kate with a light laugh. "I'm scarcely advanced enough yet in my sporting proclivities to be able to shoulder a rifle. Somehow the slaughter of the stag possesses no attraction for me, but, as regards the hunting-box, if all advertisements were not such abominable cheats and delusions, if they did not convert every tumbledown cottage into a commodious mansion replete with modern conveniences, every wretched little two-acred field into an undulating and well-timbered park, every dilapidated outhouse into a substantial stone building, and every miserable evergreen into a thriving shrubbery; in short, if it were possible to believe in any*thing* or any*body* in this wicked world of ours, I should be greatly tempted to declare that I *had* found what I wanted; but alas! though young in years, it is my misfortune to be old in experience, and experience has taught caution, distrust, and suspicion."

And the girl shrugged her shapely shoulders with a gesture of unbelief so hopelessly cynical that it verged on the ludicrous.

"Come, come, Kate!" returned Mary Whitbread remonstratingly. "While you have been amusing yourself by a sweeping condemnation of advertisements in general, please to remember that I remain in a state of Egyptian darkness as to this one in particular. Won't you take pity on my ignorance and deign to enlighten it? At present I feel thoroughly mystified."

"Really? Then I will proceed at once to do away with the mystery, if mystery there be. But," she went on in tones of mock despair, "although, as before remarked, the advertisement in question *sounds* the very thing, I am much too sceptical to be really sanguine."

Whereupon Miss Brewser, once more taking up the newspaper from the table, proceeded in a clear and distinct voice to read as follows:—

"'To be let, for the winter months, or by the year, as agreed upon, a most perfect, commodious, and well-arranged hunting-box, late in the possession of Reginald Rich, Esq., known by the name of Sport Lodge, and within three-quarters of a mile of the market-town of Foxington, in the county of Huntingshire. The residence is replete with every convenience, and the stabling, which has just been put into thorough repair, is unexceptionally good, consisting of six loose-boxes, four stalls, double coach-house, wash-house, and excellent accommodation for the men. The Critchley, the Scottesmore, and Sir Beauchamp Lenard's hounds hunt the immediate neighbourhood, while the Horn, the Lever, and the South Garrick are easily attainable by rail. For particulars and cards to view apply to Messrs. Fulton, Brown, and Son, estate agents and auctioneers, Foxington.'"

"There, Mary! What do you think of that?" exclaimed Kate, as she came to a conclusion, looking up with an air of prospective ownership, already strongly visible in spite of her vaunted prudence. "Does not that sound everything the heart of hunting man or woman could desire?"

"It sounds too good, almost," suggested the cautious Mary, who, less talkative, and with fewer theories, was in some ways more practical than her friend. "The number of packs of hounds is positively overwhelming. If so inclined, you could apparently hunt every day of the week. Despite such attractions, there is, however, one thing I emphatically protest against—at least so far as you and I are concerned."

"And what might that be, dear Miss Propriety? Some social hesitations, I suppose, as usual?"

"Well, to tell you the truth, Kate, it's the name. I call it positively dreadful. Indeed, I can't conceive any one in their senses bestowing such a heathenish, outlandish title upon a dwelling-place. No doubt Mr. Reginald Rich and gentlemen of his calibre may have found Sport Lodge eminently suited to their peculiar propensities; but fancy **two** respectable young women, like ourselves, guiltless of all male belongings, going to live in such an abode! What *would* the world say of us? Ugh! there is something horsey and fast and utterly disreputable in the very nomenclature! Does not *Sport Lodge* conjure up all sorts of bachelor extravagance to the mind? Can't you smell brandies and sodas in the air, a fine aroma of stale tobacco in every habitable room; in short, spirits and pipes impregnating the entire atmosphere with their nauseous fumes? Oh! I can imagine it so well! A small square drawing-room, with hermetically sealed windows, a dirty dingy carpet, fusty red or green rep curtains, an arm-chair or two, covered in a hideous chintz, with the inevitable wool antimacassars of every colour under the sun. Come, Kate, you must confess my sketch of a bachelor apartment is not far out on the whole."

"I confess no such thing. Besides which my imagination is not so lively nor my olfactory organs so sensitive as your own. We have only to show ourselves proof against the insiduous attractions of a "B and S," or calumet of peace, in order to render poor Sport Lodge absolutely harm-less. Now to show how tastes differ, I, for my part, consider there is something quaint and original about Sport Lodge—something a trifle removed from the everlasting common-places of everyday life. I am quite sick of Mount Pleas-ants, Hermitages, Bellevues, etcetera, etcetera. The same-ness and monotony about such names wearies me extremely, especially when in nine cases out of ten the misnomer is palpable to the most indulgent eyes. If only for the sake of variety, I welcome Sport Lodge as a positive relief, and Mr. Reginald Rich, instead of being abused, deserves a fair meed of praise as a daring and original innovator; and both courage and originality, in this prosaic age, are qualities entitled to the highest respect."

"Why, Kate," interposed Mary, smiling in spite of her inward convictions at the dexterity of the other's argument, " what a funny girl you are, to be sure! You talk like a regular old grandmother; nevertheless I am far from being convinced, and stick to my assertion that Sport Lodge sounds decidedly fast, and the chances are if we go to live there the greater portion of the community will pronounce a similar verdict upon you and me."

"And what if they do? Do you suppose *I* care what people say?" retorted Kate contemptuously. "Let them make what ill-natured remarks they like."

This was all very well in theory, Kate Brewser having not yet arrived at an age to recognise what a tyrannical mentor the world is—what a harsh, uncharitable, fault-finding, scandal-loving taskmaster; but the criticisms, if made, would probably have caused the young lady a considerable amount of vexation.

"People situated as I am can't expect to escape tittle-tattle in some form or other," she continued loftily. "I know perfectly well how every woman who hunts is condemned beforehand. She is dubbed masculine and unfeminine, while nearly every man she comes across congratulates himself in his heart of hearts that *his* wife, *his* sister, *his* womanly belongings do not join in the pursuit, but are content to sit at home stitching their eyes out over a piece of trumpery fancy needlework, tinkling the last new waltz upon the piano, or enfeebling their mental faculties by the perusal of worthless and highly sensational novels. Do not the vast majority of men and women fail to see because a girl is high-spirited and independent, she need not necessarily be lacking all feminine attributes, and because she can put a horse fairly well at a fence, is fond of sport, and all honest, healthy, outdoor pastimes, it does not by any means follow that she has unsexed herself and laid all womanhood aside. If I speak warmly it is because I *feel* warmly on this subject. Now, according to my notions, the pursuit of the fox calls forth, firstly, courage; secondly, cool judgment; thirdly, presence of mind, and that sort of independence which teaches a person to rely upon him or herself alone. Will any one deny the excellence of such qualities? A woman who hunts, and who hunts well, is not likely to scream and faint away like a log directly any accident occurs—will not talk, but act—not hinder, but help —not lose her head at trifles, but in every emergency has all her wits about her, and, if necessary, is calculated to steer her own course with tolerable coolness and dexterity through the varied shoals of life."

"Moral. No man, therefore, ought to marry unless the lady of his choice be qualified to scamper over fences at the risk of life and limb. According to your theory, Kate, I'm afraid my chances of matrimony are well-nigh nil. A fireside and a cat comprise my future prospects."

"Don't forget the man," interrupted Kate playfully. "You are one of those sweet, yielding individuals who could never encounter the world without masculine assistance and support. But to return to the subject under discussion. If we *really* go to Sport Lodge, I'll tell you what I'll do. I'll stick a large placard on my back, and print on it in enormous letters, 'Beware. I'm a most improper young person; I *hunt.*' *That* ought to satisfy everyone's scruples."

"Kate, Kate, you are incorrigible!" laughed Mary Whitbread. "Argument becomes impossible when opposed to such levity. But seriously, don't you think you are going ahead just a little bit too fast? You seem to have decided straight away that Sport Lodge is to be our future destination. Under these circumstances it is useless my entering any further protest. Nevertheless, I fear you may be disappointed."

"Well," said Kate, "it's a funny thing, but somehow or other I have a curious presentiment, too strong to be accounted for, that Sport Lodge will see us this winter. You know, Mary, what a fancy I've always had for going to that part of the world and seeing some first-rate hunting. An overwhelming desire possesses me to behold a bonâ fide Huntingshire oxer and a genuine blackthorn bullfinch. You don't hunt or care for the sport, and wonder often at what you term my enthusiasm; but I tell you, you miss *one* of the greatest, if not *the greatest*, pleasures in life by not doing so. It is a simply glorious sensation, mounted on the back of a thorough good horse, to go bounding over each intervening obstacle. At every fence left behind, every easy sweeping stride, the spirit rises. The blood warms in the

veins, a delicious glow of pleasurable excitement, intensified
by the element of danger, pervades the whole frame, you
set your teeth, cram your hat on your head, forget every
care in the world, and, intoxicated with the brief transport
of present joy, ride like," pausing breathless in search of a
suitable metaphor, "like old Harry. There is nothing in
the world to compare with it."

"It strikes me *your* hobby-horse runs away with its mistress
altogether," observed Mary Whitbread with a species of semi-
indulgent sarcasm.

"Ah! you should hear Captain Fitzgerald on the subject
of hunting," continued Kate, now thoroughly roused. "You
know he has hunted everywhere—Cheshire, Gloucestershire,
Ireland, the Vale, Bicester, &c., &c.—and he says that for a
real good all-round sporting country, with wild, straight-
running foxes; for the finest grass and fairest flying fences
in England; for a steady workmanlike pack of hounds, who
can both hunt their fox in the good old style, sticking to him
with patience and perseverance, and yet go the pace when
required, whose noses, speed, dash, and stoutness are undeniable; and for a huntsman who never turns his head from
mortal thing, who has the eye of a hawk, the seat of a
centaur, and the heart of a lion—give him the Critchley!"
And Kate, as she finished speaking, looked up with the light
of a thorough enthusiast shining in her great grey eyes, and
her whole face sparkling with that animation and joyous
belief in the good things of the future which is one of the
most precious attributes of youth and, it must be added, inexperience. She could depict to herself the delights of safely
negotiating the most formidable obstacles, but the reverse
side of the picture—the tumbles, the vexations, the accidents,
and the broken bones—never found even the smallest
dwelling-place in her imagination.

CHAPTER II.

THE DIE IS CAST.

"Oh! So that is Captain Fitzgerald's experience, is it?" returned Mary. "Poor little man! I am not particularly fond of him, but doubtless he took his dismissal to heart, and retired quite as much discomfited as the majority of Miss Brewser's admirers."

At this speech of Mary's Miss Brewser reddened perceptibly. She had indeed, a short time ago, refused the gallant Captain, but was not aware that her friend had discovered the fact. Now, however, it appeared useless to attempt denial.

"Miss Brewser's admirers have a bad time of it," she observed demurely.

"That state of things may not endure for ever," said Mary.

"Yes it will. The fact is, I don't seem to care about men. They bore me, after a certain point is reached. They are all very well to talk to and sharpen one's wits upon, but my predilections end there. There are exceptions, of course, to every rule, but the majority of the young men I come across are a weak, selfish, and luxurious lot, living only to gratify their own tastes and their own inclinations. Pleasure, not duty or honest wholesome work, is the goal of their aspirations, the aim and object of lives which are frivolous and commonplace. When they contemplate matrimony they do not consider or seek the welfare of the girl, but their own. 'How much money has she? How much can she contribute to our ease, how little detract from our requirements?' These appear to me the principal ideas permeating their brains. Now I happen to be particularly happy and comfortable as I am, and therfore require great inducements to effect any change in my position. Seriously, Mary, it seems to me there is little or none of the old heroic spirit left nowadays. The spirit that breathed in such men as Raleigh, Sir Richard Grenfell, Cook, Columbus; the intrepidity, the restless craving for distinction which in those times impelled men to action ; the chivalry, the stern sense of honour, accompanied by that bulldog pluck and capacity for fighting which made England's name what it was—seem slowly fading away, absorbed by the luxury and effeminacy of an ever-increasing civilisation. The free nomadic spirit that taught us to be self-reliant and self-dependent is dying out, giving place to a fatal ease and slothfulness. Instead of being able to shift for themselves, ladies and gentlemen in these days require constant waiting upon and attendance. They cannot do without their valets and their ladies' maids. Mentally and physically they are little better than big, grown-up babies."

" True wisdom, to my mind, consists in making the best of things as they are," remarked Mary, to whom Kate's strivings after an ideal perfection appeared highly chimerical. " You and I can't alter the world by grumbling at it, and I dare say people are not more degenerate nowadays than formerly. As for Captain Fitzgerald, he is no worse than his neighbours, and I must say you are altogether too hard on his sex."

" Am I ? I think not. I fail to see why Captain Fitzgerald should be considered an object worthy my pity. He is far too fond of number one ever to care for anybody else as much as he does for that all-important personage, and, according to my old-fashioned, or perhaps romantic, notions, when a man marries, his wife ought to occupy the foremost place in his thoughts. Now, Captain Fitzgerald simply looked upon me as a harmless, inoffensive sort of girl, who, as she possessed a satisfactory number of thousands a year, justified him in disposing of his dapper, divinely tailored person, soft drooping moustache, curly eyelashes, and killing blue eyes in the matrimonial market, thinking by so doing to gain some material advantage. No doubt, had I been a

properly minded young person I should have perceived and
been duly grateful for the vast honour thus conferred. As it
was, my perverse disposition made me look upon the whole
affair in the light of an ordinary bargain, into which neither
affection, mutual respect, or esteem were allowed to enter,
being regarded as entirely superfluous. Well, the bargain
did not suit me, and nothing more remained to be said. No
doubt my taste was lamentably bad. Nevertheless, the fact
remained. Had I been a Hottentot Venus, with a sufficient
number of money-bags hanging round my waist, Captain
Fitzgerald would have proposed just the same. I, as an
individual, had nothing to do with the offer, lucre alone
being the attraction. You may say I ought not to think such
things, but how can I help doing so when they are so self-
evident? I can't go through the world with my eyes shut,
and in keeping them open they are apt to see too clearly.
And, in my opinion, a man who seeks a woman for the
sake of her fortune, and strives to shelter himself at her
expense, is lucky if he escape without incurring her deep
contempt."

And Kate, recalling the discomfited guardsman's amazement and incredulity, and the utter bewilderment with which
he had received his congé, laughed a bitter little laugh that
sounded strangely from the fresh young lips.

"Now, Kate, it is my turn to be angry," said Mary
Whitbread, who had listened to this oration with symptoms
of marked disapproval, rendered still more conspicuous
when the lords of creation were under sweeping condemnation. "After all, there is good in everybody, and often we
only are to blame for not discovering the merits of others.
I am quite sure if we were as keen to do so as we are to
pick holes, the world would be a much pleasanter place
than it is. Now you, individually, have worked yourself up
into the absurd belief that, because you happen to be an
heiress possessed of a handsome fortune and good yearly
income, nobody will ever care for your own self, just as if
you were some horrid old frump, instead of a—well, never
mind what; it won't do to make you too conceited. Anyhow,

such a notion is preposterous, and if you go on encouraging these foolish ideas, your money, instead of proving a blessing, will end by being nothing but a curse. Your belief in human nature will grow weaker and weaker, disinterested affection appear an impossibility, until finally the crown will be set on this happy state of things by your driving from your side some straightforward and honest fellow who loves you dearly, and which sentiment in your heart of hearts you reciprocate. Oh, Kate! take warning in time."

Mary Whitbread spoke with such unusual earnestness that, in spite of herself, Kate felt moved.

"When that extraordinary occurrence comes about," she answered, with a half-incredulous sigh, "either somebody falling genuinely in love with me, or me falling genuinely in love with somebody, I'll give you due notice of the fact, Mary. In the meantime, all I can say is, such a contingency appears highly remote, and I am perfectly content to remain in my present state of spinsterhood. As you know, I like my own way, and, what's more, am used to having it; and I often think it would require an immense amount of devotion to render me amenable to the dictates of a husband. No, no; depend upon it I am better as I am. But, Mary, since you plead so speciously in favour of matrimony, and give such sage advice, I am more than half inclined to believe you yourself are harbouring some romantic absurdity. Come, make a clean breast of it, and confess on the spot."

"I have nothing to confess," said Mary, with evident truth, though the tell-tale blood rushed to her fair cheeks; for Kate's remark recalled the one solitary romance of her pure but uneventful life, when, in olden days, a certain long-legged, lank-haired, narrow-shouldered, telescope-necked curate had lain himself—not his fortune, for he had none, but just himself—at her feet, and sworn undying, unalterable affection. The episcopalian demonstration had been nipped in the bud, nipped before the poor fragile blossom had had time to expand in the sunlight of answering love. Mary's father, since dead, was a practical man, who promptly dismissed the idea of bliss in a cottage on twopence a year as a lunatic hallucination bordering on downright madness. The unfortunate wooer, though ardent in the face of opposition, became timorous and blighted, and after a melancholy interview, during which tears were freely shed on either side, took a long and last farewell of his innamorata. But the gentle Mary, having once tasted the sweetness and known the importance of being considered a Dulcinea in a pair of masculine eyes, continued to cherish sentimental recollections of the past, which, united to a species of vague indulgence towards the opposite sex, rendered her consciously, though modestly, hopeful of a future time when some other candidate might step forward and ask her to become the sharer of his joys and partner of his life.

"Why, Mary, you are blushing! positively blushing!" exclaimed Kate in mischievous glee. "You dreadful little hypocrite. I am more confirmed than ever in my opinion that you have a sneaking sort of hankering after a dual existence. Fie, for shame! What sentimental follies are you cherishing in that foolish head?"

So saying, Kate, in an unusually tender mood, put her arm round Mary Whitbread's neck, and kissed the sweet pale face held up to her own.

The conversation somehow seemed to have affected them both, for there was a tear glistening in Mary's eye as she said—

"Oh, Kate! how can I ever thank you for all your kindness?"

"By not making the smallest allusion to it. But now, instead of talking any more nonsense, let us return to the subject of Sport Lodge, from which we have indeed wandered far. If you will consent to waive your objection to its unfortunate name, I had better sit down at once and write to Messrs. Brown, Fulton, and Son."

"I do not think my objection—as you call it—was really formidable, Kate. It was made more in fun than in earnest."

"Bravo. You funny little person! You quite took me in by the gravity with which you protested. However, all's well that ends well You have had your say and I mine;

therefore we both feel considerably relieved. Some of my ideas are rather crude, no doubt, and it is a good thing for me, your putting an occasional check upon them. As it is, we argue and wrangle until between us we manage to strike upon a vein of tolerably good common-sense. So now for the famous letter."

Whereupon Kate Brewser sat down to write to Messrs. Brown, Fulton, and Son at Foxington, after the fashion of her sex, demanding every possible and impossible particular concerning Sport Lodge, and specifying a certain day, in the event of a favourable reply, on which it would please her majesty to run down and personally inspect the premises before taking the residence on lease, for on that point her mind was quite made up. She intended to devote the forth-coming winter to the pursuit of the fox, and for carrying out such an intention, what place could possibly be more convenient, handy, and suitable than the famous Foxington, celebrated from time immemorial in all annals of the chase?

CHAPTER III.

KATE BREWSER'S ANTECEDENTS.

KATE BREWSER, as already intimated, was an heiress—a good, solid, bonâ fide heiress. None of your unfortunate land-endowed proprietors, whose tenants, in these days of radicalism, assassination, and agricultural collapse, give notice, politely or impolitely, as the case may be, of their inability to pay any rent; but a real unquestionable heiress, possessing an income of some six or seven thousands a year, invested principally in Consols and securities of a similar nature. Being an only child, it may naturally be inferred that Kate Brewser had inherited this large fortune from her parents. Such, however, was not the case. Colonel Brewser, who once commanded an infantry regiment, had served with great distinction during the Indian Mutiny, and gained for himself a character for courage and uprightness from all those with whom he came in contact. During the storming of Delhi, single-handed he had succeeded in keeping a dozen of the enemy at bay, and prevented their blowing up a large powder-magazine, and for this truly gallant defence was rewarded by the bestowal of the then-coveted distinction of the Victoria Cross, which in those days was more highly esteemed and less easily obtained than at present. Like many others of his profession, the honours thus received, however gratifying to Colonel Brewser's military pride, were not of a nature to replenish an always scanty purse. Glory was cheap and cost nothing, but substantial rewards were not for the men who had shed their life's blood and ruined their health in the service of so great a country as England.

Fêtes and banquets by the score were organised in honour of the sun-dried warriors, but money wherewith to enable them to withdraw from active service and "heal them of their grievous wounds" was not forthcoming. In Colonel Brewser's case worse results ensued; for too proud to solicit favours, too retiring of disposition to push his own interests when peace was proclaimed and the rebellion crushed, the War Office, by some singular fatality, overlooked his claims to promotion, and placed younger and less scrupulous men over the head of ·a veteran who knew what war was in deed not only in name. The disappointment was so great that Colonel Brewser never recovered from the blow thus inflicted. As he lived he died, a brave and fearless gentleman, rich in nothing but honour and truth, lacking oftentimes the humblest necessaries, and constantly struggling to make both ends meet.

His wife, whom he had married for a pretty face and a sweet temper, which, in spite of many trials, had enabled her to make their modest home a very happy one, after the birth of a son, who died in infancy, and of an only daughter—our heroine, Kate—seemed never to regain her strength, but faded slowly beneath the scorching sun of the Indian climate, like some pure and fragile lily, so slowly and so imperceptibly that not until death was imminent did the sorrow-stricken husband fully realise the situation. Then it seemed as if he no longer cared to exist without her he had loved so well, and after a year or two he too fell a victim to the grim pursuer of mankind. Thus it came to pass that at the early age of five Kate Brewser was left a well-nigh penniless orphan—a solitary fatherless and motherless child

Her only living relative happened to be an uncle on the paternal side, who many years before had set out for Australia, possessing at that time nothing but an eager, resolute spirit, a large share of ambition, and an excellent constitution, added to a fixed determination and powerful will to succeed in whatever he undertook—one of those steadfast, lion-hearted men who, fixing their eyes on a given goal, allow no petty interests or trivial amusements to divert them from their path, but whose whole thoughts ·and energies are concentrated on the object for which they labour. Slowly but surely Campbell Brewser, mounting one by one the rungs of the ladder, in course of time carved his way to fortune. Then, and not till then, when through incessant work his health began to give way before the magnitude of this self-imposed task, though the indomitable spirit of the man was still undaunted, he turned his face towards his native land—that glorious land of rugged hills and changing skies, of brown bracken, rushing streams, red heather, and keen mountain air ; where the cock grouse cackles to his mate, the wild red-deer sniffs the bracing breeze, and where such men as Campbell Brewser are born and given forth to the world—men cast in an iron mould—adventurous, shrewd, self-reliant, and self-confident in the highest sense of the word—formed alike by nature and by temperament to be the pioneers of every fresh enterprise, every hazardous undertaking ; men on whose broad and capable shoulders the burden of life sits fitly, and who, with that innate love of the beautiful land of their birth which in far-off climes clings to them like perfume to a flower, given out more strongly when the day is well-nigh o'er, return when the struggle is at an end, the battle won, to lay them down and die in the oft-remembered home of their youth— the home where they trotted about the winding burns, where they pressed the springy heather with their little bare red feet, where they fished and bird-nested, and where their mother, dead long since, breathed a nightly prayer over their innocent couch. Ah ! the man's heart must be cold indeed who can forget such early days, and who in his old age does not yearn to revisit the scenes of childhood.

With Campbell Brewser, as the years went by, the yearning became so intense that nothing short of fulfilment could appease the longings of his weary heart. And now, in her time of need, this man, whose lofty nature seemed to stand alone, who, though not despising, had never yet sought solace in a woman's love, took care of the little houseless orphan. He, who in his far-off home in the bush hardly knew the sound of a child's sweet shrill voice or sturdy pattering footsteps, in the autumn of life resolved to shield and protect the lonely creature, his own kith and kin, his niece, the daughter of the dead brother whose image he had never ceased to worship. He, too, was alone but for a nephew, his sister's orphan, whom he had adopted, for lack of any nearer relation on whom to pour out the wealth of affection that had so long lain dormant in his breast. Therefore Campbell Brewser, when he heard of his brother's death, immediately determined Kate should live with him and be his charge in the future. And as the years rolled on, the strong, resolute man, who in youth, when love should have come naturally, as it does to the birds and the beasts, had been too absorbed in physical labour to render any tender passion admissible, realised for the first time that a void had existed in his heart which this tiny creature filled.

This large-eyed, high-spirited, resolute, and fearless child, who in many ways so closely resembled himself, appealed to his better nature, teaching him softness and humility, sympathy and love, while in return he imparted to Kate much of that energy and force of character which had always rendered him conspicuous amongst his fellow-men, and which, added to an austere simplicity and innate nobility of disposition, commanded not only obedience but affection. Thus little Kate became the very apple of his eye, the poetry and romance of his declining years. It seemed as if a new element of brightness and refinement had entered into his hitherto somewhat prosaic life, tinging it with a golden light. To be with Kate was a perpetual source of wonder and of joy. It was enough for him to hear her innocent prattle, to watch the sudden illumination of her expressive countenance, and to endeavour to keep pace with the quick strange workings of her childish mind; its pleasures, its sorrows, its questionings, its simplicity and shrewdness, were all equally novel, equally charming and delightful. Not only did she become his playfellow and idol, but also his companion, for the child was unusually quick of comprehension, and clever beyond her years.

Kate fully reciprocated Campbell Brewser's affection, or rather idolatry She was never so happy as when with him.

and her chief delight consisted in endeavouring to induce him to narrate some of the adventures and stirring incidents of his Australian life.

An unerring instinct, possessed by all children and dumb animals, told her that, although outwardly rough, her uncle was good and true. Therefore, in her turn, she loved him with all the intensity of an ardent nature, with the reverence and hero-worship which are so inexpressibly beautiful in the young towards the old, when the youthful imagination is apt to exalt its object, perhaps even beyond its intrinsic merit.

The other inmate of this happy household, Herbert Munro, Mr. Brewser's nephew and reputed heir, was some five years Kate's senior. Yielding and pliant, easily led astray, full of good resolutions, but without the strength of character or moral energy requisite to put them into force, delicate both physically and mentally, it seemed as if the boy and girl should have changed places. Kate, with her strong vitality, keen intelligence, and unquestionable ambition, ought to have been the man; while Herbert, as a woman, would have made one of those dependent and trustful creatures who appeal insensibly to the masculine nature, and who are often preferred to their sturdier sisters.

In spite of such differences both of character and constitution, the cousins were excellent friends; but although Herbert possessed a considerable advantage in point of years, even in these early days he failed to assert his superiority. In all their pastimes and pursuits Kate invariably proved the leading spirit, hers the master mind; for she directed, patronised, and advised, while Herbert followed her with unquestioning obedience. He lacked that boyish confidence and roguish assumption of self-assertion, whose very impudence possesses an undoubted charm for the feminine mind, ever prone to worship the strength which so quickly establishes an ascendency over it.

Kate, at this time, was far too young to analyse such feelings. She only knew that when with Herbert she somehow always felt herself the most capable of the two, stronger, both bodily and intellectually, while in her uncle's presence it was exactly the reverse. At his side she was nothing but a weak little child, humble, ignorant, loving, eager in quest of knowledge, and realising with thankfulness the advantages derived from the protection she received.

She could never forget that had it not been for her uncle, and her uncle's care and affection, she might have been left utterly alone in the world. She had no fears, no doubts, no hesitations or distrust when Campbell Brewser was there. She believed in him as she believed in her God. In her eyes he was the best, the kindest, the cleverest, the nicest, and the most superior of human beings. Compared with him, Herbert appeared a weakling and a nonentity; besides which, poor Herbert's nature happened to be somewhat timorous, while neither Kate or Campbell Brewser appeared to know the meaning of the word fear. There seemed to them something wrong, unnatural, uncanny, in the boy's want of courage, in his instinctive shrinking from everything at all unpleasant or dangerous. They were fond of him, certainly; but, almost unconsciously, a large sprinkling of contemptuous pity was mingled with their love. He seemed fashioned of such different stuff to themselves—more like some beautiful fragile flower, fair to look upon, but so delicate as to be unable to face the slightest storm, bowing to the earth at the first gust of wind—a thing deficient in hardiness and vitality, only fitted to be pampered in a heated hothouse; while they were as the sturdy upthrusting thistle, forcing its glossy purple head over the barrenest plot of ground, with lordly indifference to rain, cold, and climate, defying them all with its sharp spiky leaves. And perhaps, though quite unintentionally, this pair of kindred spirits were apt to be a little hard at times, and to underestimate the tender alien nature of the youth. Their judgments inclined towards harshness, and their estimations of Herbert's worth leant somewhat towards disdain, with the result that the lad grew still more silent and reserved. And so mid sunshine and shade the years repeated themselves. The trees in the picturesque old garden in due season put on

first their green, then their red and yellow, finally their
meagre black raiment, preparatory to sleeping the long
winter through, as if mourning the beautiful bygone
summer days. Then, when the spring once more came
round, the life-giving sap burst out into tender, curled-up
leaves, which unrolled themselves gently in the sunshine.
The birds carolled their love-songs in loud, triumphant
notes, fighting, courting, building, mating, until the young
ones came forth, and in course of time, feeling strong and
gladsome, stretched their wings and flew away, obedient
to that great law of nature that dictates the desertion of
parents when no longer useful and necessary. In the green
fields, starred by golden buttercups and sweet-smelling
clover, the white lambs frisked and gambolled in pure
light-heartedness, wagging their supple tails, bleating with
soft, persuasive voices, stretching their long, ungainly limbs,
and courting the rays of the sun in a state of dreamy
enjoyment and blissful ignorance of the future. Little
recked they that all life, however strong and beautiful, ends
in death, come it by the cruel butcher's knife, by disease,
or the slow process of natural decay. They, poor innocents,
like Herbert and Kate, were happy in the present, demanding, thinking, realising nothing more!

Oh! glorious youth! knowing not regret, remorse, nor
aught but transient sorrow, whose joys are keen and pain
short-lived, to whom the past is a void, the future a blank,
and the present—the happy, fleeting present, here to-day and
gone to-morrow—all-sufficing, all-engrossing, how we envy
thee in old age! How lovingly and with what reverent
recollections, do we not look back upon and cherish thee!
In thy innocence and joy thou art more lovely than anything on the face of this wide earth, and yet so evanescent,
that ere we have learnt to fully appreciate the inestimable gifts
which thou conferrest—the heedlessness, the freshness, the
exquisite light-heartedness, the animal strength and spirits,
which are a part and parcel of thyself—thou art gone. Either
gently faded by the unflagging hand of time, or else killed by
some rude shock, which, rousing mankind from this short

period of unthinking content, sets a mark upon his life for evermore, bringing him, once for all, face to face with the stern realities and complex problems of existence!

Even now, slowly, though surely, was the shadow creeping up, destined to plunge the peaceful household in grief and envelop it in a shroud of darkness. Death, that delays for no man—the dread reaper with his sickle—was at hand, intent on adding another to the long list of his reluctant victims.

CHAPTER IV,

A SUDDEN ILLNESS.

IT was upon Kate's seventeenth birthday—how well here-after she had cause to remember that day!—and Herbert, who was then at college, but had lately returned home, was in his twenty-second year—that in the middle of the night the girl was roused from her dreamless slumbers by the entry of the old housekeeper, who, apparently scared out of her senses, shook her violently by the arm until she awoke, with a beating heart, wondering what dreadful calamity had taken place.

"Get up, Miss Kate, dearie, get up at once," cried the seemingly distracted woman, in a hurried and tremulous voice. "Your uncle hae been taken vera ill."

"My uncle!" ejaculated Kate in that state of uncom-prehending bewilderment incidental to a sudden awakening at an unusual hour. "What of him?" Then roused to a sense of uneasiness by old Maggie's flurried manner, she added, "Oh, Maggie! why do you look so strangely at me? Is anything the matter?"

"Joost that," answered Maggie solemnly. "If I am no mistaken there's vera much the matter."

"With whom? With my uncle?" cried Kate, springing out of bed, and now thoroughly awake. "But no," as if trying to reassure her fears, "there can't be anything serious, for when I wished Uncle Campbell good-night at ten o'clock he was then perfectly well and in good spirits."

"A guid deal may happen between ten and one o'clock," replied Maggie sententiously. "Come, come, noo, Miss Kate, dinna lose time in talking—we may both be wanted for aught we ken; but put on your claes as fast as ye can. Here, throw this dressing-gown over your shoulders, for the night air is unco keen, and it wadna do for my bonny bairn to catch cold. There! that's right," as Kate meekly did her bidding. "And noo we wull depart."

"Oh, Maggie! suspense is the worst of all to bear. Tell me quickly what you know," said poor frightened Kate as she clung to the kindly old woman's arm.

Thus adjured, Maggie commenced her sorrowful tale.

"Weel, then, Miss Kate," she said, "ye maun know that your uncle had a fit o' some sort, though I canna tell ye rightly what the name o' it wad be, never having had any experience in sic-like dreadful matters—"

"Yes, Maggie," interrupted Kate breathlessly, "go on."

"Weel, then, my dearie, after ye had gane up-stairs to your ain room, Mr. Brewser rang the bell and asked for some hot whuskey and water. Jock happened to be oot, so I fetched the drink myself, and made it strong and guid, thinking it wad do the master no harm, since he complained o' a bad pain in the head, and said he felt dizzy and out o' sorts. When I brought the wee drap into the study I noticed Mr. Brewser looked unlike himself. His een were vera wild, and his face so flushed that, had I na been acquainted with his temperate habits, I might hae suspected he had already been drinking mair than was guid for him. However, I joost made up my mind to sit up all night in case he wanted a bit help. I canna tell ye what induced me to do so, but I had a kind o' presentiment something evil was going to happen. I went and sat in the corridor ootside, and by-and-by I heard him begin to tramp up and doon, up and doon the study, joost like some caged animal at a show; then on a sudden came the noise o' a heavy body falling to the airth, after which all was still again. I rushed in as fast as my puir auld legs could tak me, and, wae's me"—beginning to cry bitterly—"there I found my dear kind master lying all in a heap on the floor, and looking for all the warld like a corpse. Oh Miss Kate! it was awful, joost awful!"

And Maggie, true to her class, determined that the narrative should gain rather than lose in solemnity in the telling, sobbed with more vehemence than ever.

"Poor uncle; poor darling uncle," exclaimed Kate repeatedly, as they hurried through the long passage which led to the dying man's bedroom, for dying he was, although neither yet comprehended the fact. Already the honest, manly countenance appeared changed and distorted by pain, and the stalwart form stricken,. like some fine old oak uprooted by the vehemence of a passing storm or flash of lightning. In the space of a few short minutes Death had performed his task with certitude, stamping his imprint on the suffering features.

Meanwhile Campbell Brewser lay totally unconscious, his slow and stertorous breathing alone giving sign that life had not yet altogether departed or the brave spirit fled from its earthly tenement. But for the first time in the whole course of her recollection did Kate's passionate grief and terrified entreaties fail to rouse him. Never before had kiss of hers met with no return. The very thought filled her being with a nameless dread. Perhaps it was well for him that he could not witness the girl's deep sorrow. It would have wounded his loving heart sorely to have seen Kate's slender form shaken by a very tempest of uncontrollable sobs, while she prayed aloud in her agony that he would speak to her.

"One word, Uncle Campbell, only one word, just to show that you are alive," she repeated over and over again, almost mechanically.

Alas! the words of Campbell Brewser in the future were destined to be but few, if any, for the family doctor, who had been sent for with all haste, on his arrival pronounced Mr. Brewser to be suffering from an attack of apoplexy of a most fatal description. Of course, "While there was life there was hope;" but according to ordinary practice nothing short of a miracle could restore Mr. Brewser to health. Therefore it was false kindness not to speak the truth, and prepare those attending him for the worst. So spoke the straightforward country doctor, unversed in the evasive arts of his town-dwelling brethren.

For two whole days and nights Kate never left her uncle's side. Love did everything suggested by experience, and if love alone could have saved Campbell Browser's life it surely would have been spared; but the tenderest tendrils are torn asunder and severed by the ruthless reaper, and it was ordained otherwise by One who watches over poor suffering, impatient humanity, and to whose decrees, however hard they may occasionally appear, we are all bound to submit. For to our mortal and finite comprehension faith in the unknown and the infinite is difficult to acquire, especially when the blood runs warmly in the veins, and the world in the springtime of youth seems only beginning to unfold and open out before us. Kate's mind was full of rebellious thoughts against the workings of Providence as on the morning of the third day she sat by her uncle's bedside, weary mentally and physically, while the tears rained down unheeded on her listlessly clasped hands.

Suddenly a voice, very faint and weak, but yet recognisable, broke the death-like stillness of the chamber. Kate started violently as she saw her uncle's eyes fixed upon her own with every appearance of returning consciousness.

"Kate," he said, "don't cry, my darling. I cannot bear to see you shed tears."

The joy and the surprise of hearing him speak, in her exhausted condition, were almost too much. She jumped from one extreme to the other, without reason or reflection. So great an improvement in the invalid must mean that the miracle to which the doctor had distinctly alluded had already taken place.

"Oh, Uncle Campbell! Uncle Campbell!" she exclaimed, in hysterical delight. "I shall have no need to cry now that, thank God, you are better. You will make haste and get well, darling, won't you, if only for my sake? You do not *know* what I have suffered since your illness, or how miserable I have been."

She looked at him with tears of affection dimming her beautiful grey eyes, and a soft, quivering smile playing around the corners of her trembling mouth. He knew better, however, than to encourage vain hopes — hopes which he realised too well would never be fulfilled in this world.

"Don't deceive yourself, my precious one," he said softly. "Something tells me that my time on earth is over, and nothing remains but to try and face my fate like a man. It is no use repining over the inevitable. God bless you, Kate, and keep you from all harm, until we meet some day in heaven. You have rendered the closing years of my life happier than any I had known before, and I am thankful to my Maker for His goodness, even although he has chosen to call me hence sooner than we ever contemplated. It seems hard to have to leave my little Kate, does it not? But *His* will be done."

There was something inexpressibly touching in this strong man's patient resignation, in his unselfishness, his tenderness and compassion for the sorrow which he so clearly perceived overwhelmed the young girl.

"Uncle Campbell, dear Uncle Campbell, you whom I love and honour more than anybody in the whole world, you will break my heart if you talk so," protested Kate vehemently. "You *shan't* die. Don't *speak* of dying. I won't *let* you. I will sit up night after night, never leave your side, and nurse you ever so carefully. You shall pull through yet. You *must* pull through. Oh!" with a bitter intonation of voice, "Oh! it cannot be. God would never show such cruelty towards His creatures. If He is really good and kind, as people say, He won't take you away—you who are father and mother both in one. Uncle Campbell, I could not live without you."

Mr. Brewser at her words raised his hand from the coverlet in feeble reproach.

"Kate, my own darling," he said, appealing to her with tender pity, "you don't want to make a woman of your poor old uncle, do you? You must help him to bear this trial as you have helped him to bear many others. Don't you remember how brave I always thought you, how proud I used to be of your courage! I recollect as clearly as if it

Page 27.

She took fright and ran away for miles.

only took place yesterday, one Monday, long years ago now, when you rode the little black Shetland pony, Thekla, and she took fright at something or other, ran away for miles, and ended by throwing you over her head violently on to the hard high-road. What a fright I was in, to be sure! You were a wee bit of a lassie then, not more than six years old, and when I came up, with my heart standing still through fear, though your poor little arm was all bleeding and badly cut from the elbow downwards, and your face as white as the ox-eyed daisies growing by the hedgerow, what did you do but stretch out your tiny hands towards me and say, 'Don't be frightened, dear Uncle Campbell. I am not much hurt, and please do not be cross with Thekla. It was not her fault, and I should like to get on and ride her home.' Do you remember that, Kate? For if *you* don't *I* do. And I said to myself, ' Bless her little heart! The child is of the right sort, and no mistake. Game as a bantam cock. She takes after her father, who was a true chip of the old block, a regular Highland Brewser.' And now, my darling," looking at her with dim, but loving eyes, "you are not going to do anything to make me alter my opinion, *are* you? If for *my* sake I ask you to be brave, in order to please *me*, you will try, won't you, Kate dearest?"

He had a way about him of overcoming resistance that went straight to Kate's heart. She felt it impossible not to endeavour to comply with a request so touchingly worded.

"I would do anything in the world for your sake," she returned fervidly, "anything that you could possibly ask of me. But oh!"—with a fresh burst of grief—" this—this, Uncle Campbell, is so hard to bear."

Campbell Brewser passed his hand hastily across his brow ere he replied.

"I know it is, darling, hard for you and hard for me, very hard for both of us to have to part. We have been such good friends, have we not, Kate. Somehow or other, from quite the beginning we seemed to get on and understand each other's ways. Mine, too, must have been funny, rough ways often and often to a wee bit slip of a girl; but you never seemed to mind them, Kate, as most children would have done, or as Herbert did, for instance. Why, the very first day we met, when I went to fetch you from off the steamer, instead of being shy and frightened, or wanting to hide behind your Nannie's skirts, you looked up into my face with those great truthful grey eyes of yours, slipped your little hand inside mine, and won my heart upon the spot. Heigh-ho! how the good old times come back to one to be sure!"

His mind seemed to wander to the past, and for a few seconds silence prevailed in the chamber. Then, with an apparent effort at concentration of purpose, Campbell Brewser continued—

"But the minutes are precious, and while I am yet able I wish to speak to you about yourself. Have you ever thought what was to become of you, Kate, if this should happen which is now happening?"

There was no mistaking the meaning of the question. She hid her face in her hands, while a shudder ran through her frame. All power of speech seemed to have forsaken her; for what did she care about the future when he was dead and gone? Everything looked equally dark and blank and colourless.

She almost went the length of feeling vexed with her uncle for bringing the subject under discussion, and wondered how he could talk so composedly when on the eve of leaving her for evermore. She herself could not keep calm when she reflected that she might never see that dear, rugged face again, or listen to the grave and loving voice. Life without him appeared impossible. All the reasoning and argument in the world could never make her think otherwise.

"You see, my darling," continued Mr. Brewser after a pause, during which Kate's reply was evidently not forthcoming, "you are very young to face existence all by yourself, and when I go Herbert will be your only living relative— the only one left who will have the right to care for and tend you. I believe him to be a right-thinking lad at heart, though in many ways he has not grown up as I could have wished, and since he went to college has occasioned me considerable anxiety. Still, I hope everything may come right in the end, and you, Kate, possess courage and determination enough for both. I make no secret of my plans, and if Herbert only accedes to them, I tell you frankly he will then inherit the greater bulk of my fortune. So long as I lived I was your fitting and natural protector, but at my death it becomes impossible for a young man and a young woman of your and Herbert's respective ages to live together without giving rise to comments of a more or less malicious nature. Don't you begin to comprehend, or is it necessary for me to speak more plainly still? Well, then," as Kate's countenance assumed a somewhat mystified expression, "I must impart the scheme which for many years past I have cherished, and which would provide against any such contingency. For—Kate, surely *now* you can guess what I mean?"

She did at last, as was evident from the downcast eyes and the hot blushes that dyed her girlish face.

"Do you mean you want me to *marry* Herbert?" she faltered, in a voice she hardly recognised as her own, for the proposition had come upon her with the shock of a great surprise.

"I do. You are fond of Herbert, and have been brought up together. Therefore, what can be more natural and proper? Unless I am greatly mistaken, Herbert will make you a kind and good husband."

"I don't *want* a kind and good husband," flashed through poor Kate's mind, but she dared not give utterance to the thought, for fear of vexing her uncle in his present state.

"Of course," continued he, "I should never dream of forcing your inclinations on either side. Nevertheless I confess I fail to perceive any other plan so well calculated to secure your mutual advantage."

"I don't care two straws, uncle, about our mutual advantage," broke in Kate tempestuously. "The thing is, will such a scheme really and truly make you happy? That is all I want to know."

"Undoubtedly. The knowledge of your being actually

engaged to each other would remove the one care harassing
my mind.

"Say it again, so that there cannot possibly be any mistake," repeated Kate, with a strange insistence and feverish
eagerness. "If I marry Herbert it will make you really and
truly happy?"

"Really and truly happy," re-echoed Mr. Browser, wondering a little at her earnestness. "It will realise the fondest
visions of my dying days."

"Then that is quite enough. I cannot, of course, answer
for Herbert, and I trust to you, uncle, not to place me in any
false position, but as regards myself I promise faithfully to
fulfil your wishes."

Truly indeed had Campbell Brewser spoken when he said
this girl was brave, and a real chip of the old block. She
liked Herbert as a sister likes a brother—nay, with even a
more lukewarm affection, for his faults had not improved
with age, and she was keenly alive to the weakness and want
of stability inherent in his character. Her whole soul re-
volted against this prosaic, dispassionate *mariage de convenance*.
Girl-like, she had formed her own notions of an ideal man,
who should in all things closely resemble her uncle, and who,
like him, should be capable of inspiring respect and confidence, while she on her side was to acquire a certain influence, and use that influence gently and for his good, so that
she might uphold him in all great works, cheer his drooping
spirits, comfort him in failure, rejoice in his success, quietly
and unobtrusively identify herself with every pursuit. Something such as this was Kate's ideal view of matrimony, for
whose illusions youth and inexperience must be her best
excuse. Kate was too clear-headed to deceive herself. In
agreeing to her uncle's request she was conscious of having
made a great sacrifice, and one that in after life she might
very probably repent. To be as it were bartered away, to be
won without being wooed, to become a wife from a sense of
convenience and mutual interest, was hateful to her; but to
please her uncle, the one being in the whole world whom she
loved heart and soul, she would cheerfully have laid down

her life. Therefore, once certain that this promise would satisfy him and comfort his last moments, she never hesitated. Had he been well and in his usual health, she might not have yielded so easily, might have argued the matter roundly; but now she could not vex or cross him in any way. Hers might have been mistaken courage, but surely it was courage in its highest form—a courage in its forlorn heroism closely akin to that of our soldiers when, obedient to orders, they hurled themselves against the iron guns of the countless enemy in the "grim valley of death."

"Let us send for Herbert," said Mr. Brewser, "I should like this matter settled at once."

So Herbert was sent for, whereupon Mr. Browser proceeded to unfold the nature of his much-cherished scheme.

The young man appeared, if possible, even more disconcerted than Kate. He blushed up to the very roots of his hair, and displayed signs of the liveliest emotion, which were by no means lost upon Mr. Brewser, who, from various causes, had recently begun to view Herbert's proceedings at college with suspicion.

"It is impossible, perfectly impossible," he muttered, as if speaking to himself; "I cannot marry Kate."

"May I ask if you have any objection?" asked Mr. Brewser, with growing distrust.

"No, not exactly any objection," returned Herbert prevaricatingly. "Of course I like Kate, just as I hope Kate likes me, but—but—"

"But what, man? For God's sake speak out. What do you mean by all this shilly-shallying? If there is any reason why you cannot marry Kate tell me the honest truth. In justice to her and to myself it is only right that you should do so."

"I have nothing to tell," said Herbert sullenly.

"Very well then," returned Mr. Brewser, whose wrath now appeared fairly roused, while Kate stood by ready to drop with humiliation, "I will proceed to explain the nature of my will, as it is just possible it may influence your decision."

"Oh no, uncle, please don't!" interrupted Kate in an agony. "You are exciting yourself far too much, and neither Herbert nor I care the least about your money."

"Speak for yourself, Kate," returned Mr. Browser. "I'm not so sure of Herbert. Now listen both of you to what I am about to say. If you two marry I have left nearly the whole of my property to Herbert, with the sole condition he shall assume the family name of Brewser. Kate has already signified her willingness to enter into this contract. She agrees with me in thinking such an arrangement the most suitable one under the existing circumstances."

Kate here endeavoured to speak, but Mr. Brewser continued, unheedful of the interruption—

"It now therefore only remains for you, Herbert, to follow your cousin's example. Understand once for all I have no power to force your inclinations on either side—in fact, I only seek to secure your welfare. When, however, you say 'the thing is impossible,' I not unnaturally beg that you may state your reasons. If they be legitimate ones, Herbert my boy, don't fear to name them, and I will endeavour to act justly and fairly; but"—and he fixed a keenly suspicious glance upon the young man—"if you are deceiving me, if you are so behaving as to wrong Kate or wound her natural feelings, I swear to God I will make some other provision for her future, and give you cause to repent your unmanly conduct."

So saying Mr. Brewser fell back exhausted on the pillow, while his countenance resumed a fixed and rigid look.

Possibly this direct allusion to his will sufficed to convince Herbert of the imprudence of not carrying out the invalid's wishes, for with a sudden compliance strangely at variance with his previous statements he now expressed himself willing to become engaged to Kate. As for Kate, mortification and perplexity racked her whole being. Herbert's reluctance to the bargain was perfectly clear in her eyes. *She* might find this proposed marriage distasteful, but it was evidently doubly so to *him*. Maidenly dignity and pride were sorely wounded, and already she began to fear that, with the best possible intentions, her uncle was committing a grievous error. For almost the first time in her life she questioned any action of his, and of the three human beings now occupying the apartment, he alone who was so shortly destined to quit this earth seemed thoroughly contented. Nevertheless, by Mr. Brewser's desire, they plighted their troth there and then, pledging themselves to become man and wife six months after the date of his decease.

The end came soon—sooner, in fact, than any one foretold. The return to consciousness proved but the last flickering of the lamp of life. After a prolonged interview with his lawyer, during which neither Herbert nor Kate were allowed to be present, Mr. Brewser fell into a tranquil sleep, and in sleep his spirit passed away, so peacefully and so calmly that even Kate, who had reoccupied her place by the bedside directly the legal business was transacted, failed to perceive that in this quiet slumber the soul had soared from its earthly prison, leaving for ever all the aching weariness, the void and unrest of life.

No need to describe Kate's passionate grief, or the horror of death which now fell upon the girl. A blight had over-taken the hushed and saddened household, whose cheerful-ness and mirth could never be restored. Then the dead man's body was laid under the ground, and after the funeral his will was formally read. With the exception of one or two legacies to old and valued servants, and a sum of five hundred pounds per annum to be paid to Kate, Mr. Brewser left his entire fortune to Herbert Munro. Attached to the will, how-ever, was a sealed codicil, with instructions that it should not be opened until the day appointed for the wedding, and it was upon this recently executed deed that Mr. Brewser had evidently been employed during his last remaining hours of existence.

Time now passed slowly and monotonously away, Kate struggling hard to adapt herself to the changed order of things. She was much alone, for Herbert rarely remained at home, pleading his collegiate duties in excuse, and moreover during his brief visits he appeared absorbed by some internal care, and curiously preoccupied.

D

Over and over again Kate endeavoured to gain his confidence, but he repulsed all her advances. In fact, so visibly did he shun her society that the intercourse between the cousins became more and more constrained. It can easily be imagined, therefore, that poor Kate, as the months went by, completed her humble preparations with a sore and aching heart. For three whole weeks Herbert had never come near the place, and yet their wedding-day was fixed for the morrow. Surely a stranger bridegroom it would be hard to find anywhere; so at least thought Kate as she stood before the glass trying on a plain white silk gown purchased for the ceremony. She had not yet recovered her uncle's death, and her heart felt very heavy. Nothing indeed but the knowledge that she was acting in entire accordance with his wishes could have sustained her in the present ordeal. Suddenly the door opened and old Maggie came in, bearing a telegram that had just arrived. It was from Herbert, and contained but a very few words, yet they were enough to change the whole course of her future career.

"Forgive me, Kate," it said, "I have deceived you cruelly. There can be no marriage between us, for I was married this morning to another."

So she read, and with a great, unconscious sigh of relief the crisp pink paper fell from her white fingers to the ground, where it lay totally unheeded. Even the exclamaions of Maggie, who with the privileges of a confidential servant promptly made herself mistress of its contents, failed to rouse the girl to a full sense of the situation. In that first moment of astonishment she was only aware that some crushing weight that had been hanging over her for months was removed. Her liberty was restored, she was free once more! Free to love where and whom she pleased, free to follow the dictates of her own heart, at the eleventh hour saved by another's fault from ties which she now recognised had been insupportable from the first.

The feeling of relief was so intense that she thanked God on her knees for this providential escape. Not till many hours afterwards did she begin to inquire into the cause of her escape, or realise the fact that she had been shamefully treated. Nor until she learnt the full particulars of Herbert's disgraceful marriage did she harbour any ill-will against her cousin. But when she heard the sort of woman he had chosen —ignorant, illiterate, and of low extraction—and discovered how, when engaged to this person, he had lied to his uncle on his death-bed, and professed his willingness to marry herself, solely through fear of being deprived of his inheritance; how, for many months afterwards, ashamed to acknowledge the truth, he had systematically deceived her until compelled to make known the actual state of the case—then Kate's indignation broke loose. The wrong she had suffered was nothing compared with the meanness and cowardice of Herbert's conduct. She could not forgive him.

But curiously enough, when the codicil before mentioned came to be read, it really seemed as if Mr. Brewser, with his usual powers of intuition, had divined Herbert's intentions from the first; for in the event of his committing a *mésalliance* such as the present, Mr. Brewser directed the five hundred a year to be paid to his nephew, and the residue of his fortune was placed at Kate's disposal, with absolute control to do as she pleased with it save in any way augmenting the income of her cousin. But these events had turned the bright, impulsive, affectionate girl into a thinking, reasoning woman, shrewd beyond her years, and experienced in the ways of the world. Moreover, they had imbued her with a disdainful distrust of the opposite sex, with a hearty scorn of everything paltry and mean, which, however admirable in the abstract, rendered her at times somewhat cold in manner to all but a chosen few who had successfully inspired her respect and gained her confidence. In fact, to use a vulgar simile, she was a an instance of "once bitten, twice shy."

Mary Whitbread, however, had completely won her affections. Gentle, refined, amiable, pure in thought and in deed, in short, a thorough little lady, Kate had not been slow to recognise the inherent sweetness distinguishing her character, and the two girls were close friends and allies. The first shock over, and the programme of life now thoroughly

altered, Kate began to look about her in search of a congenial
companion, and immediately thought of Mary Whitbread,
whom she had known intimately when at school. Consequently she wrote to Mary, telling her what had happened,
and offering her a home—an offer that Mary Whitbread,
having recently lost both parents, only too thankfully and
gratefully accepted. So the two young ladies set up house
together, and for the last four years had contrived to live
most amicably. They travelled, went about, and amused
themselves after the manner of happy, idle folks possessing a
large capacity for enjoyment, to whom money is no particular
object, and whose desires have only to be expressed in order
to meet with gratification. That such an existence might
not have had some attendant drawbacks in the shape of
increasing egotism and satiety was open to question; nevertheless both Kate and Mary had so far escaped any deteriora-
tion of character. They possessed an unusual share of sound
common-sense, which not only prevented the perpetration of
any egregious follies, but kept their eyes open to the dangers
as well as to the pleasures of their somewhat peculiar position.

Kate, as the heiress, was of course exposed to the greater
temptations of the two. Foreign counts, German barons, and
Russian princes, when abroad, vowed allegiance by the score,
and even at home she became the mark of many a penniless
youth and scheming, matchmaking mother. As a rule she
was a great favourite with men, being bright and amusing,
and though equally indifferent, equally courteous to all; but
it must be confessed that maturely seasoned girls viewed her
with envy and malice, while the class of juvenile married
women, now so fashionable in London society, abused her
heartily. In short, Kate's fault was that she occupied too large
a share of masculine thoughts and masculine attentions to be
pleasing to the other competitors for such honours. Nevertheless, her admirers were received with a coldness and a
composure decidedly discomforting to the majority. The
truth was, that so far no man had come up to her ideal. Either
people were weak—an unpardonable fault—vain, conceited,
self-satisfied, stupid, prosy, dull, unintelligent, vapid, idiotic,

or something. At all events they failed to touch Kate Browser's heart, and she reviewed the different candidates for her hand "in maiden meditation, fancy free." She had plenty of offers but no flirtations. She never descended to them. It was not in her nature, or consistent with her creed of honour, to encourage any man to believe she cared for him when she did not. She was a brave, honest girl, greatly to be envied, said the world. But at the same time she was so diffident, so incredulous of her power to charm, apart from her fortune, that she had well-nigh persuaded herself that a man disinterested enough to love her for her own sweet sake did not exist; while Mary Whitbread, who, as a bystander, saw most of the game, and not only appreciated Kate's sterling qualities, but knew how thoroughly calculated she was to make any real good fellow happy, told her, and told her not once but many times, that she erred, and was in danger of ruining her future prospects.

CHAPTER V.

THE CUB-HUNTING SEASON.

THE crisp brown leaves were falling fast. Their short span of life was ended, and as fluttering softly one by one to the ground they rested peacefully on the bosom of mother earth. The hedges began to droop and their foliage to wither; the luxuriant woodbine's long tendrils shrivelled and shrank, the flowers hid their pretty heads, and the hardy bramble, clothed in autumnal tints of red and yellow, did its best to enliven the aspect of vegetable decline, while already clusters of wizened scarlet berries betokened the early approach of another hunting season.

And who amongst us, loving the "sport of kings," and enjoying health and fortune wherewith to participate in its delights, has not ere now rejoiced in such yearly recurring symptoms of nature's wintry sleep? Rejoiced with a glad heart at the gradual clearing of ditches, and thinning of hedges, and stripping of bough and bush, and welcomed as an old friend the first crisp frosty mornings, which recall many a well-remembered run and stirring thirty minutes over the broad and undulating pastures for which Huntingshire is justly celebrated—mornings when the trusty steed has had to strain every nerve in order to keep within view of the flying pack, as with a breast-high scent the beauties tore along, close in pursuit of their travel-stained fox.

It wanted still ten days, however, to the regular inauguration of the hunting season—ten days to that formal and ceremonious epoch, the first publicly advertised meet, when men, doffing the distinct comforts of pot hats, blucher boots, gaiters, and eccentric checks, affording any amount of scope to the individual fancy of the wearer, appeared in all the glory of glossy tiles, scarlet coats, spotless leathers, immaculate tops of the last fashionable hue, and ties whose scrupulous neatness compelled admiration for the deftness of the masculine fingers that had tied them ;. while the fair sex, not to be outdone, donned the latest triumph in the way of exquisitely fitting habits, moulded to the figure by artists of such repute as Messrs. Höhne, Creed, Stechlebach, and Co.

Nevertheless cub-hunting was in full swing, and so great had been the sport already shown even at this early period by Sir Beauchamp Lenard's hounds, that several of his staunchest supporters and keenest brother-sportsmen, congregating from different parts of the world, had put in an appearance in the hopes of a few preparatory gallops before the opening day.

Therefore the little town of Foxington was waking up from its normal condition of stagnation, throwing off its summer slumbers, and putting on that air of life and general activity which characterised it during the months of the hunting season. For some weeks past, every morning, weather permitting, at an early hour, long strings of sleek conditioning horses, enveloped from ear to quarter in warm hoods and monogramed clothing, were to be seen sniffing the keen air through their distended nostrils, and looking warily around with sidelong glances, as giving an occasional switch of the tail they marched demurely by. Later on in the day, somewhere between morning and afternoon feeds, grooms and helpers were wont to assemble in small knots of twos and threes, hanging about the angles of the principal street, interchanging words of welcome, imparting the last piece of gossip or scandal, and failing that, falling back on a severely impartial discussion of the studs under their charge, and the merits and demerits of their employers.

The inhabitants of Foxington just now seemed to have been seized with a sudden fit of cleanliness, and on all sides the scrubbing of doorsteps grown green through damp and disuse, the forcing open of paint-stuck windows, their adornment with smart white curtains, and the free application of white-wash, betokened the expected arrival of visitors.

The town of Foxington itself was a small, old-fashioned, unpretentious place situated on a level flat, round which the country rose gently in every direction. It was bounded on the north and east by a sluggish brook, which in summer time revealed a muddy, unsavoury bottom, but which during heavy rains was apt to overflow its banks and inundate the principal thoroughfare, in which the best-patronised shops were situated. At these, thanks chiefly to the ignorance of the bachelor element of the community, who so long as its wants were gratified cared little for the cost, most of the necessaries of life could be purchased at truly extortionate prices, greatly exceeding those of the metropolis.

If some individual, more venturesome or long-headed than his fellows, attempted to remonstrate on this preposterous state of affairs, he was well snubbed for his pains, the sleek tradesmen either explaining blandly or expostulating indignantly, but in either case with similar results. The foe retired discomfited, the honest vendor of goods triumphed and continued his prosperous career; for, as Mr. Morton the saddler, who, having contrived to amass a large fortune, was looked upon as a great authority, sagely remarked to his friend and neighbour Mr. Cowley, the opulent grocer, when discussing the matter confidentially over an evening glass of whiskey·punch, "The long and short of the 'ole thing is this, Cowley: them as can hafford to 'unt can hafford to pay like gentlemen, and them as can't had better keep away. They're no good to nobody, and nobody wants 'em in this part of the world. It's all very well in your provincial countries, but *we* "—with an unmistakable intonation of pride—"*we* are a cut habove that."

And Mr. Morton inflated his capacious chest, and looked as if he really thought himself and Mr. Cowley, as Foxing-tonians born and bred, superior to all the rest of mankind.

Such sentiments, however, appeared to Mr. Cowley fraught with so much common-sense, that they elicited his entire approval and most cordial sympathy, at the same time en·

couraging him to maintain his tariff of prices unaltered, and by no means to make that change in the cost of black pepper and loaf sugar which in a weak moment he had rashly contemplated, but which he now clearly perceived was quite unworthy of him.

Mr. Cowley's shop occupied a prominent position halfway down the High Street, which terminated abruptly in an open space or sort of square, surrounded by red-brick houses, in the centre of which stood the church, a building laying claim to great antiquity and architectural beauty. It was built of solid grey stone, from whose crevices sprang bunches of green moss and lichen. The windows were quaintly latticed with ivy-grown arches, and the massive doors curiously wrought in iron, while the tall, slender spire stood out as a beacon for miles around. Some couple of hundred yards further off you came upon the market-place. Here, every Thursday, rested droves of meek-eyed, long-horned cattle, fat porkers, whose shrill, squeaking voices were loudly raised in self-defence each time the blue-bloused butcher attempted to prod them in the ribs, timid sheep huddled together in crowded pens, rough-coated, shaggy-tailed colts, quacking ducks, cackling hens, smelling fish, hardened cheeses, meat, bloaters, gingerbread, cheap crockery and female finery, boots, shoes, toys, sweets, oranges, apples, lemons, in short, goods and chattels of every description, displayed either on the ground or on rudely constructed booths, round which the neighbouring farmers with their wives and daughters congregated. Here, too—presumably for the sake of cheerfulness, that of cleanliness or quietude being out of the question for this one day in every week—were situated the majority of those diminutive and unpretentious-looking dwellings, overshadowed by palatial stables some six times their own size, which in Foxington were considered the hunting box proper.

Some of these houses had been oddly named by their inmates. The Snuggery and The Retreat were only divided by a handsome stone-faced seminary for young ladies, whereat the daughters of opulent graziers received a liberal education;

while some eccentric individual, doubtless of the masculine sex, had actually so far outraged the proprieties as to christen his abode "The Loose-Box." Others again rejoiced in the high-sounding, and it must be confessed somewhat inappropriate, titles of Bellevue Mansion, Beauchamp House, &c., while the sporting element found vent in Fox Villa, Covert Lodge, and Hunt Hall.

On the evening of Thursday, October the 22nd, 188—, four sportsmen were seated round the dinner-table of the hospitable residence known as "The Retreat." A bottle of sixty-eight Lafitte—warmed to a nicety—was being freely discussed, while the quartette, rendered thoroughly comfortable in mind and body by a most excellent repast, gave themselves up to the pleasure—no slight one—of talking over in all its bearings, and from every point of view, the brilliant sport afforded that very morning during a racing five-and-twenty minutes over the cream of the country by the flying ladies of Sir Beauchamp Lenard's pack, who by good luck had happened on an old dog-fox in an outlying field, and were not to be denied.

"By Jove! Clinker, my boy!" exclaimed Terence McGrath, a plump, volatile little man about five or six-and-thirty years of age, speaking in a strong brogue, which displayed his nationality, addressing himself to his host, a tall, good-looking young fellow, "that's what I call something *like* a run—a downright clipper from start to finish. Could not have been better had it taken place in the middle of the season instead of during the cub-hunting. Bedad! but I never thought for one moment, when Pretty Lass stole through the hedge into the stubble beyond, and enticed all the young hounds after her, that there was going to be such a deuce of a scent! Why, the beauties flew, literally flew," concluded Mr. McGrath with Hibernian enthusiasm.

"They certainly went an uncommon pace," assented the others. "It's not often one sees hounds travel faster, even in this country, than they did to-day."

"Faith! but that's true enough. The pace was something terrific. Gad!" and Mr. McGrath thumped the mahogany triumphantly by way of giving forcible expression to his words, "old Juniper had to bustle along and put his best leg foremost to live with them at all, at all."

"Without wishing to wound the natural pride of a master possessing so distinguished an animal," returned Colonel Clinker with good-humoured sarcasm, "may I be allowed to inquire which *is* old Juniper's best leg? It strikes me any selection would be most invidious under the circumstances."

"Come, shut up, Jack. None of your chaff."

"Well, but Terry," returned the other laughing, "you must admit that old Juniper's understandings are not much to boast of."

"Nor are a good many folks'," replied Mr. McGrath, with severe reprisal. "However, I'll tell you exactly how it was. You know, Jack"—and his voice here dropped somewhat of its severity, and assumed a semi-apologetic tone—"that poor old Juniper's hocks were originally fired over in Ireland, when he was only a four-year-old. In my native counthree they consider prevention better than cure, and last winter, when he got that infernal splinter of wood in the off-fore-fetlock joint, which literally played the divil with it, firing seemed the last resource. So says I to the vet. when he came, 'Begorrah! my man, but we had better make a clean job this time all round, for it would be a damned unhandsome thing of us to leave one leg out in the cold, and render it conspicuous-like. So we'll make em all match, and then they can start quite fair and square again.' The vet. looked me full in the face and said. 'Sir, I honour you. Your humanity is truly beautiful.' Whereupon the operation was performed without much more ado. It took place last spring, and this is the first time I have been on the old horse's back since then, but he galloped in rare good form, and if he only stands sound after to-day will serve me faithfully for many a year to come. Bedad! but he's not likely to have such a breather again in a hurry. Lord, how we raced!"

Mr. McGrath chuckled audibly as he complacently recalled the doughty deeds performed that morning, for self-satisfaction happened to be one of this gentleman's idiosyncrasies. He

chose, however, utterly to ignore the fact that his varied
exploits, feats, marvellous doings, and escapes in the hunting-
field proved a source of constant amusement to the Foxington
world, which was ill-natured enough to assert that most of
Mr. McGrath's statements were highly coloured, and often
devoid the smallest substratum of truth.

His imagination might command a certain amount of admiration, but only at the expense of his veracity. Such was
the verdict passed upon Mr. McGrath's sporting adventures
by the public at large, who it is to be feared regarded the
loquacious and quick-witted Irishman in the light of an
impostor, at least so far as riding was concerned.

" You've made a capital start anyhow, old man," said Jack
Clinker, who knew his friend's little harmless weakness by
heart, and regarded it with magnanimous indulgence. " It
is very evident, Terry, that the brilliant nerve for which you
are so renowned has not disappeared since last winter. I only
wish I could say the same for mine. Increasing years, heavy
dinners, late nights, and long cigars are not particularly con-
ducive to courage, so it is pleasant in your case to witness so
gallant an exception. I'm awfully glad, old chap,"—with a
covert wink at the other guests—" that, *according to your own
account*, you were so well up, and really saw something of the
run. It would be hard to say which of the two deserves the
most credit, you or old Juniper."

" Honours are easy," returned Mr. McGrath. " But "—
after a moment's reflection, during which he appeared to
detect some hidden irony in his companion's speech—" I like
your cheek. What do you mean by saying, ' according to *my
own account ?* ' Isn't it good enough for you? Do you doubt
my word? Do you consider me capable of exaggeration?
Have you ever known me distort facts or speak anything but
the truth on all occasions ? "

" Never," replied Jack Clinker with ludicrous solemnity.
" You are a perfect specimen of candour and honesty."

" Very well, then," continued Terry, working himself up
into a state of excitement, " perhaps you'll admit I've not
hunted here all these years without knowing as much about

hunting as my neighbours. Faith! but there are some people
born so sceptical that they will hardly believe their own
mother brought them into the world, and I really think you
are one of them, Jack. Once for all, let me tell you it's not
in my nature to magnify anybody's performances in the
hunting-field, least of all my own ; and what's more, it is not
always those who talk the most, and who puff themselves up,
who are the best sportsmen."

And Mr. McGrath drew his portly person on high as much
as to say " There, what do you say to that ? "

" Hear, hear ! " interrupted the Honble. Jack Clinker,
colonel in Her Majesty's Grenadier Guards, approvingly.
." A most laudable and commendable sentiment. Post-prandial Nimrods are plentiful enough, are they not, Terry ? Pluck
and fluency are boon companions when no more formidable
obstacle presents itself than the polished mahogany laden
with bottles. Ha, Bacchus ! thou art a merry fellow, and a
right good one to boot ! Which reminds me thou hast suffered
neglect too long. Come, Terry, old chap, pass the claret this
way. We are uncommonly thirsty on our side of the table.
and your innings is fairly over for the present."

" You're pat enough with your tongue, Jack ; you always
were," observed Mr. McGrath, whose offended dignity had
not yet been restored to its pedestal, "and I flatter myself I can take chaff as well as most people ; but as for
going hard in the hunting-field, well, I never pretend to be a
crack-brained, harum-scarum fellow like yourself, who can't
even get within a hundred yards of a fence without wanting
to cram at it like a downright lunatic."

" Don't be abusive, Terry. Remember I am not to bo
held responsible for the deficiencies of my cerebral condition.
Some scientific cove, I believe, stated the fact that only one
in five hundred human beings is born with decent intelligence ; therefore do not be too hard on the four hundred and
ninety-nine. It's unkind."

" That's not my idea of riding to hounds," continued Mr.
McGrath, completely ignoring the other's remark, "though "
—with withering contempt—" it seems to be some people's.

Pluck is all very well, but there are a great many other qualities essential before a really fine horseman can be produced. Valour without discretion resembles the clumsy beast of the field, deprived of reason. What say you, Fuller?"

"That Mr. McGrath's powers of language and choice of metaphor are simply beautiful," returned he readily. "What would I not give to possess such grace and fluency!."

The antecedents of the gentleman thus appealed to were shrouded in mystery, but the Foxington world had come to accept Captain Fuller as the best ecarté-player, the most inveterate gambler, the coolest hand, the most amusing story-teller, and greatest authority on sporting matters (Colonel Clinker alone excepted) in the place. Added to these qualifications he rode undeniably well to hounds, was in with all the dealers, and never refused a decent profit on a young horse. He rarely meddled in other people's affairs unless directly invited to do so, and kept a singularly quiet tongue in his head with reference to his own. When asked his opinion on any subject he gave it with a decision that carried weight, and which had gained for him a reputation for wisdom and cleverness perhaps greater than he was fairly entitled to.

"What is it you want to know, McGrath?" he asked, raising his eyebrows in a slightly supercilious manner. "Whether valour should be tempered with discretion, eh? Why, of course it should, and in nine cases out of ten generally is. The majority of men funk at heart if only they had the courage to acknowledge it, but instead of doing so, when they come to a nasty place they take great pains to explain how they fully intended jumping it, only they thought the ground was too hard, or there really was no occasion, or they feared they might stake their horse—any excuse, in short, that comes to the mind. However, talking of a combination of the two qualities, I was fortunate enough to witness a very striking instance this morning. Do you happen, McGrath, by any chance to remember that first little blind gap we came to just when hounds had begun to settle to their work? The ditch was towards you, and almost completely overgrown with long yellow grass. Well, you came up to it, and you looked at it, and were doubtless at that moment brimful of courage, but you refrained from doing anything rash. Your discretion was of the highest order. Still, by the time you had waited a few minutes, during which hounds were streaming away in the distance, and the passage of some twenty horsemen had reduced the dangerous nature of the impediment to a minimum, you took heart. 'Hang it all!' you said once more, 'it's not such a bad place after all. Here goes for a shy at it.' Valour, you see, came to the front. Your mind was made up, and without further hesitation you charged the reduced gap with that heroic and indomitable courage born of an empty flask and stimulated spirits for which you are so deservedly esteemed by a large and admiring circle of friends. But now, what does that beggar, old Juniper, do? Does he feel impelled by the same eager desire for distinction as his ambitious rider? No, not he. He whips round with such velocity as considerably to disturb Mr. McGrath's centre of gravity, gives an obstinate shake of that wicked old head of his; having in the interim spied a convenient gate some twenty yards or so to the right, he makes promptly for it, like a sensible and confidential animal. And now, Terry, your judgment came to the fore, for had you been a regular bruiser, like our friend Clinker here, you would probably have remained at that blessed gap for the best part of an hour, endeavouring to force the obstinate brute over it, and by so doing lost your temper and your run at the same time. But you, like a true philosopher, discreetly yielded to old Juniper's better judgment, and, after passing through the gate, must have made most wonderful dispatch, since I gather from your statements that you had pretty well the best of the run throughout. Therefore I drink to valour and discretion in the persons of Mr. Terence McGrath and old Juniper, than whom no worthier representatives could possibly be found in all Huntingshire."

And Captain Fuller raised his glass and drained its contents with evident approval of their quality.

His speech was greeted by a chorus of laughter, while a

complacent smile overspread Mr. McGrath's ruddy countenance, for curiously enough, sharp as he was at detecting
a joke at another person's expense, his share of the national
vanity was so great as to render him perfectly proof against
any but the bluntest sarcasm, while Captain .Fuller's witticisms were so insidious, so artfully intermingled with judicious
flattery, that they not only failed to wound Terry's suscepti-
bilities, but actually restored him to a state of high good-
humour and self-satisfaction.

"Ha, ha! a capital story!" exclaimed Colonel Clinker.
"But I say, Fuller, if it is not an impertinent question, how
was it you witnessed all this by-play? It's mighty seldom
you stand looking on and allow some twenty horsemen
to take precedence, even if the obstacle be not a more
formidable one than a blind gap. Come, what were you
about?"

"Well, to tell the truth," answered Captain Fuller, "being
rather short of horses at present, owing to that beastly
influenza having broken out in the stable, and never thinking
for a second hounds were likely to run in the way they did, I
merely rode out on my hack, intending to potter about. She
is only a four-year old, quite a pony, and as ignorant as a
baby where jumping is concerned. Knowing, therefore, that
she could not possibly get over the fences, particularly in
their present leafy state, I contented myself with bringing up
the rear, and making sundry judicious cuts along the roads
whenever they were possible. I should be sorry to say how
many of my neighbours I came across, or what curious phases
of character revealed themselves to my observant eyes. It's
wonderful what a lot one sees. I know almost every shirker
in the field. The Grangeton brook was rare fun. I made a
first-rate nick just about that time, and got on to the road,
which runs almost parallel with it, exactly when the leading
men came charging down at the water. I tell you what,
Clinker, that's a rare good nag you were riding to-day; not
the bay, the one you rode home, but that young roan mare
who carried you so brilliantly through the run. By Jove!
she's a nailer! She flew the brook like a bird. I never saw

anything prettier in my life. You happened to pick out rather a nasty place, where the banks were steep and under-mined, and although the mare had nothing in front to give her a lead, she never hesitated one single second, but pricked her ears and went at it straight as a die. I have not seen an animal that takes my fancy so for a long time. She jumps in such beautiful form, as lightly and as quickly as a stag. Why, she must have covered close upon twenty feet when she took the brook."

"It was a pretty tidy jump for a young 'un," said Jack Clinker, who, little as he was given to bragging about his own performances, like all true lovers of the noble animal, dearly liked, when he possessed a good conveyance, to hear its praises sounded. "I picked her up this summer when down at Newmarket with the Governor. She's clean thorough-bred, by Hyperion out of Emerald. You may, perhaps, recollect the dam. She is an Irish mare, not unknown to fame, having about six years ago won one of the big steeple-chases at Punchestown, while Hyperion has some of the finest blood in the country running through his veins, as everyone who has studied his stud-book knows. Directly I set eyes on Opal—that is the young 'un's name—I fell in love with her. I knew she was bound to race and jump, not only from her pedigree, but from her make and shape. If you were to cast your eye over her you would be surprised how deep she is in the girth, and what great square hips she has got. She wants furnishing, but her bone and muscle are quite remarkable for a four-year-old. She belonged to a racing farmer, who knew her value, and for a long time the price proved a stopper. A man ought not, perhaps, to praise his own cattle, but though I say it who should not, Opal, bar none, is the very best four-year-old I ever threw a leg over. She is handsome as paint, bold as a lion, and clever as a cat. As for jumping, it comes naturally to her. She never saw hounds until to-day, although of course she has done a bit of quiet schooling at home."

"Well, she could not have gone better had she been the most mature old hunter," said Captain Fuller. "And what's

E

more, she ought to win between the flags. Has she any turn of speed?"

"Speed! I should rather think she had. It's extraordinary how she gets over the ground with that long, sweeping stride of hers. Of course, hunting is a different thing altogether to racing; nevertheless you know to-day how fast hounds went, fast enough at any rate for most of them, but they never succeeded in extending Opal. From first to last she was going well within herself, and hardly turned a hair. No, if only she grows the right way, unless I am greatly mistaken she is good enough to pull off one of our big steeplechases."

Now it is a common-enough delusion of most gentlemen possessing a second-rate animal that can gallop a trifle faster than its companions in the hunting-field, that the said animal is likely to prove a mine of wealth, and has been a hitherto-undiscovered treasure, whose light only requires to be rescued from the bushel in order to shine forth and take the sporting world by storm. Jack Clinker, however, was well qualified to give an opinion, and was not likely to be led astray in his judgments through any momentary enthusiasm occasioned by Captain Fuller's encomiums. In all matters connected with sport he was thoroughly conversant. His knowledge and experience were both considerable, for at the early age of thirty he had attained the proud position of being recognised as the finest rider, the best man to hounds, and the most successful gentleman-jockey, both on the flat and between the flags, of the day. So great, indeed, had his prestige become, that it was almost sufficient for it to be known beforehand that the Honble. Jack Clinker would ride any given horse in a race, for that horse immediately to be installed favourite. Like the invincible Archer, he had his herd of blindly worshipping followers. At cross-country meetings his success was astonishing, while even professional jockeys respected him as no unworthy opponent, and pronounced him, for an amateur, "a wonderful good judge of pace." His friends—and they were legion—declared Jack Clinker to be the best fellow in the world, whose only fault consisted in a harrowing impecuniosity, which at times led him into considerable difficulties; while his enemies—for what man has none?—took pleasure in asserting he was a regular scapegrace, a ne'er-do-well, and a shamefully extravagant young dog.

Whichever party might be right, despite sundry scrapes and adventures, chiefly of a financial nature, not a soul had ever breathed a word against Jack Clinker's honour, or accused him of any impropriety in connection with his transactions on the turf. If he were, as was generally admitted, *sans peur*, he was equally *sans reproche*. Colonel Clinker's father—Lord Nevis—a rare old gentleman of a fast dying-out school, had inherited the title and a heavily-mortgaged estate through the unexpected demise of a somewhat distant relative. Lord Nevis spent most of his days upon the property, struggling hard to free it of encumbrance, so that at his death it might be handed down clear of debt to his only son, whose comfortable settlement in life was his one great wish. To effect this result, the unselfish and devoted father economised in every possible way; while, if the truth will out, Master Jack made such frequent applications to the family purse that he quickly disposed of any small surplus accruing therein. Put into the Guards at an early age, Jack's chief difficulty had always lain in endeavouring to make both ends meet. An allowance of eight hundred a year proved totally insufficient to defray the debts he incurred. Generous to a fault, open-handed and kind-hearted, with a perfect passion for horseflesh and sport of every description, up till now he had found it impossible to live within his income. His resolutions were excellent, and his desire to retrench sincere, yet somehow or other at the end of each year the same old story repeated itself. Bills came pouring in, and money wherewith to meet them was not forthcoming. Now and again, when his lucky star was in the ascendant, Jack Clinker managed to pull off some "good thing" on the turf, the proceeds of which, impartially divided among his numerous creditors, served for a space to stay their clamorous tongues, and staved off the evil day; but alas! these "good things" were few and far between, oftentimes succeeded by shockingly bad ones, during which poor Jack went about in a dejected mood, cogitating the alternatives of an immediate and comprehensive scheme of reform, or an abode in that last retreat of the destitute, *i.e.* the workhouse. Nevertheless, so sanguine was Colonel Clinker by temperament, that even when most bowed down by difficulties he firmly believed in something or other turning up. The final crash certainly loomed in the distance, and year by year appeared more imminent, but by hook or by crook the crisis had hitherto been delayed, while in the meantime the gallant Colonel's life was not otherwise than a pleasant one. In the summer he idled about town, forming one of the highly esteemed " gardenia division," attended all the smart parties given by the leaders of society, was idolised by fashionable spinsters and professional beauties, went to every race-meeting almost in the United Kingdom, from 'Appy 'Ampton to aristocratic Goodwood; later on shot grouse and slaughtered stags on his own native hills, paid innumerable visits, contrived to kill time more or less successfully until the hunting season came round, and altogether spent a pleasant, profitless existence, such as generally falls to the lot of young men possessing just enough to keep them in idleness, to the detriment of all their higher qualities and legitimate ambitions. Jack Clinker was no fool. He had fallen into a groove which, on the whole, suited him fairly well; still, in his more serious moods, he fully recognised the fact that it might be wise to turn over a new leaf; only the pages of the book had stuck together, and a commencement was so hard to make!

At the present moment he was supremely happy, recalling Opal's meritorious performances, and looking forward to an excellent season's sport. During the winter months, in common with his argumentative friend, Terence McGrath, he rented the snug little hunting-box at Foxington in which we find the pair located, and which, owing to one or two uninvited visitors who occasionally put in an unwelcome appearance, had facetiously been christened " The Retreat." Captain Fuller lived next door but one, and had contrived to establish himself on terms of tolerable intimacy. Although possessed of no ostensible means, the Captain was one of those fortunate individuals who, living no one knows how, are quite content so long as they enjoy the best of everything at a neighbour's expense. With this end in view he had constituted himself dry nurse to a wealthy inexperienced young man, one Robert Grahame, son of a millionaire merchant, whom he had persuaded into making his *début* in the hunting-field. The fatherly interest he took in Mr. Grahame, familiarly known as the Chirper, was truly beautiful to behold. He relieved him of all trouble, managed his stud for him, ordered in the forage, rode any awkward or fractious horses, engaged the servants, wrote out long lists of delicacies to be obtained from the stores, paid all the household bills regularly once a week, harangued the tradespeople, and in return for such inestimable services demanded nothing but an occasional cheque wherewith to keep things going. And Mr. Grahame, who hated trouble, and who received from his wealthy parent just as many thousands as Jack Clinker did hundreds a year, with an injunction, to boot, to spend his money royally, conceived that he could not possibly be obeying the parental wishes better than by allowing Captain Fuller to constitute himself administrator-in-chief of the finances—an arrangement which afforded that gentleman infinite satisfaction, and which so far appeared to have suited Mr. Grahame equally well. Naturally somewhat shy and of a retiring disposition, he not only in all things allowed Captain Fuller to take the lead, but effaced himself so completely that strangers were apt to put him down as a bigger fool than he was. Robert Grahame went through the world with open but good-humoured eyes, and being at the same time both indolent and rich, had no objection to be preyed upon by his friends up to a certain point. Captain Fuller had the sense to understand this, and never to go beyond the boundary line. Hence their apparent sympathy and cordiality.

CHAPTER VI.

AN EVENTFUL BET.

THERE comes a time when even the subject of a good run may be worn threadbare, and conversation for lack of incident begins to droop. So it was now. Every fence had been recalled, the performances of each individual horse and rider discussed, the blindness of the country animadverted upon, and the appearance of hounds and handling of huntsmen freely criticised, until at length a pause resulted—a pause which Mr. McGrath, whose chief merit certainly *did not* lay in silence, quickly proceeded to break by an interrogation which he evidently considered of great importance.

"By-the-bye, boys," he asked, "have you heard the news? the news that is, or ought to be, agitating the heart of every blessed bachelor in Foxington. You, Jack, in particular, should feel interested. Such a chance may never come your way again."

"Indeed, then I had better make haste and profit by it, especially as there seems likely to be a good deal of competition," returned the Honble. Jack carelessly.

"There'll be plenty of that, I'll be bound," said Mr. McGrath with a comical twinkle of the eye, looking exceedingly mysterious.

"For goodness sake, Terry, don't be so enigmatical. If you don't look out you'll be a terribly prosy old man some of these days. Get to the point of your story, if any point exists, of which I have my suspicions."

"Well, you *are* a sceptical beggar, if ever there was one. I declare I've half a mind not to tell you after all."

"Don't, Terry, I'm not the least curious."

"Oh! I like that! Come, now, what would you say to the arrival of two young ladies on the scene of action—both young, both good-looking, and one of them rich?—so rich, indeed, that they say she does not know what to do with her money or how to spend it."

"I always mistrust what 'they say,'" responded Jack coolly, puffing a cloud of smoke from the long cigar he had just lighted. "'They say' is the most inveterate scandal-monger in the world, and at the same time the most untrust-worthy one. Who are 'they?' Answer me that question. Can *you* point them out? Can *anybody* point them out? However, if you ask my opinion, that's a different matter altogether. *I* say the young lady to whom you allude must either be a phenomenon or an idiot. I can conceive of no intermediate condition. To be the happy possessor of more money than one knows what to do with appears to my limited comprehension an utterly impossible state of affairs. I can-not bring myself to believe in it. The very mention of such a thing conjures up dim visions of bliss."

"Visions which might come true," murmured Mr. McGrath under his breath.

"Where did you pick up this exciting piece of news?" asked the Chirper, displaying an unusual amount of interest, most gratifying to Terry's feelings of self-importance, which had been rather damped by the Colonel's unbelief. "Is your informant to be relied upon? I hope so, for two nice girls would be a great addition."

"Well done, Chirper; your sentiments do you honour," exclaimed Mr. McGrath approvingly. "Nevertheless, in ask·ing such a question you display profound ignorance. There is but one person in this neighbourhood capable of answering to the term 'informant,' and she is *facile princeps!* If you want to know the intimate affairs of your bosom friend, better almost than he does himself, ask Mrs. Forrester. If you wish to be posted in the latest fashionable scandal, the ail-ments of every animal in the county, with the means to cure them, the peccadillos of the fair sex, the last *bon mot* among the men, again, I say, ask Mrs. Forrester. That woman is a

regular walking encyclopædia. How she manages to retain
so much knowledge would baffle the holy St. Patrick himself.
Nothing escapes her ! She's just as sharp and as clever as
she can hang together. Gad," bringing his plump red hand
with a resounding smack down on the table with such force
as to make all the empty glasses jingle, "if Mrs. Forrester
was only some twenty years younger, and not nearly old
enough to be my mother, I declare I know no woman I have
a greater respect for or would sooner ask to become Mrs. T."

"I was not aware up till this moment," remarked Captain
Fuller, "that the sentiment which prompted people to commit
matrimony consisted of respect alone. However, since you
entertain such extremely sensible views, I can tender no better
advice under the circumstances than 'Go in, my boy, and
win.'"

"Yes, go in, my boy, and win," laughed the others in a
chorus.

"Thanks for your good wishes," said Mr. McGrath with
melodramatic accents ; "but my friends," and here he gave
a solemn shake of the head, "widows, even the most fascinating, are a dangerous class, besides which a man does
wrong to place himself in a position where comparisons are
sure to be drawn, and generally to his disadvantage. A
second husband is a striking exception to the adage, '*Les
absents ont toujours tort.*' The dead cannot rise up to disprove
facts and contradict statements, and for this reason—No. 1
once safely under the sods is invariably right, and No. 2
invariably wrong. Therefore I am too chivalrous to desire
to do the defunct Colonel Forrester's memory such injury."

"I suppose you and the old woman have been chattering
together as usual," said Colonel Clinker. "What else did
she tell you ? Did you meet her in the town ?"

"Certainly," returned Mr. McGrath, with a comical
assumption of dignity. "I disapprove of clandestine assigna-
tions, even though the female be aged—"

"Say rather *because*," interrupted Captain Fuller, with a
laugh.

"Ah! sly dog!" ejaculated Mr. McGrath. "However, to

get on with my story; this afternoon, after my ride, feeling a
bit stiff and sore, I determined to stretch my legs by going
for a short stroll up the street. The first person I met was
Mrs. Forrester, who, having divested herself of her habit,
had driven in to fetch some medicine for a sick cow at the
chemist's.

" ' Come here,' she said to me; 'I've something to tell
you. You've heard the news, of course?'

" I was obliged to confess that, having only arrived yesterday, I was somewhat behind the times, and consequently not
posted in the topics of the Foxington day.

" ' Well, then,' continued Mrs. Forrester, ' Sport Lodge is
let for the season—let to a young lady, Miss Brewser by
name, who, it appears, is a great heiress, and what's more,
she is one of our set, for she is fond of hunting. There is a
companion, a Miss Whitbread, and they both came to-day.
I sent my groom down to the station on purpose to have a
look round. The horses arrived by the 3.30 train, and I
have just this instant seen them go by. There was no mark
on the clothing, so I stopped the man and asked him whom
they belonged to. Three hunters, a pair of uncommonly
smart cobs, a hack, and a brougham-horse formed the lot.
One of the hunters—a chestnut—looked a perfect beauty, and
the bay took my fancy also. Depend upon it the money is
all right, and just think what a chance for some of you young
men! There's Clinker, for instance; you tell him from me
to keep his weather eye open. Such plums as this Miss
Brewser require care and delicate handling, they do not
grow on every tree; but though they hang high, every now
and again they are apt to fall with a real good thud to
the ground. Don't forget, but be sure and give Jack my
message.' So saying, Mrs. Forrester whipped up her horse
and departed."

"Hang it all," growled the Honble. Jack, "why the
devil can't people leave me alone? I hate hunting women,
most confounded bores, who get in your way on every occasion, can't ride one little bit, and yet who, to make matters
worse, have any amount of pluck—a pluck born of sheer

ignorance. I declare it makes my blood run cold to see nine women out of ten come tippiting up to a big place, with no more idea how to go at it properly than the man in the moon. Ugh! don't talk to me of hunting women! With a few exceptions I'm sick of them!"

And Jack, remembering how only last season he had been jumped upon and narrowly escaped complete annihilation by a gorgeous but unfortunate young person attired in a bright blue habit, with yellow curls and golden brooch and earrings, shuddered in unmistakable disgust at the recollection of this beautiful but untimely apparition, as it had burst upon him when struggling on the small of his back in a moist ditch, and a pair of brown heels inflicted sundry bumps and bruises on his prostrate form.

"And yet," said Captain Fuller thoughtfully, "there are many worse *modus vivendi* than a wealthy marriage. As for a harmless fancy for hunting on the part of the lady, I think nothing of that whatever. Obstacles soon intervene, and if the money is only secure, well invested, and regularly paid, the chances are you, as the husband, will have the spending of the greater share, and do pretty well what you like with the interest, even if the capital be strictly tied up. Now-a-days nothing opens out so fine a prospect to impecunious youth as a well-to-do marriage. It is a safe and comfortable haven, not difficult of attainment if properly approached. Women love a judicious mixture of hardihood and flattery. The whole secret of overcoming their scruples lies in that."

"I don't agree with you, Fuller," said Colonel Clinker coldly. "Women are not such fools as you seem to imagine."

The one subject on which he and Captain Fuller never agreed or could agree was that of the fair sex. Jack Clinker thought of his dead mother with reverence. He believed in the purity of women, while Captain Fuller affected to despise it.

"Well, well," returned he, "you can do as you like. After all too many aspirants are undesirable, and I'm not at all sure I shan't have a cut in at this Miss Browser myself."

And the Captain, who was exceedingly vain of his personal appearance, twirled his scanty moustache with a complacency all the stranger as two at least out of his three listeners were aware that any matrimonial intentions on his part could only be executed under extreme difficulties.

"Bedad," interposed Terry on behalf of his friend, "but Jack must have the first innings. None of us are so hard up as he is. And if we can do him a good turn we will."

"Thanks, old boy," said Jack, with a kindly gleam in his clear eyes, "it's something to have such a backer. Besides which, what you say about my being hard up is sensible enough; things financially don't improve; in fact they get worse and worse, so its no use attempting to disguise the truth. I shall have to take the bull by the horns and do something desperate before long, the only difficulty when— and how?"

A shadow passed across his open countenance, rendering it for a moment unusually serious. There were times, though as a rule not of very long duration, when even Jack Clinker felt depressed by the increasing difficulties of the financial situation.

"*We'll* settle all that for you," replied Mr. McGrath cheerfully. "The 'when' shall be this winter—or perhaps, in consideration of your both being hunting people, we may allow a little grace, and defer the happy event until the spring—and the 'how' matrimony. Faith, me dear boy, but I quite agree with our friend Captain Fuller in thinking that excellent institution a grand refuge for the destitute, so much so that I declare to you I've had serious thoughts of trying it myself, only somehow or other the girls, bless their darling hearts, are fanciful, and require more pin-money than I can afford. It's a curious thing, but whenever I propose they begin to laugh, and nothing kills sentiment like ridicule; it shrivels it up just like a cold wind does a rose-leaf. Now you, Jack, in spite of your poverty, have looks, position, and just that sort of celebrity that the fair sex appreciate. They like a man who is somebody and who is talked about. Why," waxing enthusiastic, "the girl would be a born fool who would refuse to marry the best seat on a horse and the finest hands in England. She never could do it, the thing is a simple impossibility."

"The young lady might not be possessed of any sporting tendencies, Terry," returned the other with an amused smile. "and then what you are good enough to designate as 'the best seat and finest hands in England' would be rather thrown away upon her, would they not? It's not exactly complimentary, all one's boon companions displaying such exceeding solicitude to get rid of one; and this Miss Browser is not the only girl in the world with money. I've met others before now, and managed to escape their charms without any serious wound being inflicted on my heart."

"The more fool you, Jack. You are your own worst enemy, and always have been."

"Possible. But may I ask what you desire? Would you have me throw myself as a perfect stranger, without receiving an atom of encouragement, at this young woman's head, simply because she happens to be, or is reported to be, an heiress? A fellow must be awfully thick-skinned for that sort of work."

"Not at all. I would have you make up to her in a proper and sensible fashion. There is no occasion to fling yourself at anybody's head in the absurd way of which you speak. If any flinging is required, let it be at the lady's feet. She'll not leave you there long, I'll be bound. You know, Jack, you're a deuced agreeable fellow when you choose to take the trouble. Come, boys, fill your glasses just once more, and drink to the health of Miss Browser that now is, the Honble. Mrs. Jack Clinker that will be."

"We've had about enough of this stupid chaff," said the bridegroom-elect. "Can't you chaps talk of something more sensible?" Then, as the toast was repeated, he added as if half speaking his thoughts aloud, "Poor Mrs. Jack! She will have but an indifferent time of it, I'm afraid. A gambling, racing, betting, idle husband, head over ears in debt, and no sooner out of one scrape than into another, is hardly the sort of man for a nice young girl to marry."

"Just the sort of man she adores," observes Captain Fuller, who happened to overhear the remark, and enunciated the opinion with a decision probably arising from long experience. "Women may like and esteem the respectable goody-goody members of society, but their love is reserved for the black sheep."

"You certainly entertain the oddest opinions of the sex," said Colonel Clinker. "However, your assurances are exceedingly comforting to those who, like myself, belong to the latter class. According to your theory the bigger blackguard a man is the greater affection he inspires."

"That's about it. Women's hearts are awfully soft, but their heads are weak in proportion. We may thank our stars the majority of the sex are not sharper than they are, and possess such sweet credulous natures. Now, I'd like to bet you ten to one, in the event of your proposing to Miss Brewser, that she accepts you."

"That's rather a strong order, is it not?" said Jack Clinker, with increasing impatience. "For goodness sake let's drop the subject."

"There, I have booked it!" said the other, taking out the neatly bound volume from his pocket without which he seldom stirred. "If you win I pay you ten sovereigns, whereas, in the event of losing, you only pay me one. The odds are handsome enough in all conscience."

"Done," said the Colonel abstractedly, "on the condition I hear no more about it between this and then."

The conversation clashed with his nicer instincts of chivalry, and he wished to put an end to it. He felt vaguely irritated and incensed. He therefore rose from the table, rang the bell, and voted an adjournment to the next room, where the card-table was already spread, and all things in readiness for the amusement of the evening. Captain Fuller proposed loo, and overruled the objections of Mr. McGrath, who greatly preferred a quiet rubber of whist at half-a-crown points. The Captain, however, desired a more lucrative game, being an adept in the art of gambling. So they sat down and played with varying fortunes until the clock struck mid-

night.   Then Colonel Clinker pushed back his chair, and
said—

"It seems inhospitable to turn you fellows out, but I make
it a rule, in the hunting season, never to keep late hours."

"Just one more round," pleaded Captain Fuller, who with
glistening eyes was engaged in counting over a little heap of
i.o.u's placed before him.   He was in his element now, and
the gambler's spirit rife within him, but the Colonel proved
inexorable.   He had been a steady loser, holding miserable
cards throughout, and evidently considered it useless going on,
in the face of such bad luck.

"What an insinuating cove that fellow Fuller is, to be
sure," he remarked to Terence McGrath when their guests
had departed.   "Neither you nor I wanted to play high, and
yet he somehow forced it upon us.   I've lost close upon a
hundred pounds to-night, worse luck."

"He's a rum un," said Terry,   "I never can quite make
him out.   But I say, Jack, old fellow, another time I do wish
you'd put your foot down, and be firm.   If we begin the
winter in this sort of way, we shall have to finish it in Queer
Street.   You and I can't afford to lose a hundred pounds at
cards."

"I can't for one," Jack said with a sigh, as they went up-
stairs.

"Brewser," he muttered during the progress of undressing.
"That's a Scotch name.   I wonder what family this girl
belongs to?   Ugh! what beasts she would think us if she
had only heard us all discussing her up and down in the way
we did to-night.   I declare I felt positively ashamed."   The
fair head was on the pillow by this time.   "I'll enter Opal
for the Grand National, and win a big coup," with which
consoling determination the Honble. Jack blew out the candle,
rolled himself round, and before many minutes were over was
sound asleep, dreaming of steeplechase courses and runs
across country.

CHAPTER VII.

MISS BREWSER ARRIVES AT SPORT LODGE.

SPORT LODGE, the present residence of the young lady and her friend who, quite unconsciously, had by their arrival aroused so considerable an amount of curiosity, possessed the advantage of being situated on rising ground, some half-mile distant from the low-lying town of Foxington, which it overlooked.   From the modern plate-glass windows of the building field after field of green undulating pastures, unbroken by plough or vestige of arable land, were to be seen, while on all sides great up-standing bullfinches met the eye, composed of stiff, unyielding blackthorn, fenced in by stout wooden oxers; for the country within a radius of a couple of miles of Foxington was renowned as the biggest in England, none but the best mounted and highest couraged horsemen daring to ride over it.   Fortunately, however, gates were plentiful in the immediate neighbourhood, often indeed proving the only means of egress, straight going being rendered still more difficult by the presence of a canal, a railway, and an unjumpable brook.

Sport Lodge was a square-built, old-fashioned, comfortable abode, the solid red bricks of which its walls were composed being mellowed by the hand of time and the warring of the elements into a subdued and harmonious tint, which contrasted pleasantly with the glossy leaves of the ivy clinging to their surface.   The house stood in its own grounds, consisting of a short carriage-drive, small flower and kitchen gardens, and an extensive paddock.   Inside, the rooms, though not exceedingly numerous, were spacious and airy, while the furniture, in spite of being many degrees removed from the lofty standard of cultured æsthetes of the Oscar Wilde school, was neither glaringly vulgar nor obtrusively hideous, thanks to an abhorrence on the part of Mr. Reginald Rich to anything that might be considered the least loud. Therefore, quiet colours and small patterns predominated, much to both girls' satisfaction, when soon after their arrival they commenced a searching and exhaustive tour of inspection, accompanied by old Maggie, the latter, however, being more taken up by the state of the blankets, bedding, and kitchen utensils than with the taste displayed by the late tenant. The drawing-room, as might have been expected, came in for the principal share of abuse.

"Did you ever see anything so awful?" ejaculated Kate, though in her heart of hearts she felt conscious things might have been a very great deal worse.

But half an hour's labour worked wonders. The girls hauled about the obnoxious articles and stowed them away in unobtrusive nooks, produced yards upon yards of pretty, bright-coloured chintz, with which they draped the mantelpiece, strewed books and knicknacks about the room, stuck up some photographs and Japanese fans on the walls, and in a very short time completely metamorphozed the apartment, bestowing on it that air of refinement and comfort which feminine fingers alone know how to impart.

"There!" exclaimed Kate, feeling all the satisfaction derived from successful effort, "we have not allowed the grass to grow under our feet. No one can say, considering we only arrived this morning, that we have wasted our time."

"Certainly not," replied Mary. "Your activity and energy are something quite remarkable. At least they appear so to me. I do not know what I should do or how I should manage without you to goad me on. I feel positively certain, if left to myself, I should not accomplish as much in a week as you get through in a single day."

"Oh yes you would, Mary. It's a mere question of strength. You happen to be the more delicate of the two; besides which you are blest with a naturally calm, equable, and unexcitable disposition, which, I fear, I do not possess.

Nothing ever puts you out; I never remember seeing you in a rage in all my life, whereas I—well, a very slight cause suffices to upset my temper. I don't believe people can help themselves; it's constitutional, and just depends under what conditions they are born. You have the good luck to own a placid mother and father—you are placid also—if not, not. Now nothing worries me more than to see things left lying about day after day never tidied up or put in their places. 'We will do so-and-so sometime' is a saying constantly heard, but one which always makes me angry. Sometime is no time in my estimation. Folks who are perpetually intending but who rarely perform delay and delay until at length, if by any chance they happen to put their purpose into execution, the day has gone by when pleasure can be derived from its fulfilment. They end by outgrowing all capacity of enjóyment, and the long-deferred intention, when finally realised, becomes but Dead Sea apples. If you wish to pluck fruit from a tree you must choose the moment when it happens to be ripe and your appetite good. Procrastination only serves to rot the one and take the keen edge off the other. At least so it seems to me."

"Really, Kate, you have mistaken your vocation, and ought to have been a popular preacher. Why don't you become an exponent of woman's rights? Would not such an occupation open up a field worthy of your talents?"

"Certainly not; I don't approve of that sort of thing. If a woman cannot obtain what she is pleased to call her rights by the help of soft looks, pretty ways, and feminine attractions, I very much doubt her being able to do so by stumping about the country, addressing crowded assemblies from heated platforms, and arraying her person in masculine and unbecoming garments. A woman's real strength lies elsewhere, in my opinion."

"Well, Kate, you relieve my mind of a considerable burden," said Mary playfully. "But, with all due delicacy, I beg to mention that for the last five minutes, while you have been indulging in idle talk I have been pursuing the even tenor of my ways, and worked with a perseverance beyond all praise. There, Miss, what say you?"

F

And Mary proceeded, with an almost unnecessary display of vigour, to hammer a tin-tack into the wall preparatory to hanging up a sporting print, representing Mr. Jorrocks endeavouring to coax his favourite steed over a diminutive obstacle, which work of art Kate, as a sportswoman, regarded with feelings of the most intense veneration, and insisted on its occupying a prominent position.

"You're a duck, Mary," she remarked, "if only for the patient manner in which you listen to my nonsensical observations."

"The substantial form of Mr. Jorrocks looks beautiful," said Mary, in reply. "He exactly fills what otherwise would have been an ugly vacuum. And now to descend carefully from my exalted but not altogether secure position." Whereupon Mary cautiously placed one foot on the lower rung of the steps on which she was mounted, and returned to mother earth. "I wonder if any visitors are likely to call this afternoon," she said presently, looking out of the window in a speculative sort of way. "I ought to go and tidy myself up a bit in that case."

"I should think it doubtful," said Kate. "Anyhow, we are ready for anything or anybody, from a pious ecclesiastical visitation to a regular influx of the aborigines. By-the-bye, I wonder why it is that wherever one goes the divines, male and female, are invariably the first to pay their respects? Is it for our sins, for our moral welfare, or for the off-chance of an invitation to dinner? The problem is one I have never yet succeeded in solving to my satisfaction. It will take some little time, I daresay, before people know of our arrival, though, I suppose, sooner or later a certain number will do us the honour of calling, the little fry first, and the big last, as is nearly always the case."

"I suppose so, and perhaps we may have more visitors than we anticipate, for I thought the agent told you Foxington was an extremely gay place during the winter months, and full of hunting gentlemen."

"Oh! so he did. But I don't much believe in agents."

"Kate, you horribly sceptical young woman, I should

like to know what you do believe in. Your incredulity is something amazing, not to say preposterous."

"I believe implicitly in a little person called Miss Mary Whitbread," was the laughing rejoinder. "She at least inspires me with sentiments of profound esteem."

"And quite unworthily so. But now, Kate, if you can but be serious for two minutes together, I feel perfectly certain that in a place of this sort there are sure to be any number of nice people about, people you will like."

"That depends very much on what you call nice people. They are so difficult to define, and so exceedingly few and far between. My experience leads me to believe that the majority of human beings are neither nice nor nasty, and that the utmost feeling they inspire is one of absolute indifference. They are too insipid to be loved, too vapid to be hated. I wonder where they all go to ? If we were either angels or murderers by nature, heaven and hell would be perfectly intelligible, but where is the intermediate place, suitable to the enormous mass of living souls, that never rise above or descend beyond the dead level of mediocrity ?—the mass, who are neither vicious nor virtuous, bad nor good, but who go through their lives in a commonplace, monotonous fashion, performing neither any exceedingly noble actions nor yet any very wicked ones ? Is there no heaven for such as these ? Must they either be unduly rewarded or equally unduly relegated to eternal punishment ? Oh! Mary, I cannot understand it, but my mind rebels against both these alternatives. Justice appears so deficient in such an arrangement."

"Hush, Kate! I really wish you would not talk like that, or propound such extraordinary ideas. They are quite unfitted to your age, and only make one feel uncomfortable."

"Perhaps so. But what am I to do if such thoughts insist upon coming into my head ? They are not solicited, but enter uninvited."

"You are a strange girl, Kate, and far too clever for your neighbours."

"Not at all; I am afraid it is the other way about, and

they are cleverer than I am. Do you know, Mary, I think now-a-days people ought to be born either fools or geniuses. The competition is so enormous, and the intermediate stages so exceedingly unpleasant. To possess aspirations without the talent necessary to lead to their fulfilment is a most fatal gift. It is like the fox and the grapes. One yearns after something, only the fox displayed superior sense by retiring when he found the clusters beyond his reach, and in persuading himself they were sour. *Our* grapes are not sour, but very sweet, if only we could reach them, which we never can. They dangle temptingly over our heads, but are not to be grasped. Therefore I say the blind, the dumb, and the insensate are happier than a person like myself, possessing just sufficient brains to recognise the full extent of her own deficiencies, and yet not enough to supply the remedy, or win renown in any walk of life."

"Ah! Win renown in any walk of life! There speaks the bold, ambitious Brewser spirit. Kate, you ought to have been a man, like your uncle, and then you could have gone out into the world, and given full vent to your energies."

"I wish I had had the luck, that's all!"

"Well, as the fates were unkind enough to determine otherwise, you must content yourself, at all events for the present, by winning renown in the hunting-field, and with that end in view how would it be if you were to go out and interview the excellent Stirrup, who else, I fear, may feel hurt at his mistress's non-appearance?"

"Happy thought!" exclaimed Kate, with one of the sudden transitions natural to her, descending from the abstruse study of the psychological to more terrestrial subjects, "and I think I will profit by the suggestion."

So saying Kate fetched a neat little black felt hat from the peg on which it was hanging in the hall outside, stuck it jauntily on her pretty head, put on a pair of dogskin gloves a few sizes too large, but which she kept for similar visits to the one she now intended paying, and after a certain amount of fumbling succeeded in extracting several large lumps of sugar from the recesses of her well-filled pocket, which preliminaries terminated, she proceeded to take her departure.

Kate's entrance into the stables was the signal for various impatient neighs of welcome, while Stirrup, the stud-groom, who had been busying himself in the harness-room, immediately stepped forward to greet his young mistress with smiling alacrity. A cockney *pur sang* by birth, his features were somewhat hard and *dour*, yet they possessed that look of unmistakable honesty which never fails to win confidence.

Stirrup's hair was grizzled, and his face puckered into many wrinkles, but the keen eyes were as bright as ever, and the whole countenance full of shrewd common-sense. Short of stature, standing about five feet six inches in his boots, his legs possessed that peculiar curve which so frequently reveals the horsey individual. In fact, a man must have been the veriest tyro not at one glance to determine Mr. Stirrup's profession.

"Good-morning, Miss Kate," he said, advancing to meet her, and touching a respectable black billycock by way of salutation. "I'm afraid everything 'ere be rather in a muddle for the likes of you."

"Good-morning, Stirrup," she replied with a laugh. "The ' *likes* of me ' is not so particular as all that, I hope. It takes some little time to settle down. However, we shall be all right, I've no doubt, in a day or two, and I trust that, on the whole, you feel tolerably satisfied."

"*Tolerably*, thankee, Miss," with an emphasis on the "tolerably" which implied the very reverse. "There be one or two little matters I should wish to make so bould has to mention. There's them air 'arness-stands wants looking to just terrible. I don't know 'ow people managed afore us, but *our* 'arness won't 'ang on 'em no 'ow. Then the 'andle, it 'as dropped off the coach-'ouse door of its own accord, so to speak, for d'reckly I cum to turn it down it falls, which makes the door uncommon awkud ; and the bedsteads in the men's room hupstairs they be only fit for babbies to sleep in. Why they bain't more than two feet across—quite ridiklous

for grown-up people, let alone such fine strapping young
fellows as Dan and Tom."

"Yes, Stirrup, and what else?" enquired Kate resignedly.
"Do the harness-stands, the coach-house handle, and the men's
legitimate requirements comprise the lot?"

"Certainly not, Miss," he returned with dignity. "I'm
only telling you of just what comes uppermost in my mind.
I've not the smallest doubt but what by the end of the day a
great many hother needfuls will crop up."

"I've not the smallest doubt but that they will, Stirrup.
I'm positively certain of it—at least, as certain as one can be
of anything in this world."

Stirrup looked at her and shook his head.

"You allers love a joke, Miss Kate," he said, in an indulgent, semi-protesting manner. You *must* 'ave your larf whatever 'appens. Ah!"—as he caught sight of one of the
understrappers endeavouring to raise the handle of the pump
—"that reminds me that air machine be hawful bad to work.
It took a couple on us to get the 'osses their water this fore-
noon; and them fine windys, too, be all for show. Not one of
'em can be made to hopen; they be stuck quite fast. And the
boiler in the wash'ouse it are wrong, not a drop of 'ot water
to be got, and one of the gas-cocks won't turn proper, so that
the gas escapes, and the smell is enuff to pison the 'osses, and—"

How long Stirrup, being once launched, might have added
to this fresh list of grievances it is impossible to say. Kate's
patience was fairly worn out.

"That will do, that will do," she interrupted, making
believe to stop her ears. "I shall never remember one half
of what you have told me. Send for a man, a dozen men if
needful, and get everything put straight that you don't like.
I don't suppose," she continued "that these stables have
been occupied since last winter, but except a few small de-
fects, even you, Stirrup, must admit them to be very nearly
perfect."

She was anxious, if possible, to coax him into some expression of approbation, but Stirrup was equal to the occasion,
and would not allow himself to be thus entrapped.

"They will be well enough in their way, Miss," came the cautious reply. "I 'as seen better, and I 'as seen wus. For my part, I never swears by them there tiles, they be very dazzling to 'osses' eyes. Such-like new fangled fancies please some folks, but I am not one of those to run after every fresh craze that is started; old-fashioned ways and old-fashioned hideas be more to my mind."

"Well, well, Stirrup! Let us have a look at the horses," said Kate, seeing it was useless attempting to argue the question further. Her stud, as before stated, consisted at the time of her arrival of three hunters, a pair of ponies, a hack, and a harness-horse. First and foremost came King Olaf, who considering himself neglected during Kate's colloquy with Stirrup, had all the time it lasted been violently pawing up the straw with his hoofs and endeavouring to poke his soft nose between the iron bars of the box. In colour he was a bright golden chestnut streaked with white, becoming more pronounced at the root of the tail, and testifying to the Bird-catcher blood which ran through his veins, while a white blaze down the forehead and three white stockings on the two hind and near forelegs rendered him, quite apart from his good looks, an animal not easily forgotten when once seen. Clean thoroughbred, by that well-known sire Norseman, erewhile a winner of the St. Leger and other important races, King Olaf's pedigree defied the closest inspection. He stood about fifteen three—if anything perhaps a trifle under than over—but the deep girth, wide hips, great muscular thighs, and clean short legs, added to the beautiful compact frame, all gave evidence of an unusual degree of power. A better shaped or more symmetrical animal would be hard to find. King Olaf's forehand was simply perfect. A slender arching neck, strong yet supple, with a crest like iron, finely sloping shoulders, in which the muscles stood out like swelling balls, small pointed ears, always on the alert, a lean well set-on head, with large brown eyes, whose clear blue pupils seemed an index of the horse's character, and told both of courage and docility. The best judge in England would have found himself at a loss to pick a hole in him, and it was with

natural pride that old Stirrup was wont to remark when called
upon to display his favourite—

"There, I warrant he's about as good as they make 'em."

And Stirrup was not far wrong, for King Olaf was one of
those rare animals, few and far between, who did not know
what it was to turn his head, whose gallant heart would take
him anywhere his rider wished, over, through, or under, as
the case might be, resolute as a prizefighter, bold, active,
flippant, yet withal gentle and kind—a horse such as with
the greatest good luck it falls to one's share to own but once
in a lifetime.

That Kate knew, and not only knew but thoroughly appreciated his merits was clear at a glance. A cordial understanding existed between the pair. King Olaf treated his
mistress, that sharp young mistress whose clever tongue often
made the golden youth of the period abashed and confused,
quite *sans cérémonie*.

He gobbled up the sugar with the greediest avidity, and
then began rubbing his beautiful head against her shoulder,
as if coaxing for more, but finding he had partaken of his
share, he contented himself with calmly licking the buttons
down the front of Kate's dress, an operation that did not
benefit those articles very highly.

"You dear old greedy thing!" exclaimed she, patting the
glossy neck bent down before her, "you have had all your
sugar, and I must keep the rest for the Duckling and Grisette.
What! another piece, just one tiny one? Oh, King Olaf,
you are a sad glutton. You really are, only you ask so
prettily, I can't resist."

It was quite nice to see them together. Kate talked and
cooed to the horse, and he listened with an air of intelligence
almost human.

"I suppose *he's* all right?" continued she addressing
Stirrup. "I hear the hounds meet somewhere pretty close
to-morrow morning, and I should like if possible to go out
for an hour or two, just to have a look at them. I must
begin to get into condition you know. It won't hurt King
Olaf, will it, Stirrup? We ought to produce our swagger

horse when we make our first appearance in the Shires, so as to impress the natives favourably. Don't you think so?"

"Most certainly, Miss," he said emphatically, "and wot's more, I don't mind wagering a shilling to a golden sovereign there baint many 'osses out as can 'old a candle to 'im. I've been a groom now pretty nigh forty-five years, and I've never seen the one yet that could beat 'im. No, no, I am not afraid of the 'Untingshire cracks, for all the talk there is about 'em."

And Stirrup cast his eye over King Olaf with unmixed pride and satisfaction, glancing at Kate meanwhile in pure delight.

"Has he fed all right, Stirrup?"

"Fed? Why, lor bless you, Miss, that ere hanimal would eat 'is very 'ead off. I never seed a finer grubber in my life; he's a credit to 'is hoats, that's what he is, and I only wish we 'ad more of the same sort in our stable. There's that Grysetty now" (the real name of the mare in question was Grisette, but not being an accomplished French scholar, Stirrup adopted a pronunciation of his own on the principle of phonetic spelling), "she's a poor, delicate, fanciful crittur if you like. There baint a bit of stamina about 'er. She'll never make a good doer, she won't, and if you take my hadvice, Miss Kate, you'd get rid of 'er on the first hopportunity. She looks pretty well now she 'as done no work, and it is just possible some flat may take a fancy to 'er. There's lots o' these young sparks as don't know a 'oss from a cow."

"You would not have me take one of 'these young sparks' in, surely, Stirrup?"

Stirrup's eyes twinkled as he replied—

"I would not 'av you take anyone in, Miss Kate, but all the same if you get the chance of parting with Gry-setty, you do as I say. You let 'er go. She'll stand no work, and by the end of the season will be a regular bag of skin and bones, a discredit to hus both. I often think, Miss," continued Stirrup loquaciously, "as 'ow 'osses 'ave wonderful charakturs. They vary just as much as 'uman beings. Some be brave and lion-'earted, like King Olaf, and others again is regular

cowards. Look at that there Duckling for instance! Do
you mean to tell me he aint got just as much in that cunning
little 'ead of 'is as arf the folks one comes across? I'll be
bound that if 'is brains was weighed against many of 'em
he'd beat 'em 'ollow. He's awful hartful that 'oss is."

"He knows a tiny bit too much, I suspect. Stirrup, eh?
With all his good qualities he's terribly obstinate at times,
and insists upon having his own way out hunting. In common justice, however, I am bound to state that that way is
usually the right way. There is nearly always some cause
for the Duckling's actions. Why, as a proof of his cleverness, only the other day when I rode him, seeing a low,
inviting-looking hedge, I thought I would pop over it just
for fun, when, to my indignation, Master Duckling declined
in the most persistent manner. Well, do you know, Stirrup,
there was *wire* stretched all along the top, which I had not
noticed, but which he had seen in the twinkling of an eye.
Yes, the Duckling is a safe conveyance, and don't mean
falling. We have got used to each other's little peculiarities,
and I have long since come to the conclusion that whenever
a slight difference of opinion arises between us it is better to
yield to his superior knowledge and defer my judgment to
his."

"You bain't much wrong either, Miss Kate. They all 'as
their faults, but he 'as decidedly fewer than most of 'em."

So saying Stirrup turned up the Duckling's clothing, and
gave him an affectionate smack on the hind-quarters, which
that animal promptly resented by whisking his tail from side
to side and seizing hold of the manger between his strong
teeth. Neither so handsome or quite so well bred as King
Olaf, he looked all over a game "varmint," wear-and-tear
sort of hunter. Nor were his appearance and character at
variance, for the Duckling, fortunately for his owner, was
one of those invaluable creatures always to the fore, with an
iron constitution, never sick or sorry, ever ready for his turn
or to replace an invalid, placid, averse to needless exertion,
a voracious feeder, and sound as a bell. He stood on the
shortest and cleanest of legs, and was altogether a horse of a

good old-fashioned stamp but rarely met with.   He was now
seven years of age, and, bar accidents, appeared likely to carry
Kate in the hunting-field for twice that number more.   If he
had a fault it was that, unless in for a real good run, he
sometimes inclined towards laziness, appearing to recognise
the futility of any needless waste of vital power.   But if
hounds ran, then he would settle to his work in downright
earnest, prick his ears when he came to a fence, and jump as
if he loved jumping for jumping's sake, not merely as a
means to an end, to be accomplished with the smallest possible amount of exertion.   And if the run only lasted long
enough to choke off the majority, the Duckling was pretty
nearly certain to show to the front, for although other horses
might possess superior speed in a short scurry, but very few
were endowed with his extraordinary staying qualities.   Indeed, the further he travelled the better he seemed to go.
Plough was indifferent to him, heavy ground he simply
romped through.   He went pegging along at the same
steady, even pace up hill and down, and contrived to get over
the land in a truly wonderful manner.   Such was the Duckling.   Like many other good performers, if a slow beginner
a sure finisher, and one who, his blood once fairly roused,
proved himself uncommonly hard to beat across country—
a thoroughly excellent, confidential, and sensible animal
all round.   Many a good ride Kate had already enjoyed
on the back of the stout, honest little beast, and although
perhaps not *quite* so brilliant a performer as King Olaf, he
nevertheless ran him very close in her affections.   She liked
each best in his turn, and never wholly succeeded in given
one a decided preference over the other—a state of things
which all hunting men and women will probably regard as
highly satisfactory.

Kate in the stables, with Stirrup to talk to, was in her
element.   She stood by watching him hog the manes of the
two smart Welsh cobs, rejoicing in the names of Brandy and
Soda, which she intended driving out to covert on the morrow.
Anyhow, time passed so quickly that she was astonished
when a sonorous gong was sounded with discordant thumps

by a male domestic, summoning her to lunch in the most imperious manner.

"How time flies to be sure!" she exclaimed. "Why it only seems a few minutes since I came here. However, I suppose I must be off now. Well then, Stirrup, let me see. I think you quite understand your orders for to-morrow? The hounds meet at a place called Doddington, about six miles from here, at ten o'clock. We will start punctually at nine, so as to have plenty of time to rectify any errors, and shall drive the pony phaeton out. One of the helpers had better ride Grisette, and lead King Olaf on to covert. I should think that would be the best arrangement."

"Certainly, Miss," answered Stirrup. "But I don't much like the idea of your going all alone, particular to start with, in a new country, and heverything strange. There's the Duckling, he's fit and well, and ready to jump out of 'is skin. It would do him good to go out for a 'our or so."

"Which means, Stirrup, I suppose," said Kate with a smile, "that you intend to accompany me?"

Whereupon she ran back hastily into the house, feeling she had been keeping Mary Whitbread waiting an unconscionable time for her midday meal.

"Humph!" ejaculated Stirrup, as he watched Kate's retreating form, and apparently gave vent in outward expression to a train of inward reflections. "Talk of swells, indeed! Where is the pair as can show near 'er and King Olaf? Bless 'er dear 'art! What a clever, bright crittur she be to be sure! *She* ain't stuck up, or full of nimminy-pimminy ways, like most females. Why she talks to a poor old fellow like me exactly has if 'e was an hequal. Lor! If she don't take the shine out of some of these 'ere nobs to-morrow, why my name ain't R. W. Stirrup, that's all."

With which soliloquy Mr. Stirrup re-entered the harness-room, and before long was vigorously engaged in applying a chamois-leather to the brass mountings that Brandy and Soda were destined to sport on the morrow.

CHAPTER VIII.

MRS. FORRESTER MAKES A RECONNAISSANCE.

MRS. FORRESTER belonged to the active and energetic order of beings that does not allow the grass to grow under feet. Procrastination could not be included in the category of her shortcomings. Whenever any fresh arrivals appeared in the neighbourhood she immediately constituted it her duty to call upon them without loss of time. This mode of procedure had among the circle of her intimate friends become such an entirely understood arrangement that its various members regarded the lady in the light of a distinguished and perspicuous *avant-courier*, in whose reports, bad or good, implicit confidence might be placed, and according to which the actions of the district were determined.

An unfortunate couple, man and wife, had arrived at the Rest and be Thankful Hotel only so lately as last winter, with all the credentials conferred by youth, good-looks, and a large fortune ; but when, thanks to Mrs. Forrester's investigations, it became known the lady's antecedents were not exactly all that could be wished, the Foxington world, in a body, declined to leave that thin strip of pasteboard which leads to acquaintanceship, and felt grateful to its pioneer for having saved it from the vexations of a false position Perfect trust was reposed in Mrs. Forrester's decisions. Her ultimatum was generally law, and saved much trouble, while the keen interest she took in everything that concerned the affairs of others rendered her self-imposed task far from an unpleasant one. The reward came in the shape of knowing more than her neighbours, of being able to impress them with a sense of superior information, of having a finger in

everybody's pie, and of finding herself in universal request.
This feeling of importance flattered Mrs. Forrester's pride.
She was fully alive to the value attached to her opinions, and
spared neither time nor trouble in pursuit of gossip wherewith to gratify or astound her numerous acquaintance.

Left a widow in middle life, and possessing a competence
which, though not large, was sufficient to enable her to live
in tolerable comfort, her tastes being both frugal and simple,
Mrs. Forrester, some ten or fifteen years ago, had purchased
a small property at a propitious moment, when land happened
to have considerably deteriorated in value. This domain,
consisting of a dwelling-house and a couple of hundred acres,
was well situated within two miles of the town, and extremely
handy for the larger portion of the meets. The land Mrs.
Forrester farmed herself, and there was no better judge of
stock, or more judicious buyer and seller of beasts, in the
whole country round. The 'cutest grazier could not show
more favourable accounts, or turn a larger profit in a shorter
time.

She dabbled in science and chemistry, and thoroughly
understood the importance of supplying bone-forming and
fatty materials where scantily provided by Nature. She
believed in the possibility of improving upon that great mistress, and thereby scored over a large number of less enlightened brethren. Moreover she held the courage of her
opinions, and did not hesitate now and again to try experiments which the easy-going, half-educated farmers regarded
as the height of lunacy, but which not unfrequently ended by
carrying conviction to the narrow-grooved agricultural mind.
With much practical knowledge and energetic supervision,
Mrs. Forrester was one of the fortunate few who made the
cultivation of their native soil pay its working expenses. No
one, having once made the lady's acquaintance, could fail to
perceive that she possessed striking originality of character.
Although between fifty and sixty years old, she still retained
traces of having been in her youth a singularly good-looking
girl, though now spare in figure, and consequently deficient
in the comeliness that often improves middle-aged women.

All the features were good, in spite of the cheeks being bronzed and wrinkled, and the complexion dyed to a deep saffron by the combined effects of sun and wind and rain, though it was easy to see at a glance that she gained nothing from borrowed plumes, and utterly disdained such female frivolities as fashionable dresses and useless finery. Her clothes fulfilled the primitive mission of covering the human body with regard to warmth and comfort rather than to effect. She wore no frills, no furbelows, no such abominations as a dress-improver. False hair, false busts, false fronts, false teeth, were to her things unknown. Nevertheless, the neat head, with its covering of dark glossy hair, as yet untouched by the hand of time, the quick intelligent eye, the oval-shaped face, small mouth, and delicately arched nose, all bespoke a person of gentle birth; while neither exposure to the elements nor utter indifference to outward appearance had been able wholly to efface those good looks with which the Creator had at some period or another undoubtedly endowed Mrs. Forrester. The most startling thing about her was her voice. Deep in tone as that of any man, clear and sonorous, it yet possessed a brusqueness which strangely impressed the unaccustomed listener. To all intents and purposes it might have emanated from the deepest recesses of the ground, it sounded so sepulchral. Mrs. Forrester's ordinary attire consisted of a short and perfectly plain dark cloth petticoat, guiltless of trimming or superfluous adornment, beneath which appeared a pair of stout, broad-soled, square-toed, hob-nailed shooting boots, above which again, it was whispered, a masculine garment that shall be nameless was donned, which the observant professed many a time to have seen. Anyhow, underpetticoats were evidently not patronised, else why that dual suggestion conveyed to the mind? The upper portion of Mrs. Forrester's attire was composed of a loose cutaway jacket, also made of cloth, opening over a checked flannel waistcoat, varied, on grand occasions, by a spotted bird's-eye; a white silk tie, held in its place by a silver horseshoe pin or gold fox's head, a pair of stout dog-skin gloves —that is to say when gloves were worn at all, which was

the exception rather than the rule—and a black felt pot
hat, under whose brim the abundant hair was rolled away on
either side the face in the good old-fashioned style, finished
off at the back by a velvet bow, the only piece of finery in
which Mrs. Forrester rejoiced, if finery indeed such a brown,
rusty, greasy adjunct could rightly be considered. The whole
constituted a most convenient costume, easily modified for
equestrian purposes by the substitution of a riding-skirt for
the ordinary walking one, and of a pair of Wellingtons in
place of the shooting boots. Mrs. Forrester's gait was highly
characteristic, displaying a sideways roll, half-way between
the heavy dragoon and the jockey. So closely, indeed, did
it resemble the lords of creation that it was extremely
difficult at a slight distance to determine to which sex
she actually belonged. In fact those who put her down
as forming one of the masculine community could easily be
pardoned so natural an error. Morally Mrs. Forrester possessed undoubted ability. She had great powers of observation, a keen appreciation of the ludicrous, an innate love
of fun, coupled with a wonderful insight into the motives
actuating mankind, which prompted her on all occasions
to turn the ordinary transactions of everyday life into a
joke, or at least to perceive their facetious element. Intelligent, well-informed, clever, amusing, and above all, unlike
the commonplace herd of human beings, no wonder Mrs.
Forrester was considered excellent company, and gladly welcomed by her fellow creatures in spite of the humorous pro-
pensity which prompted her to concoct all sorts of tales at
their expense. True this versatility of speech occasionally
brought her into trouble ; nevertheless she was so thoroughly
jolly, kind-hearted, and good-natured with it all that people
forgave her little peculiarities, pocketed pride, and laughed
at the exaggerated accounts of their own doings and sayings
which were freely circulated throughout the county. Mrs
Forrester had earned the not unenviable reputation of
being "a character," and characters are generally privileged
individuals who can say and do things not allowed the
rest of the world. Her father, in her youth, had kept a

pack of foxhounds.   Mrs. Forrester, therefore, had been
brought up in a sporting coterie, and was passionately fond
of hunting.   No one in the whole county, not excepting the
huntsman himself, was so thoroughly conversant with the run
of a fox, or the difficulties connected with his successful
pursuit.   Often and often it happened that when the officials
were at their wits' ends which way to turn, and were on the
eve of abandoning the chase in despair, a quiet hint from
Mrs. Forrester gave a clue to the direction in which the hunted
animal had most probably effected an escape.   She not only
knew every hound by name, but was conversant with their
respective merits.   She could tell how Gaylad was the foremost in Sir Beauchamp Lenard's pack, how Garrulous ran
mute, how Prettylass suffered from bad feet, Finder from a
weakly constitution, and how Goliath could live through the
longest and the most tiring day without exhibiting any symptoms of weariness.   She knew them all, and loved them all, as
if they had been her children or she their kennel huntsman.
In the saddle Mrs. Forrester was absolutely at home, and
there were but few men who even now, in her declining
years, when she took it into her head to ride straight, could
beat the gallant old lady.   They tell a story still of how some
few winters ago the whole field came down to the celebrated Grangeton brook.   It might not have measured more
than about twelve to fourteen feet across, but the banks were
steep and crumbling, the bottom treacherously muddy, and
the water as it gurgled swiftly by looked coldly dark and for-
bidding.   For an hour or more the assembled company had
been walking after a fox, during which horses and riders had
lost much of their matutinal ardour, without indulging in the
excitement which often stands in good stead, when all of a
sudden the hounds splashed through the brook and picked up
the scent on the opposite side with renewed zest.   Heads
down, sterns up, they streamed away over the big grass field
of ridge and furrow.   A moment's hesitation ensued; then
the huntsman, closely followed by two or three of the more
adventurous spirits, endeavoured to ford the stream by jumping in and clambering up the rotten bank on the other side.

it was so boggy, however, and they rescued themselves with such extreme difficulty, that upon one of their number floundering into a hole, and horse and rider disappearing bodily into the water, those pressing on from behind, after witnessing the disaster, declared the attempt to be fraught with so much danger as to render it positively unsafe, if not to themselves, at all events to their steeds. In fact the occasion was one when the risk to animals became unusually prominent. While standing deliberating on the whereabouts of the nearest bridge, and racked by that uncertainty as to whether to stake all and proceed, or to hazard nothing and retire which every fox-hunter doubtless has experienced during his career, suddenly, and to the inexpressible astonishment of the beholders, no less a person than Mrs. Forrester was seen to resolutely take her horse by the head, cram him along in a manner not to be denied, and charge down at the bottomless gulf. A moment of breathless anxiety followed as the animal reached the brink, and for a second paused in his stride ; but he happened to be a particularly good clever hunter, who thoroughly understood his work, and in less time than it takes to tell he landed on the opposite side with a bit of a scramble, owing to a portion of the bank giving way, but still without mishap. A murmur of applause ran through the ranks of the spectators. "Bravo! bravo!" they cried with one accord. And now, ashamed to be outdone by a woman, and an aged one to boot, a noble sportsman, inspired with fresh courage, endeavoured to follow Mrs. Forrester's example, but alas! the undermined earth once more gave way, and his horse having jumped extremely short, was precipitated into the cold ungracious element, while the aristocratic rider, after executing a neat somersault, landed on *terra firma* on the crown of his head, thereby completely annihilating a smart new Lincoln and Bennett. These catastrophes overcame the field. Helter-skelter, men, women, and children, accompanied by a trailing hound or two, galloped off in all haste to the bridge. For the rest of that day, and for many a day to come, Mrs. Forrester's gallant feat was the theme of every tongue. To her was accorded that admiration

And in less time than it takes to tell he bowled on the opposite side.

Page 92.

and that meed of applause which courage, accompanied by success, invariably elicits.

With fine hands, a strong if not a graceful seat, and aided by all sorts of curious combinations in the way of bits, nose-bands, gags, and martingales, she could master animals which none of her own, and but few of the sterner sex, were capable of managing. She consequently bought at a low figure, never by any chance giving long prices for her horses, and, as was generally the case, they improved under her tuition, and in the course of a few months became decently tractable, she was enabled to pass them on at a consider-able profit. No one could gainsay the fact, seeing the risk and trouble incurred, that that profit was fairly Mrs. For-rester's due, and honourably gained by her own exertions. She was on terms of the closest intimacy with every dealer, farmer, and breeder of horses in the whole country round, and by frequently introducing good customers, whose purses were oftentimes longer and more fully stocked than their heads, secured their hearty good-will, which at odd times was displayed by the propitiatory gift of an ailing, vicious, or unsound quadruped, which donation the lady invariably accepted on the assumption that lead was cheap, and that anyhow these afflicted animals formed an interesting subject on which to pursue scientific experiments not yet thoroughly tested by the Veterinary College. Now and again, thanks to her really marvellous knowledge of horseflesh, and to the virtue of innumerable recipes accumulated during many years, she succeeded in effecting extraordinary cures. Then Mrs. Forrester's triumph was complete. When she had conquered some obstinate spavin, patched up a ricketty back-sinew, or doctored satisfactorily any long-standing complaint through remedies peculiarly her own, she experienced a sen-sation of genuine pleasure. So great, indeed, was the respect in which her healing powers were held by the simple country folks, that they were wont to aver Mrs. Forrester was worth all the skilled practitioners put together. It therefore was not unnatural if these gentlemen viewed so formidable a rival with envy and suspicion, declaring her to be a person of

inferior experience, professing to know more than she really
did. Every morning of her life regularly when the clock
struck six, in the depth of winter or the height of summer,
Mrs. Forrester rose from her bed and spent the hours before
breakfast in going the round of the farm, inspecting the stock,
examining the hedges, and cross-questioning the men; afterwards she retired into an inner sanctum, a sort of half
laboratory, half carpenter's shop, on whose shelves were
carefully stowed away the lotions, draughts, and cunning
compounds wherewith she sustained her reputation. On non-
hunting days she employed herself by nailing, hammering,
planing, sawing, mending, and manufacturing the various
articles in use on the premises. Sometimes she appeared for
a day or two with her arm in a sling or fingers bandaged up,
due to some such untimely accident as the slip of a chisel, the
shutting of a knife, or splintering of a bit of wood. In a
virgin country where man must depend upon his own exertions to supply his daily wants, such a woman as Mrs.
Forrester would have been regarded as a valuable auxiliary—
a helpmate who could turn her hand to anything; but among
an enervated, over-civilised population, her accomplishments
often failed to be appreciated at their full value, calling forth
ridicule rather than respect, while the verdict of the public
was "A clever but original old lady, who ought to have been
a man." Public opinion, however, did not disturb the even
tenor of her ways. She was made of too strong metal to be
wafted backwards and forwards like a feather by every puff
of wind. She had her own ideas, and stuck to them through
thick and thin.

On the afternoon of the day following Kate Brewser's
arrival at Sport Lodge, Mrs. Forrester determined on a
reconnaissance in force. She therefore ordered out her dog-
cart, into which was harnessed an antiquated hunter who
rejoiced in the somewhat singular name of Resurrection. He
had been snatched from the very jaws of death by his present
mistress, who during an obstinate and well-nigh fatal attack
of tetanus had treated him with frequent injections into the
veins of nitrate of amyll, and thus christened the patient in

memory of the event. Mrs. Forrester mounted on to the box-seat, took the reins in her hand, gave the whip a playful flourish, and started, with the intention of calling upon Miss Brewser before anyone else had done so, in order to be able to report as usual. Ready as she invariably was to make new acquaintances, the two girls, by their youth and isolated position, inspired her with a more than customary interest, rendering her intent on forming an opinion as to their merits as quickly as possible. She drove steadily along until she came to Foxington town, where she encountered her particular friend, Mr. McGrath, who, not yet entirely recovered from the effects of the pigskin, had declined to rise at the preposterously early hour of half-past six o'clock in order to jog close upon sixteen miles to covert, and was therefore wiling away the afternoon by strolling gently up and down the High Street, flattening his nose disconsolately against the shop windows, and smiling fraternally at every decent-looking young woman he happened to run against in the course of his peregrinations. Mrs. Forrester's arrival was a perfect godsend to the idle, ennuied Hibernian. He made such frantic gestures that in an instant she, nothing loth, brought the vehicle to a standstill.

"Hulloa!" she said in her friendly unceremonious fashion. "What are you doing here all by yourself, like a lost sheep? Where are the others? Gone hunting?" as Mr. McGrath nodded assent. "Pray why did you not go too? Nothing amiss with the stud, I hope? It's too early in the day to begin with invalids."

"No, no, the stud is right enough," answered Mr. McGrath with a shake of the head. "Faith, but I wish the master could say the same. He's very bad."

"Bad? Why, what's the matter, man? You look in the rudest of health."

"Ah! Looks are deceptive. It always *was* my fate to appear best when I suffered most. I'm in great pain, I can assure you."

"I'm sorry to hear it. But why so mysterious? What is this malady from which you are suffering thus terribly? I declare you have roused my curiosity."

"An injured, abrased, and inflamed cuticle," replied Mr. McGrath with perfect gravity, "which, however slight it may sound, renders horse-exercise an extremely unpleasant mode of locomotion. Now don't laugh. 'Pon my life it's no laughing matter," he added something querulously, as the lady's sides shook with mirth.

"You're exactly like all men," she said, looking at him in friendly contempt. "When the least thing goes wrong, you've no more pluck than a barn-fowl. A prick of a pin is enough to make you think you're going to die. Men are so awfully frightened about their precious selves. They haven't half the courage of the women."

"Don't kick a poor fellow when he's down, there's a dear good soul. I came to you to be cheered, not to be lectured on the shortcomings of my sex. Gad! but if it's your own superiority you wish to prove by the argument, I am willing to admit it. There aint many people in this world like Mrs. Forrester."

"You are incorrigible, Terry," she said with a conciliatory smile. "But come now, since you say you are suffering such agonies, allow me to propose a remedy. Have you ever tried a mixture of vinegar and glycerine in cases of a similar distressing nature? Three parts vinegar to one of glycerine. It's a recipe of my own, and a most efficacious one, only you must not mind if it smarts a bit at the first application. You must endeavour to bear the pain heroically. I constantly use the mixture in cases of cuts and sprains among the gees, and find it very successful."

"Thanks. I promise to try the prescription this evening, and shall hope to derive such benefit from its use as to enable me to turn out to-morrow with the Critchley at Doddington. I see they don't muster until ten o'clock, which, thank goodness, is a slightly more reasonable hour. These early meets are positively deadly, and play the bear with my delicate constitution."

"*Your* delicate constitution suffers from late nights, big cheroots, and black bottles, my friend, not from early rising. I declare I've no patience with you young men. You begin

by setting the fundamental laws of nature at defiance, burning
the candle at both ends, expending the vital forces without
supplying any fuel to the furnace, and then you wonder that
the fire is feeble, and abuse your constitutions.   Just as if
they were to blame, indeed!   If you were only taught a few
scientific truths in your youth, and the most elementary
principles of physiology, you would know very differently,
and learn that nine times out of ten you have only yourselves
to thank for your ailments.   Abjure smoke and turn teetotal-
lers, and your health would soon improve.

"You are in a very severe mood, Mrs. Forrester.   I withdraw my luckless remark."

"No need to do that.   And what's more, a few home truths
do you men a lot of good now and then.   Things are made
far too pleasant for you in these days."

"Mrs. Forrester, I wonder whether you would condescend
to answer a question that has troubled my mind for long?"
asked Terry somewhat irrelevantly.

"That depends entirely on what it is.   I make no rash
promises."

"Well, since you entertain so profound a contempt for my
unfortunate sex, how did you ever bring yourself to commit
matrimony?"

"Because my sentiments have grown with age and experience, and because, being a woman, in my youth I possessed
a woman's foibles, and was not proof against the voice of the
charmer.   Because," and her voice trembled ever so slightly,
"I was not happy at home, and I liked Colonel Forrester
better than I did anyone else.   My mother struck me once in
a fit of passion, and he took my part.   I felt grateful to him,
and when he asked me to be his wife I gave my consent.
Now," with a change from grave to gay, now, Mr. Curious,
you know all about it, and I hope you feel satisfied."

"Forgive me, Mrs. Forrester," he said, if I have done
anything to recall unpleasant memories."

Somehow he felt sorry for having asked the question.

"Terry," she replied bending forward and laying her hand
on his shoulder, while a kindly expression swept across her

weatherbeaten face, "I daresay there are episodes in the lives of most of us which we do not care to dwell upon, and an old sore is hard to heal. You are a goodhearted creature, and would never wound anyone intentionally. If I had had children of my own, if I had been a happy woman, I might have been very different. Do not let us talk of it. And now I really must be getting on, or the chances are I shall have had my journey for nothing and find my young lady out."

"Your young lady? Pray who do you intend honouring with a call?"

"I gave you credit for more discernment. Why, slow pate! Miss Brewser, of course. Who else do you suppose? That reminds me; did you ever give that gay friend of yours my message, or did you forget it altogether?"

"No, not I. I not only delivered it in full, but embellished it by various little additions of my own. There's nothing like serving things up spicy when you are about it. A little exaggeration does no harm."

"Well!" ejaculated the lady, forgetting her hurry, and administering a soothing tap to Resurrection with the butt end of the whip. "This is interesting. What did the great Colonel say to our plan?"

"Faith! I hardly know. Jack's a rum chap in some ways. He takes ideas of honour and so forth into his head every now and then, and one might just as well talk to a pig as to try and dislodge them. You can't get at him either when he's in a mood of this sort, for he declines to give out his opinions. Bedad! but we had real sport last night. Fuller did the gentleman; offered Jack first innings, and refused to spoil the market, just as if he had a chance against Jack, indeed! However, nothing would satisfy him until he succeeded in getting up a bet on the subject. You know his mania for gambling in every shape or form."

"But about this bet, Terry. What sort of bet did he make?" said Mrs. Forrester, pricking up her ears at the prospect of a bit of gossip. "Who did he bet with?"

"Why, with Jack. To tell the truth, the latter seemed so annoyed altogether by the conversation and by our recom-

mendations he should marry the heiress, that I verily believe
he hardly knew the nature of the bet, but Fuller booked it
fast enough.   Ten to one on the Honourable ; it's down in
black and white."

" Well, I wish Jack success, I am sure.   Ready money is
sadly needed in that quarter, and an infusion of wealth into
the family would be cordially welcomed."

" Yes.   He went and lost a lot to that devil Fuller only
last night, worse luck."

" You don't say so ? I should have thought after all that
has come and gone he would have had a little more sense.
Well, we must try and precipitate matters if we can.   I tell
you what, Terry," in a confidential whisper.   " You and I
will bring the young couple together and give them a helping hand.   Friends are often very useful on these occasions.
Jack is a real nice fellow with all his faults, and I know no
one I would sooner do a good turn to ; therefore I'll go this
minute and see what can be done to pave the way.   Ta-ta,
Terry.   Hope to find you out to-morrow with a renovated
epidermis.   Don't forget, three parts vinegar to one of
glycerine."

" Shan't I see you again before then ? " he asked wistfully,
thinking how very hard it was to kill time in the absence of
companions when left to his own devices.   " You won't spend
all the afternoon with Miss Kilmansegg, surely ? "

" Meaning to say I had better devote a portion of it to
Mr. Terence McGrath, eh ?   Well, if you feel sufficiently
active to step out to my place about tea-time, you shall be
treated to a cup of that comparatively harmless beverage, and
hear my report in full.   There, is your discontent appeased ? "

" Entoirely.   I feel now I have something to live for—
something to look forward to."

" So much the better," came the rejoinder.   " It's a thousand pities you do not cultivate some legitimate ambition in
life instead of wasting your abilities and frittering your days
away.   There's good stuff in you, Terry, only circumstances
have done their best to spoil it.   Au revoir."

CHAPTER IX.

A SLIGHT REBUFF.

WITH this parting salutation Mrs. Forrester once more coaxed the docile Resurrection into a trot, and without any further interruption to her progress proceeded to Sport Lodge, driving up to the door in her handsomest style. To ring the bell and enquire if Miss Brewser were within was but a second's work. It was, however, with no small satisfaction she found the interrogation answered in the affirmative. So leaving Resurrection in charge of the small boy who officiated as carriage-groom, and taking care to adjust a large rug over the animal's attenuated quarters, she entered the house, and was promptly ushered into the drawing-room.

Mrs. Forrester's eye was more accustomed to horseflesh and cattle than to elegant furniture; nevertheless even she perceived a considerable improvement had been effected since Mr. Reginald Rich's tenancy. Only a few seconds, however, were accorded her in which to make observations, for Kate almost immediately appeared, and advancing with both hands outstretched, and every sign of the liveliest pleasure, said—

"This is indeed good of you, Mrs. Forrester, to come and see me. I know you quite well from repute, and have so often read of your doings in the *Field* and sporting papers that I feel as if we were already acquainted.

Now Mrs. Forrester, free as she was from feminine vanity, had still her weak spots, and the artless and evidently sincere flattery of Kate's introductory speech flew straight to one of them. Had she been told she possessed good eyes, a pretty foot, or becoming headgear, she would have laughed the idea

to scorn, and it would have made no more impression upon
her than upon a dried-up old piece of shoe-leather; but to be
told that she was a celebrity, that outside people knew of her
exploits in the hunting-field, and admired and respected her,
was a different thing altogether.

She looked into Kate's fresh, honest, smiling face, and said
to herself—

. "Humph! You'll do; you're a nice sort of girl—not one of
the stuck-up, airified creatures I abominate."

She did not give outward expression to the thought, being
far removed from the army of gushers, but answered instead
in a remarkably gracious manner—

"You make me blush, Miss Brewser," though such an
occurrence was a distinct impossibility, "and it is my turn to
feel flattered by so kind a reception. My renown, if renown
indeed I have, is but of a very humble order. However, I
predict that you and I will be good friends. You hunt, of
course?"

"Yes, in a feeble, inexperienced sort of way. I feel quite
bashful in coming to the shires."

"Ah! no matter. You will be one of us—one of our
innermost circle, so to speak."

"That, I fear, is an honour to which I am scarcely qualified to aspire," returned Kate politely. "You see, I am
really new to the work, having only hunted regularly for two
seasons, and that in the unfashionable provinces, but I have
ridden all my life, and always loved horses. And now please
tell me something of the people I am likely to meet in this
neighbourhood, so that I may not appear an absolute ignoramus. Are they *very* formidable?"

"You must judge for yourself. It depends a good deal
upon whether you are easily frightened. I may as well tell
you, however, that as a rule the folks here are not particularly
sociable, especially towards strangers. Most of them fancy
themselves a good deal, and think it confers distinction to be
extremely exclusive. Our big-wigs, the Earl and Countess
of Huntingshire, are of a totally different order. People who
are somebodies have nearly always pleasant manners. It's

only the small fry that consider airs and graces *comme il faut.*
Our magnates generally go abroad about this season of the
year on account of her ladyship's health.   She is very
delicate—suffers from a pulmonary complaint.   This winter,
however, I am told they intend remaining if possible.   If
they do so, you will probably meet the only daughter, Lady
Anne Birkett, a nice unaffected sort of girl, and a universal
favourite.   She is passionately fond of hunting, but only
possessing one old screw, does not get out very often.   After
the Huntingshires come the Stapletons of Stapleton Hall.
They give out that they are descended in direct male line from
the Stapleton who came over to England at the time of the
Conquest, and in consequence seem to fancy themselves
higher and greater than the rest of the world.   Just as if
God's creatures were not alike, and had not each two eyes,
a nose, and a mouth !   It's such rubbish, when the only
trouble they have taken is that of being born into the world
with a golden spoon in their aristocratic mouths.   About once
a year they ask some few of us to a duty dinner, which we
attend from pure motives of curiosity.   On other occasions
we remain uninvited, for the Stapletons, male and female,
are renowned for thoroughly understanding the mutton-chop
for the beefsteak style of entertainment."

   "What is that?" said Kate, with pardonable curiosity.

   "Have you never heard of it, my dear ?   Well, after all,
it is only another name for the *quid pro quo* principle so
thoroughly in vogue in modern society—that elementary
law of exchange and barter which even the savages of
Southern Africa appreciate, and which seems inherent to the
genus *homo.*   What I give I expect to receive, what I receive
I expect I shall *have* to give—a perfect system of reciprocity
well calculated to annihilate all real generosity or kindliness
of heart.   Do you not understand this simple rule ? "

   "I call it a *disgusting theory,*" replied Kate warmly.   "One
that does away with our faith in human nature, and teaches
the impossibility of caring for our fellow creatures for what
they *are,* instead of for what they have *got.*   I *hate* such
worldliness and despise it thoroughly."

" So you may, so may I ; but all the same it's human nature. Half society is composed of mean, grovelling parasites, who prey upon the other portion. How can you expect such creatures to *give* anything, unless they get *back* in return ? They are always trying to crawl higher and higher out of their proper sphere. Those whom they might be friendly with they profess to despise, and those whom they would be friendly with despise *them*. But," she added, suddenly remembering it might be unwise to run down her neighbours to a comparative stranger, even though that stranger was apparently a kindred spirit, "I ought not to influence your opinions beforehand. You will probably form them fast enough for yourself."

" I have done that already," said Kate, " and feel far from prepossessed by your account.

Then, after a slight pause, she added with natural curiosity, " But tell me, have you many good lady riders ? Many besides yourself I mean ? "

" Dear me, yes. We are overburdened with women. Not ones," thinking the speech might be taken in an uncomplimentary sense, "who can ride, but ones who know nothing about it. Last year we had a professional beauty. Somebody asked her if she could hunt ? ' Hunt ? oh, dear, yes. Extremely fond of it ! ' Well, Captain Fuller, for he was the offender, mounted her on his best horse, with strict injunctions to follow him. The lady appeared exquisitely got up, little golden curls peeping out from beneath her hat, pearl brooch, diamond earrings, jewelled whip, and half a packet of violet powder upon her fair face. Everyone was on the *qui vive* to see the famous Mrs. X's performances. Well, my dear, the very first jump settled her. It was quite a little place, but too big for the beauty, who flew from the saddle, and executed a remarkably neat voluntary under the very eyes of the field. Alas ! however, the bodice happened to be tight, the lady plump, and buttons rolled in every direction. A dozen men rushed to the fair one's assistance, who on her return to town spread wonderful reports of her own prowess in the hunting-field. This is only a specimen of a portion of those who come out. Of course we have some ladies who go really well, and show a lot of the men the way. There's a Miss Palliser, for instance, who rides uncommonly hard; she is very tall and very thin, sits bolt upright in the saddle, and looks severely out at the world from between her animal's ears. Her pluck is undeniable, but she bustles and shoves at the gates, cuts in, and jumps upon people at the fences in such a manner that she is far from popular; nevertheless, in every good run she is always to the fore. The young men make forcible remarks; but there! very few care to see a woman's skirt fluttering in the distance. It conveys an uncomfortable suggestion of inferiority, not to say of cowardice. Then we have Mrs. Paget and Lady Beckley, Lady Anne Birkett, and Mrs. Phipps, wife of the Foxington dealer. Altogether not more than half a dozen who really follow hounds. You see it is a good big country for a lady to get over."

"I suppose so. It certainly looked formidable enough coming along even in the train. I must confess a good many of the ditches struck me as being uncommonly wide."

"They take a bit of doing certainly, but it is wonderful how soon the horses get accustomed to them. You asked me for my advice just now, Miss Browser, so I give it. Whatever other mistakes you may commit, always remember to go a good pace at your fences; the best horse alive can't clear width without the necessary impetus."

"Thanks very much for the hint," said Kate gratefully, " and I will endeavour to bear it in mind. Two of my horses inspire me with entire confidence, but the third is quite untried. However, no doubt I shall find out her capabilities before long. What I fear most is my total ignorance of the country, even to finding the way about. I wonder whether any very—*very*—VERY good-natured individual might be induced to take compassion upon an unprotected female, and constitute himself her pilot for a few days, just till the novelty wears off and she is able to get on alone? I begin to feel quite nervous."

"You need'nt. You will find plenty of candidates ready

to apply for the vacant situation, and the principal difficulty
may consist in making a judicious choice. Oddly enough
when a women elects to follow any particular man, he is
always pleased, and seems to think her doing so sheds a sort
of reflected glory upon *himself*. He accepts the risk of being
jumped upon with equanimity for the sake of the distinction.
Besides, the pilotee can always see what *he* is doing, how
hard *he* rides, how well *he* goes. However, to return to our
subject, if you want to go real downright hard, and are sure
of your horses, you can't possibly do better than follow
Colonel Clinker. No one in these parts is a patch to him.
Captain Fuller, too, though not so brilliant, is a good steady
man with hounds, who knows what he is about, and who
never takes more out of his nags than is necessary. On the
whole, I would reckon him a safer escort for a lady. He
is always well in front, and the Colonel is sometimes a trifle
overdaring. The three brothers Johnson are also reliable
pilots, and sure to turn up at the end of every gallop. On
the other hand, if you just want to ride about and coffee-
house, and, like many young ladies, consider the hunting-field
a fine arena for flirtation, you cannot do better than stick to
Mr. McGrath. He has lots to say for himself, and is a most
amusing companion."

"I don't *want* an amusing companion," answered Kate,
feeling as if Mrs. Forrester had somewhat underrated her
powers of equitation, "and I despise people who go out
hunting in order to flirt. Its ridiculous to begin with, and
wholly unsuitable to the occasion. Such eccentricities of conduct are better indulged in in private, and not under the
critical gaze of some one or two hundred horsemen and
women. My ambition soars higher, even indeed to trying
to follow this Colonel Clinker of whom you speak, although
probably at a respectful distance."

"Bravo! The ladies are all fond of Jack. He's a sad
dog in his way."

"Do you mean that he is nice?"

"Well, most people think so, but you had better judge
for yourself. I almost wonder, Miss Brewser, that you have

never made Colonel Clinker's acquaintance at some of the numerous race-meetings. He's about the best gentleman-jock of the day."

"You don't mean to say he is the *celebrated* Colonel Clinker," exclaimed Kate, vivaciously. She felt greatly impressed by the fact, for during the perusal of those sporting papers which formed part of her daily literature she had constantly read of this accomplished gentleman's successes, and was prepared to esteem and admire him accordingly. "I had no idea of that."

"Ah, I thought it strange his name seemed to awake no answering chord. But, my dear young lady, if you are still bent on following the Honble. Jack out hunting, allow me to whisper one word of caution."

"What is it?" said Kate, thinking Mrs. Forrester's warning would probably prove a recommendation not to be too foolhardy or adventurous.

"Oh! nothing," replied the artful old lady, "at least nothing very particular, only don't you go and be falling in love with him, that's all. Jack's a terribly fascinating fellow, good looking, pleasant, well-bred—just the sort of man girls take a fancy to, but he can't afford to marry, more's the pity."

"Really Mrs. Forrester, I am exceedingly obliged to you, but the state of Colonel Clinker's finances is not likely to affect me in the slightest. I am not at all matrimonially inclined, neither am I in the habit of losing my heart so easily to every chance individual I happen to come across."

"I did not for an instant intend to convey so erroneous an idea to your mind, but you know what young men are, and I thought it only fair to give a quiet hint, taking the circumstances into consideration."

"Thank you, but I am not aware that they demand any particular circumspection; impecunious gentlemen are common enough. I suppose there are no unusual features in the present case?"

"Not exactly; but when a certain lady becomes the subject of a bet amongst men, it is only fitting and proper that that lady, especially if she be a stranger, should be informed of the occurrence."

"And do you mean to declare men have been betting about ME?" asked Kate, with flashing eyes. "Has *my name* been bandied about already?"

"Don't be vexed, my dear," said Mrs. Forrester soothingly, beginning to feel a little alarmed at the commotion which she herself had raised. "Very likely the whole thing was intended as a joke. Very likely my informant may have been wrong. The affair came to my ears quite casually."

"I call it odious, horrible, and unmanly of them," continued Kate angrily.

"It is not nice, certainly," murmured the other, sympathetically, for she always made it a rule to go with the stream.

"Nice? I should think it wasn't indeed. People in these parts seem to have funny manners."

"I don't suppose they are worse than they are anywhere else," replied Mrs. Forrester sedately, considering it incumbent upon her to defend the absent.

"Perhaps you will be good enough to inform me of the exact nature of this *said* bet," returned Kate, with increasing dignity. "I object to semi-confidences. They go too far in one way, and not far enough in another."

Mrs. Forrester began to think that this seemingly pleasant young lady might, under certain conditions, prove more formidable than she had anticipated. She therefore concluded that the moment had arrived to try the effect of more conciliatory overtures.

"Tell me what has been said," demanded Kate sternly.

"My dear, you take this matter too seriously altogether. No importance should be attached to such a trifle. Even if Captain Fuller *did* bet ten to one that Jack Clinker would propose and be accepted, you surely can afford to smile at so foolish a wager. No one can *make* you marry a man against your will."

"No, thank goodness!" exclaimed Kate fervently; then setting her white teeth with a vicious expression, she added,

"According to my present way of thinking, *nothing* shall *ever* induce me to marry at *all*."

"Ah! you will change that opinion some of these days."

"I know I never *shall*."

"Then it is needless for me to warn you against the fascinations of my friend Jack. Needless to tell you what a desperate flirt he is."

"Quite needless. *Your friend Jack*," placing a marked emphasis on the words, "is nothing to me or I to him. All I desire is that we may remain complete strangers one to the other. Any wish on my part to make his acquaintance has completely disappeared. I ignorantly fancied him a sort of hero, a veritable 'admirable Crichton,' but my ideas have undergone a most complete transformation."

"And yet I assure you no better fellow lives on the face of this earth."

"In which case I prefer less immaculate beings. They are more to my mind."

"Upon my word, you carry resentment too far. It's ridiculous that you and he should be at loggerheads, all about nothing too."

"That depends on what you *call* nothing. *I call* Colonel Clinker's offence a most serious one, and one which few women in my position would forgive. Why should he want to bet about my marrying him? Simply because he fancies me to be rich, and because—as you yourself admitted just now—he is out at elbows. Do you call *that* gentlemanly conduct, pray?"

"Poor Jack! you have evidently taken him *en horreur*, as the French put it, and nothing I can say or do will suffice to convince you of his good qualities. Perhaps some of these days you may find cause to alter your opinions, and to view what at most can only be regarded as a slight and natural indiscretion with greater indulgence."

Kate felt aggravated by the above remarks.

"Perhaps," she echoed scornfully. "Mutability is the law of nature and the prerogative of women; still we shall see. I doubt your prediction ever coming true.

"One would not think every winter, when the trees to all intents and purposes are dead, that they will blossom once more
into life, sending forth vigorous young shoots, and yet they do.
It strikes me, Miss Brewser," fixing a keen, inquiring glance
upon the girl, "that your heart is not unlike the trees, *i.e.*
enjoying a wintry sleep, from which it will awaken sooner or
later. I am an old woman, and have studied the frailties of
my sex."

"Nevertheless, Mrs. Forrester, for once your deductions
are wrong. My heart is enjoying *no* wintry sleep, but simply
reposes in its normal condition. But come, we are degenerating
into nonsense."

"A signal for me to be going," replied Mrs. Forrester,
looking at her watch, "particularly as I have an appointment
with Mr. Phipps, the dealer, on my way back through the
town. I hope, my dear, we part amicably, and that you
will not bear malice for what I almost fear has proved an
officious and unwelcome act on my side. At least give me
credit for good intentions, and believe I meant only kindly.
And if—" hesitating slightly, "you would be good enough
to keep the subject under discussion an entire secret, it wil
confer a great obligation."

Kate Brewser drew herself up to her full height, and cast a
bold steady glance upon her companion. "Mrs. Forrester,"
she said proudly, "I am not in the habit of repeating
confidences or retailing gossip. You need fear nothing from
me; besides, I am not likely to circulate a story so galling
to my pride."

Mrs. Forrester brightened considerably at this speech,
although for once in her life she felt as if she had received
a severe snubbing. Fond as she was of meddling in other
people's affairs, she had been the least little bit afraid of her
own handiwork. It was a relief to think she could trust
Kate, and that she was not likely to bring her into trouble.
She began to respect the girl. Evidently she had more in
her than she had given her credit for, and was very far removed
from the ordinary run of young ladies she was in the habit of
encountering.

"After all," she said, trying the effect of conciliatory diplomacy, "after all nothing is easier in this world than to avoid people one dislikes. Colonel Clinker need never trouble you much," whereupon Mrs. Forrester rose from her seat, thinking it better to let well alone, and shook Kate by the hand with every appearance of cordiality.

"Good-bye, my dear," she said, "I shall come and see you again before long. You and I will be good friends I predict, in spite of our unfortunate little discussion."

"Don't blame yourself in any way, Mrs. Forrester. On the contrary, I feel very grateful to you for your communication. I might have jumped down this gentleman's throat in my foolish admiration for his powers of equitation, and now—why now—forewarned is forearmed."

"That's all right," responded the other cheerfully. "All's well that ends well, and I should hate to make mischief between my fellow-creatures." With which benevolent and highly laudable sentiment she effected an escape while the moment appeared propitious.

For five whole minutes did Resurrection pursue the even tenor of his ways undisturbed. His mistress seemed preoccupied, her brow clouded by abstruse thought. Gradually, however, it cleared. Mrs. Forrester was herself again, and the whip descended with a sharp click of reprimand on the quadruped's lean sides in reproof for his previous neglect of duty.

"Yes, of course!" said the lady half aloud, speaking like one who had successfully severed a Gordian knot. "Everything is certain to come right. The great secret of overcoming a woman's heart is to inspire it with interest. Love, pity, hatred, contempt, no matter what the sentiment, so long as it is not indifference. Now after I am gone, this Miss Brewser will sit down and go over every word I have said. She'll begin by detesting Jack with all her might, and fly out at the mere recollection of him, but in a little while she'll cool down, and then she'll set to work and wonder what he's like, whether he's really such a bad lot, why he takes so kindly to flirtation, what the ladies see in him and so forth.

He will engage her thoughts if nothing else, and that's half the battle. Pique and wounded pride can be trusted to do the rest. Some horses must be driven by the law of contrary, and some women are exactly the same. Ask them to do a thing and they refuse, ask them *not* to do it and it is done directly. If Miss Brewser is warned not to fall in love with Colonel Clinker, I bet she's head over ears in no time. Ha, ha, ha! Jack, my boy! I promised Terry to do you a good turn when I could, and I flatter myself I have advanced your cause not a little. To-day's work has set the ball rolling in earnest."

Which might be true enough; but whether Mrs. Forrester was justified in all her surmises seems open to question. She herself, however, was supremely satisfied at the delicate and discriminating manner in which she considered affairs had been conducted. She had recovered from the effects of Kate's sarcasms and possessed a sanguine disposition.

Meanwhile Mr. McGrath was ensconced in Mrs. Forrester's drawing-room, studying Youatt on the horse, and impatiently awaiting the lady's arrival. The sound of carriage wheels produced a thrill of welcome expectation.

"Well," he exclaimed interrogatively, advancing to meet Mrs. Forrester at the front door, "what's she like?"

"She'll do," came the decided reply. "Quite a good sort, but rather high-mettled, wants riding on the snaffle, with a running martingale. The least touch of the curb makes her chuck her head about like an unbroken colt. She's spirited, but very light in the mouth, and requires delicate handling."

From which refined remarks Mr. McGrath gathered Mrs. Forrester was unusually impressed in Miss Brewser's favour.

"Humph! A high stepper, is she? proud I suppose, and stuck up?"

"Not the least. She's very unaffected, but I fancy has a bit of a temper. However, she has got plenty of brains as well, and I would not give the snuff of a candle for a woman who does not possess the two combined."

"I prefer the brains without the temper."

"You don't know what you're talking about. You require

the one to sweeten the other, certainly, but the dish loses piquancy if too uniformly seasoned."

And then the two friends retired to the drawing-room, where over a cup of strong Souchong they discussed the results of the visit in all its bearings.

"I'm afraid she'll never take to Jack," prophesied Mr. McGrath in tones of dismal foreboding, after he had listened to a partial unfolding of the tale. "She'll never forgive him if she hears of that unfortunate bet."

"Nonsense, Terry," said Mrs. Forrester, with a severe glance of reprimand. "You're a regular ignoramus, and understand no more about women and women's ways, despite your thirty odd years, than a baby, probably not so much. Now listen to me. I know quite well what I am about. I have studied the psychological side of the feminine character, and I tell you girls like Miss Brewser, with plenty of dash and spirit, cannot be dealt with as the ordinary run of women. They require peculiar and judicious treatment. You leave it to me."

What would Mrs. Forrester have said in justification of her "peculiar and judicious treatment" could she at that moment have seen the girl of "dash and spirit" crying her heart out with mortification and the effects of wounded pride? Would she have been *quite* so confident in the success of her undertaking, or so satisfied with the result of her labours? Might she not have realised that sometimes "Where ignorance is bliss, 'tis folly to be wise," and that there is such a thing in the world as carrying even friendship too far?

CHAPTER X.

THE next morning Kate was up betimes. She had only spoken the truth when she confessed to a certain feeling of nervousness at making her first appearance in the hunting-ground of so crack a county as Huntingshire, and it was this sensation, which prompted a more than ordinary solicitude as to the correctness of her equestrian attire. She was determined that it at least should come up to the most critical standard and be pronounced well-nigh faultless, for two seasons' experience had sufficed to teach how the smallest deviation from existing fashions would surely be remarked by sharp and condemnatory feminine eyes, whose acute glances delighted rather in censure than in praise. From the men Kate feared nothing, but of her own sex she often avowed herself to be honestly afraid. Therefore she took unusual pains on this particular morning, devoting quite an extra half-hour to the exigencies of the toilette.

But on looking into the glass, and scrutinising with friendly partiality the image therein reflected, a faint smile of satisfaction played around the corners of her mouth, for she could not help noticing how admirably the plain, close-fitting habit, dark-brown in colour, set off her trim figure to advantage, or how smart and natty the general effect proved.

"Thank goodness!" she exclaimed, with a sigh of relief, not wholly devoid of elation. "My new habit is a success. Without a wrinkle anywhere, and fits like a glove. Well, they won't be able to pick holes in my clothes to-day, however hard they may try!"

Now as no woman living, whether strong-minded or the

reverse, is utterly indifferent to outward appearances, the consciousness of being well-dressed and properly "got up," as the saying is, endowed Kate with comfort and fortitude, and restored her self-possession to a degree which, under less favourable circumstances, might have been lacking.

"What an age you've been, Kate!" exclaimed Mary, on that young lady making her appearance. "I feel half in· clined to preach you a lecture on the evils of unpunctuality. Do you know what the time is?"

"The clocks are wrong," said she with a smile, "and my white tie proved more than usually obstinate. However, now let's be off."

The morning was bright and cloudless, with a clear pale blue sky, brilliant sun, and gentle breeze, which, save for an occasional sharpness, might have recalled the departed summer, and as the two girls drove merrily along, at a good smart nine-miles-an-hour trot—for Brandy and Soda were no laggards when once fairly started—their spirits rose. The exhilarating sensation of being borne swiftly through the air sent the colour to their cheeks and the light to their eyes. Before long their excitement increased on seeing strings of grooms and second horsemen, the latter leading riderless animals at a slow jog-trot out to covert. At this spectacle Kate's doubts about finding the way were finally set at rest. The road after a bit led through some huge grass-fields, larger than any she had ever seen before, at each end of which were placed five-barred gates, to prevent the cattle from straying away, and opening these kept old Stirrup pretty well employed, forcing him to clamber in and out of the vehicle with an agility rather trying to his aged bones, and still more so to his new boots. Fortunately the mud was not deep, and inflicted no serious injury, otherwise Stirrup's pride would have been greatly hurt, for he, like his mistress, was bent on putting his best foot foremost, and on upholding the credit of the establishment to the utmost of his feeble ability. To that end, ever since the small hours of the morn· ing he had been busily engaged with a chamois-leather in furbishing up the brass buttons on his coat and the various bits and buckles adorning the horses.   No effort on his part had been wanting to insure the fulfilment of his aspirations, *i.e.* that Kate should burst like some bright new star upon the hunting world of Foxington.   All his hopes and ambition were centred in her and the stud entrusted to his care.

Talk of horses, indeed.   Where was the pair could be shown against King Olaf and the Duckling?   while if it came to riding, he flattered himself he knew somebody who could hold her own with the best of them!   So mused Stirrup as he triumphantly surveyed Kate's back-hair from the hinder seat of the pony phaeton, and thought how impossible it was for anyone to compare with this incomparable mistress of his. Poor old Stirrup.   Doubtless he entertained many delusions; but they were mostly of so pleasing and innocent a nature that the man must have been very hard-hearted who endeavoured to rob him of a single one.   Happy are those who at the age of sixty believe in something and somebody.

Doddington, the place of meeting, proved an old-fashioned farmhouse, standing in a good big enclosure, which offered ample accommodation to hounds, huntsmen, and the multitude at large.

As the two girls drove up, a pretty sight met their eyes. The sun was shining down quite pleasantly and warmly on the solid grey stones of the picturesque building, lighting up with glorious tints the fading russet leaves of a large Virginian creeper, which entirely covered the porch.   It glinted off the quaint latticed windows in scintillating rays, whose brilliancy almost blinded the spectator, and flickered lovingly on the purple asters, red sweet-williams, and golden sunflowers, drooping slowly in the autumnal air.   Overhead the pale sky rose like a fathomless vault flecked with delicate streaks of snowy cloud, against which the tall old elms stretched their straight branches, while numberless rooks cawed and fluttered amongst the topmost twigs, circling round and round their home in a state of manifest anxiety, caused by the appearance of such unaccustomed intruders. On the green grass, lay, stood, and lounged the white-and-tan beauties, with their noble heads, thoughtful brows, and great dark wistful eyes, the elders taking their ease at full length, like sensible creatures, as if cognizant of the work in store; the youngsters, walking and sniffing, rolling, playing, bounding, gambolling, like so many children loosed from school, giving vent now and again to an occasional yelp when reminded by the crack of the whip that there were certain limits not lightly to be overstepped. In their midst, motionless, save for the glances of his quick, far-seeing eye, sat the huntsman, mounted on a grand chestnut horse, a magnificent specimen of the weight-carrying English hunter. Dressed in a scarlet coat and a black velvet cap, he looked a thorough workman from top to toe. That he loved his hounds, and they him, was clear at a glance. Every time they tried with upturned jowl and waving stern to leap to his side, Will Steadall's otherwise somewhat grave countenance relaxed into a smile, and with a word of caress he tossed each one in turn a morsel of biscuit. For thirteen years—years in the commencement full of toil and trouble—had he carried the horn in the Critchley country, and thanks alone to his steady handling, judicious treatment, and unwearied care, the pack now occupied the proud position of being considered about the best in England, while every winter the fields increased numerically, until at length the old frequenters of the hunt exclaimed violently against these monster gatherings, the result of success and fashion. The Critchley, however, had not always been thus favoured, for when Will Steadall first took them in hand he found the hounds a wild, ragged, riotous lot, unequal and uneven, without the smallest idea of discipline, and wont to run a hare almost as readily as they would a fox. But since those days things had mightily changed and improved, and the last season or two the sport shown by the Critchley had, even by envious competitors, been admitted truly exceptional. Therefore people flocked to their meets by the score.

To-day Will Steadall waited as usual for the master to give the signal for an onward move. Meantime, folks continued to arrive singly and in groups. Scattered about in various directions were dismounted grooms buckling up straps, altering stirrups, finally adjusting girths, loosening nosebands, and straightening manes, while in most cases a redcoated runner or astute rustic stood near at hand eagerly pressing his services, in the hopes of gaining an odd coin or so wherewith to enable him to retire promptly to the nearest public and expend the donation in a drop of "something comforting." Carts, gigs, pony-chaises, waggonettes, Victorias bearing pretty fur-wrapped women, and barouches with haughty matrons, all served, despite the somewhat early hour, to swell the crowd and block the only available means of approach and egress. The hospitable owner of the farm, who was a staunch supporter of fox-hunting, aided by sundry labourers, was engaged in passing round among the company trays of bread and cheese, supplemented by huge jugs of frothy beer, which he kindly pressed upon not un-willing friends and neighbours, while, sherry decanter in hand, he begged numerous gentlemen of his acquaintance to partake of a glass, if only "for the good of the house." Alto-gether it formed a bright, pleasant, bustling, active scene, such as we nowhere meet with out of the mother country, in whose sons and daughters love of sport appears almost universal.

And now a move was apparently imminent. Stirrup, therefore, led King Olaf forth from the outer shed, where he had already excited considerable admiration, greatly to the worthy man's gratification. Handing the ribbons over to Mary Whitbread, and telling her to keep the ponies out as long as she felt inclined and was enjoying herself, Kate, casting aside her ulster, lightly sprang into the saddle, and gently took up the reins, while Stirrup proceeded to adjust her skirt satisfactorily and place her feet in the elastic straps.

All being at length arranged, he clambered up on to the Duckling. When they saw the hounds, and began to under-stand winter had come round once more, bringing with it the delights of the chase, both horses pricked their ears, snorted, and manifested every sign of lively pleasure. King Olaf bent his head, arched his beautiful neck, which shone like burnished gold in the sunshine, and pawed the ground impetuously, as if eager to be off without further delay,

while Kate, sitting firm and square, with true balance, **left**
shoulder forwards, hands down, elbows in, and upright
carriage, remained perfectly still, seeming careless enough,
but prepared for any little vagaries which King Olaf, in the
exuberance of his heart or heels, might be prepared to give
vent to. These two were finely suited, and no strangers one
to the other, and Kate knew full well that, with light mouth
and high courage, all King Olaf required was quiet handling
on her part. He did not like being pulled at ; he wanted
leave *to go !* And when hounds ran, go he could, without
mistake or even temporary hesitation.

On horseback the girl felt in her natural sphere. At
crowded parties, in mixed assemblies, among a large con-
course of people, a curious sense of loneliness, of unsatisfied
longing, constantly overtook her, while each advancing year
rendered the frivolity and the insincerity of the world of
fashion still more apparent. But in the saddle such feelings
knew no place. They vanished as if by magic, leaving her
supremely happy. She thoroughly enjoyed the sensation of
power and management—the springy movements, the play of
the bit, the life, the stir, the action, the excitement, and above
all, the independence conferred by horse exercise. She loved
horses, often declaring she preferred them to human beings,
and what's more, knew that she could ride, perhaps not so
well as Mrs. Forrester (*she* was an artiste), but certainly
infinitely better than the majority of women. Without
undue vanity, she could not help being aware of the fact
she possessed " good hands," a gift apparently inherent, and
rarely acquired, though one without which no individual
can be considered a horseman, in the true sense of the word,
for good hands go farther than any other qualification to
establish that cordial *entente* between man and beast—that
secret affinity which can afford to defy danger and triumph
over every obstacle.

Kate now looked about her in the hope of discovering her
acquaintance of the day before ; but Mrs. Forrester, too old
and cunning a sportswoman not to save her horse every
possible inch, invariably ascertained from the master before-

hand the covert first to be called upon, and seldom put in an appearance until the hounds had reached their destination. Coffee-housing at the meet, however agreeable and amusing, she considered of comparatively smaller value than an additional quarter of an hour in the stable given to her animal. The selling of horses was a legitimate business, and only to be conducted under the most favourable circumstances; therefore anything that conduced in the smallest degree to any adverse conditions was to be utterly and entirely condemned.

The young thoroughbreds she generally rode were nearly always impetuous and excitable, and it answered Mrs. Forrester's purpose better, and appeared sounder wisdom, not to send them on to covert in company, when loquacious individuals of an inquiring turn of mind were apt to find out more about them than was desirable, but rather to jog them on quietly herself, and turn up just when the fox had broken away, and people were too greatly occupied with their own affairs to bestow much attention on their neighbours. Such were the tactics pursued by Mrs. Forrester—tactics which fully accounted for her non-appearance at the meet.

Meantime Kate could not remain unconscious of the exceedingly rude way in which some of the ladies present stared at her, just as if she had been a savage beast at a show; but although such conduct appeared extremely underbred, she was too happy and too light-hearted to allow it to disturb her serenity. Although warned to a certain extent by Mrs. Forrester of the exclusiveness of a particular clique, she had failed to understand how it regarded every fresh arrival with suspicion, as an "outsider," and how only after years had gone by could she hope to be incorporated as "one of themselves," or as belonging to the class denominated by it "the right sort." In fact, it took this coterie about five years to make up its fastidious mind whether the stranger were worthy the honour of being called upon, yet another five before anything like intimacy could take place, but by the end of fifteen it suddenly awoke to the fact that Mr. or Mrs. So-and-So was an exceedingly pleasant person, and very much improved since his or her first entry into the county.

Such were Huntingshire manners, and only Kate's ignorance induced her to ascribe to them an unusual degree of
incivility. If they summed her up, she in her quiet little
way could do the same, and she pronounced the men cold and
self-satisfied, the women rude as only ladies can be. These
were her first impressions, subject to some modifications.

But now at length a move was really made, and as they
jogged on in one long procession—carriages, equestrians, and
foot-people all interspersed—Kate's faculties were fully
engaged in restraining the ardour which prompted King
Olaf, with a squeal of delight, to bound up, all fours at a
time, into the air, and then edge nearer and nearer to the
hounds, until every moment he was in danger of treading
upon them, as first one and then another dallied by the roadside, unheedful of the angry admonitions bestowed by the two
whips on their procrastinating tendencies. Although the
company assembled was so large, cub-hunting, not the legitimate chase, still remained the order of the day, and far too
well did Will Steadall understand his business to allow for
one moment of its being otherwise, or (despite various suggestive hints) countenancing the smallest deviation from the
lawful work of the day—namely, the slaughter of the juveniles.

As usual on such occasions, particularly at the commencement of the season, the keenness displayed by the field,
and the impatience to indulge its jumping proclivities, was
something quite remarkable. Nearly every other man
appeared possessed with the insane idea of showing off his
own or animal's capabilities. Several cock fences proved too
enticing to be resisted by a certain portion of the community,
whom Will Steadall eyed with an air of undisguised contempt.

" *They* call themselves sportsmen, indeed!" he exclaimed
in disgust. "Why, these young sparks would just as soon
jump on a 'ound as look at him. They're nothing but a
combination of swagger and ignorance, and I declare I've no
patience wi' em."

Very shortly afterwards the hounds were put into covert,
and before many minutes had gone by the music of their
tongues made itself heard, ringing out on the still air **as they**

rattled the cubs up and down, and crashed through the stiff undergrowth in a steady, resolute fashion which left Reynard but little leisure, and filled the parent foxes with anxious forebodings anent the future of their young. Every now and again, with bewildered mien, heaving sides, and hanging tongue, a youthful and inexperienced hound leapt out of covert, gazing around in a state of vague uncertainty, until sharply admonished by the whip. Then a sudden stillness would ensue, broken only by a faint, tremulous whine, until once more, as one by one they took up the scent, the hounds burst forth into a joyous chorus of sound, and the horses turned with the well-loved voices like the practised hunters most of them were, while the young ones, mad with excitement, danced about on their hind legs or snatched impatiently at the restraining bit.

It was quite an hour or more before a well-grown cub, deserted by his companions and goaded by a courage probably born of despair, ventured to face the open. In an instant a deafening noise ensued, and horsemen by the score galloped frantically in the wake of the retreating animal. A few seconds elapsed before Will Steadall emerged from the centre of the covert, vociferously blowing his horn. One glance sufficed for his practised eye to take in the situation. Horsemen to the rear, horsemen to the front, horsemen on the roads, horsemen on every side, horsemen determined on leading the way, with or without huntsman and hounds.

"Hold hard, gentlemen, *please*," screamed Will Steadall indignantly. "You can't hunt without any 'ounds. Give 'em a chance, now do. You're only a-spoiling of your own sport. There ain't a bit of use in hurrying, not a bit."

But he might as well have whistled to the four winds as to have attempted to restrain a Critchley crowd in its matutinal ardour. No general upon the face of the earth could have marshalled it into order after a summer's interregnum, with a fox viewed away, and two or three convenient gates in close proximity. Therefore Will Steadall gathered his favourites together as quickly as possible, leaving the whips to collect the missing hounds, and with the dash for

which he was renowned, got them out of covert without delay.
Meantime the hustling, jostling multitude charged the nearest
gate in a body, jamming through it with hot haste, regardless of oaths, abjurations, and kicking horses, and Kate,
hardly realising what she was about, found herself engulphed in this moving mass of equestrians, all eager to
push through the narrow opening simultaneously, and all
selfishly bent on the advancement of Number one. Not until
the crush subsided, and people began to scatter in a huge
grass-field, did she perceive the hounds, with Will Steadall in
close attendance, streaming away immediately in front. Then
for the first time that day she was able to give King Olaf
his head, without fear of treading on the heels of those in the
van, and could let him sweep along at his will over the rolling
ridge and furrow, which, with short, quick, active strides, he
seemed to skim like a swallow. Kate's heart rose within her,
and already the excitement of anticipated pleasure danced in
her grey eyes. They were coming to a fence—her first one—
for half through fear of making a fool of herself and half
through an innate caution which prompted her to regulate her
actions in a strange country by those of the majority, she had
hitherto virtuously refrained from jumping, and gone sedately
through the gates, in spite of an intense desire to follow
the example of the larkers. But now she must do one of
two things. She must either go straight ahead, and, like
the leading horsemen, take the fence boldly, or else she
must cast in her lot with a large section of the field,
who immediately instituted a manœuvre in apparently an
opposite direction to that in which the hounds were running. Kate's mind was made up instantly. The obstacle
now facing her was a hedge of ordinary size, rendered
dangerous, however, by the presence of a wide and extremely
blind ditch on the taking off side, into which a couple of
horses had already blundered, pitching their riders over their
heads. Kate, however, was still too young, and her nerve
too good, to be deterred by such trivial misfortunes. King
Olaf and his mistress were apparently in entire unison, for no
sooner did he catch sight of the fence than he cocked his

small veined ears, laid hold of the bit, and quickening his
pace went at the obstacle with a determination not to be
denied. Kate loved jumping as well as he did; she therefore kept his head straight, and in the last stride or two just
steadied him a wee bit. The horse took off beautifully, and
the next instant landed far into the field beyond, having
cleared the hedge like a stag.

"By Jove! Did you see that? What a nailing good
fencer to be sure!" observed the Honble. Jack to his immediate companion, Captain Fuller, as galloping side by side
they endeavoured to regain the ground lost by a bad start.
"There aren't many horses out to-day know their business
better, I'll wager a sovereign."

"I dare say not, he's a nicish horse; and what's more, the
girl can ride a bit. It's Miss Brewser, I believe," responded
the other, somewhat incoherently, for his arms were being
almost pulled out of their sockets by the long raking animal
he bestrode. "Who-ay! Bessie lass—take it easy now," as
she yawed her head in the most unmerciful manner. "No
need to tire both of us out so early in the day."

"Miss Brewser, did you say? She's not half a bad-look-
ing girl either. I declare she rode at that fence in regular
steeplechase form—both hands steady on the reins, and never
raised them an inch. It's not often one sees a woman do
that, and I began to wonder who this new Diana was."

"Fancy your doing such a thing! Why, she's *your* heiress
Clinker."

"Not *my* heiress more than anybody else's," he replied with
a frown. "I wish all you fellows would drop that stupid
chaff. It's not fair to the girl, more especially to a nice one,
as this Miss Brewser seems to be."

Captain Fuller, feeling he had imprudently started a vexed
question, made no answer, but allowed Bessie to snatch at
him with a trifle greater freedom, whereby she soon distanced
the Colonel's more sedate and comfortable mount.

During the above short colloquy hounds had continued to
run fairly well; but alas! cubs as a rule lack the stamina of
their parents, and quickly yield up their lives to a clamorous

I

and bloodthirsty pack.   Already the hunted fox began to twist and turn in every direction, rendering it clear that this merry little spin was destined to be of very short duration, brief as sweet.   Having just flown a flight of rails, to her own and King Olaf's intense satisfaction, Kate was sailing away, well in front, with Miss Palliser only a few lengths behind.   But that lady's ambitious soul brooked no opposition, and the sight of a rival's skirt fluttering anywhere in her vicinity filled it with envy and malice.   She urged her big bay onwards by every means in her power, but though a good stout game horse he was no match in point of speed for King Olaf.   The chestnut could gallop away from him with the greatest ease, as Miss Palliser quickly discovered, to her no small mortification; while Kate, quite unconscious of having roused any inimical sentiments, joyously pursued her way.   But just when horses and riders were really warming to their work, and the glorious excitement of the chase sent a glow through their frames, Reynard's heart failed him, and he made a last convulsive effort to retrace his footsteps and return to the shelter of the friendly covert he had so recently and so rashly forsaken.   At first this stratagem appeared likely to be successful, but when within a hundred yards of the desired haven the foremost hound—old Caroline—ran at him with a rush, seized him in her long sharp teeth, and rolled him over in the yellow eadish which doubtless had often been witness to his infantine gambols.   Poor cub!   If his life had been short, his death at least was a swift and merciful one.   Out of harm's way, fat fowls, early lambs, and young rabbits would henceforth be indifferent to him, while the sharp teeth of old Caroline were surely less torturing than those of a trap.   In a second Will Steadall was on his feet, surrounded by the hounds.   "Who-oop leu leu, pull him! leu leu, pull him!" he cried in tones of encouragement to the young ones, as they tore at Reynard's remains and fought for some choice morsel.   "Down, Prudence! have a care, Christobel!"   While the usual obsequies were being performed, the field came galloping in from all sides, highly delighted with so satisfactory a kill in the open and the part each individual had played. "Nice little spin," they said one to the other, though most of them had arrived nearly a quarter of an hour after time, and could have seen but little of it. "Looks like a good scent." So they stood and chatted amicably, while the hounds lay down on the grass and rested for a few minutes after their recent exertions, the day being warm and sun somewhat overpowering, and decidedly antagonistic to active exercise.

Meantime Kate, who had been wondering what had become of Stirrup, now spied him among the crowd, and beckoned him to come to her side. She could contain her elation no longer, and felt she must impart it to someone; therefore, who better and more sympathetic than he?

"Oh, Stirrup!" she said in a triumphant whisper, "we've had such fun! I'm so glad we came, aren't you? I've broken the ice, too, and taken my first fence in good style. I wish you could have seen King Olaf. He covered himself with glory, and jumped it most beautifully, though two horses came to grief right under his nose."

"I seed 'im, Miss," returned Stirrup in tones of unqualified approval. "'Ow other 'osses misbehaves of 'emselves make no odds to '*im*. Ee don't mean falling, not ee. Why lor bless you, Miss Kate, ee jumped that ere 'edge with at least a yard to spare. There was not another 'oss cleared it in the same form. I seed two of them young swells looking at 'im, as much as to say, 'Ee's a good un, ee is.' King Holaf will hopen some of their eyes afore long, I'll be bound, for all the airs and graces they gives 'emselves, just as if they were better nor other folks. Lor, Miss Kate," he continued in a confidential undertone, "but the way some of these fine gents shirk is something hawful. No one would believe it as 'ad not seen it with 'is own eyes. Why, there aint a 'arf nor yet a quarter as rides a yard. It's all show and purtence. They likes to dress 'emselves up and jog about in company, and that's pretty nigh all they do do, except talk. Bless my 'art, once the danger is at an end, they can talk a cat's 'ead off. Mahogany sportsmen, I calls 'em. Does all their 'unting with a good bottle of wine, and their legs under the table, but werry little when they are either side of a 'oss.

Kate laughed. "What do you imagine the next move is likely to be?" she asked.

"They is pretty shure to 'ang about 'ere for another 'our or so. There be two or three more cubs left in covert, and the 'untsman will roust 'em up a bit more afore ee leaves 'em alone. Maybe its 'is last chance this season."

"In that case, Stirrup, it seems almost a pity to keep the Duckling out longer. He has just had a nice morning's exercise, and I shall want to ride him myself the day after to-morrow in all probability."

"And 'ow about you, Miss Kate? I don't like leaving you all alone. There's them there gates to open, and some of 'em be uncommon awkerd for a lady to lift."

"No matter! Depend upon it I shall manage somehow," she answered confidently. "Perhaps I may ride home in company; and if the worst comes to the worst I can always get off and walk."

"Now look ee 'ere, Miss Kate, dear, if I goes away and leaves you by yourself, don't ee go riding so forrard. The ditches is just hawful blind this time of year, and the werry best of 'osses is liable to make mistakes. Bear the saying in mind, 'Afore Christmas old 'ard, after Christmas ride 'ard.' So do be careful; and if I might make so bold as to advise, don't keep King Holaf out werry late. Remember it's 'is first day, and ee'll be wanted later on. An excitable animal like 'im takes a lot out o' hisself."

With which parting admonitions as to the welfare of the two beings he loved best on earth, old Stirrup somewhat reluctantly turned the Duckling's head towards home. He had a vague, confused idea that, in spite of her command, he was not acting rightly in leaving his mistress unprotected to find her way back alone in a new county, where she herself was quite a stranger. Orders were orders, however, and had to be obeyed. When Kate said a thing Stirrup knew she expected that thing to be done, and resistance beyond a certain point was unavailing.

CHAPTER XI.

FEMALE CRITICISM.

MEANWHILE Mrs. Paget and Miss Palliser, standing almost within earshot, had been engaged in an animated exchange of ideas, of which Kate Brewser, happily for her, was the unconscious object.

"What do you think of our new lady?" asked Mrs. Paget confidentially, edging up to her friend, and setting the ball rolling. "Is she likely to prove an acquisition?"

"*This* Miss Brewser I suppose you mean?" returned Miss Palliser, with an animation so simple a question seemed hardly calculated to provoke.

"*Yes*, this Miss Brewser. This wonderful heiress every one is talking about, and who, they seem to say, will turn all the heads of the Foxington bachelors?"

"The Foxington bachelors, in that case, cannot possess any very great modicum of brains *to turn*," said Miss Palliser sarcastically. "Are they in the habit of running after every strange young person who enters the country?"

"Ah, my dear, that's exactly it. *I* call her position a most questionable one. Two girls, without any chaperone or female escort, setting up for themselves in this independent manner, hardly seem to my mind, quite—quite the thing."

"Who are they? Does any one know anything about their antecedents?"

"Miss Brewser is Scotch, I believe. Beyond that I can say little."

"She may not even be *respectable*," said Miss Palliser, with an air of extreme propriety. "I wonder whether people intend to call?"

" Mrs. Forrester has done so already."

" Just like her, and at her age I dare say it can't signify much one way or the other; but you and I, my dear, really ought to be more circumspect."

Miss Palliser had reached the borderland when ten years more or less are not supposed to make much difference; nevertheless she still considered her reputation a pearl of spotless price, to be kept from contamination just as carefully as in the days of her girlhood. In fact, from her manner and conversation she appeared quite oblivious of the fact that that sunny period had long ago been left behind.

" I suppose the men are sure to make up to her," continued Mrs. Paget.

" My dear," and Miss Palliser fixed a severe glance upon her friend, " *whenever* and *wher*ever in this world the slightest *soupçon* of impropriety exists, the smallest symptom of something wrong, there you may be sure the men will always flock. They have *no* morals, *no* principle, *no* resolution. The faster and the worse style this Miss Brewser is the better they will probably like her, and the more they will run after her. Nowadays virtue is not appreciated." And certainly, if represented by Miss Palliser, it could be easily believed, for a sourer, more malignant-looking, and uglier woman it would be difficult to imagine. From the moment King Olaf had shown his superiority she had sworn eternal enmity against Kate. Personally she knew nothing in the girl's disfavour, but the mere fact that she had proved herself capable of holding her own in the hunting-field was sufficient to render her an object of envy and detestation.

" I'll tell you one thing," whispered Miss Palliser mysteriously.

" Yes," said Mrs. Paget, all attention. " What is it?"

" Why, she can't ride one little bit; she came at a tiny flying fence just now a hundred miles an hour without the smallest control over her horse, and all but knocked me over."

This was untrue, and Miss Palliser knew it, seeing that when Kate had jumped the fence in question she (Miss Palliser) had happened to be quite a couple of lengths in

the rear, but it answered her purpose just as well as any
other statement, and served to establish a *casus belli*.

" She's plucky," observed Mrs. Paget, actuated by a higher
sense of justice.

"Plucky! So's the bird that dashes itself against the iron
railings of its cage; so's the dog that threatens to bite you
when his bone is withdrawn, and the beasts of the field, and
the birds of the air. Plucky, indeed! I tell you she's as
ignorant as a babe in swaddling clothes; I doubt even if she
knows how to stick on, let alone set a horse at a fence.
People like that ought to stay at home, and not come out
hunting. They are a perfect nuisance, and positively dangerous. As for judgment, she has not a scrap, and from her
manner is not likely to acquire it. No, no, depend upon
it the kindest thing we can wish Miss Brewser is that she
may get a rattling good fall, the sooner the better, which
will either teach her caution or lay her up for the rest of the
season."

"Oh, I dare say she knows nothing about riding. How
should she, poor thing?" remarked Mrs. Paget compassionately, who, being younger than Miss Palliser, was inclined to
look upon Kate's shortcomings more leniently than the elder
lady. "Nobody, to my knowledge, has ever heard of her in
the Shires before now."

Mrs. Paget was the wife of a retired brewer, who considered
Huntingshire the acme of fashion and the hot-bed of aristocracy, and who had once been heard to assert that he only
cared for hunting on account of the good society to be met
with in the hunting-field.

"I should think not," said Miss Palliser, with a sneer.
"Do you know, I should not be the least surprised if she
turned out no better than she ought. Such things have happened before now."

"Well, anyhow she rides good horses. That chesnut is a
perfect beauty."

"Yes; it's a sad pity to see such a fine hunter so completely wasted. However, I suppose money is no object.
But tell me, my dear, what do you say to her figure? Don't

you call it rather—rather"—pausing in search of a suitable
adjective—"*peculiar* ?"

"Well, I don't know; there is something a little odd about
it, perhaps. But until you called my attention to the fact,
I was inclined to consider it tolerably good. She carries
herself well."

"Good? Well I never heard such a thing! Fancy *you*
thinking it good, Mrs. Paget. I really should have thought
you would have known better."

"Did I say good?" seeing she was in danger of losing
caste, and overcome by the other's superior decision. "Let
me have another look. Oh yes, I was mistaken after all;
only moderate—very moderate."

"Plenty of padding," suggested Miss Palliser, considerably
appeased. "Looks like a hen turkey with its breast well
trussed."

"Ha, ha! An excellent simile, and uncommonly neatly put."

"I dare say," continued Miss Palliser in tones of deprecia-
tion, "that *men* may admire Miss Brewser's figure, but all
right-minded people know how to value *their* admiration at
its proper worth. Their ideas on such subjects are so extremely odd, to say the least of it. Personally I care a great
deal more for the opinions of my own sex than I do for those
of a parcel of silly, wild, flighty boys. However, that's
neither here nor there. If they see anything to admire in
Miss Brewser they are free to do so for aught it affects me;
all I can say is, that she is not *my* style of beauty. *I* prefer
something quieter, more refined, and less masculine."

Miss Palliser's cheeks were of a uniform sallow hue, all
the colour in her face having unkindly settled in the extreme
point of her nose, and it was a remarkable fact that during
all the years she had hunted in Huntingshire no living soul
had ever yet been able to discover what *was* her "*style*" of
feminine beauty. Never had any one proved so fastidious in
her tastes. Thin ladies she objected to altogether; also
stout, tall, obese, long-waisted, short-legged, medium, dark,
and fair ones. The only conclusion possible to arrive at was
that the single style Miss Palliser honestly and genuinely

admired was her own, and as nobody else did, it showed how wise and how merciful was the invisible Providence ruling over us.

"I don't think Miss Brewser has altogether such a *very* bad seat on horseback," observed Mrs. Paget, after a slight pause. "I've seen worse."

"Mrs. Paget, I *did* think *you* knew what a seat was," returned Miss Palliser scornfully, "*you*, who've hunted here, off and on, ever since your marriage; and I'm sorry to be unable to agree. But here's Colonel Clinker," as that gentleman passed close by, "*he* knows what's what: I'll ask *his* opinion."

The Honble. Jack knew the ladies well, and disliked both, especially Miss Palliser, but at mention of his own name he felt bound to stop and inquire if he could render them any service.

"What do you want to ask me?" he said in a cold but courteous tone. "Anything very important?"

"Oh, no, Colonel; not exactly important," said Miss Palliser insinuatingly, "only Mrs. Paget here declares that Miss Brewser has a good figure and a good seat on horseback, and knowing you to be an authority, I thought I would just make an appeal at headquarters. *You* don't think so *surely?*" and she looked at him out of her little colourless eyes.

Years ago Jack Clinker had seen through the petty spite and jealousy of which Miss Palliser's nature was capable, and despised her accordingly. As often as she made advances, just so often did he rebuff them. Captain Fuller's remark had left him in no mood to discuss the heiress, and after seeing her ride certainly not to do so unkindly. Besides, he took a pleasure in aggravating Miss Palliser.

"Mrs. Paget is quite right," he answered brusquely. "Miss Brewser has one of the prettiest figures and nicest seats I have seen for a long time, and there are very few women can ride over a fence in the way she did a few minutes ago. Added to these advantages, she appears to be a thorough lady." With which cutting remark Jack Clinker slightly raised his hat and rode off. "What brutes some women are, to be sure," he muttered to himself in disgust. "Old devil! why can't she leave the poor girl alone. And all because she cut her out in a miserable little ten minutes' spin. Faugh! I declare it's enough to sicken one with the sex altogether."

Miss Palliser turned green, and looked completely dumb-foundered. She had expected to find an ally, instead of which a daring and determined enemy had confronted her, unexpectedly, but none the less surely. Besides which Colonel Clinker's opinion carried considerable weight throughout the county.

"You've put your foot in it nicely," said Mrs. Paget, with an attempt at consolation which did not prove altogether satisfactory to its intended object.

"I don't care if I have," returned Miss Palliser angrily. "I can see through a stone wall as easily as most people, and I call it positively disgusting. Do you suppose that if this Miss Brewser were a penniless lass Colonel Clinker would constitute himself her champion in this ridiculous fashion? No, not he! It's the money he's after. That's as clear as clear can be, and I repeat, I call it disgusting. If you and I were heiresses *we* should have all the men toddling round us in just the same way."

But even Mrs. Paget ventured to think, in spite of this assertion, that Miss Palliser laboured under a slight delusion. She was weak, easily influenced, and entertained the most profound respect for Colonel Clinker as a scion of that aristocracy which she revered next only to her Creator.

"I think you were a *little* too much down on Miss Brewser," she said, beginning to waver in her allegiance.

"Tut, Mrs. Paget, do you suppose *I'm* going to follow your example, and model *all* my opinions by those of the Honble. Jack?" responded Miss Palliser with a sneer that made Mrs. Paget blush to the roots of her hair. "*You* may look up to the nobility if you like, *I* don't care twopence about them." Whereupon, after delivering this Parthian dart, which went quivering straight to poor guilty Mrs. Paget's heart, Miss Palliser turned her horse wrathfully aside, and put a close to a conversation which had ended less harmoniously than it had commenced.

Meanwhile the morning was wearing away, and a fresh move was made in the direction of a covert some two or three miles distant, which necessitated a long jog at that back-breaking pace so extremely trying to ladies. Mrs Forrester now came up and shook hands with Kate. "Good morning, Miss Brewser," she said. "I have seen you several times in the distance, but never had an opportunity of saying a word, and have contented myself with admiring your horse. I want to introduce you to our master, Mr. Bingham. He's very quiet, but a nice sort of man when you get to know him, and he's just been asking who you were."

"Really," answered Kate, "I am very much flattered, and shall be happy to make his acquaintance. Upon which Mrs. Forrester promptly effected an introduction.

"Make yourself civil," she whispered significantly into the master's ear, "for it's worth your while to conciliate an excellent subscriber. The young lady is rolling in wealth, and sure to be good for a couple of ponies."

"Thank you, Mrs. Forrester," returned he with a wink and a smile. "You've always an eye to the main chance, even when on pleasure bent."

Whether owing to this remark of the lady's or not it would be impossible to say, but before long Kate was surprised to find how exceedingly chatty and pleasant the " quiet, nice sort of man " could be. They got on famously, and soon made friends, so that the remainder of the jog to the covert was performed under favourable circumstances. Arrived at their fresh destination, the number of foxes appeared truly bewildering, and such a long time was spent in tow-rowing the cubs that the prospect of a run became more and more remote. It was now half-past two o'clock, and Kate, remembering Stirrup's parting injunctions, determined on making tracks for home, especially as she heard the hounds were likely to draw farther and farther away from Foxington. She therefore inquired the way from a ruddy-faced and obliging farmer who happened to be near, and he assured her she could not possibly mistake it, provided she was able to open sundry gates. Thus enlightened, Kate turned King Olaf's head towards Sport Lodge. The horse had fretted a good deal during the long period of inaction that had taken place. He was still very fresh, and exhibited a decided reluctance to quit his companions; but once fairly out of sight and sound of the hounds, he quickly settled down into a long swinging trot, which soon put a considerable distance between them. Kate followed the high-road till she came to a recently painted hand-post, where she had been directed to turn sharp to the right, keeping on a bridle-path which led across the fields for a couple of miles, when once more she would emerge on the turnpike close by Foxington. Now, as we have seen, Miss Brewser was an exceedingly independent young person, accustomed to rely upon her own resources; therefore she felt in no wise disconcerted at the prospect of riding home alone, as a good many ladies similarly circumstanced might have done. The only drawback consisted in King Olaf's dislike to gates. Instead of standing quietly while his mistress endeavoured to raise the latch, he was always in such a desperate hurry that he insisted on trying to force his way through before the gate was fairly ajar, thereby often occasioning Kate various rather unpleasant bumps and bruises. Horses, like people, are not made absolutely perfect, and King Olaf must be forgiven for possessing this one fault.

Despite sundry of these little casualties, Kate managed to get through the first two or three gates tolerably successfully, and was just beginning to congratulate herself on her achievements, when a slight damper was put on her self-esteem by a barrier that baffled every effort, and remained obstinately closed in spite of both force and persuasion. It was doubly fastened with a bar and an iron hook. This latter, after repeated essays, Kate did manage to undo, but the gate itself remained immovable, requiring a man's strength to heave it up from the ground. In the midst of her difficulties, and by way of making matters worse, King Olaf growing suddenly impatient, began to back away, and during one of these slight vagaries her hunting-crop was torn from her hand. It was engraved with her name, and having been given to her by her uncle, she would have sacrificed a good deal sooner than lose his present; besides, without it now she was completely handicapped. For a few seconds the girl felt almost *nonplussed*, but she possessed a resolute disposition that could not bear to be beaten in anything it undertook. She wanted to get home, and she wanted to regain her lost crop, and the only way to arrive at these results appeared to be by dismounting. In her pocket she invariably carried a stout leather strap, which, in the event of an emergency like the present, she was in the habit of buckling on to her stirrup, and by this contrivance was able to reach her foot up far enough to place it in the lengthened loop and then swing herself into the saddle. But what you can do with a quiet, steady, tired-out animal at the end of a long day's hunting, and what you can do with a remarkably fresh and high-couraged one after only a few hours' easy exercise, are two very different things, as Kate now discovered to her cost. To descend from the saddle was comparatively simple, but to regain it a most laborious and difficult undertaking, for every time she made an attempt King Olaf dodged and fidgeted, fidgeted and dodged, till Kate was fairly worn out, and her temper raised to an unwonted pitch of exasperation so that she actually went the length of applying the epithet "brute!" to her favourite but certainly tantilising hunter. She looked around, but not a soul was in sight to come to her assistance. Once more her resolutions were quickly taken, and she decided on trudging the rest of the way on foot, consoling herself meanwhile with the philosophical reflection that "What cannot be helped must be endured!"

Picking up her habit in one hand, and taking hold of King Olaf's bridle with the other, she started off at a good round pace. She had not, however, gone above half a mile, and had already begun to discover that patent leather riding boots and lengthened pedestrian exercise were highly incompatible one with the other, before she was startled by hearing a voice close behind say—

"I hope you have not met with an accident."

Her first impulse was one of relief, her second to notice that
the horseman who thus addressed her was mounted on a
sporting black mare, and was decidedly good-looking.   He
had fair hair, honest grey-blue eyes, a smiling open countenance, and a manly upright carriage, which impressed Kate
favourably at first sight.

"Is anything the matter?" he repeated riding up alongside.   "Have you had a fall?"

"Oh dear no," answered she airily, now that help was at
hand, determined to make light of her adventures.   "I could
not open the last gate, it was so heavy, and after bungling for
a long time, dropped my hunting-crop.   Being a favourite
one, I got off to pick it up, and then was unable to remount,
consequently was obliged to have recourse to Shanks's mare.
Are *all* the gates about here equally refractory?"

"Some of them *are* awkward I admit, particularly for a
lady.   To tell the truth, I wonder you got on as well as you
did.   Many fair equestriennes of my acquaintance stand in the
same awe of a five-barred gate as of a full-grown bull, and
cannot stir without a groom riding close to their horse's tail."

"They ought not to come out hunting then," said Kate,
decisively.   "Women have no business to be so stupid and
such cowards."

The stranger laughed, seemingly amused at her sentiments.

"Don't you think the farmers are more to blame," he said
with a smile, "who fasten up their gates by all sorts of such
odious contrivances, that even we men are often at our wits'
ends how to undo them, and were it not for such things as
hinges would many a time be stopped in the midst of a good
run?   The ladies are not so much in fault as you appear to
imagine."

"I am glad for *their* sakes they have found so chivalrous
and so courteous a champion," answered Kate politely, though
a trifle sarcastically.

He looked at her, as if not quite sure whether she were
joking or in earnest.

"You are too flattering," he replied in the same tone.
"But the courtesy of which you speak is not very apparent

so long as I remain seated and you standing. Allow me to assist you to your horse." So saying he jumped down to the ground.

Now the human voice is a wonderful index of character, and possesses immense powers of attraction and repulsion. A pleasant-toned voice goes far towards creating a favourable impression, and the new-comer's had a soft truthful ring which inspired Kate with confidence, and made her forget that this gentleman was an utter stranger.

"Do you know how?" she asked saucily. "I'm awfully heavy, remember."

"I'm not afraid of that," he replied, apparently confident in his own powers. "Try me."

Kate placed her foot somewhat coyly in the palm of his broad hand — she noticed it was broad, and thought men's hands ought to be so—and the next instant with a dexterous hoist he sent her flying into the saddle.

"Capital!" she exclaimed, not a little pleased to find herself there again. "Stirrup himself could not have done it better."

"Who's Stirrup?"

"Oh! Stirrup's my groom, and such a dear old man! Still, as he does not always accompany me out hunting, the very first time I come 'to grief' I shall know now where to apply for help. There's nothing like a friend in need."

"Do. Let that be a bargain. All the same, I hope," turning the frank blue eyes full upon her, "the day will never come when you may meet with a bad accident. If there is one sight in the whole world I hate more than another, it is seeing a lady fall. Their limbs are so delicate, compared to ours, and so much more easily injured. However," with a cheerful smile, "it's much too early in the season to talk of broken bones. They're bad enough at any time, so no need to think of them beforehand. Now," giving Kate the reins, and loosing King Olaf's head, "are you *quite* comfortable? Is there nothing more I can do for you?"

"No, nothing, thanks," she said, wondering if he meant to depart, and wishing he would stay a little longer, at least until she had reached the high-road. "I cannot thank you sufficiently for the trouble already taken on my behalf."

"Please don't mention it. I feel only too proud to have been able to render any service, and am already amply repaid by the pleasure of your society instead of riding home alone." He did not intend trotting on then after all. His next speech rendered that fact still more evident.

"There are still two or three gates to be opened," he said, as he once more remounted. "So, if you will allow me, I propose seeing you safely through them."

He spoke with such an air of calm decision that there was nothing to be said, and Kate gratefully bowed assent. The presence of this handsome stranger was far from being displeasing. He had a courtly way of speaking, which appealed to her sense of refinement and put her at her ease. Some such thoughts ran through her mind, as for a few seconds they rode on in silence. Her companion was engaged in a critical examination of King Olaf. Presently he said, resuming the conversation—

"May I be forgiven for expressing my extreme admiration for your horse? He is a real beauty," once again running him over with the eye of a connoisseur. "A trifle small perhaps, but a rarely well-shaped animal. He's a good one, too, I know, for I saw him jump a fence this morning in grand style. There happened to be a blind ditch on the take off side, and I noticed him particularly, because, to tell the honest truth, I thought you were riding just a wee bit too fast at it, but the chesnut steadied himself exactly at the right moment, and evidently requires no teaching. You're lucky in having such a good hunter."

"That I am," said Kate, charmed at hearing her favourite's praises sung, and stooping down to pat his glossy neck. "Even *my* bad riding can't make him go wrong."

"Please believe I intended to cast no aspersions on your horsemanship; on the contrary—I—I—" checking himself suddenly.

"Well, what?" she asked, with all a woman's love of flattery.

"I admired it."

Kate blushed without exactly knowing why, and endeavoured to start another topic of discussion. Nevertheless she felt pleased that the stranger considered her *début* in the Shires had proved creditable.

"I thought I was wrong," she said, "in going quite so fast, but Mrs. Forrester had specially warned me against the dangers of slow riding, and her advice carried the day. You see," turning towards him with a frank humility, "I am only a novice as yet."

Her candour was attractive, and pleased him. Coquettes and flirts he had met by the score, but straightforward, outspoken girls, with no humbug about them, were comparatively rare.

"Do you know Mrs. Forrester?" he asked.

"Yes, a little. She called upon me yesterday. We had a long chat together, and she told me a variety of news."

"Ah! she's a regular old gossip, but a good soul all the same, if only she could be persuaded to leave horse-coping alone. This animal that I am now riding once belonged to her."

"Indeed!" said Kate, speculating as to whom her companion might be.

"Yes," continued he, "I bought her at the end of last season, and I call her M'liss, for a wilder young savage never looked through a bridle. You remember Bret Harte's story, don't you?"

"Ah! poor M'liss. I always felt so sorry for her, and she possessed such an intense capacity for suffering. Her emotions were almost *too* keen. I hope *your* M'liss does not resemble the original one in that respect."

"No, *my* M'liss is a very sulky, thickskinned creature, or rather *was*, for she has marvellously improved lately."

"Perhaps she too loves the schoolmaster," suggested Kate, with a little air of finesse.

"Not so much as she fears his reprimands in the shape of a sharp pair of spurs. Talking of horses, however, I should like you to see a four-year-old of mine, who is *almost*, if not *quite,* as handsome as the one you are on. Ah! I see "—as Kate made a cynical gesture—"you find that hard to believe?"

"Very. You must excuse my scepticism, but even if your animal were as beautiful as Venus herself, she could never compare with King Olaf in my eyes. Perhaps it sounds conceited to say so, but you see, when you have ridden a horse a season or two, been well carried, and found out all his good qualities, you learn to regard him with a peculiar pride and affection which prevent any other filling his place, or even approaching him in the smallest degree."

"Bravo! That is honestly spoken. I see you are fond of horses."

"*Fond?* I *love* them. The gift of speech, after all, is a dangerous one. Our friends bother us perpetually with their ill-timed chatter, our horses never. I like dumb things— things with no tongues to irritate and madden."

"Still even horses are vexatious enough at times. They are not *all* good, quiet, placid, amiable-tempered creatures."

"I know; but whatever their faults they cannot speak. Silence is golden."

"Well, your ideas strike me as rather peculiar. Would you like to play at mumchance for the rest of the way home?"

"Certainly not," said she with a laugh, "I was indulging in generalities, not in personalities. Besides, there are exceptions to every rule."

"I suppose *I* could not acquire this desirable dumbness?" he asked playfully.

"It does not appear likely," she answered, while a demure smile trembled upon her lips.

"Ah! you think I am a chatterbox?"

"I did not say any such thing."

"No, but you implied it."

"Conversation by implication is always unpleasant, and liable to lead to misconstruction. Suppose, instead, you were to tell me where we are?"

For they had quitted the green fields, and were now pacing down a good wide road.

"Don't you recognise that house?" he said, pointing to one on the left-hand side.

"Why, it is Sport Lodge, surely. I had no idea we were so near home."

"Yes, Miss Brewser," he said, "it is Sport Lodge, and I am afraid I must wish you good-bye, for my way leads more to the right."

"Stay," she exclaimed, impelled by a sudden desire to learn her companion's name. "You possess an unfair advantage over me. Before we part, at least let me know to whom I am indebted for so much kindness?"

The sun was sinking in the horizon, and its rays caught the stranger's fair hair, turning it into golden as he raised his hat from his head and said quietly—

"I am Colonel Clinker."

He was not, however, prepared for the effect produced by these apparently simple words. Kate's countenance fell, assuming an expression of unfeigned astonishment, for the announcement came upon her as an overwhelming surprise. The possibility of this pleasant, agreeable young man turning out to be the depraved individual who gambled, betted, and vowed *nolens volens* to make her his wife, had never entered her mind. The disillusion was complete. Her interest had been aroused once or twice during their short ride home, the soft voice had thrilled her strangely, and now, when she recalled these things, her animosity found vent in regret.

"Colonel Clinker!" she echoed impulsively. "Oh! I am so sorry."

The next moment she could have bitten out her tongue. How could she make so foolish, so idiotic a speech?

"Sorry!" he said, feeling in his turn somewhat surprised and scarcely flattered. "Why sorry? What has sorrow got to do with my identity?"

"Oh, nothing," she answered coldly, striving hard to conceal her confusion.

"You are enigmatical in the extreme, Miss Brewser. You first do me the honour of wishing to know my name; then, when you hear it, you tell me you are sorry. What inference am I to draw from such a speech?"

"I—I—really don't know."

"Miss Brewser," he said, looking Kate full in the face, "you are equivocating. You know perfectly well, and are concealing something from me."

The hint of deception touched her to the quick.

"Well, then," she said, with considerable heat, "if you *must* know I will tell you. I thought before I knew who you were that you were nice, and now—" hesitating how best to conclude the discourteous sentence.

"You are sorry because I am *not*."

An awkward silence ensued. Colonel Clinker was evidently both hurt and perplexed, but when he spoke again all the anger had died out of his face.

"After all," he said, "why should I be vexed at your frankness? Very likely you are right, and I am a worthless fellow. It does one good now and again to be taken down a peg or two in one's own self-esteem. Tell me, is there nothing I can do to become nice, or at all events *nice*-er?"

She felt beaten. This humble appeal went far to disarm her wrath and raise her respect in spite of his previous shortcomings, but she was not going to let him see that he had gained the smallest advantage.

"That," she replied coolly, "is for you, not me, to ascertain."

"Miss Brewser," he said, with visible annoyance, "you appear to know of something to my disadvantage, and therefore I feel as if I were groping in the dark, being ignorant of any possible cause of offence. Can you not tell me what it is?"

"No."

"Then you admit that there *is* a cause?"

"I admit nothing. And really, Colonel Clinker, I hope you will excuse me, but I must be going. I don't want my horse to catch cold."

"At least you will give me the opportunity of endeavouring to regain that good opinion which I seem to have forfeited?" he urged, with a persistence that surprised himself, but she had piqued his curiosity and wounded his pride. "I shall do myself the honour of calling," he added, taking a sudden resolution.

"It's hardly worth your while," was the encouraging reply, though Kate, as she uttered the words, felt ashamed of their rudeness.

The Honble. Jack opened his blue-grey eyes in surprise, and gazed steadily at her; her own sank to the ground. Once again victory rested with the assailed, and the assailant encountered a serious rebuff.

"You must allow *me* to be the best judge of that," he said calmly, and then, raising his hat, without looking to the right or to the left rode away in the direction of Foxington.

Kate unconsciously watched his retreating form. Certainly this Colonel Clinker was a cool hand. She had signified clearly she did not wish him to call, and yet he had announced his intention of doing so. Evidently he intended carrying off the money-bags with the smallest possible amount of delay. Such conduct was outrageous. She quivered with indignation as she walked King Olaf up the hill that led to Sport Lodge.

"It is abominable!" she said to herself. "What a fool I was not to tell him what I think of him when I had the chance! I can't imagine what made me such a coward!"

Could it be possible that the low tones of that truthful voice, or the pained look of those honest, wondering eyes were to blame for a fault not often attributable to Kate Brewser?

"Bother the man!" she exclaimed, working herself up to a still further pitch of indignation. "I wish to goodness I had never seen him. I—I—I—*hate* him!"

But even while she spoke the words she knew they were false, knew that though Jack Clinker might have—aye, and probably had—a hundred faults, he was both a man and a gentleman. Nevertheless, Kate, when she reached home, did not feel so satisfied with the results of her afternoon's ride as to communicate any portion of them to Mary Whitbread. Neither did Colonel Clinker, though he dined out that evening with Captain Fuller and the Chirper, and was plied by them with questions as to his early disappearance

from the hunting-field, consider it necessary to inform his
friends how he, that afternoon, had made the heiress's acquaintance.   Perhaps the circumstances were not so pleasant
as to justify him in doing so.   Anyhow, he acted upon that
remark of Miss Brewser's in which she had alluded to the
special value of silence.   But though he spoke little he
thought a good deal, and his mind dwelt freely on the
strange manner in which she had expressed her sorrow at
hearing his name, and the frigidity she had afterwards displayed.   That any kind friend had informed the young lady
of a certain bet written down in Captain Fuller's betting-
book never entered his head.   In fact the bet itself had
been forgotten as soon as made, sharing the fate of many
another post-prandial transaction, and had entirely escaped
his memory.   Mrs. Forrester's "good turn" was, however,
already commencing to bring forth fruits.   The seed carefully
sown by her judicious hand was sprouting into life, though
whether adverse storms might not beat it to the ground and
stamp out all its vital germs still appeared uncertain.

CHAPTER XII.

AN INVITATION TO DINNER.

MRS. FORRESTER, having once undertaken a benevolent mission, had no idea of allowing it to remain at a standstill. Like an experienced general, she considered the position in all its bearings, and despising inertia as a condition only worthy chrysalises and dormice, at once threw out skirmishers and determined upon immediate action.

It was owing to the decision thus arrived at that on Sunday morning, when she made her first appearance downstairs, Kate received the following epistle, written in a bold, manly handwriting.

"DEAR MISS BREWSER,

"Will you and Miss Whitbread excuse a short invitation, and give me the pleasure of your company at dinner tomorrow night at 7.30 o'clock? I have asked Colonel Clinker and one or two of our Foxington exquisites to meet you, but it will only be quite a small party, for, to begin with, I dislike any others; and secondly, have neither the appliances nor the establishment suitable to a large 'function.' That, I believe, is the correct word nowadays, is it not? With kind regards,

"Believe me sincerely yours,
"JANE FORRESTER."

"P.S.—I shall consider it a *particular* favour if you will come, and by so doing prove that my unfortunate mention of a certain little episode, which shall remain nameless, has been forgiven."

Clever old lady! She felt convinced that this artfully worded postscript would clinch the matter.

" The girl's as proud as Lucifer," she said to herself with a chuckle while sealing up the note, " and will come, rather than let me think she is afraid to meet Colonel Clinker, unless my experience of human nature be fallacious." And Mrs. Forrester's previsions turned out as correct as usual, her observations on mankind being second only in perspicuity to those on horseflesh and cattle.

Now since the preceding afternoon Kate's indignation had cooled to a very considerable extent—often the case with people who having indulged in a fit of anger, before long experience a natural revulsion, which makes them begin to inquire how far their conduct has been justified, and whether passion may not have overruled common-sense? The human mind is so constituted that it often renders a sort of dual vision possible, which presenting both sides of a question, opens out a plea of extenuating circumstances, until, like a ball on the rebound, whose every spring grows feebler and feebler, wrath dies away altogether. Kate had by no means arrived at this peaceable frame of mind, nevertheless, she was undergoing that preliminary stage when the conduct and actions, glanced at retrospectively, did not appear so wholly and entirely satisfactory as they had done only a few hours before.

Various emotions disturbed her when she recalled the passage of arms she had had with Colonel Clinker on the day before. She resolved in future to treat the offender with a cool civility, far more galling than paltry words, which should maintain her womanly dignity and prevent any relapse into vulgar retaliation. She was conscious that she had not come out of the fray with flying colours, but having made these resolutions, it appeared unpardonable folly, quite unworthy of the masterly position she intended assuming, to decline to meet Colonel Clinker at the house of a mutual friend. Would not the very act of avoiding him be a sign of cowardice and defeat? and would not her doing so invest that gentleman with an importance he was very *very* far from possess-

ing? So far as Colonel Clinker affected her, Kate Brewser,
he was an absolute cipher, and likely to remain so. Under
these circumstances, why should he be so honoured as to
influence, or even be supposed to have the *power* of influenc-
ing, one of her actions? The thing was ridiculous, absurd,
preposterous! So she repeated to herself, each time with
increasing conviction. After all, Mrs. Forrester had been
right in saying she was her own mistress, and could follow
her own inclinations. What if Colonel Clinker *had* backed
himself to marry her? It took two to make a match, and in
the meantime might there not be a certain fitful pleasure in
discomfiting the adventurer, in fighting him with his own
weapons, in rendering coolness for coolness, sarcasm for sarcasm? The idea fascinated her. It would be like acting in
a farce, and she felt thoroughly equal to the part, diamond
cut diamond! Her mind was made up, and she vowed whenever they met to treat him with frigid indifference. Mrs.
Forrester's appeal had struck a right chord, and found Kate
in a suitable mood for its reception.

She therefore sat down and wrote an exceedingly civil little
letter to Mrs. Forrester, in which she took the opportunity of
assuring her that the incident referred to was of so little
consequence that she had forgotten it long ago.

And Mrs. Forrester, when she read the contents, once more
chuckled complacently, and said to herself, " Aha! that Miss
Brewser is a deep 'un, deeper and prouder even than I
thought her. All the better. If it comes to pitting her brains
against mine, we shall see who gains the day. Poor Jack!
He's a dear good fellow; but it's lucky for him I took the
thing in hand, he never could have pulled through by himself. The fact of the matter is these heiresses get spoilt, and
are as artful and as crooked in their ways as an old vixen in the
month of March. There's no running them straight anyhow."

With which reflection Mrs. Forrester took off her Sunday
gown, replaced it by her work-a-day skirt, and retired to the
pigsty to administer a dose of sweet nitre to an expectant
mother, whose hopes threatened to be blighted by a troublesome cough.

On the following morning Kate went out with Sir Beauchamp Lenard's hounds. Being a wet day, Mary Whitbread
preferred remaining in the house, and Kate elected to hack
out to covert. In the event of meeting Colonel Clinker
she had decided on bowing politely but frigidly, avoiding
any attempt at conversation. Curiously enough, however,
that gentleman's conduct appeared to have been regulated by
precisely the same train of thought, for when he saw Kate he
made an icy salutation, and throughout the day never once
offered to come near her. No one seeing the pair would
have guessed they were not only acquainted, but had ridden
amicably home together, side by side, for several miles.
Colonel Clinker treated her like a stranger, and evidently
declined to presume upon an introduction so informally
obtained. At first she was not ill-pleased by this state of
things, feeling it removed much cause for embarrassment,
but as the hours passed on and she began to fancy that
he not only kept at a distance, but did so intentionally,
her feelings underwent a curious and unaccountable revolution. She felt hurt, and thought, in spite of their little tiff,
he need not have been quite—*quite* so stand-off. If *she* were
ready to forgive, so at least might *he* be. Women, indeed,
are strangely contradictory beings, hard to please, and often
scarcely knowing themselves what they really wish for.
Had Jack Clinker come up to Kate early in the morning
and tried to make his peace, she would certainly have
shown him the cold shoulder, and probably seized the very
first opportunity of establishing a quarrel; but as he behaved
in exactly the same way that she had chosen, and never
volunteered to address a single remark to her, nor after
the first formal bow to give the least sign of recognition,
she felt exceedingly mortified and displeased. As for
Jack Clinker, had his conduct been the result of the most
profound strategy, instead of wounded vanity, he could not
possibly have displayed more truly Machiavellian tactics, or
any more calculated to bring the young lady to her senses.
Nevertheless, he was guiltless of such astute diplomacy,
and simply kept aloof because he did not know how his

advances might be received, and because he was too proud to place himself in a false position. Kate, on the contrary, had so construed his parting words as to imagine he would seize the first opportunity of renewing her acquaintance, and when she found he had no intention of doing so felt decidedly humiliated. Such is woman's nature. An adorer whose love is true, and whose conquest is assured, meets but with cold reward; while the fickle, unsteadfast, inconstant, slippery wooer occupies her whole thoughts and attention.

That afternoon Kate Brewser once again rode home by herself, but the ride was comparatively tame and uneventful. The gates were easy ones; the Duckling stood like a lamb, and pushed them gently with his nose, and no knight-errant's services were required for the relief of a distressed damsel. Under these favourable conditions it might reasonably have been expected the damsel herself should prove content, but she returned in a dissatisfied and taciturn mood, not wholly to be accounted for by a moist day and the heavy unpleasant clinging of a saturated habit.

"Have you enjoyed yourself, Kate?" asked Mary Whitbread, who, sitting before a cosy fire, was warming her little feet on the fender.

"Not a bit. We've had a wretched day's sport. Done absolutely nothing, and all I've got for my pains is a thorough good soaking."

Whereupon Kate stalked up-stairs without deigning to enter into any further explanations concerning the short-comings of the weather and the uncertainty of fox-hunting.

"Nothing is so nice as one expects it to be," she mused dismally. "Fruition brings but Dead Sea ashes."

Whereby it may be seen the young lady was inclined to take a very desponding view of life on this particular evening, which did not, however, prevent her from bestowing an unusual amount of thought as to which garment in her possession—black, white, pink, or blue—would prove most becoming to her special style of beauty.

Kate ended by choosing a simple white gown, made of some

soft, clinging material, which fitted her to perfection, setting
forth the lines of her slim yet rounded figure admirably. A
single row of pearls encircled her slender white throat, above
which the shining hair was arranged in smooth dark coils.
Twenty minutes sufficed to bring them to their destination,
where, after they had deposited their outer wrappings in the
hall, they were shown into a small but well-lit room, plainly
and comfortably furnished in an old-fashioned, substantial
style. A bright fire flamed on the hearth, and around it Mrs.
Forrester and three or four men were already congregated,
deep in the horsey-foxey conversation which usually prevails
in the Shires during the hunting season, when all other
topics pale before the absorbing subject of the chase, and
even politics are lightly touched upon and as lightly left
alone.

"How do you do, Miss Brewser? So very good of you
to come on such a short informal invitation," said their hostess
significantly, as she advanced to welcome her guests. She
was dressed in a high dark silk, with a white cap, stuck a
little awry on the top of her head, suggesting the idea of
having been perched there by accident rather than design,
and in this attire so much more closely resembled her sex than
in the daytime, that Kate at first scarcely recognised her
quondam acquaintance. "I don't pretend to give grand
dinners," continued Mrs. Forrester. "My *chef de cuisine* is
not nearly accomplished enough for that. You see a lone old
woman does not require much in the eating way, and gas-
tronomic luxuries are really wasted upon me. Personally, I
care for nothing but a little plain mutton or beef, and detest
all your made up kickshaws. However, I told you beforehand,
you must not expect much, and that we should only be a
small party."

"I'm so glad of it," said Kate, pleasantly. "I think large
London dinner parties something awful; and depend upon it,
from six to eight is the right number."

"We have hit on a happy medium then, for we are exactly
seven," replied Mrs. Forrester cheerfully. "But now let me
introduce you and Miss Whitbread to my friends Captain

Fuller, Mr. Graham, Mr. McGrath, and Colonel Clinker. The latter is a celebrity, so I need say nothing about *him*, and is looked upon as our Foxington lion by the rural population, whose minds are fascinated by his achievements."

"Does the lion growl?" asked Kate maliciously.

"Jack," said the old lady. "Come here and answer that question for yourself. Miss Brewser wants to know if you growl?"

"Yes, and show fight too, when unfairly attacked," he replied, with meaning. "The lion may be a noble animal, but there are limits even to *his* endurance."

Kate blushed. "Lions are useful occasionally," she said, with a sort of half apology, determined to produce some change in his cool demeanour. "I think we have met before."

"I remember the circumstance well, Miss Brewser."

"Indeed? Your memory appeared to me uncommonly short."

"Not shorter, if you will forgive me for saying so, than other people's."

"What!" here interrupted Mrs. Forrester. "Do you mean to say you two are old acquaintances?" She felt disappointed at finding an introduction had already been effected without her intervention. Her besetting foible consisted in liking to be considered as the mainspring of a clock, without which the works could not fulfil their functions. For the clock to go without her being instrumental in setting it in motion was a direct infringement of her natural rights.

"Not precisely *old* acquaintances," corrected Kate, emphasizing the adjective, "merely very casual ones."

"Yes, *extremely* casual ones," assented Colonel Clinker, with a readiness which somehow exasperated her not a little "so casual, indeed, that Miss Brewser appeared, when we last met in the hunting-field, to have totally ignored the existence of so humble a person as myself."

"Why, I bowed to you. What more would you have had me do?"

"Oh! nothing," with irritating *sang froid*. "A frigid

inclination of the head was sufficient to satisfy my aspira· tions. I am not ambitious."

"Few men are at your time of life, but you appear highly contradictory."

"Do I? If so I cannot lay claim to any originality. Even ladies are inclined to be so at times."

Kate coloured again. She began to find this exchange of witticisms less favourable to her own powers of retaliation than she had expected. Her temper was rising.

"Come, come!" Mrs. Forrester exclaimed, once more intervening. "I can't have you two sparring at each other. Jack! I'm curious, and want to know how you made this young lady's acquaintance?"

"That's easily explained," said he. "Miss Brewser happened to stand in need of a little assistance one day coming home from hunting, and I was fortunate enough to be able to render it, in place of a groom. Indeed, I'm not quite certain she did not mistake me for one. She probably intended offering me a vacant situation, for that is the only way I can account for the profound sorrow she expressed on discovering my ineligibility."

He spoke jokingly; but his eyes fastened themselves upon Kate with an expression of quiet sarcasm. She was clever and quick-witted, and in her intercourse with men often felt herself intellectually superior, but for once, beneath that calm exterior, she recognised a master spirit. She would like to have trampled upon him, to have beaten him down into the dust, to have shown her own greater power, and then perhaps to have ultimately displayed forgiveness; but now, to her great surprise, the tables were turned, and *she* appeared likely to suffer defeat, instead of inflicting it.

CHAPTER XIII.

DISCUSSING THE LADIES' STEEPLECHASE.

In the meantime dinner was announced, giving her an opportunity of collecting her wits, for Colonel Clinker offered his arm to the hostess, Mr. McGrath came forward to claim Kate, while Mary Whitbread fell to the portion of the fascinating Captain Fuller, who, however, having lost a considerable sum at his club in town on Saturday night—or rather Sunday morning—happened to be in a less sprightly and more taciturn mood than usual. After a little preliminary bustle, they seated themselves at table, when Kate found the enemy had taken up a strong position on the right, while Mr. McGrath supported the left division.

"You're looking a little pale this evening, Mrs. Forrester," said he. "Nothing the matter I hope? You're not feeling seedy?"

"A liver attack," she replied with her customary bluntness. "Not very serious, only requires plenty of fresh air and exercise. One gets fat and lazy in the summer. By-the-bye, Miss Brewser, that was a nice useful-looking nag you were riding to-day. Not so showy, perhaps, as the chestnut, but with capital good points, and looks like a wear-and-tear sort of customer."

"You've described him to a nicety," said Kate in reply. "The Duckling is a stout, honest little beast, never sick or sorry, but until he gets excited inclined to take life almost too easily. He lacks the chestnut's dash."

"Have you ever ridden him with a spur?"

"No, I can't say that I have. To tell the truth, I feel somewhat afraid of applying it indiscriminately."

"Oh no you wouldn't. You take my advice, and ride him in one, if only for a time or two. The least touch is often sufficient to rouse a sluggish horse. They are apt to get cunning when ridden by ladies, and an occasional reminder does them all the good in the world. I know many people object to a one-sided spur, and say it's worse than useless, but my experience is exactly the reverse. I consider it a most valuable auxiliary, especially with a certain class of animal."

"Faith! and a better authority does not exist in the whole of Great Britain," interposed Mr. McGrath, looking round the table with an expression of conviction which seemed to say, "There! I defy any one to contradict that statement!"

"Now, Terry, keep your national blarney for those who appreciate it," returned the old lady vivaciously, "and don't waste your soft sawder upon me. I'm too ancient for that sort of thing, and past the market."

"Begad! but its rale unkind that ye are, Mrs. Forrester, mavourneen," exclaimed Mr. McGrath, adopting the very strongest brogue. "And a clever faymale like yerself can always command a market."

"Thank you, my good friend; you are exceedingly flattering, and were I a young girl my head would be quite turned with such a complimentary speech."

"Shure, Mrs. Forrester, and if ye were but a wee bit spalpeen, it would be for trying to persuade ye to become Mrs. Terence McGrath that I should aspire."

"Then it's lucky for you that I am not, and you are deterred from committing so crowning an act of folly," retorted the old lady amidst a general roar of laughter. "Your heart's too big for your body, Terry, and as for your common sense, it is nowhere, so let us change the subject. Jack," turning to Colonel Clinker, "I've got something to tell you, something I was particularly requested by a fair admirer to consult you about. Are you all attention?"

"Am I not always so when addressed by Mrs. Forrester?" returned he gallantly. "Who is the lady, and why does seek advice from so incompetent a person?"

"A great friend of yours, Lady Anne Birkett, and she is mad about getting up a ladies' steeplechase. You remember there was some talk of doing so last winter, only the project fell to the ground through want of proper backing. But this year it appears the old Earl has taken up the affair *con amore*, and has signified his intention of allowing the race to be run over his land, provided some competent person—yourself, for instance—will undertake to choose a suitable course, and see that the fences are not too large and dangerous. It won't do, he says, for the ladies to come to grief, neither will he allow the thing to be made public in any way, but if a few of us choose to get it up among ourselves, and can ensure some four or five starters, he will present a handsome silver cup to the winner. Now Lady Anne, when she heard you were coming here to-night, particularly asked me to seek your opinion on this momentous question, and engage, if possible, your active co-operation. In fact, she wants you to become the moving spirit, and take the whole thing in hand from first to last."

"Very kind of Lady Anne, I'm sure. But who and what is the field to consist of? Have you any notion?"

"Why, there's Lady Anne herself. She's as keen as mustard about it, not that she will possess the ghost of a chance of winning, unless the Earl puts his hand in his pocket and gives her a decent mount. Miss Palliser, too, is always game for anything in the riding way. Her ambitious spirit would simply revel in the excitement of a race. I lay any money that she jumps at the idea."

"I wish the old scarecrow would jump off the hooks. Nasty spiteful creature! I hate the very sight of her out hunting! Well, go on, who else?"

"Then there are Mrs. Paget and Mrs. Phipps; perhaps one or two others; and lastly, with a little persuasion—myself."

"Yourself? Capital! That puts a different complexion on the matter altogether. Why, every man in Foxington would turn out to see the celebrated Mrs. Forrester come galloping in between the flags on a winning

mount. We shall have another feather added to your cap
yet."

"Or another censorious dart placed in the hands of my
enemies," said Mrs. Forrester, whose eyes failed to be completely blinded by the honour and glory of this redoubtable
prospect. "I shall be called an old fool for my pains, and
not without some show of reason, for what's the use of going
gallivanting over a country at my time of life? However,
Lady Anne left me no peace until I half promised her I
would make one of the number."

"And quite right too; the race would seem but a very
half-hearted affair without your support."

"Oh, nonsense, Jack; things would go on exactly the same.
Only I help to swell the rank of lunatics, and the more the
merrier. Perhaps Miss Brewser may be induced to take part
in the proceedings. What say you?" appealing to Kate.
"Will you throw in your lot with our daring band of horse-
women?"

"There's nothing in the world I should like better,"
answered she, with glistening eyes. She had already pictured
to herself the glorious sensation of piloting King Olaf past
the winning-post, and had listened breathlessly to everything
that had passed between Mrs. Forrester and Colonel Clinker.
"*But*," she added rather lamely, catching an expression of
stern disapproval on Mary Whitbread's face, opposite, "but
—but ——"

"Well, what?" interrupted Jack Clinker. "Don't be
afraid to mention any scruples you may entertain. Perhaps,"
and Kate fancied she could detect the least possible sneer,
"the project appears too dangerous, and if so, my sympathies
are on your side altogether."

"Your sympathies are entirely misplaced," said she tartly,
feeling deeply wounded by any implication on her courage.
"I am not *quite* so timid as you seem to imagine, and was
not deterred by the possible danger; only," gathering confidence, "should not we be apt to scandalise the good people
of the neighbourhood, and make ourselves somewhat conspicuous?"

"You are right, Miss Brewser, and display sound wisdom in being afraid of their comments. No doubt you will gain a very bad name."

He was laughing at her, and she could not endure chaff from him, of all people in the world, when up to this moment he had more or less ignored her existence, and studiously addressed all his conversation to Mrs. Forrester.

"I *do* wish you would not employ that word 'afraid,'" she said irritably. "I detest it; and once for all let me tell you I'm not *afraid* of anything, certainly not of a few ill-natured remarks from people who are perfect strangers to me. So please banish the idea from your mind."

"The beauty of it is," said Mrs. Forrester intervening. "people *can't* talk, for nobody is to know anything about the race outside our own immediate circle, and snobbishism reigns so supreme that when folks hear the Earl of Huntingshire has been the chief patron and supporter of it, scarcely a dissentient voice will be raised. In order to maintain as much privacy as possible, he proposes that even the place of meeting should be kept a profound secret, and only divulged some four-and-twenty hours before the race. However, my dear," turning blandly towards Kate, "we wish everybody to please themselves, and if you have the least hesitation about riding do not scruple to say so."

"Hear, hear!" chimed in the Honble. Jack approvingly; "them's my sentiments, and if I were you, Miss Brewser, I should decline."

"But you are *not* me," she retorted in an undertone, "and all I decline is the advice so gratuitously offered. Perhaps you will allow me to judge for myself, and," looking round with an air of defiance and speaking aloud, "my mind is made up. I intend to compete, since Mrs. Forrester has been good enough to ask me to do so."

"That's right, my dear!" exclaimed the lady approvingly. "I told Lady Anne I felt almost sure you would join our party; besides, it would be a shame not to give that beautiful chestnut an opportunity of showing us all his heels. He ought to have an uncommonly good chance of winning. Can he stay?"

"Yes, I think so," answered Kate more placidly.

"Have you heard what the distance is to be?" asked Colonel Clinker. "So much depends upon that, especially with untrained horses, generally as fat as so many bullocks. I should say a two to a two and a-half miles course would be amply sufficient. A longer one will only give rise to a variety of mishaps. I lay ten to one La Palliser comes in as blown as a Liverpool chaser."

"Well, all such details will probably be left to you to decide," said Mrs. Forrester. "Lady Anne wants you to go over the first day you can in order to settle preliminaries. You know the big grass-fields, within half a mile of the Castle? There was some talk of making one of them the starting-point. But you will settle all that, since everything is to be placed in your hands."

"An exceedingly invidious honour, pretty sure to call down on my devoted head no end of abuse. I never knew the man yet who undertook to make out a steeplechase course and did not come in for almost universal condemnation. The riders consider the obstacles too large, the public think them too small; the one finds fault with the distance, the other complains of its brevity; and so they go on. It's impossible to satisfy everybody, even under the most favourable conditions; but when it comes to pleasing half-a-dozen ladies, and providing both for their safety and amusement, I confess to shrinking from such a difficult and delicate undertaking. It already weighs upon my mind like an 'incubus.' Imagine the tremendous responsibility of selecting the fences, when I think at each particular one that some frail-limbed woman may come to grief over it. I don't fancy the job in the least, and nothing but my friendship for Lady Anne would induce me to countenance it for one minute. However, since you ladies appear resolved, put me out of suspense at once by telling me when the celebrated female Foxington steeplechase is likely to come off?"

"I won't have you speak of our purpose in that disparaging manner," said Mrs. Forrester reprovingly. "And I back the ladies to acquit themselves quite as creditably as if they were men. Now, Jack, don't be disagreeable, for if you begin by giving yourself airs and turning up your nose in disdain the whole thing will collapse, and Lady Anne be terribly disappointed."

"I should be sorry to disappoint her ladyship. She's a real good sort, and I certainly would go out of my way to render her any little service that happened to be in my power. Has she fixed the time?"

"Oh dear no! In fact the idea has only just been broached. But I fancy she wants the race to come off pretty soon, probably about the beginning of December, but any way before Parliament meets. Their plans after Christmas are generally rather unsettled."

"The horses will have to be trained, of course," remarked Colonel Clinker, speaking with professional authority. "That is a *sine quâ non*. I suppose you are prepared to put the chestnut into regular work, Miss Brewser?"

"Really," said she, "I have hardly thought of it yet Won't that mean losing his services in the hunting-field altogether? And just at present I am too short of horses to be able to dispense with my best one."

"Short, are you?" interrupted Mrs. Forrester, who seldom allowed the chance of doing a little business to go by unmolested. "Are you on the look out for another? Because if so, I wish to dispose of an animal that would suit you down to the ground and carry you just like a bird. He's a bay, rising seven, and a first-rate fencer, as the Colonel there will tell you. As a rule I dislike selling to friends, but the Peer is a *bonâ fide* article, that I am only parting with owing to several younger horses coming on. He's a made hunter, and cheap at a hundred and twenty guineas, the price I'm asking for him."

It flashed through Kate's mind that if the Peer were really so good as represented, it seemed hardly worth Mrs. Forrester's while to sell him at the very commencement of the season, but she was not aware that his original price was twenty-five guineas, and that for a profit of a hundred pounds the lady would have parted with every animal in her stable.

"You are very kind," she answered diplomatically, thinking it well not to appear too keen. "I may probably have to purchase an extra horse or two later on, but just now I am in no particular hurry for a few weeks."

"May I be allowed to offer another piece of advice, in spite of the severe snubbing you took occasion to administer a short time ago," whispered Colonel Clinker a second or two later, when their hostess's attention was engaged in another quarter.

"Certainly," said Kate, feeling rather conscious of the rebuke, but still somewhat surprised at the request. "What is it?"

"Don't you let yourself be persuaded to buy any of Mrs. Forrester's horses, that's all. She's a dear old soul, and I'm awfully fond of her, but I should be sorry to see one of her so-called 'made hunters' palmed off upon you. Do you understand, or have I once more committed an offence?"

"Not at all, but please explain what is your meaning."

"Why, you see Mrs. Forrester is both able and clever. She rides awful brutes, and manages to get rid of them to advantage somehow. But they are not suited to other ladies, and therefore I should be sorry to see you buy one. Purchase a horse *with* Mrs. Forrester if you like—there is no better judge in England, when the cheque comes out of somebody else's book—but not *of her*. The risk, nine times out of ten, is too great."

"She must be a wonderful rider!" said Kate.

"That's exactly what she is, but I should grieve to see a young lady of your tender years imposed upon, and I *know* the Peer would not suit you."

"I'm not so young as all that. I was twenty-two last birthday," said Kate, impelled to make the statement by a species of brusque honesty, characteristic of her disposition.

"A mere child," said he looking at her and thinking how much too young she was to face the world alone. He noticed also how bright and large her eyes were, and how perfect the pose of the small head. "You are not angry with me for what I have said?" he asked, feeling as if he should like to be good friends with her in the future.   "I have not annoyed you *this* time, have I ? "

She hesitated for a second and then said—

" No."

" I know how independent you are," he continued apologetically, " and half feared you might resent my interference."

"People *ought* to be independent, and able to shift for themselves in this world."

" I entirely agree, so far as *our* sex is concerned, but in yours it becomes a question whether independence may not be carried to too great an extent—whether it is not apt to give women a certain brusqueness and hardness, scarcely in harmony with their character, at least from a manly point of view ? "   The sentence no doubt was uttered without any particular intention, but curiously enough Kate chose to put a personal construction upon it, and the spirit of opposition once more grew rife within her.

"Oh ! " she said flippantly, " I suppose you are like most other men, and care only for the pretty blue-eyed, flaxen-haired doll type, which looks up to you and worships you like demi-gods.   Brains don't signify ; the fewer the better for then dolly is less likely to see flaws in her idol, or to detect that what she takes for pure metal is nothing but a base alloy.   These clinging, lichen-like creatures appeal to a man's vanity if not to his nobler instincts, and in return they are rewarded by a lukewarm, half-contemptuous affection. The natural position of things is reversed, and *c'est l'homme qui se laisse aimé, pas la femme !*   It saves a great deal of trouble, and the limpets make excellent and obedient wives. *They* at any rate are not too independent."

" You are sweeping in your condemnations, Miss Brewser. Luckily for me, however, I have escaped the wiles of these beautiful but inane playthings of whom you speak.   Matrimony is an expensive luxury, rather superfluous than otherwise in my estimation, especially nowadays, when young ladies expend a moderate fortune on their clothes, and the dressmaker's bill would nearly cover the expenses of a season's hunting.   A man must either be very bold, very rich, or very, very foolish to undertake the modern girl of the period."

"Girl of the period indeed ! What an odious expression ! Just as if there were not hundreds and hundreds of nice, quiet, sensible girls about, if only the men had sense enough to appreciate them ! Instead of which, because their frocks happen to be a little behind the fashion, or their boots country made, and their gloves a size or two too big, they call them frumps, guys, gawkies, dowdies, every name under the sun. Why should we all be judged by our outer garments to such a ridiculous extent as to veil our eyes to inward merit ? Answer me that question if you can."

"But I can't. It's much too abstruse for my feeble comprehension."

"Well, then, do you believe in the law of demand and supply ? Are you by any chance a political economist ? "

"A political economist indeed ! Why, my dear Miss Brewser, I am not even a domestic one, and find it impossible to practise that virtue at home. A poor devil like myself, head over ears in debt, has quite enough, and more than enough, to do in minding his own affairs, without bothering about those of the nation."

"Ah ! you don't understand me. What I meant was simply this. You men as a body complain of the girls. You say they are fast, frivolous, and extravagant. Well, I ask in their defence, who make the girls so if not the men themselves ? They create a demand for a certain style of woman, and that demand is promptly supplied in order to gratify their tastes. If there were no demand there would be no supply. It is merely a fundamental law of nature—that's all. In support of my theory, enter any ball-room almost that you like, and you will see rows upon rows of quiet, *good* girls sitting partnerless by their chaperones, while the loud, noisy, fast ones have nearly every man in the place dangling after them. True, the lords of creation may return to their homes, and after devoting themselves all the evening to Mrs. A. or Miss B., declare they thank heaven their sister, wife, daughter, as the case may be, does not resemble the divinity, but with what result? Why their belongings, who probably have spent a dull evening, totally neglected, put two and two together, and after a bit begin to make comparisons. That stage once reached, the end soon approaches. They find that if they paint their cheeks, dress showily, talk immodestly, and altogether are 'bad form,' they too become a centre of attraction, and need no longer sit in retired corners alone, 'chewing the bitter cud' of desertion and isolation. They become different beings, but you men alone are to blame for their degeneration, though in the words of that arch-sneak Adam, when the mischief is done you turn round and say, 'It's not me, it's the woman.'"

She had forgotten where she was, and who she was speaking to, being carried away by the bitter earnestness of her subject. Unlike many girls of her age, she had seen a great deal of the world, and that under such peculiar circumstances as to render her unusually clear-sighted. Her cheeks now were flushed, and her whole face sparkling with animation, and Colonel Clinker, looking at her in astonishment, could not restrain his admiration. He dearly loved a highly-mettled steed, and Kate in this glowing mood reminded him of some gallant and spirited young creature. He had never met any one like her before, so clever, so original, and yet so honest and simple. She impressed him by her strength of character as well as by her good looks. And he himself possessed a strain of candour which forced him, unaccustomed as he was to hearing the shortcomings of his class thus roundly taken to task by so young a girl, to acknowledge in great measure the truth of what she said. It began dimly to dawn upon his mind that it was just possible the world might contain better things even than horse-racing and horse-riding, and that a dear little woman at his own fireside might possibly exercise a more salutary influence over him than did the life of restless excitement he was in the habit of leading—a life of wasted ability and unprofitable pleasures, whose only results consisted in embarrassing his father's old age, and squandering the patrimony he otherwise might have inherited. This child, this outspoken girl, with her honest

voice, fearless eyes, and daring opinions, clad in her simple
white gown, had appealed most strangely to his better nature,
raising in him suddenly a vague unsatisfied longing after
nobler things. Such sensations seemed too unreal to be
encouraged—only a passing weakness—to be crushed in its
infancy, such as the sight of a pretty woman, the glance
of an eye, the turn of a head, will often give rise to. With
a forced laugh and a sigh he roused himself from his meditations.

"You are a hard hitter, Miss Brewsor," he answered, "and
I scarcely know how to defend my sex against so forcible an
attack. You speak, however, as if your own experience had
been unfortunate. At twenty-two one's views on mankind
and one's knowledge of its deficiencies are not generally so
matured."

Kate coloured up to the very roots of her hair.

"Yes," she said, after a pause, while her voice quivered
slightly, "you are right. I *have* been unfortunate in my
experience, but please do not let us talk about it."

"Here, Terry!" cried Colonel Clinker to his friend, with
ready tact, seeing the conversation evidently began to
distress her, "come to the rescue, and help me to defend
myself against this young lady's shafts of sarcasm. We men
as a body have been catching it terribly hot all round. Can't
you say something neat on our behalf? I never came out
head of the class in argument, but you're a real tiptopper
at it."

"I should not dream of contradicting a lady," said Mr.
McGrath politely, in answer to this appeal. "Bless their
dear hearts! I love them all!" Which amorous sentiment,
delivered at the top of his voice, with a hearty expansion of
lung, forthwith created so much amusement that the conversation once more became general, until Mrs. Forrester made
a sign for the ladies to retire by nodding her head at the
end of the table, and thereby caused her cap to lose its
equilibrium and to roll sideways on to the floor.

"Now you young men," said she impressively, as she dived
under the mahogany in search of the missing article, and

suddenly came in contact with Mr. McGrath, bent on a similar errand, "you're to make haste, and not sit drinking and smoking *all* the rest of the evening. We want you to amuse *us*, and not *yourselves*, for once in a way, and if everybody is agreeable we can play a round game of cards by-and-by."

The gentlemen, thus admonished, made the most solemn promises not even to allow the charms of tobacco, wine, and anecdote to detain them, which promises they, for a wonder, kept nobly, appearing in about a quarter of an hour. Meanwhile Mrs. Forrester had not been idle. With the assistance of the two girls she cleared the centre table of its books and covering, and placed four shaded candles in their stead ready for a start. In thorough harmony with the sporting side of her character, the old lady dearly loved a quiet " gamble," and so long as it did not go beyond a certain limit, it afforded her the heartiest satisfaction to win small amounts from her friends, though that satisfaction was a trifle less apparent when she herself was called upon to disburse.

" Can you and Miss Whitbread play nap or poker?" she inquired of the two girls. "They are our great games, though I set my face against anything higher than three-penny points. Still these are exciting enough."

" I don't think Mary knows either game," said Kate, answering for both. " As for myself, I have played a few times only, just sufficient to master the first very elementary rules, and to appreciate the value of a flush or full hand."

" Ah! I see you are *au fait*, and any little mistake you may commit some of the gentlemen will easily correct. Mr. Grahame," addressing that individual, who was shyly warming the small of his back before the fire, and caressing an invisible flaxen moustache with great solicitude, "you'll bank with Miss Whitbread, won't you ?"

The Chirper thus appealed to started violently, turned crimson with confusion, but expressed his extreme willingness to assent to the proposal. He had sat by Mary Whitbread's side during dinner, and had been fairly astonished at his own garrulity. For once he had come across a girl who not only did not alarm or set her cap at him, but who listened with becoming attention to his every utterance, and who attended to the narrative of his personal affairs with an interest as genuine as it was charming. The young people had no objection whatever to being paired off at cards, and began counting their counters with amicable gravity. Not so Kate, who when asked by Mrs. Forrester if she would condescend to play with Colonel Clinker, said in the most marked manner—

"Thank you, Mrs. Forrester, I prefer my independence, and dislike all partnerships, preferring to stand or fall alone."

"Miss Brewser is quite right," said he ironically, "alliances are always to be avoided, especially between people so dissimilar in character as ourselves. We should fight like cat and dog over some miserable rubbishy hand. We two are better apart."

There was no getting over him. Every remark she made he promptly capped, and hitherto she had been decidedly worsted in each separate encounter.

"Yes, far better apart," she said with a toss of the head. "It is fortunate that for once we agree."

"*Most* fortunate," he echoed, but inwardly he exclaimed, "deuce take the girl! What the devil does she mean with her partnership? Does she suppose I want to force myself upon her, or is it nothing but her infernal conceit?"

And Kate, on her side, thought, "I never met any one so horribly sarcastic in all my life. I don't like him one bit, and yet he can be nice enough when he chooses. However, since he evidently wishes for war—war let it be to the knife."

So the two antagonists sat and glowered at each other across the green baize cloth, and played on all sorts of foolish hands, just for the sake of opposition. But when the game came to an end, and they counted up their losses, the gain to neither party had been great.

"I think we'd better consent to bury the hatchet next

time we play poker together," said Colonel Clinker. "We
should have been clear broke had we gone on at this rate,
and had it not been for the limit."

The girls had declared they must be going, and he made
the above remark in an undertone when he followed them
into the hall, and helped Kate on with her cloak. His voice
sounded soft in her ears. It had a peculiar *timbre* which
touched her in spite of herself, and he looked so thoroughly
manly and gentlemanly as he stood there, pretending to
fumble over her cloak, that she said in reply, with all the
indifference she could assume—

"Very well, we will avoid the bankruptcy court if possible,
else our creditors might have a rough time of it."

Was it not an unfortunate coincidence that these two, even
although unintentionally, always contrived to wound each
other on their tenderest points? Kate had been innocent of
any evil intention, nevertheless Jack Clinker's feelings were
sorely hurt by what he imagined was marked reference to his
pecuniary difficulties.

"That was a nasty speech, Miss Brewser," he said coldly.
"You don't like my advice, but for the third time this evening
I tender it. You are rather fond of hitting the right nail on
the head, but take care you don't get into the habit of striking
it too hard. It's an evil and an unkind practice, apt to grow
unawares upon those who indulge in it."

And now suddenly she remembered what Mrs. Forrester
had told her of his financial embarrassments, and the construction he had evidently put upon her words grew clear to
her mind.

"Oh!" she cried hastily, while a flush of shame dyed her
face, "I did not mean it. I'm so sorry—so awfully sorry.
Will you ever forgive me?"

His brow cleared at once.

"Never mind," he said, in quite a different tone. "It was
my fault. I'm a stupid fool to be so huffy. Good-bye, Miss
Brewser." He handed her into the carriage, shut the door,
and then added persuasively, "You'll let me come and see
you, won't you?"

She could not have told herself what was the instinct that
induced her to look him straight in the face with a smile and
say, "Yes." After all he could be nice when he chose; and
though she was in no danger of falling a victim to his fascinations, she began to understand that Mrs. Forrester had
perhaps spoken truly when she declared Jack Clinker to be a
dangerous man. She had not acted quite as she had intended
throughout the evening. But there was no fear of his proving
dangerous to her—not the least. That was quite a different
thing.

Meantime Mr. McGrath was holding a private conference
with his friend Mrs. Forrester.

"Well," said he, in an anxious whisper, "how do you
think they are gettting on? It struck me it was rather a
slap in the face for poor Jack when she turned round and
told him she detested partnerships! What do you suppose
she meant by it?"

"Oh, nothing," answered Mrs. Forrester, soothingly. "She
runs a bit contrary, that's all. Don't like the whip. Jack
was pretty free with the lash, you know, and she showed
some temper. Nothing more than might have been expected,
however."

Which declaration was a highly magnanimous one, seeing
that Mrs. Forrester had not imparted to Mr. McGrath the
manner in which she had betrayed his confidences.

"But do you think matters are progressing satisfactorily?"
said he.

"Admirably; how could they possibly be going on better?
Why, they did nothing the whole evening but spar and quarrel
like two great overgrown babies who could not leave each
other alone. What on earth would you have more?"

"I don't know. Do you call squabbling a good sign?"

"A good sign? Yes, certainly; I tell you it's a. *capital*
one!"

"Don't you consider it looks somewhat like a case of
mutual aversion?"

"Terry, you're really a very simple individual. I tell you
it's no such thing. It's the law of attraction and gravitation

which makes warring elements unite. Why, where's your natural history, man?"

"Well," said Terry, but half-convinced, "you may be right. You're a clever woman, Mrs. Forrester; but it's not the way the boys do their courting over in Ireland. Love-making there is done at the first intent, so to speak, and does not require all this beating about the bush and groping in subterranean alleys."

"Subterranean alleys! What nonsense you're talking, Terry."

"It's true, though, all the same. In our country the boys make up to the girls in a straightforward fashion, and give them a slapping good kiss on the cheek without all this roundabout sort of palaver."

"And a slapping good snub Jack would get for his pains if he were to try that game on. No, no, Terry, make up your mind that your countrymen's conduct cannot be implicitly followed on all occasions; and believe, besides, that most women are not won in that ploughboy manner. They *like* what you call 'round-about palaver.'"

"Well, it beats me altogether, and I give it up as a bad job. All I can say is, appearances are not entirely satisfactory."

"And I tell you appearances are *exceedingly* satisfactory, could not be more so, in fact; and that you know no more about the ways of 'a man and a maid' than my old tabby cat there," pointing to one on the rug. With which remark she bade him farewell; and, having turned her guests out of doors, retired to rest, well pleased with what she considered had proved a most successful evening.

The Honble. Jack Clinker, at all times subject to curious fancies, took it into his head to walk home, and firmly declined the companionship even of Mr. McGrath. So he put on his greatcoat, lighted a long cigar, and trudged away steadily. The yellow moon shone like a clear sphere in the dark heavens, anon brightening all the landscape, and making the trees and hedgerows stand out in delicate *silhouette*, again hiding away behind a mass of heavy cloud, while the merry stars twinkled and played at hide and seek in their far-off homes.

"Only twenty-two," said he, pursuing a train of reflection evidently uppermost in his thoughts, "and hates partnerships! Dash it all! It's not natural at that age to talk like a woman of the world. She said her experience had been unfortunate. I wonder *how* and in what way? I'd give a pony to know the story of her life. She must have been disappointed or badly treated some time or other. Perhaps it was some d—d fellow, which is the reason she's so awfully hard on the rest of us. Poor little soul! How pretty she looked when she was laying down the law. She reminded me of a snowdrop in her white frock, and her eyes sparkled just like two jewels. Talk of dolls, indeed! There's mighty little of the doll about her! What a spirit she has got, and—yes—" with a smile, "what a tongue as well. Never mind, after all she means no harm by it, and her heart is in the right place. I don't think your milk-and-watery creatures would suit me in the long run. One soon tires of them, just as she said. Now there would be no sameness, no monotony about *her*. She'd keep a man up to the mark, and prevent his wits from wool-gathering. Why, she made even *me*—ME—Jack Clinker—feel inclined to turn over a new leaf, and regret the past. I wonder, now, whether it would be possible to begin afresh and kick clear of the old groove? Things can't last much longer as they're doing. A smash sooner or later is inevitable. Pshaw! what a fool I am to be sure! I can't think what's come to me to-night, or what has put such ideas into my head. It's not likely a girl of Miss Brewser's wealth, surrounded, too, with every luxury, would ever care for a poor devil like myself. Enough of such nonsense. These confounded stars make a fellow maudlin."

He puffed vigorously at his cigar, and looked up into the cool, dark sky. The soft night air, laden with moisture, kissed his cheek, and seemed to lull his senses to rest. The peace of nature shed her charm around him, sinking petty every-day worries and actions into triviality.

"What an awfully jolly evening!" he soliloquised once more, knocking the ash away from his nearly smoked Havannah. "It makes one feel inclined to wander about all night, dreaming of half-fledged thoughts and wishes. Were it not for that bothering money I have everything a man could want—good father, position, health, friends, and spirits —and yet, every now and again there seems to crop up a curious void, just as there did this evening. I wonder what it is, and why on earth that girl in her white frock made such an impression upon me. Heigh-ho! It's a funny, unsatisfactory world in many ways!"

And with this unoriginal conclusion to his moralising, Jack Clinker found himself standing by his own hall-door, which he entered with a latch-key, and making a bad headache an excuse for not sitting up to the small hours of the morning, discussing the evening's events over a brandy and soda with Terence McGrath, he went up-stairs at once. He did not care to listen to his friend's opinions of "that smart young woman in white." He could fancy Terry using the very words; and he was in one of those fastidious, uncertain moods when comments are apt to be distasteful, and therefore ungraciously received, and when one's feelings are so highly strung that chaff irritates and banter jars.

Those "confounded stars" had certainly a good deal to answer for.

CHAPTER XIV.

A FRIEND IN NEED.

By time-honoured custom the opening meet of Sir Beauchamp Lenard's hounds was invariably held at Stapleton. In
olden days, during the life of the late lamented Squire,
Stapleton Hall had been renowned for a generous hospitality. From the richest to the poorest, people were liberally
regaled, and nobody was ever sent' empty away from the
doors of the most popular and best-hearted fellow in the
county. Such was the verdict of the public. But, alas! life
is fleeting, and in course of time this excellent gentleman was
gathered to his forefathers, and his eldest son, Duberly
Stapleton, took up the reins of office. The latter cared little
for sport, and, although a staunch preserver of foxes, seldom
honoured the county hounds with his presence.

Stapleton Hall was a fine old structure, built in the Gothic
style of architecture. It stood on an eminence, from which
an extensive view of the surrounding country was obtainable.
In a hollow immediately to the rear of the house lay a large
piece of ornamental water, on whose smooth surface a pair of
stately, long-necked swans swam gently to and fro, turning
their slender necks from side to side, while their white
plumage gleamed like snow in the morning sun. From the
left bank of this lake a well-timbered wood, known by the
name of Stapleton Hillside, and intersected by many winding
paths, rose steeply up, while in front of the residence an
unbroken expanse of undulating grass, not unlike the billows
of the sea, presented itself to the eye.

About three hundred yards beyond the house a depression
in the ground formed a sort of valley, from whose sides sprung

a couple of thickly gorsed coverts several acres in extent. They were renowned as a veritable stronghold of foxes, from which the "varmint" was hard to dislodge; but numerous as these were in point of numbers, and apparently fine, healthy, well-grown animals, it was a most unusual thing for a home-bred Stapleton fox ever to do' much more than vacillate between gorse and Hillside, until the patience of hounds, hunts-man, and field fairly came to an end. All through the fore-noon, directly a move was made, Reynard slunk hither and thither, at least half-a-dozen being on foot at one time, and the screeching, hooting, shouting, and galloping never ceased for one moment, to the intense delight of the swarms of foot people who made the opening meet an excuse for forsaking their legitimate occupations, and taking a regular holiday. But when little by little the crowd began to disperse, and the Stapleton foxes had once more fully sustained their unenvi-able reputation, Dick Slant, the huntsman, by order of Sir Beauchamp, trotted the hounds straight away off to Mad-dington Gorse, from which place a worthy yokel had just brought the welcome piece of intelligence that a fine old dog-fox had been viewed by himself stealing up the warm and sheltered sides only a few minutes previously. To Stirrup's intense consternation, King Olaf having during the preceding day given utterance to one or two ominous-sounding coughs Kate at the last minute had found herself obliged to fall back upon Grisette. Now all through the morning the grey had proved exceedingly fractious and irritable, refusing to stand still for one single second, anon plunging her head violently forwards with an impatient jerk which almost dragged the reins out of Kate's hands, again suddenly tossing it on high, till her face was in imminent danger. The short gallops hitherto indulged in between the gorse and the Hillside, alternating with periods of prolonged inaction, had apparently roused the mare's impetuous temperament to a dangerous point, and rendered her a far from pleasant mount. Added to this, she displayed the still graver fault of lashing out in the gateways, so that having badly kicked an unoffending quadruped that had pressed upon her more closely than she deemed advisable, Grisette

had quickly gained for herself a disagreeable notoriety, and
was pointed out as "that brute" by people who had been
eye-witnesses of the transaction. When, therefore, directly
hounds went into Maddington Gorse, the welcome "Tally ho!
tally ho!" followed by a prolonged and delighted screech of
"Hark forrard! Gone away!" reached her ears, Kate felt the
prospect of a scurry, however short, to be a positive relief.
One thing was certain, Grisette could not possibly behave
worse, and the chances were in favour of some of her irri-
tability subsiding, once hounds were fairly under weigh. At
the first sounds of Dick Slant's horn, the field started into
sudden vitality, and galloped as usual for the most convenient
gate. Alas! it chanced to be securely bolted, and the work
of dismounting and heaving it off its hinges, owing to the
extreme impatience of the crowd, proved unusually long,
several minutes of valuable time being thus unavoidably lost,
while people stood by and cursed and swore as if the most
terrible calamity had happened, and their very lives depended
upon the instantaneous removal of the unwelcome obstacle.
Now immediately to the right stretched a very big but nevertheless jumpable fence. It was a bit too big, however, at
starting, when jumping still bore the charm of novelty, and
practice had not as yet rendered seats secure and nerve confident. The huntsman, though, could not afford such considerations when his hounds were in full cry, so without more
than a passing hesitation he charged the fence and got over,
followed by a Colonel Clinker on a grey horse, who cleared
the whole thing beautifully, and these two thus gained quite
a fifty yards' start on the barricade division. Mounted on
King Olaf or the Duckling, for either of them inspired her
with courage, Kate would have dearly liked to follow suit, but
it appeared decidedly rash to attempt doing so on an untried animal, who so far had certainly not succeeded in making
a very favourable impression on her mistress. There are
occasions, however, when the actions are determined without
voluntary effort, and this was one—at least so far as Kate
was concerned—for while she was standing a little outside the
crowd, fearful of Grisette's heels inflicting further injury, and

waiting for the gate to be removed, the mare took the bit
between her teeth, and pulling like a demon, in a set
resolute fashion which defied any attempt at resistance,
charged full tilt at the fence before Kate fairly realised
what she was about. Finding herself absolutely powerless
to control the animal's movements, she wisely desisted in
her endeavours to do so, and thereby probably saved
herself a fall. She sat perfectly still, gave Grisette her
head, and the next minute with a crash and a smash which
sounded decidedly alarming in the ears of a novice, and
which sent the topmost twigs flying in every direction, the
mare landed far into the next field. The noise of breaking
branches caused Colonel Clinker to turn round in his saddle,
and, when he perceived the girl, to cry out "Bravo!" approvingly. But seeing Kate safely over, and no harm done,
he did not diminish his speed, for now the hounds were
simply racing in their front across the big grass pastures,
pointing as if for Stornow, a thickly fenced and very un-
negotiable bit of country, which took a deal of doing, as
Colonel Clinker had often found to his cost. In the large moist
fields the eadishes grew long and yellow, clinging to the horses'
legs, reaching almost up to their hocks, and rendering it extremely difficult to avoid the small cut drains which intersected them, and which made riding fast a work of conside-
able danger, especially with an animal not absolutely in
hand; but the pace was too great to allow of hesitation. It
really began to look as if they were in for a good thing,
and as if for once scent was all that it ought to be. As
they tore along, Kate's energies were entirely devoted to
sitting far back in the saddle and preventing Grisette from
running away altogether. She was in that unpleasant position when the consciousness of utter weakness, pitted against
brute force, presents itself to the mind. If the mare made
the slightest false step they might break their necks together
for all the power she retained of preventing any such calamity.
Still, the situation was decidedly exciting, for now, close under
Stornow village, the hounds made a sharp detour to the right,
which completely upset the calculations of the road and point

riders, constituting the great bulk of the field, who by this manœuvre were hopelessly thrown out, so that none but the immediate followers were left in attendance on the flying beauties. Meanwhile Grisette was pulling like a mad thing, and Kate's face, from the exertion of endeavouring to hold her, resembled a full-grown peony. Her arms ached and tingled from the sockets to the wrists, and worse than all, a tremulous dead sensation had begun to overtake them, depriving them of the little strength they still possessed. The fences, too, now came in rapid succession, one after the other, almost as fast as they could jump them—big, fair flying fences, guarded by ditches, out of grass into grass—a magnificent country, but one that undoubtedly demanded a finished hunter. As she swept over, or rather *through*, each impediment in its turn, the utmost Kate could do was to keep the mare's head straight and trust to Providence, for Grisette had an ugly way of chancing top-binders in a manner only too well calculated to strike terror into the heart of her rider. Nevertheless, up till now, inspired by the example of the good grey horse in front, she held her own, despite sundry narrow escapes, and kept her place close in his wake. Grisette's faults were many, as Kate had not been long in discovering; but the most heinous one of refusing could not be numbered in the category of her shortcomings. The very sight of a fence seemed to add to her natural impetuosity, and though unpleasantly chary of height, width presented no obstruction whatever. There was not much fear of her leaving her hind legs floundering in a ditch, so that after a bit, finding she got over *somehow*, even though not quite so cleanly as she was in the habit of doing, Kate grew tolerably accustomed to the mare's peculiar and rather alarming style of jumping, and became almost reconciled to the recurring sound of the breaking twigs as they flew before Grisette's forelegs like arrows shot from a bow. Her blood by this time was in a glow, fear had lost its restraining influence, caution had fled to the winds; her one idea, her one thought, was to keep near to that good grey at any hazard. Rather than lose a yard, she felt prepared to smash every bone in her body. The pace at

which they were going intoxicated her. Those who hunt
themselves, having doubtless often realised the sensation, will
recall times when they have ridden their very best under
similar circumstances, and will sympathise with what less
adventurous spirits might term this dare-devil, foolhardy mood
of the girl's.

Colonel Clinker, on Snowflake, once become conscious that
Kate Brewser was following close in his footsteps, had
several times turned round in the course of the run and
shouted to her to come fast or slow, as the case might be, at
any particular fence, and during these brief glances he perceived that in spite of Kate's courage and good horsemanship,
Grisette had completely overpowered her mistress, and was
far from being a safe conveyance. But there was little time
for reflection. Since they had left Stornow, the hounds had
never faltered for a second, but flown along with a breast-high
scent. Very few were with them. Dick Slant, the huntsman,
and Colonel Clinker cut out the work, the latter with Kate in
attendance, and behind them not more than a dozen horsemen, each riding his hardest, with eyes eagerly bent on the
racing pack, that, in a compact body, streamed on, on, on,
without a straggler or laggard among the number, in stern
and terrible silence. The yokel had been right when he
testified to Maddington Gorse holding a good old dog-fox,
who had brought them along in a style not often seen, even
in the crack hunting county of Great Britain. But now Pug
seemed to change his point, and again bore away to the
right. The pace began to tell upon *him*, as well as upon the
horses, and he sought a convenient refuge, leaving the sound
and springy turf which hitherto he had closely adhered to,
and making for the difficult country all round about Shepperton, a village conspicuous by a solitary windmill standing
on a big round hill, which formed a landmark to the surrounding neighbourhood. The fences here were regular
" man traps," guarded on one or either side by stiff wooden
rails, commonly termed " oxers." Two ploughed fields, heavy
and binding, now lay in front of the pursuers, the first of
them being separated from the arable land by a tall and un-

commonly hairy bullfinch. Dick Slant pulled his clever hunter up to a trot, and after some persuasion and jobbing in the mouth, managed to bore a way through, and then pop off the bank over the ditch on the far side, and the well-trained Snowflake did likewise. It was eminently a place where a good steady horse showed to advantage, but it was useless asking Grisette to go slowly or to double. She rushed at the bullfinch in her usual wild manner. The reins were torn out of Kate's hands, and she herself nearly dragged off backwards. Nevertheless, she got over safely, though in rather a sorry plight. Her hat was battered in, and a sharp thorn had caught her face, and scratched it to such an extent that the blood flowed freely.

"The brute!" said Colonel Clinker indignantly, as he saw the red drops making their slow way down her disfigured cheek. "Why on earth does she want to go a thousand miles an hour at everything she comes across?"

"That's just what I can't tell you," gasped Kate, applying her pocket-handkerchief to the injured part. "All I know is, it's exceedingly unpleasant."

But they had no time for further talk, for the hounds, though running rather more slowly, were still advancing steadily over the sticky clay fallows. Now there are certain horses who cannot get along at all in heavy, wet soil. Even animals that are very decent stayers on the top of the ground collapse altogether when their hoofs sink fetlock-deep in the soft earth. Directly they entered the plough, Grisette began to labour and falter in her stride. She stretched her head forwards, the white foam lathered the reins like soapsuds, while the mare's mane hung damp and straight in steaming wisps upon her dripping neck. She had clearly shot her bolt, and now dropped heavy on the hand, although she ceased pulling and snatching at the bridle. As they crossed the second of the two ploughed fields she subsided from a gallop to a canter, from a canter to a feeble lurching trot. Still it would never do to stop with the pack now well ahead, and Kate determined to struggle on to the end, *coûte qui coûte.* She was by no means insensible to the danger of riding

a beaten animal, only she could not bring herself to
cease following the hounds when up till now she had held
so good a place and entertained such a pleasant consciousness of having gone really well. Nevertheless, what but a
few short minutes ago, in spite of Grisette's little eccentricities, had appeared to her the summit of human enjoyment, gradually assumed a painful and alarming nature.
She began to speculate on the probable duration of the
run, and devoutly wished for its prompt termination, or at
least a prolonged and highly welcome check. If something
did not happen, and that soon, she would be forced *nolens
volens* to give in, for to feel that wretched Grisette sobbing
and labouring under her, to see the limp neck and distended
nostril, to hear the catching breath and palpitating heart,
going like a sledge-hammer, to watch the convulsive jerkings
of the quivering tail, and the spasmodic heavings of the
panting flank, had become both pitiful and vexatious in the
middle of a good run. Fortunately there was grass once
more ahead, and only a small straggly fence intervening
between it and the plough. With a faltering leap, followed
by a real bad peck, and a desperate struggle to regain her
footing, Grisette got over it, bearing away on her moist brow
the marks of mother earth.

"That was a near thing," thought Kate. "However, a
miss is as good as a mile, according to the old saying."

Her spirit rose within her in spite of this mishap, for she
hoped that the light going, added to some judicious nursing
on her part, might succeed in pulling the mare through after
all. But these hopes were destined to be of very short
duration, for to her dismay only about a couple of hundred
yards off loomed an immense stake-and-bound fence, newly
trimmed, with a binder running all along the top as thick as
a man's arm, and apparently ten thousand times more unyielding—an obstacle, even on the fittest and freshest of
horses, entitled to great respect. Colonel Clinker, when he
saw it in the distance took a pull at Snowflake and waited for
Kate to come up almost alongside.

"For heaven's sake," he said in a voice full of anxiety,

"take care what you are about! Your mare's dead beat, and I don't half like your going at it."

"I can't possibly show the white feather now," came the answer between her set teeth.

"At all events," he said, "let me go first. There's just a chance of Snowflake's carrying away the binder, or making a hole somewhere. Put the mare steadily at the fence, and keep her well in hand, for she's bound to scramble terribly."

But the gallant Snowflake for once failed to satisfy his master's aspirations. He collected himself for an effort, and flew the obstacle like a bird, with at least a foot to spare. There was little fear of *his* bringing topbinders away. So great, however, was Colonel Clinker's anxiety, that he pulled him back almost to a standstill, in order that he might watch how Kate fared. Urging the mare on by heel and voice, the girl rode bravely at the fence; but even before Grisette took off she knew for certain they were bound to come to grief. There was no answering response to her call, no elasticity of motion or willingness of spirit, nothing but a disheartening reluctance to proceed.

A horrible crash, a violent fall, a recollection of the mare rolling backwards and forwards over her body, followed by the death-like feeling of a heavy, crushing weight pinning her to the ground, were Kate's next immediate sensations. Far too beat to attempt rising from the place where she had fallen, Grisette laid on the helpless girl, grunting with terror, every now and then hitting out with her hind legs, which momentarily threatened to dash the head of her unfortunate rider to pieces. Each minute it seemed as if the deadly iron hoofs must prove fatal.

"Good God!" exclaimed Colonel Clinker, hastening to dismount. "I never saw a worse fall in my life; she will be killed to a certainty. Here, one of you fellows," he said to a couple of men who had just come up, "hold my horse, will you? There is not a minute to be lost. We must get her away somehow."

His face was ghastly, with not a vestige of colour left

in it; still his presence of mind did not desert him. In any emergency he was quick to decide upon a course of action, and he saw at a glance that owing to the danger of Grisette kicking out yet more violently, it would be useless attempting to draw Kate's prostrate body from under her by main strength. The best chance appeared to be to get the mare on her legs as. quickly and as quietly as possible. The risk might be great, but it must be run, there was no help for it. "The brute will struggle," he said. "However, it's a case of kill or cure, and we can only act for the best. Delay can do no good."

Kate in her dangerous position heard the words.

"You are right," she said, looking at him with a faint smile. "Delay can do no good, and I promise to keep as still as a mouse."

The relief of hearing her speak those few words and of knowing she retained her senses was so immense that it lightened half the load of care weighing on Jack Clinker's heart.

"That's right," he said more cheerily. "Trust to us, and all will come well yet. *We* shan't let any harm happen to you if *we* can help it."

She tried to answer, but her face paled suddenly, as just then Grisette gave a fresh struggle, and the iron hoofs missed her head by the eighth of an inch.

"Bless the girl!" said Colonel Clinker to himself, "what a good plucked 'un she is, to be sure! She has never screamed once, although I fear she must be in great pain."

And he was right, though she would have scorned any outward expression of the fact, for her breath came hard and slow, and a sickly sensation was stealing over her. To be so near a sudden and awful death, to realise all its terrors in that first swift, overpowering impulse of physical fear and human weakness common to mankind, was an experience not lightly to be encountered even by the bravest. Kate did not call out or faint, but in those few moments when she lay under Grisette she lived a lifetime. Suffering, retrospection, memory, hope, and doubts were all condensed in that brief period. Like an a mirror, the actions of her girlhood presented themselves to her mind—her dear dead uncle, the old home, Herbert, Maggie, Mary Whitbread, and a host of confused thoughts. How was it that the life she had often professed to disdain appeared so sweet at the first prospect of losing it? Why did she suddenly cling to it with such a strange tenacity, when one good blow of Grisette's hoofs could so easily put an end to earthly struggles? She could not have told, or given herself any satisfactory reason for this change of feeling, which at twenty-two was only thoroughly natural, being but the strong vitality of youth rebelling against possible death.

Meantime several people flocked round the spot where the disaster had taken place, for bad as human nature is represented, there are always a certain number of folks ready if an accident occurs, even when hounds are running hard, to give up their own immediate enjoyment and come to the assistance of their less fortunate fellow-creature. Perhaps the consciousness that one good turn deserves another, and that their own time may be near at hand, has something to do with the truly Samaritan spirit which unquestionably exhibits itself in the hunting-field. A man who will jump on you almost as soon as look at you will nevertheless often give up a good run in case of an emergency arising.

Colonel Clinker, aided by several kindly volunteers, now seized Grisette by the head and flank, and with all his force attempted to raise her from the ground. Twice she made a sort of half effort, and twice, her legs seeming to slip from under her, she rolled back on the girl; but at the third essay, and after a short though desperate scramble, during which Colonel Clinker held up Grisette's neck with an iron grasp, she managed once more to regain her footing, and stood on all fours, snorting and shaking like an aspen-leaf. Kate lay perfectly still, for the two last rolls had crushed her sorely.

"Are you terribly hurt?" asked Jack Clinker fearfully, bending over the prostrate form. "Dear me! she is insensible!" he added in alarm, when no immediate answer was forthcoming.

His words and anxious perturbed face braced Kate to fresh effort.

"No, I'm not," she answered bravely, though her lips quivered as she spoke. "At least," correcting herself, for she had never felt as she did now, and was not very sure what might happen next, "at least, not quite. I shall be better in a little, I dare say."

"Ah! the brute rolled right over you several times. However, I hope you will feel more like yourself in a few minutes. You've had an ugly shaking."

"Thanks," she replied. "You're all so kind to me, and I hate myself for making such an absurd fuss, but I think I shall do now."

She tried to raise herself upon her elbow as she spoke, but the movement caused such discomfort she was glad to desist from the effort.

"Give her a drop of brandy," suggested one. "Undo her habit," said a second. "Loosen her collar," advised a third. "Cut her stay-lace," hazarded a fourth. "Stand her up," exclaimed a fifth ignorant but well-intentioned onlooker.

"Do nothing of the sort, gentlemen," said Colonel Clinker, decidedly. "Let the lady have plenty of air, and don't all crowd round her together. She wants to be left quite still for a bit, and allowed to remain where she is a few minutes until she comes round. In fact," he added, with a keener insight into Kate's probable wishes than was possessed by the rest of the assembled company, "I really hardly know if it is necessary to detain you any longer. It's a pity for you all to lose your sport, and I will remain with the young lady. I feel sure she would rather you lost no more time."

"Oh, yes!" interrupted Kate, "it makes me quite unhappy that so many people should have their fun spoilt on my account. Please go."

Thus admonished, one by one the little crowd dispersed, until Jack Clinker was the sole member of it left.

"I wish you'd go too," said she, directly they found themselves alone, with a remnant of her old pride. "I've been quite bother enough as it is, and I dare say Stirrup will appear before very long. I don't the least mind being left alone, and I can't bear the idea of your not seeing the finish of so good a run."

"Hounds are miles away by this time," he answered indifferently, "and though I admit it *was* a good run, it is by no means the first, and, please God, by no means the last I shall take part in. So don't vex yourself about that. I'm not altogether such a selfish savage as to leave a lady all by herself in circumstances like the present." He hesitated for one moment, and then added, "especially you." She could not have told why, but his answer comforted her. She had begged him to leave her, but at the same time she had not wanted him to go, and now he disclaimed the intention of quitting her so peremptorily that she desisted from any further persuasion.

"You are very good," she said once more, "and I suppose you will take your own way, whatever I urge to the contrary."

"Way? Why, of course I shall; I'm used to having my own way in everything, as you'll soon find out," he answered cheerily. His admiration for her cool courage was rising fast. At that moment all thought of fox and hounds had vanished from his mind. His next action was to take off his red coat, roll it into a ball, and place it under the girl's head. "There, that's better, is it not?" he said. "Makes a sort of pillow. Do you feel cold at all? I wish to goodness I had something to throw over you and keep you warm. After all I was a fool sending those fellows off in such a hurry, but I began to be afraid they might annoy you. They mean well, but have not a bit of tact."

"I'm very glad you did," she said with a smile. "Some of their suggestions were positively alarming. But won't you catch cold without any coat?"

That simple act had touched her woman's heart, and predisposed her more in his favour than all that had gone before. It testified to a chivalrous and kindly nature.

"Not I. Do you think I'm barley-sugar to melt in the sun or the rain, as the case may be? But we must not let you stay here too long, for there is such a thing as rheumatism in this world. Do you think you could get up now if I were to help you a little? Don't be in any hurry, unless you feel inclined, only perhaps it may be wise to make an effort."

"I'll try," she said submissively. "I feel much better than I did a little while ago."

"Capital! The quiet has done you good after all! I have had so many falls of one sort and another myself that I know from experience what a relief it is, when one is knocked out of time, to be allowed to lie still for a minute or two. Officious friends either *can't* or *won't* understand that fact, and give you no peace until they have hauled you on to your horse again. Often and often have I wished them all a hundred miles away."

"Talking of horses, what has become of my unfortunate steed? Has she broken her neck or run away?"

"Neither, though the former would but have served her right for her misdemeanours. She's not very far off or likely to wander in her present condition."

The Honble. Jack cast an indignant glance over his shoulder at the unconscious authoress of Kate's misfortunes, who, tied to a gate-post side by side with the good old Snowflake, looked exceedingly wretched and forlorn, bespattered with mud from head to tail, the crutches of her saddle all dented in, and her coat, stiffening rapidly from the cold air super-vening on lavish perspiration.

"The beast!" exclaimed he, eyeing her with marked dis-favour. "I should like to shoot her on the spot."

"Don't be so bloodthirsty. What did poor Grisette do to encompass our downfall, for really I hardly know?"

"I will tell you easily enough. She never made the ghost of an effort, or rose one single inch, but just galloped straight into the fence, caught the binder with her chest, and turned a complete somersault into the field. A pretty lady's hunter!"

"Now, I won't have you abuse my property. It's not good manners; besides, remember, the poor thing was dead beat, and really was not so much to blame after all. We seemed to me to have been galloping tremendously fast, and

I don't somehow think she's much of a stayer. She did not give me the impression."

"That I can easily believe, for those tearing, rushing brutes generally do pull themselves out in something under twenty minutes, and once they begin to blow it's all up. They ride like a lump of lead for the rest of the day. I don't tumble to that class of animal. Nine times out of ten they're soft, showy, and cowardly. As for Grisette—that is her name, is it not?—you ought not to give her a chance of repeating her ill-conduct in the future. You stuck to her like a brick, and rode awfully well, but take my word for it, she's not a safe animal for any lady to hunt."

"She has her faults, I admit, but perfection is terribly hard to find, either in human beings or in horseflesh. Such at least is my experience."

She had succeeded in assuming a sitting position, but still felt unequal to the task of remounting or standing upright. It was, therefore, with some relief she saw Colonel Clinker's second horseman now appear on the scene, who, touching his hat respectfully, as if not altogether sure his presence might not be considered incompatible with certain orders he had received erewhile, said in a half-apologetic, half-explanatory sort of way—

"Beg pardon, sir! but farmer Smith 'ee told me as 'ow you was a-staying behind with a lady as 'ad met with a bad haccident, and I took the liberty of riding Hopal part of the way back again to see if I could render any assistance. I 'ope I acted right, sir."

"Quite right," answered his master, in tones of unqualified approbation, though the chances were on any other occasion poor Leatherdale might have received a severe reprimand for this breach of discipline. "And now, Leatherdale, attend to what I say. I want you to go straight to the inn and tell them to bring a trap immediately, and to wait at the cross-road for Graby until I turn up. You know the place I mean, don't you?"

"Yes, sir, woll nigh upon the old sign-post, afore you come to the seventh milestone."

"Exactly; and Leatherdale, don't forget to ask for the loan of a shawl or warm wrap of some sort or other. The young lady is sure to feel chilly after a bit, when the reaction sets in. If they make any bother about lending it, you can mention my name and give them half-a-crown. Do you understand what I want?"

"I'm to order a trap and borrow a shawl, and tell 'em to wait till you come, sir."

"That's it, and Leatherdale" turning to speak with the man aside, so that Kate might not overhear his final injunction—"it's as well to be on the safe side. If you should happen to meet Miss Brewser's groom on the way, or anyone going in the direction of Foxington, ask him to call at Dr. Baker's and leave a message saying his services will be required at Sport Lodge in about an hour's time. I fear there may be some broken bones to set."

"'Deed, sir! I'm sorry to hear that, sir!" said Leatherdale with ready sympathy as he rode off to do his master's bidding, determined, after the manner of his kind, that the ill-news of Miss Brewser's accident should lose nothing in transmission, but rather gain in point and piquancy.

CHAPTER XV.

A FRIEND IN NEED.

As soon as he had gone, Colonel Clinker said to Kate **in a** voice of quiet authority—

"And now we must get you to your feet. You have lain on that damp ground quite long enough, and will derive no more benefit from keeping still. Can you rise by yourself, or shall I help you?"

Kate shook her head, and declined assistance in her curiously independent way, but only to find a moment later, when she struggled up with great pain and difficulty, that she could not possibly do without aid.

For one instant she stood tottering and swaying to and fro like a helpless reed in the wind; then suddenly the green fields, Grisette, Snowflake, Colonel Clinker, seemed to swim before her eyes, a sickly faintness stole over her frame, and she would have fallen had not Jack supported her in his arms. She could just feel their strong but gentle clasp, and then she lost consciousness. Her eyes closed, and insensibly the small head, with its crushed and battered pot hat, sank on his broad shoulder as on a pillow.

A transient gleam lit up Jack Clinker's frank blue eyes when he felt Kate's weight. As he held her for once, as if indeed she were his very own, a swift, strange thrill of delight shot through his being. With her pale, scratched face, dishevelled hair, and blue lips, she moved him more than any woman had hitherto done in his whole life before. It was the same feeling he had experienced the night of Mrs. Forrester's dinner-party, but now it returned with twofold strength. He took out his silver flask, forced brandy through the girl's set

teeth, and waited anxiously for the first symptoms of returning life.

Gradually a faint tinge of colour, like the blush of a white
rose, flickered back into her cheeks, and the beautiful lashes
which hid the grey eyes curled themselves upwards. At first
her look was vague and wandering, but as little by little the
brain began to reassert its power, a rosy flush suffused her
whole countenance.

"I am better now," she said, freeing herself from his
arms. "I can't think what made me so silly. I have never
fainted until to-day."

He let her go directly, but even then she could not stand
alone. He held out his hand—that powerful, manly hand
she had noticed and liked before.

"Will you not take it?" he said with a half smile. "You
are proud, but you see you cannot do without me altogether."

She put her small palm in his, and he led her like a little
child to the place, some few yards distant, where the two
horses were standing tied together.

"If you could manage to sit on Grisette for a hundred yards
or so," he said gently, "just till we get to the road and meet
the trap, I think it would be better for you than walking.
Will you mind my lifting you up?"

"No," she said simply.

It was a strangely sweet and strangely novel sensation to
her, who for so many years had been accustomed to take
the lead, to decide and act alone, to find someone who could
do these things for her. It seemed pleasant to be protected
and cared for, especially when she was suffering. Many
men might have taken advantage of the situation, might have
made their kindness felt as a matter calling for gratitude;
but *he* did everything so quietly and so naturally that she
could but accept his services in the same spirit in which they
were rendered.

"Do not be afraid," he said, when he had lifted her on to
the mare. "I will lead Grisette with one hand and hold you
with the other in case you should feel giddy. Let me know
if it hurts you moving."

He walked by her side in silence, but though the motion of the animal sent a sharp catchy pain to her heart, and made her grow hot and cold by turns, she shut her lips firmly over her white teeth, determined no sound of complaint should escape them. She could not bear that he should think her a coward, and so at length they reached the roadside, where, to their no small joy, an open pony-chaise stood in readiness awaiting their arrival.

"And now," said Colonel Clinker to the man in charge, "I propose driving the young lady home, provided you can manage to ride the grey and lead the mare back. They are both pretty well tired out, and will be as quiet as sheep."

So saying he helped Kate into the vehicle, propped her up with the cushions of the seats, and, after tucking a couple of shawls round her, seated himself in the empty place by her side, and taking up the reins drove off at a good smart trot.

"The sooner we get home the better," he said, "and as the trap only holds two, I thought perhaps it might be pleasanter on the whole for you that I should come instead of the man, who would not have known what steps to take had you turned faint again on the way."

He deemed it necessary to make this explanation, although he did *not* deem it necessary to tell her how reluctant he felt to part from her, at least until he was assured she was in good hands.

"You are very kind and considerate," she said in reply. "I did not know men were so thoughtful."

She was not going to tell *him* either how completely the arrangement satisfied her. After all, it was only natural to prefer his society to that of the inn-proprietor from Shepperton.

"Ah! I forgot. Your estimation of our sex is extremely poor. Well, no matter—all the more reason for me to endeavour to raise it."

"Did you think that when—when—" she began eagerly, but checked herself as suddenly. She was thinking, "when you made the bet."

"When what?" he said, seeking for an explanation.

"Oh, no matter; only something that just happened to strike me."

"Won't you tell me what it was?"

"No, thank you; I'd rather not, especially as the thought recalled a highly disagreeable recollection."

Her tone had become cold and her manner frigid.

"In that case I apologise for my curiosity," he replied, relapsing into silence.

"So you don't approve of Grisette?" she said presently, after a prolonged pause. "Do you know, I'm afraid you're rather vindictive."

"No. Approve of her? I should think not. Confound the brute! She's a real bad un."

"Now once again I say, don't abuse my belongings; it's not polite."

"Truth very seldom is. How long has she been in your possession?"

"About two or three months. I was let in by a friend. Friends have a way of doing those pleasant little things at times."

"Yes, if you call them friends. I don't. I wish I could lay claim, however, to being one, so that I might ask a favour at your hands."

"Is friendship the *sine quâ non* which renders requests admissable?" she asked maliciously. "Are they not often proffered without any particular intimacy on either side?"

"That speech is, I suppose, intended to remind me of being without the pale. Thank you, Miss Brewser. You have a candid manner of putting things highly calculated to impress people with a sense of your honesty."

"And you of snapping up one's words and not understanding chaff. What is this favour you ask?"

"Simply that you promise me never to ride Grisette again."

"Indeed! Am I to show the white feather merely because she has given me a fall? That would be cowardly."

"No, not because she has given you a fall, but because she is a mad, headstrong, soft brute, not worth her keep. Will you promise?"

"But I can put Stirrup on her," said she, equivocating. "She'd do nicely to jog about the roads on."

"Very nicely. She would not pull Stirrup's arms off, I suppose, or run away, or go headlong into the nearest carriage? No, of course not."

"Now, don't be sarcastic. If Grisette's not fit for me to ride she's not fit for poor dear old Stirrup. But how am I to get rid of her?"

"Easily enough. Make a chop with Phipps or some respectable dealer. Depend upon it, the first loss is always the smallest in cases of this sort. There's no extravagance so ruinous in the end as that of sticking to a bad gee."

"Well, perhaps not; I'll think it over any way."

He was charmed at gaining even this concession, for he honestly only desired her welfare. A pity he could not leave matters as they were—a pity that some foolish instinct prompted him to bend over her and say, in a soft, persuasive voice—

"Will you think it over to—to—please *me ?*"

It was the first indiscretion he had committed—the first speech which deprived her of her sense of ease. Mrs. Forrester had warned her of his being a flirt. Had he already begun to practice on her? Or was he gradually smoothing the road for that ultimate proposal he had backed himself to make?

"No, certainly not," she said curtly. "If I think of selling Grisette at all it will be to please myself, not other people; and excuse my saying so, but do you not consider I ought to be the best judge of my own affairs?"

No snub could have been more direct. His face flushed as he answered haughtily—

"Certainly, Miss Brewser. I regret I should have been so foolish as to display the slightest interest in them. Henceforth I will studiously guard against any recurrence of the fault."

He flicked the pony sharply with the whip, and settled down into a gloomy silence. She felt sorry for having produced this result, and after a bit endeavoured to resume the conversation.

"What a lovely afternoon it has turned out," she said, after a quarter of an hour had elapsed, during which not a word had been uttered on either side.

No answer.

Colonel Clinker pretended to be absorbed in a profound contemplation of the surrounding landscape.

"The country about here looks good for hunting," she said, wishing more and more as they neared home to make her peace, and feeling conscious of having ill-requited his kindness and attention. "Do you often run this way with hounds?"

"Sometimes."

"The fences look very big about here."

"Rather."

"I suppose most people don't jump them, but stick to the roads?"

"Yes."

"How much farther are we from Foxington? Far?"

"No."

She looked up into his face. It was very gloomy and stern, She put her hand on his arm for one second, and said with a pretty, penitent smile—

"Won't you tell me *how* far? I hate monosyllabic replies. They're so *very* unsatisfactory—give one no information whatever."

His brow relaxed a little though he answered coldly—

"Foxington is quite close. You will see it when we pass the next bend in the road. We are just home."

She made no reply for a few seconds. She was cogitating an unwonted act of grace. They drove through the town, past the church, up the hill, then in at the gate of Sport Lodge. Another minute and it would be too late.

She turned her head away and stared at the scanty laurels which flourished ill among the clay soil.

"Colonel Clinker," she said in a low voice, "I'll promise not to ride Grisette again if you wish it. I was wrong to speak as I did, and I believe you had only my interest at heart."

It cost her a great effort, but nevertheless she felt easier when it was over. Her words surprised him so much that the staid old pony was actually suffered to fall into a walk.

He looked her straight in the face, with one keen inquiring glance. "Thank you," he said. That was all, but from the tone of his voice she knew he was pleased, and that she had not suffered in his good opinion.

"Are we friends again then?" she asked softly.

"I did not know you ever considered us as such, Miss Brewser."

"Never mind what you 'did not know.' After the great kindness you have shown me this afternoon, I should be sorry not to part amicably. We can resume our differences, if necessary on some future occasion."

"I devoutly hope, then, that it may not prove necessary. Might not 'our differences,' as you call them, be buried alto-gether?"

Kate, however, was saved from making any answer to this question by the appearance of Mary Whitbread, followed by Dr. Baker.

"Oh, Kate!" she said. "What *is* the matter?"

"Nothing very serious, I hope, only I've made rather an idiot of myself, and given Colonel Clinker no end of trouble," answered the girl.

"I wish you would not mention that part of the business," he said. "Don't you remember a certain bargain we made not so very long ago?"

"I really am ashamed to say I've quite forgotten it."

"Why, that I was to be allowed to pick you up whenever you came to grief."

"Ah! yes, of course. Little did I think how soon your assistance would be required."

"And now, Kate," said Mary Whitbread, when between them she had been helped into the hall, "you must come upstairs at once, and let Dr. Baker pronounce upon your condition. We can't allow you to stand talking here any longer."

"Good-bye, then," she said to Colonel Clinker with a smile. "You see I'm under marching orders." She put out her little hand frankly, and he pressed it in his own.

"Good-bye, Miss Brewser, I hope you will soon get well May I be allowed to wait until the doctor issues his bulletin?"

"Certainly, if you care to take so much trouble."

"I *do* care to," and then he turned away, and went and sat by himself in the small cosy drawing-room. It seemed a perfect age before any one appeared to relieve his anxiety. He took in every detail of the apartment—the books, the work, the flowers, every little sign that betrayed the presence of ladies. He turned over Kate's photograph-book, and critically examined a faded likeness which represented that young lady, in short frock and shaggy hair, at the age of fifteen.

"What a trump she is," he thought to himself, as he recalled the adventures of the afternoon. First, how she had followed him fence for fence all through the earlier part of the run, going straight as a die, without any pause or hesitation; next how, riding a beaten horse, she had gamely struggled to the bitter end; and lastly, when the crowning disaster arrived, how she had shown conspicuous courage, and never lost her presence of mind and self-control for a minute. She had roused his admiration as much as she commanded his respect. He was still sitting there poring over the photograph in an abstracted manner, when Dr. Baker reappeared.

"Well!" he said, rubbing his chubby pink hands together with an audible chuckle. "I bring good news. The young lady, after all, is not so seriously hurt as we imagine, and there are no bones broken. Her ribs have been badly crushed, which accounts for the pain in breathing. A week's rest will, I hope, work wonders. I have recommended her to keep in bed for the next twenty-four hours, but if all goes well I know no reason why a fortnight should not see her in the saddle again. She appears to have an excellent constitution and plenty of pluck, two very desirable but often missing qualities in a patient."

"Oh yes, she has plenty of pluck; I can answer for that. Most women in her place would have made a terrible to-do, but she never uttered a single complaint."

That night Jack Clinker's slumbers were very uneasy, frequently disturbed by crushing sounds, and the vision of struggling horses and sweet girl faces. The latter haunted him until the small hours of the morning, when at length he gained repose.

Miss Palliser heard of Kate's accident, as a matter of course, and when she heard of it she remarked with glee to every member of the hunting-field—

"Ah, poor thing! Just what one would expect. No judgment and no notion of riding. But there, very likely it will do her good, and by the time she has been brought back in a cart once or twice more, perhaps, she may begin to settle down and go like a Christian," which speech being interpreted meant that Kate had again shown Miss Palliser the way, and aroused in her a fierce and bitter jealousy not lightly to be quenched. *New* ladies invariably provoked hostile feelings, but a young and good-looking one who dared to cut Miss Palliser out was especially to be condemned. Insignificant ones might be tolerated, but not those who aspired to distinguish themselves in that hunting-field of which Miss Palliser considered herself the queen.

CHAPTER XVI.

ANTICIPATING VISITORS.

THE next morning Kate felt terribly stiff, and all movement was attended with such extreme pain that she could scarcely turn round in bed, and consequently, sorely against her will, was obliged to remain quietly there for the whole of that day, a proceeding she most highly disapproved of, and one which nothing but sheer necessity induced her reluctantly to submit to. At about ten o'clock Colonel Clinker and Mr. McGrath had ridden up to Sport Lodge, on their way out to covert, in order to inquire after the invalid, and Mary Whitbread, at Kate's request, had gone down to the hall-door and given them the latest particulars.

"So Miss Brewser passed a fairly good night upon the whole?" asked Colonel Clinker, with no little interest. "You say she's progressing?"

"Most decidedly. In fact she is better almost than could have been expected under the circumstances. But she is never one to give in. If you knew her as well as I do you'd say the same thing."

"Without possessing that privilege, I can fully endorse the statement. Miss Brewser has marvellous courage. Will you be so good as to tell her we called, Miss Whitbread, and hope before long to find her downstairs again. Come, Terry, we must be off, or we shall be late for the meet."

So saying the two friends had ridden away together, leaving Mary to convey to Kate sundry messages full of condolence and sympathy, which that young lady received with demure complacency.

"I thought he'd come," she remarked to Mary.

"He? Who's he?" the latter replied in astonishment.
"Oh! Colonel Clinker, I suppose you mean. Really Kate, it
is wonderful for you to speculate on the probable movements
of any man, whether he comes or whether he does not come
being generally a matter of supreme indifference to your
highness."

"And pray did I say it was otherwise? I simply remarked
that I thought Colonel Clinker would put in an appearance.
After all it was purely a mere matter of form,—an act of the
most ordinary civility."

"Certainly, Kate; only it struck me you began to display a
little more interest than usual in this fascinating guardsman."

"You're a donkey, Mary," said she in reply, though the
tell-tale blood rushed to her cheeks. "I don't care twopence
about the man, and probably never shall."

The conversation dropped for the present, but Mary Whitbread, who in her little quiet way was not devoid of observation, took occasion to remark, although she wisely held her
peace, the introduction of that word "probably." She was
accustomed to the most vigorous denials, and formed her
own conclusions on the matter. Two days elapsed without
anything taking place, but by noon on Sunday, in spite of
Mary's protestations, Kate suddenly announced her intention
of going downstairs, vowing and declaring she neither could
nor would remain longer in her room.

"You are very foolish, Kate. You know the doctor told
you to keep quiet," said Mary repeatedly, trying to dissuade
her from such a step.

"And what if he did?" she retorted. "I'm perfectly sick
of molly-coddling, and the best way to cure one's self of stiff-
ness is to defy it, and walk about all the same. There's
nothing like volition in such cases. If you determine on
doing a thing you can pretty nearly always do it. Indecision
and weakness of character are at the bottom of two-thirds
of human failures."

Accordingly, the young lady arrayed herself in an uncommonly pretty and highly becoming tea-gown suitable to the
existing circumstances, an exquisite garment composed of

pale grey satin, with cascades of dainty lace; and descending
the stairs, though not without considerable difficulty, and a
recurrence of that old pain in her chest, took up a position on
the drawing-room sofa.

"There, Mary, that's decidedly better!" she said, as soon
as she was fairly established. "But oh dear! how my bones
ache! Just as if I had been thrashed soundly from head to
foot."

"You deserve a good whipping for your imprudence in
getting up. However, I suppose 'a wilful woman maun have
her way.'"

"Of course she must, and not infrequently it turns out to
be the right way. Besides, you know, I must positively
make haste and get well, if only on account of this forthcoming steeplechase. As it is I shall be terribly out of condition. It's just my luck, getting laid up exactly when I
want to do a thousand-and-one different things."

"Kate, don't you think it would be an excellent opportunity for you to back out of this said steeplechase altogether?
I hate the idea of your riding in it, and your fall will be a
capital excuse."

"Yes, if I wanted an excuse, which I don't."

"Steeplechasing is such a frightfully dangerous amusement," urged the other apprehensively. "The very thought
of your taking part in a race makes my blood run cold.
Hunting is bad enough surely, but the cross-country business
is infinitely worse."

"And what do you call hunting, you dear little ignoramus
but cross-country business? Do you imagine everybody sticks
to the gates?"

"I know you don't, Kate, for one. I only wish you did.
Then you would not be brought back in this alarming state."

"I don't see that it's so very terrible after all."

"Do you remember Mr. Gambetta's sensible utterance
when he fought that celebrated duel of his, in the 'Tramp
Abroad?' 'It is not death I fear, but mutilation.' Fancy if
you were maimed or disfigured for life, the bridge of your
nose smashed in, an eye gouged out, or all your front

teeth destroyed. How would you like to snow yourself then?"

"I needn't show myself. I could stop at home."

"You'd soon tire of that. Solitude is not much in your line."

"Well, then, I'd purchase a new nose, a new eye, and a new row of teeth. Perhaps they might even effect an improvement in my personal appearance."

"You are digressing as usual; but Kate, will you promise to give up the steeplechase, if only to oblige me?"

"I would do a good deal to oblige you, Mary, but I can't promise what you ask."

"Why not? Have you any particular reason for insisting?"

"People would think I was afraid."

"You do not generally show yourself so sensitive to public opinion as all that. Whose criticisms do you particularly fear?"

"No one's," said she, reddening in spite of herself. "But I have given my word, and don't intend to go back from it. Mary, my dear, don't worry me any longer about the matter, there's a good girl. Besides, to tell the truth, I'm looking forward to the whole affair tremendously; it will be great fun, and though of course I'm bound to pretend I don't care much one way or the other about the result, I don't mind telling you in strictest confidence I'd give anything for King Olaf to win. Wouldn't it be glorious, Mary?"

"Well, Kate, I really don't know. I suppose it would be better than losing. He has a very good chance, has he not?"

"Yes, according to Mrs. Forrester and Colonel Clinker, both excellent authorities. I'm not a bit afraid of King Olaf making a fool of *him*self, but I am of *my*self. I might cut a voluntary before the whole assembled multitude. Imagine what an awful fiasco; yet such unfortunate contretemps are by no means rare, and the best of riders not always invulnerable. I verily believe I should pack up there and then, and hide my diminished head abroad for the remainder of the season." She paused, as if contemplating the catastrophe conjured up by her lively imagination.

"Nonsense, Kate," said Mary encouragingly. "You are

no more likely to disgrace yourself than anybody else—*not so* likely I should say, judging from the various representatives of female horsemanship I have beheld lately. However, since your self-confidence appears so deficient, why don't you get a man like Colonel Clinker, for instance, to coach you up a bit? Your determination to ride being inflexible, it is my duty to give you good advice. He knows all about horse-racing, and doubtless could impart many valuable hints."

"Perhaps so, but all the same I would not ask him for worlds."

"You need not ask him. He may probably offer to help you of his own accord. It struck me the other night at Mrs. Forrester's he was on the verge of making some proposition when you snubbed him as usual."

"Why do you say as *usual*, Mary?"

"Because I don't think you're particularly civil. You talk as if you had some sort of spite against him. Anyhow, if he comes here this afternoon and you happen to get on the subject, I can see no reason why you should not seek a little assistance from one so competent to advise."

"Has he not rendered assistance enough already, poor man, without being bothered for more? But what makes you think he will come to day?" She looked away as she spoke, pretending to be busy curling and uncurling the ribbons on her tea-gown. She herself had speculated on such an event, hoping he might call, yet feigning complete indifference. Mary Whitbread turned her quiet eyes upon her as she answered—

"Because I feel pretty sure some of them will walk up this afternoon."

It was Kate's turn to stare now. "And why should you feel pretty sure some of them will walk up this afternoon?" she repeated with considerable vivacity.

"Because," and Mary blushed rosy red, "well, because, if you *must* know, I happened to meet Mr. Grahame this morning when I came out of church."

"Oh! you *happened* to meet Mr. Grahame, did you? How very singular!"

"I wish you'd be quiet Kate, or I won't tell you another word."

"Oh! there's more to come, is there? Go on."

"Mr. Grahame," resumed Mary with dignity, "walked part of the way home with me, and in the course of conversation intimated that it was his intention to honour us with a call this afternoon."

Kate looked at Mary with a mischievous smile. "So Miss,' she said, "that is the reason why, although the morning was drizzly and the roads one sea of mud, you put on your best black silk frock. Mary, there are depths of artfulness hidden beneath that quiet exterior of yours which defy comprehension. First you insist on going to church in spite of a cold; secondly, you profess to despise the rain; and thirdly, you appear in your smartest clothes, though in an ordinary way you are an economically disposed little person. The only sad conclusion possible for me to arrive at is that these young men are turning your head. Did Mr. Grahame approve of your best black silk, or was he so absorbed in contemplation of the wearer as to be oblivious of all such minor considerations?"

"Kate! I never heard anyone talk so much nonsense in all my life. I have only seen Mr. Grahame some two or three times."

"No matter, there's such a thing as love at first sight, and yours is just the sort of tender, romantic disposition that falls a victim to it; while, unless I'm much mistaken, Mr. Grahame possesses a somewhat similar nature."

"I can't answer for Mr. Grahame's nature, but I can for my own," retorted Mary, blushing and smiling, as if Kate's accusation were by no means altogether distasteful or even impossible.

The conversation was now brought to an abrupt conclusion by the ringing of the front-door bell, and by the sound of masculine voices outside, shortly followed by the appearance of Colonel Clinker, Mr. McGrath, Captain Fuller, and Mr. Grahame.

After the first exchange of civilities was over, the Honble.

Jack placed a chair close to Kate's sofa, and seated himself, as if he had a right to the principal position near her.

"Well, Miss Brewser," he said, "and how are you? Getting over your shaking I hope, and beginning to feel more like yourself again."

"Thanks, I'm rather stiff, but on the high road to convalescence, and very considerably improved since I last had the pleasure of seeing you."

"Ah! you were being dragged up the staircase then, with Miss Whitbread on one side and Dr. Baker on the other, while I looked on and felt myself superlatively *de trop*. After all, men are but clumsy creatures."

"You did not display much clumsiness throughout the afternoon. I don't know what I should have done had it not been for your help—probably remained lying on my back like a capsized turtle to this very hour."

He looked gratified. It was no small reward to find himself received so graciously by one whose moods he had already learnt were apt to be changeable and wayward. "I wish you would cease trying to thank me," he said. "I did nothing— at least, nothing that any other man would not have done in my place."

"It depends so much on the *way* things are done," she returned. "You must not destroy my gratitude by any disclaimer."

It seemed a long time since they had said good-bye to each other at the foot of the staircase, though in reality but a very few days had elapsed. The sound of his voice and the sight of his open sunny face did her heart good, and already there existed moments when she felt that had she not known too much she could have liked him well, have made a friend of and respected him. She almost wished that Mrs. Forrester had left her in complete ignorance respecting that obnoxious bet. His actions would not then have appeared so inconsistent—would not have inspired her with confidence one minute, only by their cool cunning to fill her with disgust the next, and so continually give rise to a variety of contradictory emotions. To-day, however, any sentiments of

O

repugnance she possessed remained in abeyance, and she was determined to say and do nothing likely to destroy the harmony at present existing between them.

"Did you have a good day yesterday?" she asked, seeking to introduce a congenial topic of conversation.

"Only tolerable. Scent was poor, and foxes ran rather ringy. We missed you very much, Miss Brewser, and half my time was taken up in answering inquiries and explaining exactly how the accident happened. Dick Slant paid your horsemanship a great compliment. He confided to me that he had never seen a lady go better in 'all 'is born days.'"

"No, did he really?" said Kate, brightening up at praise so sweet to her. "I feel wonderfully flattered. Oh dear me!" with a pretty little *moue* of impatience, "isn't it tiresome, my being laid up on this stupid old sofa, instead of getting out hunting?"

"I hope you'll be all right before long. Remember things might have turned out infinitely worse."

"Yes, yes, I know; but you must admit that it's very bad luck meeting with an accident just now when we have this race in prospect, and every day lost is really of importance. King Olaf will get as fat as a pig."

"Only if you allow him to, which is easily prevented. However, talking of the race, that reminds me I've got a lot to tell you about it. I was dining with the Huntingshires last night, and after dinner had no end of a confab. Lady Anne and I put our heads together and arrived at a variety of wise conclusions."

"Indeed! What is Lady Anne like? Is she nice?" inquired Kate with apparent irrelevancy.

"That depends on what you call nice. People's ideas differ."

"Well, is she pretty?"

"No, not exactly pretty. Her features are rather insignificant, and her complexion somewhat too muddy; but she has a charming manner and expression, and altogether is a dear good girl."

"Really? Is she aware of the very high opinion you entertain of her?"

"What an odd question. How can I tell? As a rule young ladies are pretty quick at discovering the fact, but Lady Anne is superior to the ordinary run of girls. She has not a bit of humbug in her composition."

"Is not, I suppose, all things to all men—to one thing constant never? Eh? I daresay she's sharp enough in her way. Well, go on. What did you and *this* Lady Anne decide between you?"

"*This* Lady Anne and I," echoed he with a quiet laugh, which somehow produced the effect of irritating Kate, "this Lady Anne and I decided, first and foremost, that there was no use in putting the race off to some indefinite period, and that it should be run in about three weeks from now. Secondly, as regarded the important question of weight —for the competitors have all got to be brought together somehow—we determined, after a good deal of controversy, on making it twelve stone all round, with a seven pound allowance to animals under five years of age. There won't be many to claim the allowance, I'll be bound, unless perhaps Mrs. Forrester. Next we settled that the length of the course should not be shorter than two, or longer than three miles; then, as a matter of *course*—no pun intended—there must be a water-jump to show off the ladies' powers of equitation; and, lastly, that the jockeys, or rather the jockeyesses should sport silk. Don't you think we did a pretty good evening's work? It is something, if only arranging the preliminaries of so important and original an event."

"Oh, I know in your heart of hearts you don't approve of our ladies' steeplechase one bit; and probably behind our backs turn the whole affair into ridicule."

"If I did that I would rather do it to your faces than in the clandestine manner you allege. To tell the truth, I *don't* like the idea altogether; not that I consider it improper in any way, but simply on account of the danger. I should be very sorry to see my sister, if I had one, riding."

"But since we are all comparative strangers, unless, per•

haps, it be Lady Anne," said Kate, with the slightest *soupçon* of jealousy, "the sight of our tumbling about ought not to be very harrowing to your feelings."

"My feelings will assuredly suffer if I see *you* come to grief again."

He fixed his clear eyes upon her, and Kate felt the colour rising to her face. Stupidly! For what on earth was there to blush at? He had a habit of making little speeches that might be variously construed, and that might or might not contain any hidden meaning, according to the consciousness of the recipient. Yet she fancied she had detected a slight emphasis on the "you," which foolishly set her heart fluttering, and brought the colour to her cheeks. But Kate Brewser possessed, in all its ductility, that feminine tact which leads the conversation, carefully yet imperceptibly, away from the point of danger, or even of constraint. Her acquaintance with Colonel Clinker was far too recent to render open flattery acceptable; she still preferred veiled and guarded insinuations, which, while they tantalized and gave room for speculation, did not alarm. Therefore she said, returning to a previous topic of discussion—

"And how, pray, are we *jockeyesses*, as you so politely term us, to appear in strictly professional costume? The thing is surely impossible?"

"Not altogether, as I'll prove, though I'm prepared to admit certain modifications may be necessary. The boots and breeches, for instance, could hardly be carried out in their integrity."

"No, I should think not," interrupted she decidedly. "What an idea!"

"Well, but listen; surely there can be no objection to the fair equestriennes retaining their ordinary skirts, and getting their maids to run up some sort of bright silk shirt—a Garibaldi, that's the proper name, I believe. Now a coloured Garibaldi could not offend any propriety, and would yet be something bright, more easily distinguishable at a distance than a sombre black habit. Don't you think so?"

"Yes, perhaps. Was it your notion or Lady Anne's?"

"Well, to tell the truth, it originated with me; but Lady Anne accepted the idea with great vivacity, and decided there and then on sporting orange and black stripes. You know they are her brother's regimental racing colours."

"And very pretty ones, too, I should imagine. But what am I to have? Can't you give me a happy suggestion? I should like something that will look nice without being very loud."

"It's not so easy to advise a lady on such a serious matter. Their dress beats me altogether. We admire the results, but the details are positively bewildering, and calculated to send anyone into a lunatic establishment."

"And yet you know men give it just as much thought as we do; love of dress is inherent to mankind, and distinguishes him from the animal world. Horses and dogs take no thought for their apparel; men do."

"And the more donkeys they. However, what you say about the love of dress being innate is true enough. Even savages plaster their hair with castor-oil, and, all other covering failing, fall back upon cowrie shells and blue and red paint. Well, since you ask for a suggestion, and since Lady Anne is adopting her brother's colours, why should you not take mine—French grey and cerise?"

"I think I should prefer colours not quite so universally known. I might disgrace them, you know, and that would be dreadful."

"I am not very much afraid of such an event. I've seen you ride to hounds, and know better. However, since you evidently do not approve of my colours, what would you say to a judicious admixture of sky blue and old gold? The combination is a pretty one, besides being suited to the æsthetic taste of the age."

"I do not care for that half so much as I do for having something that will show King Olaf off to full advantage."

"Or King Olaf's mistress?"

"No, sir, King Olaf. Great as my vanity may be, and as you apparently imply *is*, I think more of the appearance of my horse than of my own, for the time being. How on earth am I to get him into condition, I wonder ? "

"Oh! I wanted to have a little chat with you on the subject. In spite of your disaster, which prevents your riding him yourself, you ought to let someone give the chestnut a good gallop every morning. You see time is getting short, and animals of his colour are apt to be hot and fidgety, and often more difficult to train than those of a placid, sluggish temperament. Now, in any race, no matter how short, condition is half the battle. It will always tell, especially if the going be a bit deep. Whichever way we mark out the course, there are one or two ploughed fields must be traversed, and the chances are between this and then they will be tolerably heavy. The animals that are not fit will soon tire once they get on to the clay. King Olaf, *if* he runs at all, must have every chance given him."

"I quite agree with you there ; but why do you say ' *if?*' "

"Oh! merely because I thought you might perhaps have changed your mind, and your fall would be a good excuse for not entering the horse."

"That's precisely what Mary Whitbread told me a little while ago."

"So Miss Whitbread has been giving you some sensible advice too, has she ? And what did you say in reply ? "

"Exactly what I say to you, and to everyone else who may wish to tender similar counsel—that having made up my mind, I neither want nor will accept of any excuse."

"Are you always so firm in your determinations, Miss Brewser ? "

"Always!" with a little impatient shrug of the shoulders. "How can anyone say in this changeable world what one is always ? There is no such thing as always ; besides, you know the saying, ' *Souvent femme varie.*' "

"Yes, and I should fancy Miss Brewser was a truer exemplification of it than most of her sex. But now to get back to our original topic. Does the invaluable Stirrup understand the mysteries of training ? Will he be able to undertake King Olaf's preparation, and send him to the post tolerably fit ? "

"I really don't know. You see Stirrup and I have never gone in for racing up till now; this will be our first appearance on the turf."

"All the more reason, therefore, for it to be a successful one."

"Stirrup would obey orders, he'd do anything I told him; but then I sadly fear that I myself hardly know the proper directions to give. I suppose diet has to be considered as well as exercise."

"That part of the business is easy enough. Plenty of good old oats, as many as they will eat, a few bran mashes, and little or no hay. Now the question is this—would you trust King Olaf to me?" He paused for a second, as if half doubting how the proposition might be received. His quick eye caught the shadow of misgiving which passed across Kate Brewser's face, and made him add hastily, "Don't be alarmed I did not mean altogether, or even to take him out of his own stable, but just for an hour or two on non-hunting days, when you can dispense with his services, and feel in a magnanimous mood."

"*Trust him?* Of course I'd trust him with you" she answered frankly, her momentary fears set at rest, "although I admit it's not everyone I would repose such confidence in as to confide my ewe lamb to his tender mercies."

"Thank you for so good an opinion, Miss Brewser, which I shall henceforth do my utmost to deserve. Joking apart, I was thinking that if you could arrange to let one of your stableboys ride the horse down to my place the first thing every morning, I would give him a gallop myself. We have got a beautiful little miniature course close to the house, with some half-dozen nice easy fences; nothing that a horse could hurt himself at, but still sufficient to teach him his business. I know as regards jumping King Olaf does not require much schooling, still I should like to pop him over once or twice, as the best of hunters sometimes dwell a little longer at their fences than is desirable for steeplechase form. I don't anticipate the smallest trouble with King Olaf, but he is too good an animal to be messed about, and I will take care the horse is not bullied or ill-treated, which it is just possible he might be if you were to mount an ignorant groom on his back."

He did not tell her that in order to put his proposition into effect he would have to rise between six and seven every morning for the next three weeks to come, and face the keen air before breakfast, or that such an offer, coming as it did from him, Jack Clinker, the great amateur jockey of the day, was one that half the owners of steeplechase horses in the kingdom would have jumped at. He made the suggestion as if unconscious of its possessing any value, and as if the obligation to be conferred would not be on his side, but on Kate's. Since he had held her in his arms for those few brief moments the desire to serve her had grown and increased, until it seemed almost a necessity he should enjoy once again that sweet, strange sensation of being her protector.

And on her side began to creep the mysterious longing for a safe place of refuge in which to anchor that storm-tossed vessel, her woman's heart, which even the happiest unmarried girls experience at times, and which, like some far-distant light struggling to pierce the mists of evening, speaks of comfort and security. There were moments in which her life also appeared wanting—when an aching void made itself felt, and when even riches and independence failed to satisfy the secret cravings of her nature. She had heard, indeed met with, people of complex character, where the good and the bad were so at war one with the other as to render the individual within whose breast they fought like two perfectly different beings, sometimes amiable, attractive, charming, at others exactly the reverse, according to which spirit predominated. Perhaps the wicked fairy had gained the upper hand and caused that eventful bet, perhaps Colonel Clinker had repented of it since, perhaps he might even have been led into it by others. Already she began to make excuses for him, so great was the charm of his personal presence, and the influence he possessed over her. When he was away she could reason differently altogether, and recall the plain facts of the case—tell herself he was a flirt, a pauper, and a fortune-hunter, but before the glance of his eye, the soft tones of his voice, poor Kate's prudent reflections vanished as if by magic. And now, though he made so light of it, she knew well that he was making a most generous proposal, and one that nothing but friendship or self-interest could have dictated. Yet how was it possible to believe in self-interest when he was sitting there so close to her side, looking cheerfully at her with those kind blue eyes, that seemed as if no evil thought or nefarious design could possibly lurk behind their transparent depths. Mary Whitbread had told her to ask for his advice, and now he had freely offered more than she could have dared to seek more even than she felt justified in accepting.

CHAPTER XVII.

THE HERO SMITTEN.

" It's awfully good of you," she said after a slight pause, " really, awfully good; but your time is very valuable, and I should feel positively ashamed to occupy so large a share of it."

" You, personally, will trespass but on a very small portion, I'm afraid. Come, Miss Brewser, won't you say yes, for— for King Olaf's sake?" He lowered his voice a trifle as he made the request, and pretended to be deeply interested in the nap of the glossy silk hat reposing between either knee. " Won't you put your pride in your pocket and agree, just in order that King Olaf may win?"

" My pride has nothing to do with it," she answered in similar tones, " but I feel I really ought not to accept so kind an offer, and one that entails such a vast amount of trouble. Only think what a nuisance I have been already."

He shrugged his shoulders with a gesture of irritation and dissent.

" I wish to goodness," he said, " that once for all you could be induced to divest yourself of a most absurd and entirely erroneous idea."

" What absurd and erroneous idea? Explain yourself."

" Why, that whenever, of my own free will, and to please my own individual inclinations, not yours, mind you—for," bitterly, " you accept any little attentions on my part reluctantly enough in all conscience—I offer to be of service, you immediately turn round and talk of the *trouble*. Can't you see in this particular instance how selfishness is at the bottom of all this said trouble? I have set my heart on King Olaf winning the race. You need not disturb yourself by imagining that I have any other reason than the exceedingly simple one of always liking to see the best horse to the fore, and in urging you to take the most probable steps to effect such a result I do but foster my own egotism."

"A remarkably ingenious way of distorting facts. Nevertheless, I remain unconvinced by your argument."

"Never mind about that, if only you will cease thanking me for nothing at all, and making me out to be a benefactor when I perform an exceedingly trivial action, which gives me a great amount of personal gratification. There! Do you still insist on refusing my overtures?"

"How can I after such an appeal? If I may not express my sense of your kindness, may not protest, may not say no, and may not even enter into any explanations, what can I do but yield to the wishes of so very unreasonable and headstrong a person?" He had won the day, as he could see by the mischievous twinkle in her eye, the merry smile on her lips.

"We might have settled this matter long ago," he said, "had you not displayed those very qualities of which you accuse me. However, now I trust all will go smoothly. I *want* to see you win. I would rather see you come first past the post than anybody."

"Not sooner than Lady Anne?" she asked, prompted by some vague spirit of rivalry. "You'd rather Lady Anne won, *surely?*"

"Can't we leave Lady Anne alone?" he exclaimed, with just a shade of irritation. "Why should *her* name be dragged in? What has *she* to do with my preferences?"

"I don't know. That is a matter for you to decide. I only thought," and her voice grew a little indistinct and husky "that as she was an *old* friend, and I merely a *new* acquaintance, that your sympathies would naturally be enlisted on her behalf, especially after the panegyric you pronounced a short time ago."

"People's sympathies sometimes take a queer, *unnatural* turn—fly towards those who repulse them most, and pass over the comparatively congenial. Such things are unaccountable I grant you, but nevertheless they occur not infrequently. If my sympathies have taken what seems to you a strange direction, you might still give me credit for possessing them. But you are a terrible unbeliever, I'm sadly afraid."

"I hardly know *what* I am," she said musingly. "Number one, though apparently not a very complex problem, is the most difficult of all numerals to analyse. Number one is stubborn and stiff-necked, lending itself to no divisions. It must be first or nowhere."

"You speak in parables."

"A bad habit of mine, for which I apologise freely. Half-fledged ideas run away with one at times before they can be properly bridled. They are like little chickens when they first break their shell and find themselves launched in this immense world. They wander hither and thither, without definite aim or object."

"In spite of a certain lack of method," said he, chiming in with her mood, "I prefer the rovers to the stay-at-homes. Half-fledged ideas and embryo notions are better than none at all. They promise well, even if they do nothing more. However, I frankly admit you're too clever for me, Miss Browser, and inspire me with a salutary awe. Meantime I have something weighing on my mind, but am in mortal dread of disclosing it for fear I should bring down on my devoted head the vials of your wrath."

"Do you think they are so easily unloosed, then?"

"No; but when a lady reminds a man she dislikes any interference in her affairs, he naturally bears the injunction in mind, and feels a delicacy in re-offending."

"Oh dear me. What a terribly tenacious memory you have got, to be sure. It's an awful punishment finding all my foolish sayings brought up against me in this sort of way. Let bygones be bygones."

"Willingly. I ask for nothing more. May I feel emboldened to proceed?"

"Yes, in the exact proportion that a guilty conscience commands attention," she replied playfully.

"Let me confess that Terry and I spent the hours of worship in Mr. Phipps's, the horsedealer's yard. After a bit, Grisette's name was introduced, and I asked Phipps, who I know well as a very respectable dealer, if he happened to have anything in his stable just then which he could thoroughly recommend as a lady's hunter?"

"I hope you did not commence operations by taking poor Grisette's character away altogether, for in that case Mr Phipps would naturally feel prejudiced against her beforehand, and less inclined to come to terms?"

"Now do you think it likely that anyone the least acquainted with the intricacies of horse-coping could be such a downright fool? No, no; I puffed the mare up to the skies, and made her out a wonderful animal. However, to get to the point Phipps showed me an uncommonly well-shaped blood-horse he had just bought at one of those big Yorkshire fairs, from which country he came with a great reputation. When I told Phipps who the lady was he was very civil indeed, and said if you would kindly fix an early day you could either see the animal ridden over his fences or try him yourself, as you chose. This I said, was well enough so far as it went, but that we should require a trial with hounds. Now Phipps, as a rule, like a wise man, sets his face against such a proceeding; but knowing me to be a pretty frequent customer, he ultimately consented to my demand. The horse seemed a smart, sporting, well-bred animal, and took my fancy greatly. He has capital legs, good flat bone, and some of the best hocks I have ever seen—just the sort of horse that is certain to be snapped up immediately, as he looks a Huntingshire hunter all over. Now I feel half afraid of my presumption, but I thought I would lose no time and come and see you to-day in order to give you the particulars, so that at all events you might have first choice. I have got Phipps to let me have the refusal of the horse for a couple of days. The question is, do you feel disposed to look at him?"

"Very much. After such a description I already long to possess him."

"But when do you think you will be able to go to Phipps's, Miss Brewser? Not just at present, I should imagine, for you can scarcely move."

"Can't I?" limping across the room out of pure bravado. "There, I'm getting on capitally. I believe I could go to-morrow."

"I should not dream of allowing you to do so. Besides, it's a hunting day."

"Why don't you reverse the order of your reasons, and put the last first and the first last? Well, if Monday won't suit, how about Tuesday?"

"Tuesday would do very well indeed. I could arrange to meet you at Mr. Phipps's that afternoon, at any time you like to mention."

"But I thought the Scottsmore always met on Tuesday?"

"So they do; but to tell the truth they are a long way off, and I have half a mind to run a bye for once in a way. I stumped a couple of horses last week, and an extra rest will do them all the good in the world."

In spite of two trifling casualties, his stables were still pretty well stocked; but he did not consider it necessary to mention that circumstance, nor that, until her advent, neither wind, rain, nor distance had ever in former seasons succeeded in keeping him away one single day from his beloved hounds. A change was fast coming over the spirit of his dream, and even sport was beginning to occupy a secondary place in his thoughts, though he still entertained frequent misgivings as to the probable manner in which their object might receive his advances. This feeling prompted him to add somewhat abruptly, "It's rather cool of me, offering to meet you at Phipps's, for perhaps my presence is not acceptable." How charming she was, to be sure, when in one of her gracious moods! How nice when she dropped that sharp-edged tool of sarcasm and left repartee untouched!

"I should be dreadfully at sea without you," she answered truthfully, and Colonel Clinker thought he had never seen her look so sweetly feminine before. "A lady is terribly helpless on these occasions, and certain to be worsted when it comes to pitting her wits against one whose profession demands their daily use. I often wonder why it is that a horse, who is the noblest of all animals, should give rise to such mean pettifogging actions and jobbery? The fault is not his, but surely lies in the predatory instincts of a race which teaches the knaves to outwit the fools. Horsedealers, I fancy, mostly belong to the former section."

"They would soon cease to exist were it not so. Their imaginations become sharpened, and they romance upon every occasion. There's old Phipps, now, he'll tell you one story after another in a frank and open way that would deceive his very grandmother. He means no harm by it, probably does not even know he swerves from the path of truth; but the force of habit is too strong, and makes him forget that it is sometimes advisable to be plain-spoken. Honesty pays every now and again, though some people find it hard to believe."

"Well, so long as I succeed in getting a good horse, I can afford to smile at Mr. Phipps's little idiosyncrasies. Will three o'clock be too early for you on Tuesday afternoon, or will you not have finished breakfast by then?"

"You never can desist from chaffing your fellow-creatures on every occasion, Miss Brewser. My morning meal is generally well over by the time you mention, and I shall be delighted to meet you at that hour."

"All right, then; Mary and I will be at the rendezvous punctual to a minute. By-the-bye, do you think it would be a good plan to let Stirrup ride Grisette down a little beforehand? Mr. Phipps, as one of the heads to the proposed bargain, would probably like to see her."

"Yes, most certainly. If we only succeed in effecting a deal I shall be perfectly happy, and the brute need never set foot inside your stables again."

"Poor thing! I feel quite inclined to stick up for her when I hear her so vigorously assailed. You are a very ruthless enemy, Colonel Clinker."

"A ruthless enemy but a good friend, I hope; so don't let us re-open the argument. You know what you told me when we drove up the drive together?"

She remembered perfectly well. She had told him she did not believe he was actuated by motives of self-interest, and that he only sought her good. At this moment the belief was stronger than ever.

"Yes," said she, looking down and toying with the lace handkerchief on her lap, "you are right. We settled the matter then to our mutual satisfaction, and need not discuss it any longer. Grisette's fate is sealed, and never again shall I crash through the fences on her back. I don't regret her one bit, really. The chances are that I should have sold her anyhow, though perhaps not quite so soon. I am very much obliged to you—I dare not say for the trouble, since that is forbidden—but for the pains you have taken on my behalf. Please believe I am truly grateful."

"And that I am more than rewarded by the exceedingly kind manner in which you have granted my request."

"We are getting too polite," retorted Kate with a happy little laugh. "If we go on being so civil to each other we shall quarrel again before long, if only for the sake of variety I hate monotony, don't you?"

"Like poison. Shall we break it at once?" he answered, while a broad smile illumined his face.

"It's hardly worth while for this afternoon, but we'll bear it in mind for some future occasion, and start afresh the next time we meet."

The _tête-à-tête_ was here interrupted by Captain Fuller and Mr. McGrath, and Kate, who seldom was at a loss for something to say, contrived to keep all three amused at the same time; while Mary Whitbread, making a photograph-book an excuse for retiring into the nearest window with Mr. Grahame, remained there, much apparently to the satisfaction of both parties, while the two flaxen heads bent suspiciously close together over its contents. Before long Mr. McGrath discovered a number of mutual acquaintances, whose short-comings he and Kate discussed with the usual zest, while even Captain Fuller exerted himself to be agreeable. Tea was brought in, and they chatted away so merrily that not until it was well-nigh dusk did the four gentlemen reluctantly rise to take their departure. "We have to thank you for a very pleasant afternoon, Miss Brewser," said Mr. McGrath. "We have paid you an unconscionably long visit."

"Not at all. The obligation is entirely on my side. Just think how dull Mary and I would have been all by ourselves with no one to enliven us! I hope you will take pity on us again very, very soon."

"No fear of that. We certainly shall. You will, I foresee, be favoured with too much of our society before long.

"Impossible to have too much of a good thing; eh, Mr. McGrath?"

And then at length they departed, and the two girls were once more alone together. Kate seemed lost in a brown study. Mary Whitbread was the first to speak.

"What a nice man Colonel Clinker is," she remarked tentatively.

"Do you think so?"

"Yes, don't you?"

"I hardly know. Sometimes I think he is and sometimes I think he is not. I can't quite make him out."

"How do you mean? He does not appear a very impenetrable personage. On the contrary, he rejoices in a peculiarly frank and open expression which impresses one favourably at first sight."

"Like Mr. Grahame's, I suppose?" She laid her hands on Mary's shoulders and looked her straight in the face. "Mary," she said, "what a foolish little romance-weaver you are, to be sure! Always building castles in the air, whose very existence depends upon the workings of your imagination, and which can only come crashing to the ground on the smallest possible provocation." So saying she rose from the sofa with a sigh and went upstairs.

P

CHAPTER XVIII.

AT MR. PHIPPS'S YARD.

On Tuesday afternoon at the appointed hour the two girls, accompanied by Stirrup and preceded by Grisette, drove up to Mr. Phipps's door. There, although the church clock was only just chiming three, they found Colonel Clinker awaiting their arrival.

"Well done!" he exclaimed cheerily, "how famously punctual we all are!"

"Have we kept you long?" asked Kate.

"Not an instant; I have but this minute arrived. And now we had better adjourn to the yard, where I believe Phipps already is."

Upon which he handed them out of the phaeton, and led the way. Mr. Phipps was engaged in a critical and depreciatory examination of Grisette, who, in justice it might be owned, looked uncommonly well. She had recovered from her recent exertions in the hunting-field, and was fit and fresh, added to which (on a hint from Colonel Clinker of her probable departure) Stirrup had carefully fed her with plentiful bran mashes the last few days.

"This, I presume, is the mare you spoke to me about," said Mr. Phipps to Colonel Clinker, revolving the toothpick he invariably carried in his mouth from one side to the other, and doffing his hat to the ladies.

He was a large, square-built man, with sandy hair, fresh complexion, and light brown eyes. He would have passed as good-looking had it not been for his teeth, which were discoloured and straggly, like the broken-down lichen-covered stumps of park palings, with considerable intervals between

them, which caught the eye and fascinated it, as a serpent
fascinates a bird, each time he entered into conversation.
His voice was deep, his delivery slow and momentous, pro-
ducing an impression of superior knowledge on the unaccustomed listener, while every now and again an odd twinkle
appeared in his humorous eyes, which proved catching in the
extreme, and formed a curious contrast to the general staid
gravity of his demeanour. Mr. Phipps had begun life as a
stable-helper, and had risen to the position he now occupied
through natural talent. He was not ashamed of his origin,
and in fact frequently alluded to it, holding up his career as
an encouragement to young men starting in life without
money or friends. "It's the competition as does us now-a-
days," he was wont to say, "and the bad-plucked uns give in
directly. Success is like a stone wall. You may take a
'ammer and a long nail, and try to drive the nail 'ome.
Well! most people gets dis'eartened after a very few attempts,
but if you go on 'ammer, 'ammer, 'ammer, not all day but
every day, you end by making your mark upon that stone
wall, and doing pretty well what you please with it. Perseverance and pluck together will always gain the victory in
the long run, but bless my 'eart alive, these young sparks is
in too much of a 'urry. They don't know 'ow to wait, and
wait, and wait, maybe for years, and yet keep up their pecker
all the time."

From which observations it may be gathered Mr. Phipps
was a remarkable man in his way. He now drew in his
toothpick with an action of caressing suction, and remarked
once more—

"So this is the mare, Colonel, eh?"

"Yes, Phipps, this is the animal I told you Miss Brewser
wished to part with."

"Humph!" and the ejaculation, delivered in Mr. Phipps's
peculiar intonation, made Kate, who stood by listening, think
more meanly of her property than she had ever done before,
such volumes of disparagement did it seem to imply. "I'm
not surprised at Miss Brewser's wanting to get rid of 'er. An
outsider, now, might probably consider 'er a decent-looking

quadruped, but she's terrible light in the barrel, taking into account as how we are only at the commencement of the season instead of near the end. She don't appear like much 'ard work. Whether they can stand 'unting or not makes but little odds to me, you may say, once the 'osses is sold. Very true, I answer, but then they must 'ave the appearance, even if like ourselves they sometimes turn out deceptions in the end. Now from the looks of 'er, I'd lay a pony to a shilling that mare's a bad feeder."

"Come, come, Phipps. Don't begin by crabbing, or we shall never get to business," interrupted Colonel Clinker, knowing well the man with whom he had to deal, and his prevailing rhetorical weaknesses. "You are just as well aware as I am that the heavy-carcased beasts are not always those who get along the best, and that a gross feeder is far more liable to come to grief in his wind and a variety of different ways than a moderate one. A big body with inadequate timber is a thing to be carefully avoided. I'd much sooner have the lean frame on good understandings, and the mare has capital legs of her own, as clean as a four-year-old's. The fact of the matter is, however, as I told you on Sunday morning, that she proves a little too much for Miss Brewser, and pulls rather more than is pleasant for a lady. They are not *all* Mrs. Forresters, you know, Phipps."

"Ah, no! Wonderful woman that," sticking his hands in his pockets. "Knows as much about the ins and outs of a stable as I do myself."

"Which is saying a good deal. Now this mare of Miss Brewser's would be the very thing for some of your hard-riding young customers; she goes a good pace, as I can testify, and does not know what it is to turn her head. Both very desirable qualities, not to be met with every day."

"That's true enough, Colonel," said Mr. Phipps, proceeding to feel Grisette's back sinews with professional severity. "I see she's got a windgall or two."

"Mere nothings that will soon pass away. You don't often find a seasoned hunter without them."

" *Nothings* when you're selling, *somethings* when you're buying," observed Mr. Phipps, with the twinkle before alluded to lighting up his piercing brown eyes. "Buyers and sellers are apt to examine objects from a different point of view."

"Now, Phipps, you're far to sharp for me to argue with. Before we waste any more time on preliminaries, suppose you show us the brown horse instead—Sir Richard you call him, do you not?"

"Yes, Colonel, that's 'is name. A good name for a good 'oss, says I."

"And quite right, too. Well, we'll go and have a look at him, and see if he takes Miss Brewser's fancy or not. She is the person to decide."

"By all means," said Mr. Phipps with more alacrity than he had hitherto displayed, ushering them into a roomy loose-box, piled up high with yellow straw in evident anticipation of intending visitors. "Here, Tom," calling to his principal aide-de-camp, "come and take Sir Richard's clothing off."

The man did as he was told, and in another minute the horse stood whisking his tail, laying back his ears, and catching at the manger after the manner of thoroughbred animals. Colonel Clinker's praise had not been overstrained. Sir Richard was a beauty to look at, standing close upon sixteen hands, on good short legs, dark brown in colour, with a lean intelligent head, tapering ears, flexible neck, and a compact well-put-together frame.

"There!" said Mr. Phipps with an air of assumed indifference, though he kept his eye rivetted on Colonel Clinker's countenance, trying to read every passing expression depicted thereon. "There! You don't often see a better looking 'oss than that, though I says it as shouldn't."

"Yes, he's a tidy animal," replied the other in tones of corresponding *sang froid*.

"I should rather think he *was*," responded Mr. Phipps vivaciously. "There's not much fault to be found, I take it, even by so good a judge of 'ossflesh as Colonel Clinker. A 'ole's not easy to pick in Sir Richard."

"Handsome is as handsome does," was the phlegmatic rejoinder.

"I'm not afraid of '*im*. He knows '*is* business. There's some pleasure in showing a good 'oss to a man like you, Colonel, as can rightly appreciate 'im. Why, bless you! 'arf the people who come here know no more about a 'unter," and Mr. Phipp's voice was filled with unutterable contempt, "than they do about the man in the moon. It's like casting your pearls afore swine. Now I'll tell you what 'appened to me the other day, Colonel. A party arrived who I had done various business transactions with.

"'Mr. Phipps,' sez he, 'I want a good 'oss.'

"'Very well, sir,' sez I, 'I'll do my best to serve you.'

"He likes a bit of blood, so I showed him a thoroughbred bay mare as stands in the third box from here."

"'No, no, Phipps, that won't do,' he sezs, afore ever the man could take her clothing off. 'Too underbred altogether, and don't show enough quality.'

"'She's in the stud book,' answers I, as quickly as possible, 'and has not even a stain on 'er pedigree.'

"Lor, Colonel! you should have seen 'is face! I never saw a man look so small in all my born days."

"'She aint my class, Phipps,' sez he, turning as red as a turkey-cock, and scuttling out into the yard.

"'Very well, sir,' sez I, as cool as a cucumber, 'that's a different thing altogether.'

"I ask you now, Colonel, what *is* the good of showing a gentleman like 'im a decent 'oss? He don't know one when he sees it. There's nothing dis'eartens a dealer so much, and puts 'im so out of conceit with his perfession as the ignorance of his customers. It's 'arder to bear than anything else, and yet he dare not say a word to enlighten 'em for fear of getting into their bad books."

"It must be very trying certainly," said the Colonel sympathetically, fully entering into Mr. Phipps's grievances, and the gentleman you refer to, instead of buying hunters, ought to be relegated to the nursery."

He had meanwhile scrutinised Sir Richard from top to toe, felt his legs, picked up his feet, punched his sides, examined both eyes, and peered into his open mouth. Then finding

Mr. Phipps's assertion were correct, and that there was indeed little room left for criticism, he said—

"Let's have the horse out, Phipps, and see how he moves."

A saddle and bridle were immediately produced, and Sir Richard, when all the preparations were complete, was led forth and mounted by the head man, who proceeded to ride him up and down the yard several times.

"Good action, Colonel, isn't it?" said Mr. Phipps, endeavouring to extract a few words of commendation from so wary a customer. "Moves true all round, and gets over the ground without any trouble to hisself."

"He bends his hocks well under him, certainly," admitted the Honble. Jack, not to be ensnared into any active approbation, "but," qualifying even this meed of praise, "he goes very close, much closer than I like to see."

"That don't signify so long as they don't brush, and I'll guarantee he never hits those legs of his. But wait till you see 'im jump. A finer fencer never looked through a bridle, nor a cleaner, cleverer one. 'Owsomever, if you don't fancy 'im there's plenty as will. He'll not be on my hands long. A 'oss like *that* won't stand idle for very many days. He'll sell, and what's more, sell *well*. There's Miss Palliser, for instance, who is on the look-out for an animal good enough to win a steeplechase. She'd buy 'im like a shot if you don't take 'im. He'd suit Miss Palliser down to the ground, for he's quiet and yet 'igh-couraged, just the sort she likes; and what's more he's a good stout 'oss, and as fast as greased lightning. Put 'im back, Tom. You can put him back,' waving to the man to stop. "No good knocking 'im about if he don't take the Colonel's eye," he added with an air of injured innocence.

Now Mr. Phipps knew as well as possible that Sir Richard *did* take the Colonel's eye, but he was a diplomatist, who thoroughly understood the disadvantage of making his wares appear too cheap. Tom, on his side, intimately acquainted with his master's various tactics, immediately made a great show of dismounting, preparatory to taking the horse back into his stable again.

"Stop a bit, don't be in such a hurry," interposed the Colonel, who was far too old a hand not to keep pace with every move of the game. "I'll just throw my leg over him and see what sort of a feel he gives you."

"As you like, Colonel," returned Mr. Phipps with a renewed assumption of indifference, his object being now attained. "It's all one to me. Take 'im or leave 'im *as* you please. A good 'oss can always fetch his price."

"So Miss Palliser's thinking of buying Sir Richard, is she?" said Colonel Clinker, while the stirrups were being lengthened to his satisfaction.

"Most likely. She's not seen 'im yet, though. I gave you the refusal, Colonel."

"Ah, yes, to be sure! Very good of you, Phipps."

"Do you like the horse?" whispered Kate, coming up and patting Sir Richard's neck.

"Very much indeed. But if we appear too keen Phipps will open his mouth. He's a knowing customer, not easily bested."

"So I should imagine. I should have been utterly annihilated without your help. Mr. Phipps would soon have crushed me into silence."

"One must oppose these sort of people with their own weapons; never a very easy task for a lady, even under the most favourable circumstances. But Phipps is not half a bad fellow in his way, once you get over his little pecularities of manner. He's shrewd, though at the same time wonderfully kindhearted, and I feel quite sure he would not sell you a bad horse. He always prides himself on his customers coming back again, and what's more they generally do. A clever dealer's chief talent consists in knowing exactly how and where to place his goods, to which end it is necessary he should possess a keen insight into human nature, and an intimate acquaintance with its foibles. Phipps stands preeminent in these respects, and therefore seldom makes a *faux pas.*"

"I shall get quite learned before long. Able to set up an establishment of my own," said Kate playfully. "Will you come and be my head man?"

"Head man, rough-rider, stable-boy, anything you please,"

he answered; then as he rode away he said carelessly to Mr. Phipps, "As Miss Palliser never gives much for her horses, I presume you're not asking a long price, Phipps."

"Two hundred, Colonel," replied Mr. Phipps, feeling at last the negotations were in a fair way of being entered upon. "He's worth that any day."

"H'm, two hundred is a goodish sum for a thirteen-stone hunter."

"Do you think so, Colonel? Why look at that there 'oss The Swell, as fetched four fifty at Tattersall's last week. He aint half so good an animal as Sir Richard, and eight year old into the bargain. 'Osses is terrible dear just now."

"I've never known them otherwise when one was on the buy."

"Now, Colonel, I appeal to you," said Mr. Phipps, roused to a sudden display of virtuous indignation assumed for the occasion. "Can you expect to find perfect manners, good looks, 'igh courage, and sweet temper, all combined, without having to pay summat for them?"

"Let us go into the field, said Colonel Clinker," "Miss Brewser will probably like to see Sir Richard jump one or two of those breakneck fences of yours."

"Yes, indeed, I should very much," said Kate.

Whereupon Mr. Phipps threw open a gate at the back of the yard, which led into a fair-sized paddock, where a flight of bushed-up hurdles, a low rail, and a couple of small artificial fences were supposed to test the powers of the animals about to be purchased.

"I see you've not made them any bigger since last winter," said Colonel Clinker with a smile. "You don't want your customers to come to grief?"

"They're big enough Colonel, as it is—too big for some of 'em. Now just you take Sir Richard, and pop him over one after the other."

Thus adjured Colonel Clinker did as he was told. Sir Richard was evidently no novice, and knew quite well what was expected of him; still in his case familarity did not breed contempt. He loved jumping clearly for its own sake, and cocked his small ears and went resolutely at each obstacle in succession, springing over them like a stag. Then when brought to a standstill, he stood arching his neck with gleeful impatience, while the crimson linings of his distended nostrils stood out in striking contrast to the rich tan muzzle, and the swelling veins seemed suddenly to have leapt into life.

"Lor bless you, Miss!" exclaimed old Stirrup, who had been edging nearer and nearer to Kate, "he *can* jump, and no mistake. Bea-utiful."

"Jump!" repeated Mr. Phipps in his most superior manner, and with an elevation of the eyebrow which seemed to express surprise at the tardiness of the other's discovery, "did I not *tell* you he could jump from the first, only none of you believed what I said? Jump, indeed! Why, that there 'oss would carry your young lady like a bird. Nobody would touch 'em."

"Ee's a nice 'oss," said the unsophisticated Stirrup in reply.

Meantime the Honble. Jack was putting Sir Richard through all his paces, and the horse seemed to take a pleasure in yielding to the delicate touch that directed him as with a silken thread, strongly yet lightly.

Mr. Phipps stood by, chewing his toothpick, in silent admiration. He was a devoted follower of the Colonel, whose good horsemanship had many times gained him various sums on the turf.

"You don't often come across such a rider," he remarked in confidence to Kate, who also was watching the Honble. Jack's movements. "Have you ever seen 'im ride a race?"

"No," as she shook her head in dissent.

"Well, I tell you it's the prettiest sight in the world. He never takes a yard more out of his 'oss than is necessary, but just comes in the last few strides, and wins on the post, as cool as a cucumber. For my part, I'd rather see 'im up than two thirds of the perfessional jockeys. He's got a style about his riding, and a finish, not one man in ten thousand ever attains to."

She smiled at Mr. Phipps in such a friendly way that that

gentleman, who was by no means insensible to feminine fascinations, grew still more discursive. She allowed him to ramble on at his will. He had apparently hit upon a congenial topic of conversation. She liked to hear Colonel Clinker's praises sung, and even a long recital of some famous exploit he had performed months ago at Kempton Park failed to weary her or prove too great a tax on her attention. Mr. Phipps, on his side, discovered that those big grey eyes had a charming way of looking at him, and the expressive face of smiling pleasantly. He even went so far as to contemplate whether, under pressure, he might not be induced to knock five pounds off the handsome profit he contemplated making. His meditations on this point reached no very definite conclusions, being disturbed by the return of Colonel Clinker, who throwing the reins on Sir Richard's neck, and lightly vaulting to the ground, whispered in Kate's ear—

"He'll do. He's a real nice horse, with easy paces and good mouth, and he gives you a wonderful feel over his fences. I really think he's worth the money Phipps is asking. But of course you are the person to decide. Now supposing Phipps could be induced to spring a hundred for Grisette, the question is would you let her go at that price?"

He did not wish to influence her actions in any way, feeling a certain delicacy in doing so. Nevertheless it was a relief to him when she answered without hesitation—

"Yes, I would. She cost two hundred and thirty, but I don't expect to get anything like what I gave; besides," looking up at him with a frank smile, "I have such perfect confidence in your knowledge of horseflesh that I should feel quite satisfied at any arrangement you chose to make."

He would not have been man, with man's store of vanity and human weakness, had he not felt flattered by the naïve defference contained in this speech, had not the womanly trust it displayed appealed to his self-esteem.

"You are very kind," he said, "but you ought to ride the horse yourself before coming to any final decision."

"I'm afraid I can't in my present crippled condition," she replied.

"Ah! how stupid of me, I was quite forgetting."

"Not at all. Since *you* have ridden Sir Richard, and pronounce a favourable verdict, *I* am content to accept it without reserve. What would my humble opinion be, compared to yours?" And as the liquid eyes looked up at him they sent a thrill of pleasure to his heart.

"You may be quite certain that in making any bargain, Miss Brewser, I shall do my utmost to promote your interest in every way."

"I feel sure of it. I can't think why you should be so good to a helpless young woman like myself."

She hated the words when she had spoken them, for they recalled that possible object which she strove so hard to keep in the background, and which his presence dissipated like smoke in thin air. But he, not knowing all her thoughts, allowed the gratification he experienced to appear in his face. The cool wintry sun cast a last flickering ray on the honest features, the fair hair, and drooping moustache as he stood close to her side while they held this short and whispered colloquy.

"Then you commission me to make the best bargain I can, subject to a trial with hounds?" he said, in the tone of a man asking for final instructions.

"I commission you to do whatever you think best. There! I can't say more, can I? So now to business."

"Mr. Phipps," said Colonel Clinker, addressing that gentleman, who had stood aloof, though a keen observer of what passed, "Miss Brewser wishes to see if we can do a deal together."

"Certainly," said he. . Whereupon the whole party prompty retired into an inner sanctum, where all transactions were definitely concluded, and within whose four walls many a sale had been effected, many a horse changed hands. Mr. Phipps detaching a key from among a bunch he produced from his trouser pocket, now unlocked the door of a cupboard, and as a preliminary brought forth a couple of black bottles, a decanter of sherry, and half a dozen wine glasses.

"Now," said the Colonel straightforwardly, "there's no use taking up your time, Phipps, in beating about the bush. Miss Brewser likes Sir Richard. The question is, what would you be prepared to allow in exchange for the grey?"

Mr. Phipps stretched his legs out under the table, subsided n his chair, and appear absorbed in the most abstruse calculations.

"Well, really Colonel," he replied after a considerable pause, "that's a most difficult question to answer, and one requiring a deal of thought. Would it not be better for Miss Brewser to tell *me* what price she puts upon the mare? It would clear the way, so to speak, and make it easier for both parties to come to an arrangement."

"She cost two hundred and thirty," said Kate, giving no direct reply in answer to this appeal.

"Ah! that may be easy enough. But the thing to consider is not what she *cost*, but what she's *worth*?"

"Well, well, Phipps, "it's for you to make some sort of proposition,"- interrupted Colonel Clinker. "The mare's rising seven, sound, and a likely nag, as you have had the opportunity of ascertaining."

"Would not do more than carry a boy of fourteen," objected he musingly.

"Nonsense, Phipps. She'll carry the larger half of your customers, I'll be bound."

"What, combined, Colonel? 'She would be a good 'un to do that."

"No, separately of course. Come, now, Phipps, we're wasting time, and since you don't seem disposed to make any offer on your side, I must do it on mine. If you like to allow Miss Brewser a hundred for the grey mare, she'll send you a cheque for the remaining hundred to-morrow morning. What say you to the bargain?"

Once more Mr. Phipps allowed the gravity of his decisions to be felt by a prolonged silence. Then he shrugged his shoulders, shook his head, and said deliberately—

"I could not do it, Colonel, could not do it anyhow. My expenses would not even be paid, let alone any profit.

"Come, come, Phipps! Old friends like you and I don't *want* to make a big profit out of each other. We've done one another too many good turns for that."

The stern expression of Mr. Phipps's face softened.

"Ah, Colonel!" he said relenting, "you're a terrible hand at getting round a fellow's weak side."

"And a very good thing to. If we didn't occasionally find out our tender spots and keep them fresh and green, why, Phipps, most of us would be as hard as brickbats. There's nothing like doing a kindly action now and then for softening human nature; so, Phipps, you let Miss Brewser have Sir Richard?"

He got up and held out his hand, which the other wrung with cordial appreciation.

"Very well, Colonel," he said, "I'd do anything to oblige you, though this is not business."

"We'll call it friendship then, instead," said the Honble. Jack with a pleasant smile as they left the room. "Good-bye, Phipps."

"Good-bye, Mr. Phipps," said Kate, putting her little palm in his. "Thank you very much, and I'll try and do your horse credit."

And then they went out into the street, and Mr. Phipps stood watching their retreating forms.

"Phipps, my boy," said he to himself, "this won't do; the perfession will suffer if you allow your feelings to get the better of you in this sort of way. You ought to have stuck out for another pony at least. But lor! that there Colonel is such a pleasant-spoken chap, he twists one round his little finger. That's a nice girl, too, that Miss Brewser, and it strikes me the Colonel is deuced sweet upon her. Well, he might do worse, he might do worse;" with which reflection Mr. Phipps went off to take tea with his better-half in the back-parlour.

CHAPTER XIX.

JEALOUS RIDING.

In ten days from the time of her visit to Mr. Phipps's establishment Kate was sufficiently recovered from the effects of Grisette's misdemeanours to be in the saddle again. She started modestly, merely intending to ride about quietly, and keep to the roads and the gates, while Mr. McGrath, ever ready for an excuse which banished jumping from the programme, willingly offered his services as escort, and besides proving himself a most cheerful and entertaining companion, displayed the greatest consideration towards the young lady thus placed under his protecting wing. He amused Kate vastly by pointing out in his comical way various members of the Hunt, on whom he kept up a regular fire of running commentary, describing with much humour and acumen the individual peculiarities of each one in turn.

"Do you see that man standing close to you on a handsome bay horse?" he asked, indicating the personage in question with an airy wave of his arm. "He's the Honourable Alfred Charrington, the head of the lardy-dardy, no-man-like-self division. Well, for three whole years did the Honble. Alfred and I meet continually in the hunting-field, while for three whole years did he honour me with a supercilious stare. Now there are few things more irritating to a fellow's vanity than to be calmly ignored. Argument, disagreement, even insolence, are each in their way easier to bear than that species of lofty indifference intended to convey a sensation of inferiority, and of belonging to a lower class of beings altogether. It gives the feeling of there being something *wrong* about you, without your exactly knowing *what*. Such were the terms on which we stood, when bedad, one fine day, greatly to my astonishment as you may imagine, what does my gentleman do, after looking over his left shoulder and squinting at me out of his little cock eye, but favour me to a nod, whose mixture of patronage and condescension was truly beautiful to behold, and say, 'How do, McGrath?' He had apparently become conscious of my presence at last, and took this early opportunity of recognising the fact. Faith, Miss Brewser! it made the very blood boil in my veins. You see I had got used to being a nobody in the Honble. Alfred's estimation, and any change came too much as a surprise to be appreciated. Shall I tell you what I did? I was determined on having my revenge. Every dog has his day, and mine had come at last. I looked him up and down with a stony gaze which took in every detail from the crown of his shining chimney-pot to the soles of his faultless boots; dash him! he has the best varnish in the county, and I said with the utmost severity at my command, 'Sir, it has taken you three years to make up your mind whether you would deign to know me or not; it will not take *me* three *minutes* to decline the honour of your acquaintanceship,' whereupon I stared him straight in the face and then rode away. Gad, Miss Brewser!" and Terry laughed heartily at the remembrance of his adversary's utter discomfiture, "you never saw a man look so dumbfoundered in all your born days. He was that astonished he could not find a single word in reply."

"I don't wonder," said Kate. "Such an answer was enough to take anyone's breath away. But what an idiot the man must be!"

"He only possesses the besetting sin of a good many of our neighbours about here."

"And what might that be?"

"Thinks too much of himself and too little of others. A very common failing, especially among people of narrow intellect and large vanity."

"He ought to be a warning to us all, then, not to be over self-satisfied. Don't you think some folks are put into the world solely to fill a *rôle* of determent? There are **moral** scavengers just as there are ornithological ones. The vulture is a bird of bad repute, but nevertheless he fills his place in the economy of nature, and perhaps Mr. Charrington was born as an example, which most of us should avoid rather than imitate. I don't express myself clearly, though I know quite well what I mean."

"You express yourself quite well enough for me to understand. It never struck me in that light before, and 'pon my soul I'm not sure but what you are right. If I accept the Honble. Alfred as a warning, I can look at him with far more charitable feelings than I do at present. Poor fellow! after all, according to you, he is but a social scarecrow, fitted to frighten all the human crows away. Ha! ha! That's a capital idea, and tickles me immensely."

Surely it was lucky for the Honble. Alfred Charrington that he did not catch this conversation, or it is possible that even *his* equanimity might have been disturbed, and the calm waters of self-satisfaction in which his soul lay steeped be stirred from their tranquil depths by the keen blast of ridicule sweeping over them. Would it have been an act of kindness to have torn down the delusions so long entertained, to have laid bare and exposed the shallowness of the crumbling soil on which they were raised and carefully nurtured by petty egotism? Who can say? Even the pruning-knife is apt to cut too deeply, and kill the old tree with its good and its bad together, instead of promoting a new growth and fresh flourishing blossoms. The old tree may be gnarled and twisted, decayed, covered with parasites; it may shut out the light of the sun, hide the blue skies, and cumber the earth; but when removed altogether is it not apt to make its absence felt, and the very object we have so long grumbled at to leave a blank on disappearing?

Some such thoughts flitted through Kate's mind as she looked at the gentleman on the handsome bay; but her speculations were quickly ended by Mr. McGrath exclaiming—

"But here comes another of our local celebrities," as a big, burly, broad-shouldered man of about five-and-forty, square-featured, clean shaven, and keen-eyed, mounted on a huge

Q

weight-carrying hunter, rode by. "I want you to take special notice of him because he is said to be the finest welter-weight in Great Britian. If you are quite sure you are not bored, Miss Brewser, gad! but I can tell you a good story about him too."

Whereupon Mr. McGrath commenced another piquant anecdote, well flavoured with Hibernian wit. When it came to an end Kate said, "Ah, Mr. McGrath, Mrs. Forrester was right when she told me what an agreeable companion you were, and I have enjoyed both your conversation and your society immensely."

She felt no difficulty in praising Mr. McGrath to his face. He only inspired her with friendly interest; therefore the words came readily enough. There was no cause to consider them, to weigh their probable effect, or to fear on one side giving offence, or on the other of appearing too forward and anxious to please. She experienced no constraint in his presence. He had no power to make her blush, or to send her heart beating like a sledge-hammer, and the first words that rose to her lips were merrily uttered, in pure ease and good-fellowship.

There are some men who raise such friendly sentiments at first sight, yet it is a question whether they ever succeed in establishing any loftier feeling or warmer relationship. It is their fate to go through life as the confidant, but never as the loved. Kate felt herself infinitely brighter and more amusing in Mr. McGrath's company than in Colonel Clinker's; yet the briefest sentence from the latter, his slightest expression of approval or disapproval, carried more weight than the whole torrent of Mr. McGrath's conversation put together. Nevertheless the facetious little Irishman contrived to keep her in a state of such perpetual merriment, that at last she asserted her sides ached so unmercifully that the effects were infinitely worse than a hundred falls, and she really could endure them no longer. As the day wore on, her spirits rose. In spite of Stirrup's protestations she insisted in getting off her hack and having the side-saddle put on to Sir Richard, who had come out for the first time since he had been in the hands of his new proprietor. She declared herself no longer an invalid, and fully equal to encountering the fatigues of a run.

Stirrup, who ere now had discovered the futility of argument, especially when opposed to the fair sex, was forced to withdraw his objections and yield, though somewhat reluctantly, to his mistress's wishes. And as if to reward Kate for her sudden decision, she had hardly begun to make friends with her new horse before a joyous chorus of sound broke out from the midst of a small gorse-patch the hounds were drawing, and in another minute the whole pack streamed away close at the heels of a fine, white-tagged old fox, whereupon Kate, throwing prudence to the winds, could not refrain from joining in the chase. A mile's gallop full tilt down a road running parallel with the hounds served still further to heighten her enthusiasm, so that when, at the first opportunity, some of the foremost riders branched off into the open fields, where a vista of tolerably practicable fences held out a pleasing prospect, she followed suit. When she came to the first obstacle her caution had vanished, and Sir Richard swept over it so easily and so freely that indeed none appeared necessary.

The ice once broken, she took everything that came in her way, until she began to find herself occupying quite a distinguished position in the hunt, and the brown had fairly established his reputation as a good fencer. Poor Miss Palliser, whose lucky star had not been in the ascendant lately, and whose fate appeared invariably that of chewing the bitter cud of mortification, from seeing a rival habit fluttering in advance, lost considerable ground at starting by the unfortunate banging-to of a gate, but now she was galloping like the wind in order to lessen the already diminishing distance between herself and that offending skirt, which constituted a regular eyesore in the green orbs of jealousy. She determined once for all on besting this obnoxious adversary, and showing her conclusively the absurdity and crass stupidity of attempting to compete with one so *facile princeps* as herself.

"Did you see how beautifully my horse jumped that las

fence?" she remarked to Colonel Clinker, who happened to be within hail.

He also had been delayed by the refusal of a young animal he was qualifying for a steeplechase certificate, and like Miss Palliser was intent on getting closer to hounds.

"I'm sorry to say I did not," he returned satirically. "By some extraordinary and greatly-to-be-deplored accident, for one instant my eye was withdrawn from you—a circumstance that causes me much regret."

"Indeed!" said she, not altogether easy as to the intention of this observation. "Really, Colonel Clinker, one never knows whether you are in earnest or not."

"Very much in earnest, Miss Palliser."

"Then," said she, with a smile of reassurance, "I feel extremely flattered by your good opinion. It is pleasant to find friends think well of one."

"Would you like to heighten it still further?" said he quietly.

"Certainly," she replied, a little surprised at the request, and wondering what was coming next.

She felt she could like Colonel Clinker very much indeed, if only he were always in the present amiable and complaisant mood. There had even existed moments in bygone years when she had contemplated the possibility of changing her maiden name for that of Clinker, but such dreams had gradually faded away, owing to the taciturn manner in which the gentleman was wont to receive her advances. Nevertheless, a compliment from *him*, however tardily uttered and laboriously extracted, came with double power to please, like long-sought-for honey rewarding the exertions of an industrious bee.

"Certainly," she repeated, with a feeling of pleasing expectation stirring the sluggish depths of her heart. "What can I do?"

"Why," said he ruthlessly, "you can give that young lady in front of you a little more room at her fences, and not ride quite so horribly jealous."

Poor thing! The reaction was terribly severe, and in the

first shock of it she felt too surprised even for indignation. She drew in her breath with a gasp that resembled the gurgle of a drowning man, and emitted the single mono-syllable, "Oh!"

"Yes," continued Colonel Clinker pointedly, for somehow or other he never *could* bring himself to regard Miss Palliser as a woman, and therefore felt little compunction in trampling on her feelings. "Yes, and what's more, I saw you just now, simply because Miss Brewser happened to be leading, ride on to her horse's very tail. If he had made the least peck or the ghost of a mistake at the fence you would have been on the top of him to a certainty. It's deuced unfair, and if *you* call that riding *I* don't."

During this speech the lady had partly recovered from the first stunning effects of the blow delivered, and both pride and temper now came to her assistance. But the last straw broke the camel's back. When it became a question of *riding*, *her* riding, anger assumed the upper hand, and crushed all incipient sentiment at its very birth.

"Colonel Clinker," she said, or rather screamed, while her sallow complexion suddenly flamed into scarlet, and her small grey eyes gleamed with a vicious expression, "I beg leave to state I have not hunted all these years in Huntingshire for nothing. I flatter myself I know *how* to ride at a fence as well as *most* people, at least, such is the general opinion; and I don't require *you* or anyone else to give me lessons how to behave in the hunting-field. I consider you are *most—* MOST—MOST impertinent." She had begun bravely, but her voice here died away in hysterical sobs. Her mortification was complete. Colonel Clinker bowed silently, and galloped on.

"Well, that was sharp and decisive enough in all conscience," he said to himself. "La Palliser and I have fought our first pitched battle, though many's the skirmish we have indulged in. I'm afraid I was a little rude, but the rebuke will do no harm, and the way she jumps on people is really quite abominable."

"What a fool Colonel Clinker is making of himself about

that Miss Brewser," Miss Palliser remarked later on to her dear friend Mrs. Paget.

She had sense enough to keep their little encounter to herself, but she could not refrain from launching a few venom-laden arrows by way of taking some revenge.

"A fool?" said Mrs. Paget. "In what manner? I have seen nothing to justify such a remark on your part."

"You're as blind as a bat, my dear," returned Miss Palliser contemptuously. "I tell you the man's quite gone off his head. To so great an extent, indeed, that he can't speak with decent civility to anybody else."

"I had a chat with him some little time ago, and he appeared much as usual."

"You're a goose, and never could see a thing, even when it was going on under your very nose. *My* eyes are considerably sharper; they can't hoodwink *me* in a hurry."

"But, my dear Miss Palliser, who *wants* to hoodwink you? After all there would be nothing so *very* wonderful even if Colonel Clinker *were* to fall in love with Miss Brewser. Rank united to wealth is not an uncommon occurrence. One sees it every day of one's life."

"There I agree; but don't talk of love, it's a perfect profanation to call such calculating, mercenary transactions *love*. Colonel Clinker's no more in *love* with Miss Brewser than I am."

"Then his sentiments must be extremely lukewarm," said Mrs. Paget, who took a mild pleasure in nagging at her friend.

"Not at all; mine are very much heated though, by dislike rather than affection. I think Miss Brewser an odious, stuck-up, forward, *fast* young woman; and as for Colonel Clinker, any respect or regard I may once have entertained for him he has entirely forfeited," with which concluding observation she went home, galloping past Kate, and bespattering her with mud without a word of apology.

"Phew!" said Mrs. Paget, eyeing her retreating friend dubiously. "She's very crusty! I wonder what's up now? It's a pity she's got such an ungovernable temper, but one really never feels sure what she may say and do next."

CHAPTER XX.

PREPARING FOR THE LADIES' STEEPLECHASE.

THUS, varied by hunting, heartburnings, sport, petty jealousies, and gossip, time glided by, until at length the eventful day arrived on which that source of infinitely more mixed passions, the ladies' steeplechase, was to be decided. It had been settled for a Tuesday, and though supposed a profound secret, the knowledge of its taking place had somehow leaked out. The comparatively early hour of one o'clock was definitely fixed for the start, several farseeing individuals declaring that in any attempt to bring the jockeyesses to the post a considerable delay was sure to arise, partly through their inexperience, but still more through the difficulties of the fair competitors arranging the exigencies of toilette to their satisfaction. The kind old Earl, who had thoroughly entered into the spirit of the thing from first to last, had signified his intention of entertaining the riders and their friends, when the race was over, to a sumptuous lunch, immediately after which the cup would be presented to the fortunate winner amid all the formal pomposity of speech-making and health-drinking.

The morning luckily broke fair and still. Soft grey clouds filled the sky, swept gently onwards by a mild south-westerly breeze. It had rained fast during the night, leaving each blade of grass and faded russet leaf trembling under the silvery weight of the crystal burden imposed on it, every one of which shone like a sparkling gem as the pale face of the sun struggled bravely out from amongst the misty shroud encircling it, while those hardy birds who scorned to forsake their storm-swept home for milder climes, lured by the genial atmosphere, strutted about the moist roads, head on one side, seeking here and there a precarious livelihood with a cheerfulness and an activity which seemed to say, "After all, there's no place like old England. Our companions are fools to fly away." Poor little creatures, when they sat shivering and shaking under the cold, cruel snow, perhaps they told a different tale; but to-day, at least, they were happy. Kate felt very joyous and pleasantly excited as she and Mary Whitbread drove out to the rendezvous. She had arranged with Colonel Clinker to be on the spot early, in order that they might walk round the course together, and they found him, accompanied by Mr. McGrath and Mr. Grahame, already awaiting their arrival. A considerable number of spectators had assembled, making it clear the much-talked-of privacy could not possibly be maintained in face of the interest evidently aroused on all sides. The sporting element was, of course, present in full, scarcely a man or a woman from amongst its ranks being missing, while the Foxington tradespeople, accompanied by their wives and daughters, who appeared much interested, had turned out in force. Even the itinerant gipsy was represented by a stout party in a blue skirt and tartan shawl, who went about singing atrocious songs in a still more atrocious voice, insisting on telling fortunes to people who had no anxiety to hear them. Colonel Clinker and his companion were victims not likely to escape their most favourable predictions.

"Cross my hand, pretty lady, with a silver saxpence," the woman said to Kate with whining insistence. "It will bring yer luck, nothing but luck."

"Get away, my good soul, don't you see you're bothering the lady," said Colonel Clinker, fearing she might annoy the girl.

"Not I," answered she, with intrusive confidence. "The lady has a good kind heart of her own behind that sweet face, but the poor gipsy can see what's in it. There are clouds, and darknesses, and crossings, but the fair gentleman with the blue eyes stands out clear among them all. The end will be marriage. Oh yes, the poor gipsy woman knows."

"For heaven's sake let us come," said Kate turning suddenly scarlet, and snatching her hand away from the other's detaining grasp. "I never listened to such nonsense in my life."

"Nonsense, is it?" called the woman after them indignantly. "The fair gentleman's eyes are full of love. *He* does not call what I say nonsense, at any rate."

"How horribly vulgar these people are to be sure," said Kate, feeling intensely exasperated at what she chose to consider the gipsy's impertinence.

"Never mind," said her companion, with suppressed emotion. "Don't allow yourself to be annoyed at her forecasts. Come with me and have a look at the fences instead, or you will be running out of the course, which would never do."

She felt grateful to him for covering her confusion, and incensed with herself for having displayed any. What a poor weak fool she was, to be sure! Had Mr. McGrath been her companion, the woman's prophecies would have produced no further impression than the ordinary clap-trap jargon of the profession. All she could hope was that Colonel Clinker did not attribute her vexation to its right cause. They started together on a tour of inspection, followed by Mary Whitbread and Mr. Grahame. Colonel Clinker, on whose shoulders the entire management had fallen, had spared neither time nor trouble in rendering the course as perfect as possible. It was beautifully marked out with rows of little white flags, placed at such close distances that it looked next to impossible for the riders to make any wrong detour, while the run-in was corded on either side with stout ropes, leading in a direct line to the winning-post, which stood up, tall and unmistakable, close to the judge's improvised box.

Starting at the farthest end of a large grass-field, in full view of the assembled company, the course first led somewhat uphill over very severe ridge-and-furrow, at the top of which a good honest fence with a ditch and low guard-rail on the take off side barred the entry into the opposite field, which, though bigger in dimensions, was far more level and very sound going. After this it ran across a sticky ploughed

enclosure, which Colonel Clinker had not been able to avoid;
then over a small double, leading once more into grass, and
later on, in and out a road carefully laid with tan. A rather
sudden turn to the right here revealed the water-jump. This
was a small natural brook, or rather—so steep and crumbling
were its banks—a species of gully, with bushed-up hurdles,
set in a slanting direction leaning over it, and the whole
width could not have measured much more than some ten to
twelve feet across. Any ordinary hunter ought with ease to
clear such an obstacle in his stride; but Colonel Clinker had
purposely refrained from making it larger, actuated by all
sorts of visions of dripping female forms and broken backs.
After the water-jump came three or four more fair flying
fences that each required a bit of doing without being very
formidable. These completed a good sized-ring, and the last
obstruction would land the competitors in the same field
up whose slopes they had started. Altogether it looked a
good fair course, such as no animal used to following hounds
should find difficult to encompass. Kate and Colonel Clinker
carefully criticised each fence, choosing beforehand the best
spot for jumping, and this was the verdict they unani-
mously pronounced. The ground also was in beautiful order,
neither too hard nor yet too deep. As they walked round
together Colonel Clinker proceeded to give Kate a variety of
advice as to what she should and what she should not do
in the forthcoming race, all of which she listened to most
attentively, and determined on following to the best of her
ability.

"Directly the flag drops, Miss Browser," said he, "be sure
and let your horse have his head. A good start in a three
mile race is not of such paramount importance as in a five
furlong scramble, still it is by no means to be despised.
There's nothing like beginning well. It gives a horse confidence in his rider, and tells him he means going. But
directly you get on to the ridge-and-furrow, take a good pull
and make King Olaf go well within himself. Never mind
being last of the whole lot, especially if you only feel yourself
to be so on sufferance, and can regain your lost position at any

moment you please. Nothing takes so much out of a horse
as pushing him fast up an incline at starting, before he has
warmed to his work and got his pipes all clear. Steady him
at the first fence; the chances are he will want to rush, and
might overjump himself in his eagerness. Very probably you
may find by then that you have the legs of most of your companions, but don't on any account force the running so early
in the day. Don't bustle King Olaf until you get fairly
through the plough. If, after that, he is still going strong
and well and pulling tolerably hard, you may begin to
forge ahead a bit. Remember up to this point you have to
ride a waiting race, and let anyone else lead the way who
likes. Drop your hands when you come to the double, and
whatever you do, don't go too fast at it. Give King Olaf a
full opportunity of understanding what is before him. It's
the nastiest fence of the lot, and the only one I am at all afraid
of, particularly with an impetuous horse. The same rule
applies equally to the jumps at the road; take them steadily.
Horses often jump the fence out carelessly, so be on your
guard. So far we have brought you along capitally. Take
a good firm hold of his head, and set King Olaf just as fast as
you please at the water-jump. He'll clear it by yards I know
beforehand, but if you can remember, keep close to the white
flag on your right. The banks there are both narrower and
firmer than in any other place; besides you get the inside turn,
and will gain several lengths by so doing. And now send your
horse along in downright earnest. Nine-tenths of amateur
riders throw away the race by waiting too long and not coming
soon enough. Then they get flurried, lose their heads, and
all is over with their chance of winning. By this time the
riff-raff will either have tailed off or come to grief; anyhow,
you will know pretty well which are your most dangerous
remaining opponents. If you find you have them fairly settled,
come straight away over the last two fences and past the post,
hands down, but if it comes to a contest, keep cool and collected and do the best you can. I foretell a perfect triumph
to our party," concluded the Colonel, drawing a deep breath
of satisfaction in anticipation of this desired result. After a

momentary pause he appeared however to recollect it was just possible there might exist a reverse side to the picture, and he added in calmer accents, " On the other hand, should any mishap occur—though I devoutly trust not—or should you by any chance find King Olaf is blown, for God's sake pull him up there and then. You have ridden a beaten horse once too often as it is, and there's no use in struggling on to the end under such circumstances. And now I have given you enough instructions to fill a small volume. I don't suppose when the time comes, you will remember one-third of them."

" Oh, yes, I hope so! " answered Kate confidently. " But when I listen to such excellent advice, it really makes me feel as if I were obtaining a mean advantage over my neighbours, and as if they too ought to have the opportunity of profiting by it. It hardly appears fair my accepting so many valuable hints."

"Most of them don't require any aid. There's Mrs. Forrester knows quite as much, if not more, than I do myself; Mrs. Paget, who would never understand what one wished to convey; and Miss Palliser, who would be mortally offended by any advice. No, I am perfectly satisfied, and shall be quite content if only my pupil will promise to obey the orders of her trainer. The question is," looking at her somewhat anxiously, for though as a rule his own nerve was steady as a rock, it broke down hopelessly under the strain of the possible chapter of accidents which this race exposed Kate Brewser to, " will she promise? "

" Of course she will," she answered readily. " That is to say, unless circumstances over which she has no control decide otherwise, I shall ride implicity to orders, like a six-stone nothing boy. Does that satisfy you? "

"I shan't be really satisfied," said he nervously, " until I see you and King Olaf cantering in ahead of everything else."

"You dreadfully ambitious man! And what if your pupil disappoints your expectations after all? "

" She will not. I have every confidence in the ability of herself and horse. Nevertheless, I wish to goodness the thing was well over."

She had never seen him so anxious and restless, or his calm manner so disturbed. Could it be possible that he was a coward at heart? But no, she knew better.

"What's the matter with you?" the said; "are you trying to make *me* afraid?"

"God forbid! But I can't help it. I'm horribly afraid myself."

"And so am I," chimed in poor Mary Whitbread, who in spite of the pleasure of Mr. Grahame's society was white as a sheet and trembling from top to toe.

"What nonsense!" said Kate lightly. "You two talk as if you expected me to be brought back on a stretcher. I beg leave to state I have not the smallest intention of departing this life."

"Please don't hint at such a horrible possibility, Kate," said Mary fearfully.

"I shall turn up again, never fear. I'm not a bit afraid, and I won't be frightened. So there!" She said these words with such determination as to silence her companions, while her tightly-set lips and the resolute expression of her countenance betokened a firm resolution not easily shaken.

But now time was progressing, so they adjourned to the paddock, where King Olaf had just put in an appearance. Old Stirrup walked by the side of the horse, and led him proudly round and round, while ever and again his rugged face lit up with a smile of triumph, when some such admiring remarks as, "'Ee's a good 'un 'ee is." "There goes the winner," etcetera, fell upon his ear. And indeed King Olaf fully deserved the flattering enconiums heaped upon him by the public at large, for in the last three weeks Colonel Clinker had taken great pains with his conditioning, and short as the time had been, had effected a considerable improvement in his appearance. As King Olaf walked jauntily by, swinging his tail from side to side, moving with that light springy step peculiar to him, he looked a perfect beauty, and so sleek, gentle, and docile, few would have given him credit for possessing such high courage and daring. His mane had been carefully plaited that morning by Kate's own white and

nimble little fingers, and his whole appearance was that of a
racehorse.   True he seemed a trifle lighter in the barrel than
he had done a month ago, but then what flesh he now carried
was hard and firm as a board, while the muscles on his strong
arms and thighs could almost have been counted.   Colonel
Clinker had given him his last gallop, and knew the horse to
be not only fit and well in himself, but also in all probability
(though still of course but imperfectly trained) in a far better
state of condition than any adversary he would be called upon
to meet.   He entertained small fears of King Olaf, his chief
anxiety being on Kate's account.   He called up all sorts of
imaginary dangers, and rendered himself quite miserable in
their contemplation.   She might fall, she might be cannoned
against, she might be jumped upon, she might not be able
to hold King Olaf, she might even be dragged and killed
outright.   There were no end to his anxieties, which grew in
intensity as the hour drew nigh, until they became almost
unbearable.

"Swear to take care of yourself," he whispered in Kate's
ear as she disappeared into the dressing-room.   The colour had
almost forsaken his cheeks and his voice trembled with emotion.

"Dear me, how timid we are to be sure!" she exclaimed
flippantly, trying to resist the impression he produced, but the
evident interest he took in her welfare touched her inspite
of herself, and prompted her almost involuntarily to hold out
her hand.

He grasped it warmly, and she added with a little reassur-
ing nod—

"Au revoir, my revered pastor and master.   Cast away all
fear as unworthy both of us.   I tell you everything will be
right.   Your pupil has not the smallest intention of disgrac-
ing either herself or you."

And then she vanished behind the heavy folds of the red
curtain concealing the doorway, and left him to think what
an idiot he was, and yet how impossible it was to help being
one where she was concerned.

"She's a veritable sorceress, a witch, an enchantress, and
I am her slave!" reflected Jack Clinker, as he wound his

way to the paddock in order to superintend the saddling of
King Olaf.   "I wish to God I were a rich man, I'd ask her
to marry me to-morrow, not that I expect I should have the
ghost of a chance.   There are some women one feels sure of,
but she is full of contradictions—charming one minute, cold
the next, made up of variety; tantalizing, sarcastic, lovable,
and delightful by turns, but not the sort of girl to let a fellow
think she cares two straws about him, whether she does or
not.   Well, for my part I like such women.   Easy conquests
lack piquancy, and nothing good in this world is to be
obtained without trouble, delay, and striving.   All the same,
I wish she were not so damnably rich.   It makes a man look
like a fortune-hunter, and no one gives him credit for disinterested affection.   If I proposed to Miss Brewser, kind
friends would say I cared only for her money.   Heigh-ho !
It's uncommon hard lines, in more ways than one, being a
pauper, or next door to it.   A chap's obliged to stick to his
bachelor habits when all the income he possesses barely
suffices to pay his cigar and flower bills, and yet, upon my
soul, I'm getting awfully sick of single blessedness ! "

While awaiting Kate's reappearance he purchased a card,
and looking over it found there were but six horses coloured,
namely, Lady Anne Birkett's brown gelding, Hastings, aged,
pedigree unknown ; yellow and black stripes, yellow cap
Mrs. Forrester's Singing Bird, by Musician out of Lightheart
scarlet, scarlet-and-black cap.   Mrs. Paget's grey gelding
Duncan Grey, aged, pedigree unknown ; chocolate, pink
sleeves and cap.   Miss Brewser's chestnut gelding, King Olaf
by Norseman out of Ice Maiden, six years old ; sky blue and
gold.   Mrs. Phipp's black horse, Black Anster, aged, by
Historian, dam unknown; cherry, yellow band ; and Miss
Palliser's bay mare, Coquette, five years, by the Beau out of
Scandal.

"H'm," said Colonel Clinker, when Kate re-entered the
paddock in all the glories of her racing kit.   "Out of that lot
we may dismiss two—Hastings and Duncan Grey—straight
away.   Poor old Hastings is a long sight too far gone in the
forelegs to take to steeplechasing as an amusement in his

declining years. I should not be at all surprised if he did not even get round the course. As for Duncan Grey, he's a slow, lumbering brute, who can't gallop faster than you can kick a hat along. He's no more use than a headache, and though a fairly good fencer will not prove very formidable. Singing Bird is a well-bred animal, and the best of Mrs. Forrester's lot, but with that lady's mania for purchasing cheap oats and mixing them with all sorts of experimental articles of food, I very much doubt her ability to stay. Nevertheless, though not in the same street with King Olaf, it won't do to estimate Singing Bird's chance too lightly. To begin with, as a four-year-old she takes the allowance, and, secondly, the services of so experienced a sportswoman as Mrs. Forrester will add many pounds more in her favour, so that altogether we must regard the pair as decided adversaries. Mrs. Forrester will ride a waiting race throughout, in order that if the hare comes to grief, she, as the tortoise, may profit by the occurrence. She will take advantage of the smallest error any of you commit, and won't go over a yard of unnecessary ground. In fact, so highly do I estimate Mrs. Forrester's chance, that were there any betting on the transaction she should certainly carry all my *place* money. Having disposed of her, we next arrive at Black Anster. I know him well of old as a rare good hunter, but alas! possessed with that not infrequent infirmity—shortness of breath. At the first symptom of a tussle this little defect in his respiratory organs will interfere with his powers of winning, and in my opinion annihilate them altogether. And now we come to Miss Palliser's Coquette—a dark animal, of whom neither I nor any-one else know anything—purchased, I fancy, purposely for this occasion, and pretty sure to be dangerous; so much so, indeed, that I hear she has backed herself to win for fifty pounds. All I can say is, I devoutly hope she may *lose*. However, I advise you to keep a sharp look out on that objectionable female's movements, for she is capable of anything, and if I mistake not already owes you a grudge."

"Me?" exclaimed Kate, innocently. "What have *I* done to offend her, pray?"

"You may well ask that question. Nothing, unless it be you have ridden a trifle too hard in the hunting-field to please her majesty."

"Oh! she's that sort of woman, is she?"

"Very much that sort of woman. So be extremely careful how you give her a chance of cannoning or knocking you out of the course."

"Really! I always looked upon Miss Palliser as a very harmless personage."

"And thereby displayed your intense ignorance. She's anything but harmless. On the contrary, she's exceedingly mischievous and exceedingly jealous. However, forewarned is forearmed."

"If you inveigh in such strong terms against the lady, I shall begin to suspect that you are a disappointed swain," said Kate saucily.

"A disappointed swain, indeed!" echoed he, laughing heartily. "That is capital, but your surmises are by no means correct. For many as have been the passages of arms between myself and Miss Palliser, any interchanges of a tenderer nature have been left out in the cold altogether. It will have to be a very long bow, shot by her ancient hand, that succeeds in sending a dart into *my* heart. *That*," with an emphasis on the word, "has been reserved for someone else to do."

He sent a swift inquiring glance at Kate, and those clear eyes produced so much confusion that she turned her head aside, before, after a pause, answering coldly—

"You are enigmatical, and metaphorical language is always difficult to understand. I object to Cupid's weapon, and also to Cupid himself, as a young gentleman of erratic and unsatisfactory manners. But here comes Mrs. Forrester; let us go and hear her ideas on things in general."

Decidedly Jack Clinker's tender insinuations were not amiably received, and fell harmless to the ground, like a poor wounded, fluttering bird, who strives to take wing and soar on high, and yet who at each endeavour recognises more and more its utter powerlessness. He was beginning to find it

better to stick to generalities, and not attempt a forward
policy that was pretty sure to meet with rebuff.   He gave no
outward expression, however, to his feelings of discomfiture,
but advanced to meet Mrs. Forrester with all good grace.
Neither he nor Kate could refrain from a broad smile when
they viewed the old lady, who, arrayed in a rusty brown skirt,
adorned with a huge leather patch at the knee, and a loose
scarlet Garibaldi, indeed looked as if she despised all those
effects produced by personal adornment.   Her sharp eyes
immediately detected an expression of amusement on her companions' faces.

"Ah!" she said, "you are laughing at my get-up, I can
see.   Never mind, I'm uncommonly proud of my racing
colours.   They cost me the large sum of three and threepence
halfpenny, including the cricketing cap.   I bought a remnant
of red flannel at tenpence a yard, and consider I did the thing
very economically.   Now if *I* tumble about in the dirt *I*
shan't have any fine clothes to spoil like some of you smart
young people," with a good-humoured glance at Kate.   "*My*
garments will wash, which is more than can be said of yours."

"Ah, my dear lady, *you* resemble the inestimable Mrs.
Gilpin, who, though on pleasure bent, possessed a frugal
mind," said Colonel Clinker gallantly.

"It's a pity for some people they don't rejoice in a similar
virtue," retorted Mrs. Forrester.   "If *you* were to practise
economy, Master Jack, for instance, there would be no great
harm done."

"And perhaps no great good either.   There must be some
extravagant people in the world, if only for the sake of promoting trade.   Are you going to win, Mrs. Forrester?"

"I wish I could answer that question.   I mean to try."

"I was just telling Miss Brewser that you and Miss Palliser
were the only two competitors she need really fear."

"*I* don't count for much, I'm afraid, but I hear Miss Palliser has set her heart on winning, and scoured all over the
country after a horse to her mind.   That's Coquette going by
now.   Do you see the big mare, next to Miss Brewser's chestnut?   Looks like speed."

But further conversation was cut short by the mounting of the equestriennes and the marshalling them forth in proper array. Time had long since been up, and people were getting a trifle impatient at the delay, though had they but realised the difficulties of starting six fair ladies, pulling up their girths, shortening their stirrups, adjusting their habits, and taking in their curb-chains, they might have displayed a greater leniency. However, at length all was ready for a start, and the half-dozen Amazons, round whom much interest was centred, emerged from the paddock in Indian file. King Olaf and Coquette certainly carried off the honours in point of looks. This latter proved a great big fine upstanding thoroughbred mare, showing a lot of quality, and as far as appearances went seemed likely to be the chestnut's most formidable opponent. Singing Bird came next in the public estimation, but she looked light and in poor condition. The competitors now went for their preliminary canter, which called forth many comments among the multitude, who freely criticised the ladies' seats and hands. Good-natured Lady Anne, on her dilapidated steed, beamed with fun and merriment, as if impelled to impart her own pleasure to those around. Mrs. Paget appeared decidedly nervous and ill at ease, Mrs. Phipps was exceedingly solemn and somewhat out of her element, Mrs. Forrester represented real business, while Miss Palliser looked grim yet excited, and Kate resolute.

CHAPTER XXI.

THE RACE ITSELF.

AFTER a little more delay, during which last words of caution and advice were being whispered into fair ears, the six horses were got together pretty evenly, and the flag dropped to a really excellent start. In another minute the whole half-dozen came sweeping by the spectators at a very fair pace, all in a cluster, but they had not gone more than a couple of hundred yards or so before it was curious to watch how first one, then another, began to straggle, while the horses' tails bobbed up and down like those of ducks in a pond, as they laboured uphill over the trying ridge-and-furrow. Poor Duncan Grey rolled about like a ship in a gale of wind, and lost ground at every stride; while the unfortunate Mrs. Paget, who was inclined to embonpoint, bumped painfully to and fro in the saddle. Old Hastings also plodded on with manifest exertion, and did not appear able to go the pace. Meantime Kate, bearing in mind Colonel Clinker's last admonitions, pulled King Olaf to the rear, much against the gallant chestnut's will, for he was keen as mustard, and, thanks to his muscular and compact conformation, glided lightly on and off the top of each ridge with the activity of a young chamois clambering amidst its native rocks. Singing Bird and Black Anster were both ahead, while Miss Palliser, untouched by any prudent considerations, and animated by the sole desire of distancing her opponents, was forcing the running, and already held a clear six lengths' lead. In this order they arrived at the first fence, over which they flew without any greater mishap than Hastings jumping short and bringing his hind legs down with a crash on the top of the binders, making a big gap by which Duncan Grey profited, as

he swerved half way across the course towards it, and thereby
so displaced poor Mrs. Paget's centre of gravity that she was
within an ace of cutting a voluntary, and was so long before
she recovered her equilibrium as to occasion her partisans the
greatest anxiety. They gallopped on bravely enough, the
ladies really acquitting themselves most creditably without
any material change taking place in their respective positions
until they came to the next obstacle, another flying fence,
only with the ditch this time on the far side, and here
Hastings, whose temper had probably been upset by the feel
of the thorns at the last one, whipped round to the left, and
to the intense annoyance of their respective owners, induced
Duncan Grey, very nervously ridden by Mrs. Paget, to do the
same. The other four horses got well over, and entered the
plough with nearly a hundred yards' advance of the two mis-
creants. Coquette by this time had still further increased her
lead, Singing Bird, Black Anster, and King Olaf, close together,
being a good way behind, but when they got into the deep
ground it became evident that Miss Palliser had been making
too much use of the mare, for she gradually came back to her
horses, and allowed the distance between them to diminish to
such a considerable extent that when they reached the fences
in and out of the road King Olaf was almost abreast, with
the other two in immediate attendance. Miss Palliser, irritated at seeing the trio so near, instead of steadying Coquette
as she ought to have done, raised her whip-hand and gave the
mare a smart switch, in consequence of which she landed too
far into the road, and blundered badly on jumping out,
almost coming down on her knees, and throwing Miss Palliser
well forwards; while Kate, remembering what she had been
told, kept King Olaf firmly in hand, and negotiated the double
obstacle beautifully. This little episode left her the advantage, and enabled her not only to have first shy at the water,
but also to choose the particular spot Colonel Clinker had
advised. She gave King Olaf a little cheer of encouragement,
which he knew well of old, a slight shake of the bridle, and
then set the good horse resolutely at the brook, close to where
the white flag stood on the right-hand side. But Miss Pal-

liser's jealousy was now more than aroused, and indeed had rapidly become so overmastering as to dispel any last lingering remnants of prudence. She called upon poor Coquette, and at the very moment King Olaf took off came with a tremendous rush at the identical place selected by her rival. The consequence was a violent collision occurred in the air, which very nearly upset both horses, and knocked them all to pieces for the time being.

Old Stirrup, with that mysterious affinity which tells us intuitively where sympathy is to be found, had crept up to Colonel Clinker's side, and was watching the race with alternate feelings of pleasure, hope, anxiety, and pride. The latter sentiment was gaining a decided predominance when the event above alluded to took place.

"Dash my buttons! Did you see that?" he exclaimed, trembling with indignation and excitement. "She did it o' purpus. I seed her with my own eyes, and a more deliberate or disgraceful foul I never witnessed."

Colonel Clinker put down his glasses for one second, rubbed them hastily with the corner of his silk pocket-handkerchief, and muttered between his set teeth—

"Damn that beast of a woman! She's a bigger brute even than I thought."

Stirrup overheard the words and knew that one person at least shared his virtuous wrath. He had thought well of the Colonel from the first, but now he went up greatly in his estimation as an assured well-wisher of his beloved mistress, and one who would stick to her through thick and thin.

By what, however, appeared little short of a miracle, King Olaf and Coquette managed to regain their legs, after a scramble, without any worse catastrophe arising from the encounter than loss of position. Both Singing Bird and Black Anster passed them. Nevertheless, King Olaf decidedly escaped the best of the two, for thanks to having started first, he received the brunt of the shock on his hind quarters, while Coquette, whose impetus had been greater, tumbled right down on her head, and sprawled several yards before recovering himself.

She came with a tremendous rush.

Kate could not help feeling angry. Perhaps most people would have done so under the circumstances.

"What do you mean by riding like that?" she asked severely.

"Nothing. I shall ride as I choose," came the sullen rejoinder.

She saw then that there was no generosity, no friendly competition, to be expected in this quarter, and Colonel Clinker had been right when he warned her against Miss Palliser as against a dangerous enemy. If she could do her a bad turn and prevent her winning it was quite evident she would do so. Kate's courage, however, was of the kind which rises with an emergency, and which opposition only rouses into a doubly firm determination to succeed. She resolved to best Miss Palliser at any rate.

"Certainly," she replied, with chilling politeness; "that is what I imagine you have hitherto done. Take care, however, your mare does not turn the tables upon you before long."

There was no time for any further interchange of civilities between the ladies, for Singing Bird and Black Anster were still in advance.

Kate set King Olaf going again as quickly as possible. She had ridden with great patience and judgment, and obeyed orders implicitly, but the moment had now arrived to ascertain of what mettle her horse was really made. If she allowed herself to get too far behind she might never regain the ground lost through that most provoking foul. Thank goodness, King Olaf felt strong as a lion under her, while Coquette, owing to the ruthless way in which her mistress had used, or rather *mis*used her powers, not only lathered freely, but already began to hold out unmistakable signals of distress. Still a very few more strides were sufficient to show that either had the speed of Singing Bird and Black Anster, both of whom they passed with ease, and both of whom seemed pretty well cooked. Side by side the two leaders now galloped on, taking fence for fence, King Olaf always a little in advance, but with Coquette running very gamely, and showing under different guidance what a real good mare she might have proved. Nevertheless, as they neared the last few fences, King Olaf's superior condition told more and more. The further they went, too, the greater became Kate's presence of mind. She had recovered from the first flurry of a natural excitement, and now brought all her judgment and intelligence to bear on the task in hand; while Miss Palliser, on the contrary, flushed and tremulous, seemed hardly to know what she was about. King Olaf had never extended himself even, and galloped gaily and freely. In this manner they reached the last fence of all, which the gallant chestnut flew with ridiculous ease, but just as he landed a shrill scream rent the air, and looking round in alarm Kate beheld Miss Palliser's form shoot from the saddle, apparently without any assignable reason, and come with a fierce bump to the ground, where it lay like a helpless bundle, prostrate on mother earth, leaving Coquette, who must have felt insulted by this apparent vagary on the part of her rider, to canter away with loosely flapping reins. Kate knew now that she had the race in hand, but Singing Bird and Black Anster were only a few lengths in the rear, so she wisely did not risk a finish, but came on at a good steady pace and won exactly as she pleased, while the public, whose sympathies, after the *contretemps* at the water-jump, had been entirely on her side, applauded her to the echo. The victory appeared, in fact, a most popular one, for, to tell truth, Miss Palliser's friends were few and far between.

It was a picture to see old Stirrup's face; indeed, the expression of it would have formed quite a physiological study when he saw King Olaf come cantering in. It literally rippled over with delight.

"I knowed 'ee'd do it; I knowed 'ee'd beat 'em all to fits," were the only words he could find at first to express the height of a joy so intoxicatingly overpowering.

Meanwhile poor Miss Palliser was lying on the flat of her back with her heels up in the air, vowing and declaring she was killed. A crowd quickly gathered round the unfortunate horsewoman, who before many minutes discovered this statement to be highly exaggerated, inasmuch as, with the exception of the wind having been knocked out of her body by the exceeding velocity of her downfall, she remained unharmed in aught except in spirit, which latter appeared terribly mortified.

"If it had not been for my stirrup-leather breaking just when it did," she explained to her auditors, "I *must* have won. Was there ever such luck in this world? Really it is *too*, TOO cruel."

"Was that why you tumbled off, Miss Palliser?" asked Captain Fuller in his cool sarcastic way.

"Ah, of course," retorted she in a state of high exasperation, "I know that's exactly what people will say. They will say I cut a voluntary—I who have never done such a thing in my life. I shall be greatly obliged to you, Captain Fuller, if you will contradict the statement, and allow the public to know the true state of the case. The stirrup-leather alone was to blame."

"I'm glad to hear it," responded he with an impenetrable countenance. "That's satisfactory at any rate. One always likes to find some good excuse for these unfortunate little casualties."

As for Kate, the very first person she met when she rode back into the paddock was Colonel Clinker. He came towards her with a smile of pleasure and relief brightening all his face.

"Bravo! bravo!" he cried. "You rode awfully well. No one could have ridden better, not even a professional jockey. There was not a single thing I told you to do that you did not do, and that exactly right. I feel indeed proud of my pupil."

He took her hand in his and shook it warmly. A sudden impulse seized him.

"Oh, Kate!" he added in a softened voice, "you don't know how thankful I am to get you back again. My heart stood still with fright when I saw the collision at the brook, and thought you were in for a fall. I never felt so queer in my life."

The flush of victory glowed in her veins. She was too happy, too full of the pleasures of that proud moment to remark the use he made of her Christian name. It was not till afterwards, not till the warm blood had cooled and her mind resumed its normal condition, that she remembered how he had held her hand in his and called her Kate in tones that seemed as if they could only possess one meaning, one interpretation. At the time she merely realised the subtle joy of feeling here was a person who sympathised and rejoiced at her triumph as if it had been his very own, and whose evident interest was not alone flattering to her vanity, but acceptable to some warmer and deeper emotion that now and again began to stir the pulsations of her heart.

"Thanks for your congratulations," she said; "but don't praise me, for I did nothing but stick on. Praise King Olaf instead. My success is entirely owing to him and—and to you," beaming down on the open countenance so near her own. "Without your help I should have been nowhere. You saw how Coquette stopped, purely through want of condition. Well, King Olaf's superiority was solely and entirely owing to your exceeding kindness."

Kate, assisted by her companions, now dismounted, whereupon King Olaf stretched out his forelegs and shook himself heartily, just like a dog when he emerges from the water, while she, regardless of all onlookers, put her two arms round his neck and rubbed her soft cheek against the beautiful animal's velvety nose.

"Oh, Stirrup!" she cried artlessly, "isn't he a darling? Didn't he behave beautifully? We must have his picture painted. I shall get an artist down from town to do him at once."

They were a pretty pair as they stood thus—the horse, with his mild blue eyes filled with an intelligence almost human, his swelling veins, his slender limbs, and tapering head; she with the rich colour mantling in her cheeks, her slim figure set off to full advantage by her perfectly fitting colours, and a stray lock of hair just fluttering in the gentle breeze.

Colonel Clinker felt all at once as if he hated King Olaf. A fierce and sudden longing seized him to have those sweet lips pressed to his instead of to that light tan muzzle, to feel the coveted clasp of those encircling arms about his neck instead of seeing them placed so lovingly round King Olaf's. He wanted to take her to himself and speak to her of his love —his deep, overmastering passion. It cost him no small

effort to preserve silence and turn away, but the time had not
yet come, and he preferred suspense for a while longer to a
cruel certainty that might rob him of all pleasure in life.
Besides, what had he to offer her? He had no money, no
profession, no particular brains, not even settled habits. He
had been accustomed to a round of perpetual excitement,
gambling, betting, racing, late hours. Even if she would
take him, was he fit to be married? Might not his old
bachelor habits cling to him still? Might not the same restless spirit break forth afresh? He was inclined to think not.
He was inclined to think he could make any sacrifices for her
sake, inclined to think that with her by his side fresh possibilities, higher aims, higher ambitions might open themselves out to him in the future; but as yet he was like a man
who sees "through a glass darkly." He doubted his own
powers of forbearance, of steadfastness, and perseverance; a
glimmering light had commenced to brighten the pathway of
uncertainty, casting flickering rays of sunshine upon it, but
they were not assured. The light might be put out altogether
by too hasty, too rude a breath, and so long as he could still
retain a certain amount of self-command he would run no risks.
Therefore Jack Clinker, when he looked at Kate by King
Olaf's side, turned suddenly away, so that she wondered where
he had gone, and why he had forsaken her thus early instead
of assisting her to drink the sweet, intoxicating cup of success
to its very dregs. Others crowded round to offer their congratulations, but she felt hurt at his prompt defection, torturing
herself with self-communings as to whether she could have
said or done anything that might have offended him, so true
is it that even in our most joyous moments some little tiny
sting robs them of full fruition, rendering them satisfactory
only in part.

In the meantime Miss Palliser had waddled into the paddock, her back well plastered with mud and her habit torn to
shreds. She, too, watched Kate embracing King Olaf, but
with very different sentiments.

She could not conceal her malice any longer; therefore, turning to Captain Fuller, who stood close by, she said spitefully—

"What dreadful bad form that girl is to be sure. Just look at her now. Why she makes as much fuss about winning a twopenny-halfpenny race as she could do if she had won the Derby. I call it positively sickening."

"Do you?" retorted he. "I imagine success always *is* sickening when viewed with the mortified eyes of defeat."

"Pooh! Nonsense! You need not think *I* care about being beaten. A miserable little course like this is no criterion whatever—mere child's play after the sort of fences *we* have been accustomed to. I daresay Miss Brewser imagines she has done something wonderful, but anybody who understands about racing—anybody, that is, except Colonel Clinker, whose little game we can all see through—would tell her differently. But, there, she's so horribly conceited one might just as well talk to a peacock."

Miss Palliser had taken no pains to lower her voice, and Kate overheard every word of the above speech.

She got very red in the face, but said, eyeing her adversary steadily—

"Please do not talk quite so loud, Miss Palliser. Perhaps you were not aware when you made those flattering remarks that I was within earshot."

After some self-communion she had thought it better to announce the fact.

"I don't care whether you were or not," returned the other, carried away beyond all bounds of civility. "It's nothing to me."

Kate drew herself up to her full height.

"I will not condescend to argue with you," she said loftily, and then she turned away, feeling deeply hurt by Miss Palliser's conduct. Before long she met Colonel Clinker once more. "You were quite right," she said going up to him, "to warn me against that woman; I did not believe you at at the time, but now I know you had wisdom on your side."

"What's she been doing? Anything more to annoy you?" he asked suspiciously.

"Yes, she has been excessively rude, but I do not wish to repeat such low and vulgar sayings. Miss Palliser is simply —no lady."

"Oh! so you've begun to find that out, have you? Well,

better late, perhaps, than never. It will be easier after this to keep out of her way."

"I shall certainly take care to do so in the future. I wonder," said poor Kate musingly, "why people say such nasty, horrid things? What's the good in this world of being so spiteful towards our fellow creatures?"

"Ah, what indeed! I'm sure I can't answer that question satisfactorily, and yet, wherever you go there is always a certain number of folks ready to put the worst construction on all your actions, and give you over beforehand to the arch-fiend. However, I will not have you vex yourself about Miss Palliser's rude speeches. She's not worth such a compliment. Here's the Earl coming to escort the heroine of the day to lunch. So cheer up."

As he spoke the old gentleman made his appearance, leaning on his gold-headed stick, and, after some slight delay the invited guests marched off to the Castle to eat and to drink. A merry meal followed, lasting over an hour, and at the end of it the Earl, who bore his own daughter's defeat most good-naturedly, got up and presented the cup to Kate with great ceremony, making a little speech to the effect "that he had much pleasure in bestowing it upon his dear young friend, on one whom he was sure all would admit had most gallantly earned the prize." In fact he grew so paternally affectionate that Kate hardly knew how to reply, and felt ready to sink into the earth when Mr. McGrath called loudly for her to return thanks.

"But I can't," she said in a flurried whisper. "I don't know how. I never made a speech in my life. I'd rather commit suicide."

"That does not matter in the least. You must. The Earl will be dreadfully offended if you don't. Besides, people make speeches every day whether they are proficient in the art or not, so fire away."

Thus entreated, Kate rose from her seat and said in a clear voice, though inwardly trembling with nervousness—

"Ladies and gentlemen, I thank you for your kindness. I don't really deserve it, or the praise our kind host has so freely bestowed upon me, and I feel certain any of my oppo-

nents would have won the race had they had the good fortune
to posess so gallant a horse. All the credit of the performance
is due to him, and to him alone."

Then she sat down again rather hurriedly, knowing that
if she were to harangue the company for an hour she could
not find any words which would express her opinion more
completely.

"Bravo! bravo!" cried the Earl and many of the gentlemen, who were taken by her pleasant appearance and modest
manners. "Here's King Olaf's health. Three cheers for
King Olaf!"   .

Everybody joined in the toast—everybody, that is to say,
except Miss Palliser, who could not bring herself to participate in the general rejoicings.

"What humbug it all is to be sure," she observed under
her breath to Captain Fuller, who for his sins was seated next
to her. "Such a ridiculous fuss about nothing. Colonel
Clinker is bad enough in all conscience, but I really wonder
at the Earl, who ougnt to know better, being so silly as to encourage this Miss Brewser in her affectations. It's downright
sinful."

"You don't seem to like Miss Brewser, eh?"

"No, I can't say that I do.   Why should I?"

"Oh, for no particular reason, of course.   But things have
turned out just as I anticipated.   It was simply impossible for
six ladies to compete in a race, or anything else, without
giving rise to all sorts of envy, hatred and uncharitableness.
Miss Brewser is merely paying the usual penalty of success."

"How so?"

"Does not success invariably create detractions?   Particularly feminine ones.   No, no; depend upon it the jealousies of your sex beat those of ours all to fits."

"I don't agree with you in the least, Captain Fuller. That's
just the sort of thing men delight in saying. They always
try to make themselves out superior beings, and to impress
that superiority on every occasion. Now, if this Miss Brewser
were really a decent sort of girl I should be the very first to
feel pleased at her having won, and congratulate her on her
good fortune."

"Would you, Miss Palliser?"

"Yes; don't look at me in that sceptical sort of way, as if you did not believe what I was saying. I repeat, if Miss Brewser were nice I should feel pleased at her success; but as it is, I believe I am not alone in considering she took a very unfair advantage over the other competitors."

"What on earth are you talking about?" exclaimed Captain Fuller, opening his eyes. "An unfair advantage? *What* unfair advantage, pray?"

"Oh, it's not necessary to enter into particulars, especially as we are all of us of the same opinion."

"If you do not choose to divulge what that opinion is, of course I can do nothing but guess at it," said Captain Fuller with growing curiosity. "If I happen to hit the right nail on the head will you tell me if my surmises aré correct? I fancy I have an inkling as to your meaning."

"Guess away as much as you please," said she loftily. "All I will say is, that if *we* had all been heiresses, and encouraged young men in the most shameless and improper manner, if *we* had been fast and forward, and if *we* had shown an utter disregard for our good name, it is just possible that *we*, too, might have secured the services of a professional jockey. But, thank heaven, *we* possess some pride and some self-respect, which prevent our behaving like—well, I will not say what," and Miss Palliser pursed up her lip with an expression of such extreme propriety and modesty that she might have been a girl in her teens instead of a world-hardened virgin the wrong side of forty, who, as a rule, displayed no hesitation in calling a spade a spade.

"Phew!" said Captain Fuller to himself, while a sardonic smile overspread his usually impassive features. "That's how the land lies! What extraordinary creatures these women are, to be sure! La Palliser is simply mad with jealousy. There's some fun to be got out of her. Let's have a try."

He put on his most sympathetic manner, and said inquiringly—

"I gather that you do not approve of Colonel Clinker's having rendered Miss Brewser so much assistance?"

But the lady was in no mood to be drawn.

"No matter what I approve, or what my sentiments on the subject are," she said brusquely, "I'm not an old hen to go about cackling all over the country, like our friend Mrs. Forrester over the way; but all I *can* say and *will* say is this. If "—and her voice assumed a stern ferocity—"if that young person—I will not call her young lady, for she does not behave herself as such—but if that young person fancies she is going to crow over us all she is mightily mistaken. I, for one, shall not submit to it, and shall find means to recall her to her proper place."

"And what might you consider her proper place, Miss Palliser?"

"That's my affair, not yours," said she with a sneer. "You are a man, and have all a man's weakness for money, when centred in a marriageable woman."

This was a nasty thrust, and Captain Fuller's thin mouth twitched ever so slightly; for once, not so many years ago, when it had been reported Miss Palliser inherited, or was about to inherit, a fortune, he had made himself so agreeable that on the rumour proving incorrect he had experienced some slight difficulty in executing a timely retreat. Nevertheless he parried the attack with his usual dexterity.

"I wish all women possessed your spirit, Miss Palliser," he said gallantly, though if his wish could have been fulfilled he would have regarded this earth as a perfect pandemonium. "It's quite refreshing now and again to meet with a person who, like yourself, has the courage of her opinions. Most ladies are comparatively tame."

"That's neither here nor there," said she with asperity. "I hate such trashy compliments. But I *do* pride myself on disliking all mean, unfair, and underhanded ways, so if you come across Miss Brewser you can tell her so from me. Ah! at last," she added impatiently, "thank goodnes they are making a move. What an interminable meal this has been, to be sure!"

"You are more frank than polite, Miss Palliser. I, as your companion, feel exceedingly flattered by the remark."

She looked at him contemptuously.

"You and I," she said with a sneer, "know each other too well to stand on much ceremony. You remember the old proverb anent familiarity?"

"Perfectly," assented he with exasperating calm, "though it is nice and kind of you to remind me of it. However," shooting one parting shot after her as she rose from the table, "the day has been rather trying in more ways than one, and when a lady has torn a new habit-skirt to rags, taken a fall, and endured defeat, civility and amiability of temper naturally enough go to the wall. Good-bye, Miss Palliser. When next we meet I hope to see you restored to a more equable frame of mind."

He irritated her beyond conception, but the time had gone by to fling back any suitably severe reply, and the last word, for once, remained with the gentleman.

"Hum!" he reflected. "I'll lay a monkey there's mischief brewing. The Palliser means vengeance, and no mistake Well, if you hold the sheet in your hand squalls are rather exciting than otherwise, and if any row ensues I fancy I can lay my finger on the offending party. Women who remain unmarried after the age of five-and-thirty ought to be strangled. Double-distilled vinegar resembles honey as compared with them. Poor things! It seems a pity we cannot some of us take compassion on their forlorn condition; but women are plentiful as blackberries, and therefore the ugly ones are at a discount; besides which, when they show temper as well, all I can say is, 'Lord deliver us!'"

Thus, with mingled sentiments, the participators in and the spectators of the famous ladies' steeplechase separated.

And perhaps the happiest person that day was old Stirrup. There was no sting of bitterness in his cup to speak of. The two beings he loved best in the world had acquitted themselves to his entire satisfaction, and when that afternoon he groomed King Olaf with pride and unmixed triumph, and gave him a double feed of oats after his brilliant performance, the faithful servant felt himself to be the proudest man in creation.

CHAPTER XXII.

COMMENTS IN THE "COUNTY SPORTING CHRONICLE"

THE much-talked-of steeplechase was over and done with, and ought, by all the laws of society, to have been gradually consigned to oblivion; but it was destined before many days passed to give rise to an immense amount of discussion, for on the Saturday following the day on which the race was run an article appeared in the *County Sporting Chronicle*, a newspaper rejoicing in an extensive circulation among the landed gentry, well-to-do farmers, and sporting members of the surrounding neighbourhood. This article, ably calculated to set all those connected with the race at loggerheads, gave birth to the fiercest indignation. It was minus a signature, and read as follows :—

"During the reign of Her Most Gracious Majesty Queen Victoria the progress of science and civilisation has advanced with such rapid strides that each fresh innovation, each startling discovery, rarely occasions more than a temporary feeling of astonishment. The telephone, the phonograph, and the spectroscope have come upon the human comprehension in such quick succession that it almost fails to grasp the stupendous truths they reveal. Marvellous as the advances made in the present century undoubtedly are, it nevertheless is open to question whether, in all cases, they have been attended with beneficial results. The 'Married Women's Property Bill,' and similar recent Acts passed by the legislature of the United Kingdom have, to a certain extent, prepared our countrymen at large for the insistence of that abstruse term vaguely denominated 'Woman's Rights.' These so-called 'rights' are open to a somewhat elastic interpretation. If woman seriously desires emancipation from all those usages and customs which hitherto have encircled her, care, at least, should be displayed in the means employed to obtain the loosening of those obnoxious shackles by which she loudly asserts herself to be fettered. In olden days, while her lords and masters sallied forth, crossbow and arquebuss in hand, to fight the wild boar in his native forest, or to do battle against insurgent hordes, the gentler sex was content to remain at home, engaged in the exercise of those peaceful household avocations which, in modern times, it is unfortunately apt to regard with contempt and contumely. Woman's leisure hours *then* were profitably employed in the production of those vast and beautiful tapestries whose vivid colouring, cunning workmanship, and faithful portrayal of nature are a standing monument of her industry, besides calling forth our highest admiration, not only in respect of their intrinsic merit, but also with regard to the skill and patient perseverance of their fair producers. We humbly submit that in those days woman occupied the sphere which she is most calculated to adorn; but, unfortunately, in the nineteenth century such ideas have become decidedly antiquated. Our ancestors are regarded as worthy humdrum people, who failed to understand the art of living, and who, indeed, never got the length of recognising the fundamental truth that personal pleasure is the mighty god by which nine-tenths of the world are ruled. Consequently, in the present age, throwing off many precious feminine attributes with derision, woman not only enters the lists against those physically, if not intellectually, her superiors, and boldly emulates the deeds of the manlier sex, but, not content with attiring her person in the most masculine and eccentric garments attainable, hunts, travels, shoots, smokes, swears, drinks, gambles, bets, and fishes, besides in every possible and impossible way attempting to identify herself with the male portion of the community. It has, however, been reserved for the *enterprising*, if not the *discreet*, ladies of Huntingshire to strike out an entirely new and original path, and by adding steeplechasing to the above category, to

advance a considerable stride yet nearer the pastimes, pleasures, and pursuits of the lords of creation; and if imitation
be, as is often averred, the highest, subtlest, most insidious
form of flattery, then those ladies have given distinctive proof
of their earnest sincerity. When, however, on the other
hand, we find a distinguished and prominent member of the
aristocracy, one who moves in the most exalted circles, and
is a dignitary—as he should be an example—in the land,
not only giving to such proceedings the weight of his sanc-
tion and encouragement, but actually authorising his own
daughter, a young lady barely out of her teens, of an age
when innocence should be guarded as the apple of the
eye, to be their primary instigator, it certainly seems high
time for the more soberminded among us to reflect upon
a social revolution which, headed, alas! by royalty itself,
is rapidly bringing about a new order of things, and under-
mining in their very foundations those staid, old-fashioned,
and, it is still to be hoped, *orthodox* ideas, which our
forefathers were wont to regard as the real standard of
true morality. England is a country of which all English-
men feel proud, and the national sentiments cannot be so
far perverted as to approve the unsexing of her women.
If the term appear harsh, it is, nevertheless, not undeserved;
but it seems better to make a warning of the minority while
there is yet time, than to sacrifice the majority by allowing
them to become infected with fast, foolish, frivolous, and
demoralising notions, whose ascendency can but prove inju-
rious to the feminine mind. These few words of caution may
not, perhaps, be utterly disdained by the six ladies who took
part in the race, more especially when we on our side are
willing to admit a certain meed of praise is due to their
audacity—an audacity which, had it but been displayed in a
more meritorious cause, would have called forth the plaudits
instead of, as it did, the aspersions and hostile criticisms of
the populace. For that populace has yet to be educated up
to an appreciation of beholding delicate women, attired in
fanciful and fantastic garments, riding one against the other
over a series of formidably dangerous obstructions, any single

one of which is sufficient to place their valuable lives in
jeopardy, and dislocate limbs hitherto respected as both
tender and fragile. It has still to learn wherein the beauty
consists of seeing high-spirited girls, whose energies are
surely worthy a higher outlet, and sober mothers of families,
who ought to know better, come galloping helter-skelter past
a post, scarlet in visage, muddy in person, dishevelled in
appearance, retaining none of that feminine refinement which
appeals so strongly to the masculine element, and carried
away to such an extent by spurious excitement and mixed
passions as to be utterly impervious to all sense of ordinary
decency, ordinary modesty. It is just possible that in process of time the public might grow accustomed to female
steeplechasing, as it does to many another flagrant exhibition,
but such moderation can only come with long usage, and at
present it certainly appears sounder wisdom to stamp out all
such displays in their infancy rather than allow them to take
any hold on the national mind. Fortunately, apart from a
certain amount of interest inspired by the novelty of the proceedings, the approval and applause presumably coveted by
the fair competitors was wisely withheld, thus testifying
strongly to the sound common sense and discrimination of the
public at large. The feminine character possesses many
charming, virtuous, and fascinating qualities; nevertheless
it is a pretty well established fact that amongst the foremost
of its shortcomings jealousy holds a conspicuous position.
Unfortunately we have every reason to believe that on the
occasion unto which allusion has already been made, envy
and emulation were unusually rife among the ambitious
candidates. So keen indeed was the rivalry exhibited as
to lead to the most unpleasant results—results on which it
becomes almost painful to comment. Suffice it that in more
quarters than one rumours are prevalent to the effect that
the actual winner of the much-coveted prize, a silver cup
presented by the Earl of H——, obtained an unworthy
advantage through obtaining the services of a well-known
gentleman, who, although not strictly speaking a professional
trainer, has acquired so great an experience in all matters

connected with horseflesh as to render him thoroughly
deserving the appellation. What this gentleman's motives
may have been it is scarcely incumbent on us to inquire into;
but as the turf, generally speaking, is not regarded as an
arena whereon riches are amassed, and as the lady's fortune
is reputed exceedingly large, there appears small difficulty in
distinguishing a possible object that may account for so
marked a piece of favouritism. On the fairness of such a
proceeding it is unnecessary to dwell at length. Facts are
facts, and these speak for themselves. Neither can it be
desirable to linger long over the absurd and demoralizing
spectacle of an aged female (devoid even the plea of giddy
youth, which might in some measure palliate conduct so
unseemly and so untimely) careering round a steeplechase
course on a half-starved Rosinante, and attired in a garment
which ordinary propriety would promptly have relegated to
the privacy of the bed-chamber. At a period when the meri-
dian of life has long since been left behind, it is truly
lamentable to find a woman's being centred in such frivolous
amusements. How far better and how far more suitable
would it not be if she were to pass her time in pious contemplation of that not far distant removal from a world of sorrow
which sooner or later overtakes all mankind, and in a profitable preparation for death that might fill her hours of recreation in a surely worthier manner? Instead of profaning her
declining years by the assumption of masculine pursuits
which call forth ridicule, would not such saintly conduct be
setting a higher and more valuable example to the rising
generation?

"These are questions requiring but little reflection, and to
be answered but in one way. Perhaps the only lady who fails
to fall under the ban of general condemnation to which the remaining five have unluckily exposed themselves, is she who,
owing to an exceedingly unfortunate disaster, met with so
severe an accident, and when victory appeared all but assured
was prevented enjoying its fruits. This lady, too honest and
too proud to solicit extraneous aid, stood on her individual
merits, and in so standing unluckily fell to the ground, else

the result of the race might have proved very different. In conclusion, the whole affair can only be regarded in the light of a singular and whimsical freak, which in future we trust may not be repeated; and when the competitors find they have gained neither honour, glory, nor applause by these eccentric vagaries, then perhaps they may consent to re-enter the comparative retirement of private life—that private life unto which woman is so eminently suited, and in emerging from which she makes so cruel a mistake, besides being utterly wrong in fancying the approbation of the opposite sex is to be gained in such a fashion. The more sensible and shrewd of men view with growing distrust the advanced tendencies of an age which impel woman, by leaving her natural and legitimate sphere, to become unsexed, and which renders possible an exhibition similar to the one it was our painful privilege to witness last Tuesday. That that inappropriate display may be forgotten and forgiven as quickly as may be is the most charitable wish of all rational folks, and one in which doubtless the great majority of those present will acquiesce. Let the ladies' steeplechase be buried in the annals of an oblivious past, and then once more may the fair equestriennes of Huntingshire hold up their heads and resume their rightful places among their less remarkable, less aspiring, and less notorious sisters."

So read the article, and its appearance not unnaturally gave the signal for a perfect torrent of indignation to unloose itself in every quarter, for, to tell the truth, the good people of Huntingshire had shown such lively interest in the matter of the race, that this wholesale abuse was looked upon as a personal insult, even those who had taken no active part in the proceedings regarding it as a covert act of malice. Mr. Quildry, the editor, did not escape severe objurgation, and never in the memory of that mythical personage, the oldest inhabitant, had any paragraph appeared in the *County Sporting Chronicle* that had created so great a commotion among the sporting division. This being the case, it was not to be wondered at if Kate Brewser, against whom certain sentences seemed peculiarly directed, felt deeply wounded by accusations

so disagreeable and unkind, as to rob her of any little pleasure
she might hitherto have experienced from her success. The
venomous sting had been surely aimed, causing the wound to
fester and inflame under the influence of the poisonous matter
introduced. It annoyed her beyond measure to find her name
coupled with that of Colonel Clinker, and especially that the
very thought of any unfair advantage, which had only found
a temporary dwelling-place in her own mind, should now be
advanced as a matter of fact, and endowed with all the significance of a positive assertion. These things were not to be
borne. Either they were true or they were not true, and in
any case ought to be proved. Such was Kate's feeling on the
subject. As to that other insinuation—that insinuation about
her fortune and Colonel Clinker's neediness—she told herself
she scorned it, and disdained it as unworthy of him; nevertheless, the small sharp barb of malice sped home, and re-
opened the old wound, giving rise to the old suspicions, the
old distrust. Since even a newspaper made public the
gentleman's designs, must they not have become the common
talk of the town? must there not exist some foundation for
such reports? The very idea was gall and wormwood. Her
whole pride rebelled against the thought; and yet, do what
she would, she found it impossible to banish it altogether
from her mind. When she met Colonel Clinker next her ease
had vanished, and a constraint and coolness came between
them, for he too, was enraged to a degree by the aspersions
cast upon his character. Those which alluded to his being a
professional turfite he could afford to laugh at, but those
which coarsely spoke of his relations to Kate Brewser, of his
ulterior motives in singling her out as "an object of favouritism," he could neither forgive nor forget. And yet they tied
his tongue and rendered it impossible for him to discuss a
matter in itself so delicate and so difficult to handle. He
could utter no word of self-defence to Kate Brewser as things
stood at present, though already he fancied he detected from
her altered manner how great was the impression made.
And as usual, when direct speech, direct explanation is
impossible, the results produced by a few idle words and

written sentences grew in magnitude and importance, until they acquired a wholly fictitious self-torturing ascendency. But of the various victims who writhed under the sarcasms of the author's pen, perhaps none reached to such a pitch of virtuous wrath as Mrs. Forrester. She who in her brusque way professed to despise praise and hold herself above flattery, was yet keenly alive to ridicule. Possibly the small smattering of truth, which like a vein of ore deep down in a mine, underlaid the whole composition, accounted in some measure for this result. Had the absurdities scoffed at been even more patent and glaring than they were, the derision of them might have been easier to bear than when a certain substratum of facts formed a fair working foundation. There was no denying the assertion that Mrs. Forrester *had* worn scarlet flannel, and that scarlet flannel was a material highly in favour among occupants of the bed-chamber. But the chief offence of all lay in that ruthless allusion to her age and irreligious occupations. Now Mrs. Forrester was a hearty churchgoer, who regularly every Sunday forenoon snoozed under the influence of Mr. Parker's monotonous voice, and listened to the threequarters of an hour sermon with a decorous gravity highly credible to her powers of endurance and patience; therefore she felt any remarks against her theological proclivities to be peculiarly unkind, as they were peculiarly uncalled for.

"I'll expose him. I'll never rest till I find out the scoundrel who has taken all our characters away." So said the wrathful old lady to herself, and having thus said, at once proceeded to act.

In consequence of her urgent representations and calls for speedy vengeance, a meeting of the offended parties and their sympathisers was convened forthwith, and held at Mrs. Forrester's residence on the first non-hunting day. The meeting was crowded to excess, and so far as numerical numbers went, proved a decided success, the only absentee of any importance being Miss Palliser, who pleaded a bad cold which detained her in bed as an excuse. Her non-appearance, however, was but little commented upon, for after the unladylike jealousy displayed during the race, she had fallen into even greater disfavour than usual. Colonel Clinker, who in any emergency was invariably regarded as the man to come to the front, was of course present, as also were Messrs. Grahame, McGrath, Captain Fuller, Kate Browser, Mary Whitbread, Mrs. Paget, and Lady Anne Birkett, who apologised for her father's absence owing to a press of county business. There was a great deal of whispering going on in quiet corners, and subdued expressions of the most varied opinions. Mrs. Forrester waited, however, until all her guests had assembled before formally commencing the proceedings of the afternoon. When the last carriage had disburdened itself of its occupants, she rose from her seat, and with an unusual amount of solemnity addressed the company in her grave guttural voice.

"I regret to say," she said, "that we are here to-day for no pleasant purpose. A most offensive publication has appeared in the paper, as all of you already know. We ladies have been laughed at, insulted, and derided, in a manner which it is impossible to forget. I do not know if you all agree with me in thinking that the author should be rendered responsible for what he has written, and, personally, nothing short of an ample apology could in any degree atone for the mischief he has done us. He has publicly insulted us, and therefore in my opinion ought to be made to publicly withdraw the offending statements that have exasperated so many of those present. These are my sentiments, but I shall feel much obliged if you will discuss the matter openly, and bring forward any fresh views calculated to throw light upon the affair, or which can regulate our future proceedings."

So saying Mrs. Forrester looked round with a hawk-like expression which seemed to challenge argument and invite discussion.

"You are quite right," said Colonel Clinker, who had warmly approved the lady's speech from first to last. "Something must be done, and the sooner the better. We can't allow such insinuations to be levelled against us without refuting them with the scorn they deserve. Either collectively or individually, as may be decided best, we must set to work and take steps to find cut and punish the offending party. If this sort of thing is allowed to go on we shall never have any peace, and every harmless little frolic becomes magnified and distorted into a national sin. It's utterly preposterous."

Jack Clinker delivered himself of the above sentiments with a warmth and a decision which impressed his hearers not a little. In substance they were but a repetition of Mrs. Forrester's, but observations made by a popular and good-looking young man, among an audience in which the female element largely predominates, are apt to be received with a favour often wholly disproportioned to the talent they display. Women are impressionable beings, and a stalwart stature, frank blue eyes, and well-cut features, go a long way towards convincing them of a masculine speaker's power of oratory. All the young ladies plumed their feathers and nodded their heads in token of assent and approval. Nevertheless they refrained from making any original suggestions. Everybody seemed so thoroughly persuaded of the truth of Colonel Clinker's concluding remark, that further comment appeared almost superfluous. "The thing was utterly preposterous." What could possibly be more forcibly and tersely put?

"That's exactly what my father says," said Lady Anne, after a slight pause. "He says that if newspaper writers and newspaper editors are to be allowed to behave in such a manner, all liberty of action and freedom will become annihilated. In fact, to tell the truth, it is long since I have seen my father so annoyed by what after all we can only regard as a vulgar *trifle*."

And Lady Anne, as she uttered the concluding words, drew herself up with a dignity for which few would have given her credit. But in spite of her good-nature and retiring manner, there were times when she recollected, or seemed to recollect, how the blue blood of the Huntingshire's ran in her veins, mingled with that, on the maternal side, of the haughty De Crespignys, and then Lady Anne, in spite of her smiling freckled countenance and plump little figure, looked every inch an aristocrat.

"It does not necessarily follow, because a trifle is petty and vulgar, that it loses power to irritate," remarked Captain Fuller, who had hitherto refrained from speaking, but who now joined in the fray with a quick decision that seemed to indicate superior knowledge and superior elevation to the public feeling.

"Of course not," assented Lady Anne readily. "I did not mean to convey the idea that we were not wounded by this article, but only that we *ought* not to be—two entirely different things. Practice and theories, however excellent each may be in their way, are often at variance, and as I said before, my father is more annoyed by this business than I believe he would be were he to hear to-morrow a change of Government was imminent, or the country on the eve of a fresh election. Why, do you know, he actually goes so far as to talk of instituting an action for libel against this mysterious unknown, or failing him, against Mr. Quildry. I would not be in poor Mr. Quildry's shoes for something, I know that. I wonder if he already begins to quake?"

"I'm almost afraid," interrupted Colonel Clinker, "that the Earl would hardly be able to show sufficient just cause of complaint to make out a clear case. It is always difficult to bring matters home to the offending party, and although in our own minds there can exist but little doubt as to who the designated parties are, I fail to see exactly how they themselves can bring the affair to any profitable issue."

"Why, Jack! you talk like a Q.C.," said Mrs. Forrester banteringly. "Where and when did you contrive to pick up this vast amount of information?"

"Ah! if you had had as much to do with lawyers in your time as I have had in mine, perhaps you also might have amassed a small smattering of legal knowledge, and learnt that an action for libel is a thing not lightly to be entered upon, even although backed by the Earl of Huntingshire. I predict that in giving still greater publicity to the affair we are unlikely to meet with satisfaction. The answer we should receive would probably be this, or something very like it: 'Foolish people! You choose to feel aggrieved because the cap happens to fit. How can you hold others responsible for such a result? No harm was intended, general expressions employed,' etcetera, etcetera. Don't you understand how artfully the argument might be extended? No, Lady Anne, with all due respect for your father's opinion, we must not have recourse to litigation, but," and his voice assumed a tone of stern determination, "if we can only catch the delinquent before many days have past, then we will take the law into our own hands, and make the wretch smart if we can."

"Bedad, Jack! I agree with you altogether," said Mr. McGrath with considerable warmth, "but what do you say, Miss Brewser?" turning to Kate. "So far you have expressed no opinion."

"I say," returned the girl angrily, "that if anyone believes I have taken an unfair advantage over my neighbours, I am quite willing to return the cup which the Earl presented me with. It would afford me no pleasure whatever to keep an article which I had not honestly won."

"Don't think of parting with the prize, my dear," broke in Mrs. Forrester good-naturedly. "You beat us all fair and square, and whoever says to the contrary speaks an untruth. King Olaf had everything settled at least half a mile from home."

"Thank you, Mrs. Forrester," said Kate, with a hearty glance at the old lady. "Such an assertion gives me fresh heart. I wish, however, to say a few words to those here present about the 'unfair advantage' before alluded to. I believe every one is aware that owing to my fall I was unable to ride my horse myself, besides being utterly ignorant of all matters connected with racing, and that Colonel Clinker," her face grew rosy-red as she uttered his name, "most kindly and good-naturedly came to my assistance. Being under the impression no special rules had been laid down with reference to the ladies' steeplechase, and also that owners were at liberty to prepare their horses in any way they might deem best, I gladly availed myself of his proffered services, little dreaming that by so doing I was laying myself open to a horrible charge. That Colonel Clinker's aid proved an inestimable advantage, I freely admit; but that in availing myself of it I was guilty of any act of intentional unfairness I deny altogether. I can't help feeling, however, that such a statement ought never to have been made public unless the person who advanced it is prepared to come forward and substantiate the truth of his cruel assertion. That, at least, I think I have a right to demand "

She spoke quietly, but clearly and decidedly, as she usually did when greatly in earnest. She possessed in a large degree that rare gift of truthfulness which makes itself felt, and forces conviction on an audience, however unsympathetic at the outset. Here, however, but few were found to disagree, seeing they were all gathered together with one purpose.

"I wonder ," said Lady Anne, who had listened attentively to each speaker in turn, "whether the writer of this article was a man or a woman ?"

The question created an immediate diversion. Somehow the idea of a woman being mixed up in the business did not appear to have entered the heads of many of the company, and the mere suggestion provoked a lively discussion.

"I never even gave the matter a thought," said the Honble. Jack vivaciously. "Of course it's a man, and a common man into the bargain. No lady would be capable of so mean an action."

"Are you quite sure of that ?" asked Captain Fuller quietly.

"Positive, or at least as certain as one can be of anything in this world."

"Ah ! I'm glad you put in a saving clause, for I've known women do very queer things before now—kick over the traces and run anything but kindly, especially when once their jealousy was fully aroused."

"Do you mean to tell me seriously," said Mrs. Forrester, "that you believe the culprit to belong to our own sex ?"

"I make no assertions one way or the other, although personally I entertain a very strong suspicion that a daughter of Eve soiled her fair fingers in the concoction of this very pretty pie."

" Now what on earth makes you think so ? Do you imagine that any woman, no matter how lowly her position in life, would willingly expose the sex of which she forms a part to such sweeping abuse and ridicule ? The thing appears simply preposterous, and, bad as we may be, and many of us are, we are not quite so bad as all that. If any distinct object were gained by such invective one might possibly understand it, but there *is* none—*can* be none to my mind."

" And in so fancying, Mrs. Forrester," said Captain Fuller coolly, " you for once fail to display your usual perspicuity. Now I can imagine a very distinct and conceivable object."

" Really! Well, I admit you puzzle me altogether. Go on."

" I must put the case more clearly. Suppose, then, a certain lady to be actuated by feelings of the acutest jealousy. suppose that she had been outshone by a younger and prettier rival ; suppose all her worst passions were aroused, and a thirst for vengeance, at whatever cost, had overtaken her, can you not conceive that such a lady would not easily be deterred by conventionalities."

" But even then," objected Mrs. Forrester, " she would hardly satirize her own sex indiscriminately. She would content herself with the abuse of the one particular person."

" And by so doing show her cards to all the world! No, no, Mrs. Forrester, a revengeful woman is cleverer than you give her credit for being, and one who is both crafty and malicious into the bargain, so long as she imagines discovery impossible or improbable, will not stop short at anything. The very abuse of which you complain is, in my eyes, nothing but a blind to throw you all off the right scent, and thus lessen any risk of detection. If, as I suppose, the writer be a woman, don't you see that the more she inveighs against her own sex, rails and scoffs at it, the less likely is she to be classed as belonging to it ? There is method, even reason, in her spite, which, to my mind, renders the whole thing exceed-ingly simple."

" There is something in what you say," mused Mrs. For-rester, shaken, though still not wholly convinced, by the other's reasoning.

"Enough, perhaps," continued Captain Fuller sententiously, "to give you a pretty strong clue, if followed up in the right direction."

"And what do you call the 'right direction,' pray?"

"Your own powers of astuteness will probably lead you to discover it, Mrs. Forrester, without any aid from a disinterested party like myself."

"That's mean!" retorted she testily. "Why can't you tell me straight out like a man what you know, instead of giving vent to mysterious hints?"

"But supposing I know nothing?"

"Never mind about that. You suspect somebody, I can see."

"Well, and if I do I have at least sufficient wisdom to keep such suspicions to myself until they prove correct."

"You are a regular Solomon!" exclaimed Mrs. Forrester with a species of reluctant admiration, for Captain Fuller's terse logic, although it impressed, did not please her altogether.

It was not agreeable thinking that the gentleman was behind the scenes, and not only knew more than he chose to impart, but also more than she did. Such a state of things was one which gave birth to grave dissatisfaction, and exasperated her extremely.

"I lay claim to no such exalted pretentions," returned the Captain with mock humility, "although I flatter myself I can see through a stone wall as clearly as most people. Still that's not saying much."

"And you refuse to help me?" persisted Mrs. Forrester, returning to the charge.

"How could I refuse? I merely profess my inability to discover a mystery which puzzles you all. Why should I be supposed to possess superior information?"

"You are tantalizing to a degree," retorted Mrs. Forrester, "for either you are a perfect impostor, or else you take a delight in keeping us in the dark. However, I for one won't *be* kept in the dark. I shall not rest till I elucidate this matter, and find out who the author or authoress of the offensive article was. And when I make up my mind I generally succeed in the long run. I firmly believe in the power of volition; therefore," with a highly expressive shrug of the shoulders, "if you won't help me, why I must help myself, that's all."

"And what do you intend doing?"

"Going straight to the editor and demanding an explanation. I shall call at Mr. Quildry's office to-morrow morning and insist upon his revealing who his objectionable correspondent is."

"If you do that you will prove yourself even cleverer than I imagined. But you won't get old Quildry to give up any business secrets in a hurry. He's far too knowing and too wide awake for that."

"We shall see," said Mrs. Forrester prophetically. "There's no knowing what can be done till one tries, and I mean to have a real good try, any way."

"Poor Quildry!" murmured Captain Fuller compassionately, but luckily the lady did not overhear this expression of pity.

"Quildry," continued she, "is like the rest of the sex, approachable in three ways—through his palate, through his vanity, through his self-interest. The first I shall have no opportunity of attacking, but the two last are sufficient in themselves to insure success when properly nurtured. Sometimes vanity predominates over self-interest, sometimes self-interest over vanity; but a woman with her wits about her can generally effect a masterly stroke of policy by ringing the changes on first one, then the other. My acquaintance with Mr. Quildry has hitherto been confined to a few brief notes passing between us and an occasional visit, so that I have never ascertained which of these three masculine foibles absorbs the larger share of his composition, but I shall soon discover and use the knowledge to my own advantage and to my own ends. If, by hook or by crook, I do not succeed in overcoming Mr. Quildry's objections I shall fall immeasurably in my own estimation, and have entirely to remodel my opinions on men, and the wheels within wheels by which they are influenced."

T

" Well, Mrs. Forrester," said Captain Fuller, "if you succeed, I, on my part, shall believe more implicitly than ever in the power of woman."

And then one by one her guests departed, until Mrs. Forrester remained alone.

" What a sly fox that Fuller is, to be sure!" she ruminated. "I bet ten shillings he knows exactly who has written this article. But when he talks of a woman who on earth can he mean? The paragraph is not devoid a certain coarse talent, but for once I confess myself thoroughly beaten. However, we shall see what to-morrow brings forth!"

And the old lady, like a bloodhound on the trail, kept twisting and turning about each possibility in her mind, trying to make out a furious scout which should lead straight to the desired object; but although she lay awake a goodly portion of the night, she failed to unravel the mystery.

CHAPTER XXIII.

AN UNHAPPY EDITOR.

Mrs. Forrester's energies, however, were fully equal to the occasion, and next morning by ten o'clock she arrived at the unfortunate editor's office, where she found poor Mr. Quildry looking more careworn and sallow even than usual, and up to his eyes in business. Now everybody in Foxington knew Mrs Forrester in a greater or less degree, and she, in return, knew everybody, and was acquainted with the townspeople's most private concerns. Therefore, when she made her appearance, Mr. Quildry raised his weary eyes from the pile of loose sheets they were engaged in deciphering, and wished the lady good-morning with unwonted animation.

"Good-morning, Mr. Quildry," said she, acknowledging the salutation in her customary offhand manner. "Busy, as usual, I perceive!"

"Yes, madam, very," he replied, with a sigh of dejection.

Mr. Quildry suffered from a torpid digestion, and there were times when the ills of life appeared unendurable to the harassed, bad-constitutioned, and overworked man—times when he was wont to stroll out of a summer evening after the day's toil was over and gaze at the little peaceful green churchyard, a mile or so out on the main high-road, with an aching longing for rest and a weary distaste of life crowding up in his tired brain; but now he gave a smile, pitiful from its transparency and evident effort, and prepared himself to inquire into Mrs. Forrester's wishes. She, however, anticipated his civility by going straight to the point without any preliminaries calculated to soften the severity of the lecture she intended to administer.

"I will not keep you long, Mr. Quildry," she said, "bu. I have come to say a little word about that article on the ladies' steeplechase which appeared in your paper a few days ago."

Mr. Quildry changed colour, and the smile vanished as quickly as it had been conjured up.

"Indeed, madam!" he said in a quavering voice, strongly suggestive of inward perturbation. "I hope no offence was given?"

"Now, Mr. Quildry, what a thing for you to suppose—you who have had so much experience. Why, of *course* offence was given. How could it possibly have been otherwise, considering the nature of the publication?"

She spoke with a fierce asperity which startled Mr. Quildry most alarmingly.

"I'm extremely sorry, madam," he murmured uncomfortably, fidgeting on his hard, shiny stool, "extremely sorry."

"Sorry! And well you may be. It will be a good day for you, Mr. Quildry, when you succeed in clearing yourself of any responsibility in this matter. That article ought never to have been allowed to appear in a respectable paper like yours. It was a gross piece of impertinence, and, I can tell you, has given the greatest offence in very high quarters. Yes"—as the guilty Quildry writhed beneath the indignant expression of her keen eyes—"you have put your foot into it nicely. Your wits must have been wool-gathering when you committed so heinous an act of folly, and unluckily for you the Earl of Huntingshire, who generally takes but little notice of such things, is simply furious at the allusions made. In fact Lady Anne Birkett was only saying yesterday she never remembered seeing her father so upset. A pretty position for you to have placed yourself in, Mr. Quildry, and what will come of it all heaven only knows! The town of Foxington is in a perfect uproar—Colonel Clinker, Mr. McGrath, Mr. Grahame, Captain Fuller, Miss Brewser, all of them wild with anger. There was a meeting at my house yesterday, and the long and the short of the whole thing is I am deputed to call upon you and demand an explanation or an apology. Tell me who wrote that article?"

Mr. Quildry found it impossible to evade the stern severity of this last demand. His house and premises were let to him on a yearly lease by the Earl of Huntingshire, in whose power it lay to turn him out. Therefore, when the wretched man heard how he had incurred his landlord's displeasure, he quaked in his thick, ill-made boots.

With a tremendous effort at self-control he mustered up sufficient courage to reply.

" I really can't say, madam, who the party was. It's quite against our regulations and rules of business ever to give information as to our correspondents."

" You'll have to waive those rules and regulations, then, for once," said Mrs. Forrester curtly.

" It would never answer," protested Mr. Quildry. " We should get into a perfect sea of trouble, and be tossed about on contrary waves."

He was rather given to interspersing his conversation with flowery metaphor, but such elegances of speech were completely wasted upon Mrs. Forrester.

" Never mind about the contrary waves," she said impatiently, " and as for the sea of trouble, it strikes me you are pretty well immersed in that as it is."

" You see, madam," said Mr. Quildry with explanatory brevity, " people very often send money to pay for the insertion of paragraphs just as they would do for an advertisement, and then we are more or less bound to let them appear."

" In other words, Mr. Quildry, you make friends with the mammon of unrighteousness."

" That's an ugly name for it, madam," said he, feeling there was a Scriptural flavour about the allusion distressing in the extreme to so good a churchgoer as himself.

Then, goaded into sudden exasperation, he added—

" We poor devils of printers are literally beset with difficulties quite beyond the public comprehension. We are the scapegoats on whose backs blows are showered by the score and who receive no sympathy whatever."

" Don't talk nonsense, Mr. Quildry," said Mrs. Forrester. once more transfixing the unhappy editor with a scrutinizingly stony gaze. "By your own confession you take money to publish objectionable matter—not a particularly cleanly proceeding; but surely it is your duty to exercise some discretion as to what *does* and what does *not* appear in the columns of your newspaper. You are the person to be held responsible, as the Earl of Huntingshire justly observed, and the shortest way for you to get out of the mess is to tell me the author's name without further delay. It is just possible by so doing that I may be able to conciliate the Earl in time."

"But, madam, really I cannot. It would go against my con—"

"Now, Mr. Quildry, don't be a fool," interrupted the lady. "You have got a very comfortable berth of it here, and until this unfortunate episode occurred have managed to give general satisfaction. Why should you allow one false step like the present to do away with the labour of years? Everybody makes mistakes now and again, but there is nothing like rectifying them in time, and before the mischief goes too far."

"I'm sure, madam, I am willing to do everything in my power," said Mr. Quildry, feeling resistance to be vain as opposed to such cruel, hard, practical common sense. "I've no wish to sacrifice my prospects, poor as they are."

"That's right," said she more amiably. "You are a really superior man, Mr. Quildry, whose intelligence is deserving of better things than a county office, and I should like to tell you a little story. There was once a poor weakly gosling hatched by the side of a broad stream, whose current rolled with great rapidity over the rocky boulders and smooth, rounded stones. The gosling was young, ignorant, enterprising, and ambitious. He believed implicitly in himself, and therefore, in spite of the mother goose's repeated warnings, he needs must venture into the troubled waters, full of self-confidence and self-conceit. He fancied he could swim like the sturdy old swan who sat pluming his feathers all day long in the sunlight; but alas! this foolish gosling choked, and gasped, and gurgled, until at last he got engulphed in a whirlpool, and would have sunk had not the mother goose rushed to his assistance and seized him in her strong, yellow beak.

"'There, you simpleton,' she said, giving him a push in the direction of dry land. 'Don't you understand that you are too weak to oppose so strong a torrent? Nothing is to be gained by such an act of folly. The waters flow on just the same and you are lost, whereas if you would only exercise a little sense, and float with the stream instead of against it, you would soon learn how capitally you can swim. I am your mother. Take my advice, and never do such a stupid thing again.'

"Now, Mr. Quildry, try and put yourself in the place of the gosling, and imagine me to be the mother goose. Can you derive no instruction from the tale?"

"A very pretty story indeed, madam," said he uneasily; "quite poetical."

"Don't bother your head about the poetry, man. Stick to the prose, and try and glide into smooth water once more if you can; and whatever you do, don't attempt to set yourself up in opposition to the Earl. Now I'll tell you what I'll promise. If you will be sensible, and give up the name of the person who has brought about all this mischief, I will undertake no blame shall attach to you, and that the thing shall blow over without further trouble. There, that's fair enough, surely."

"And what if I declare I don't know it?" said Mr. Quildry, completely overcome by Mrs. Forrester's forcible rhetoric, and taking up a final standing-place on the crumbling hillock of equivocation.

"I should not believe you. If you don't know it you *ought* to know it, and, moreover, can easily ascertain; so no more idle subterfuges. *You* call yourself an editor, indeed," turning down the corners of her mouth contemptuously. "A pretty editor, when you do not even know what goes on between your own four walls. Why, one might just as well be a dummy at once! However, it's no use talking. There's the article written in black and white, and here are we, the ladies and gentlemen of Huntingshire, all feeling equally insulted, and if you either can't or won't reveal the author's name, why the Earl will probably proceed to stronger measures, and take such steps as may force you to do so in the end."

Once again at this terrible mention of the magnate's name poor Mr. Quildry displayed the most profound consternation. Self-interest was dragging him one way, some few remaining scruples of honour the other, and between the two never was man more hopelessly distracted or thoroughly wretched. As a last resource the unhappy editor took refuge in pitiful entreaty.

"Please, Mrs. Forrester," he cried, with a whining and semi-incoherent voice, "be merciful. You place me in a truly terrible position, for on the one hand I run the risk of mortally offending the Earl of Huntingshire, on the other of casting a stigma upon my professional character from which it may never recover in the future."

"You should have thought of all that before allowing such an article to appear in your newspaper," retorted she, perfectly unmoved by the appeal. "It's not a bit of use crying over spilt milk; the wisest thing is to dry it up immediately, so as to do away with the stain as quickly as possible. If people *will* walk through a muddy lane instead of sticking to a nice clean pathway, they must not be surprised to find they dirty their shoeleather, and that some of the mud remains. You are only reaping the consequences of your acts, Mr. Quildry, and it is nobody's fault but your own if you find them somewhat unpleasant."

"Ah, madam!" said he, still vainly endeavouring to elicit some small token of sympathy, "the world is a hard place for a poor struggling working man like myself. There is not much charity to be found in it. You do not know what a life mine is; nothing but perpetual worry and perpetual toil from the time I raise my head from the pillow until I lay it down again at night. We have eight small children to provide for, and there's my wife expecting her confinement at Christmas, and a delicate woman into the bargain."

"More shame to you then, Mr. Quildry," said Mrs. Forrester with a severity not wholly genuine, for beneath all her eccentricities of manner beat a warm and kindly heart. "Your quiver was already full enough."

"That may be, madam," came the solemn reply, "but children are the gift of the Lord."

"Yes, like thunder and lightning, like disease and pesti-
lence. A little of them goes a long way, I should imagine.
However, we are wandering from the subject in hand, and
since you said you were busy it is a pity to waste valuable
moments unnecessarily. For the last time, Mr. Quildry, will
you or won't you give me the information I desire?"

She leant her two elbows on the table and looked him
straight in the face with her piercing eyes.

He changed colour under their sharp gaze, and shifted
uneasily in his seat with a weak gesture of despair.

"Don't be so hard upon me," he sighed.

"I don't wish to be hard upon you, Mr. Quildry," she
answered, "but you will have to do this thing sooner or later,
and therefore no good can be gained by procrastinating."

He had fought better than she expected, but the battle was
now won.

"You will think it strange, madam," he said, "that I
really do not know who wrote the article in question. I was
so busy myself writing the leading articles on our agricultural
show and other county matters that really for once I was
forced to leave the compilation of all minor paragraphs to my
head clerk, and I assure you I was as much astonished as
anybody when I saw the criticism of the ladies' steeplechase
among the columns of my own paper."

"That I can easily believe," said Mrs. Forrester grimly.

She had played her fish with great dexterity and address,
but his dying struggles were beginning to grow monotonous
and aroused impatience in the angler's bosom.

"Go at once and see your head clerk," she added imperi-
ously, "for I must be getting on, or I shall lose my day's
hunting. I am late as it is," drawing out a huge old-
fashioned watch from the recess in which it found an habi-
tual dwelling-place.

And Mr. Quildry did her bidding without further parley,
although knowing perfectly well that he had lied when he
declared that he was ignorant of the author's name, yet
having lied, determined to stick to the untruth through thick
and thin.

Presently he returned, with such a subdued and woebegone expression as surely would have struck most ordinary women with compassion.

"Well!" exclaimed Mrs. Forrester eagerly as he re-appeared.

"The article in question was handed in at our office on Thursday evening by a groom, who had orders to pay for its immediate insertion.

The words seemed literally dragged from Mr. Quildry's pale lips, but Mrs. Forrester's basilisk eyes were fixed upon him, searching him through and through, and exercising the same weird fascination that a poisonous reptile does on a defenceless singing-bird. She was completely master of the situation, and the strong will subjugated the weaker.

"Who did the groom belong to?" she asked impatiently.

Even then Mr. Quildry trembled to utter the words aloud. He leant forward and whispered one single name in Mrs. Forrester's ear.

The change that forthwith took place in that lady's face was most remarkable. The mouth opened, the eyes enlarged, the eyebrows arched themselves with surprise and indignation.

"Good gracious!" she exclaimed breathlessly. "Are you positive of this?"

"Quite positive," came the melancholy rejoinder.

"Impossible! There must be some mistake!"

"No, madam, there is no mistake. It is exactly as I tell you."

"Well I never. You *have* astonished me!"

"And you will remember your promise, Mrs. Forrester? You will do your best to shield me from the Earl's anger?"

"Mr. Quildry, when *I* make a promise I always endeavour to keep it. Rest assured that I shall use all my influence on your behalf."

"Thank you, madam, you are very kind," said he, con-siderably comforted by the turn things were taking.

"No, Mr. Quildry, I am *not* kind, only just, and"—smiling graciously at him—"I am glad to see that you are a gosling so amenable to reason, and have so quickly perceived the policy of not opposing a roaring torrent. And now I must really be going, or my poor horse will die of catarrh. Good-bye, Mr. Quildry I take my leave with a very high opinion of your intelligence, and a hope that Mrs. Quildry may spend a happy new year with number nine."

So saying Mrs. Forrester departed, leaving Mr. Quildry to digest her farewell speeches as best he might.

For a long time he remained standing mutely gazing after the receding vehicle. Then a glimmering light of shrewd reason lit up his dull eyes as he shook his head dubiously and muttered—

" A very remarkable woman that, an exceedingly remarkable woman, in fact; but all the same I'm glad she's not Mrs. Quildry, for she would worm every secret out of me just like a maggot worms its way into a ripe nut, and leave me no peace till nothing but the empty shell remained. These clever women are not pleasant to live with; they *will* have their own way, and don't understand the art of knocking under."

With which ruminations Mr. Quildry returned to his stool and tried to seek oblivion in hard work, but he was far too much worried and distressed to gain the consolation he desired, and the sound of the storm he had been instrumental in raising still seemed to whistle round his ears with an ugly persistency not calculated to enhance the merit of any literary compositions he was engaged upon.

A sombre smile overspread Mrs. Forrester's countenance directly she found herself clear of the town.

" Hum!" she said half aloud, as if speaking the thoughts that were uppermost in her mind. "It does not do to under-rate one's neighbours altogether. Tit for tat. That woman has bided her time. Nevertheless she has contrived to pay me out for the horse I sold her nearly three years ago, which happened, unfortunately, to turn unsound very shortly afterwards. Well, we are quits now at any rate. She has wiped that score from my conscience, and if she wishes for war henceforth, war to the knife let it be."

It was long since old Resurrection had felt the whip so smartly applied to his lean sides, or since he had been called

upon to get over the ground at such a slashing trot, but Mrs.
Forrester was not only in a hurry, but also burning with
impatience to impart the remarkable news she had succeeded
in eliciting from Mr. Quildry.   She anticipated a triumph
dear to her soul.   To her great delight she found the hounds
still engaged in drawing a large wood close to the meet, and
people were standing about in clusters of twos and threes
coffee-housing.   She lost no time in mounting and accosting
Captain Fuller.

"Well," said she, with an unmistakable air of victory,
"I have found out all about it, as I vowed I should do before
long."

"All about what?" he asked, for a moment forgetting their
argument.

"Why, about Miss Palliser, of course.   You knew from the
first, only you would not tell, and gave me all this trouble for
nothing."

"Not for nothing, Mrs. Forrester.   Had I mentioned Miss
Palliser's name in the first instance, the probabilities are you
would have laughed my suspicions to scorn."

"Well, perhaps I should," she admitted frankly.   "I was
a terrible old fool, but somehow or other, in spite of all the
hints you threw out she never once entered my head.   I
wonder still what her little game was."

"Oh! feminine jealousy and spite.   The Palliser is naturally of a vindictive turn of mind, and one who would never
forgive another woman for defeating her.   There is a want of
generosity about Miss Palliser's character."

"Yes, there's no denying her to be a dangerous woman.
I knew she was what the French call a *mauvaise langue*, but I
had no idea she could write.   She would make her fortune as
a critic—one of your cut-me-down, pull-them-all-to-pieces sort
of people."

"She'd fill that *rôle* beautifully.   Still she would have to
moderate the vigour of her style if she wished to keep clear
of shoals.   But now tell me what you mean to do?   Are you
still bent on revenge?"

"Most decidedly.   I shall inform all my friends **and**

acquaintances of Miss Palliser's conduct and beg them to show her the cold shoulder. Between us all I fancy we can make things a trifle too hot to be altogether pleasant."

She was as good as her word, and in ten minutes' time every soul out hunting that day, either on horseback or on wheels, had learnt who was the authoress of the offending article that had appeared in the *County Sporting Chronicle*. They one and all agreed to cut Miss Palliser dead.

By-and-by the lady appeared, quite unsuspicious, from the inner recesses of the wood, where she had been ploughing up and down through a sea of mud, and perceiving Colonel Clinker, Mrs. Forrester, Mr. McGrath, and Kate standing talking together close to the gate by which she gained egress, said with impudent assurance—

"Good-morning, Mrs. Forrester; good-morning, Miss Brewser; morning, Colonel Clinker."

The two ladies returned her greeting with a frigid stare and never moved a muscle by way of recognition, but Jack Clinker made his horse pace one step in advance, and sternly fastening his grey-blue eyes on Miss Palliser's small twinkling ones said, with a cutting dignity of manner—

"Madam, *we*, the members of Sir Beauchamp Lenard's hounds, beg to offer our congratulations on your literary talents, but at the same time we decline the honour of your further acquaintance."

The cat evidently was out of the bag, and Miss Palliser knew the game to be at an end. She turned ghastly pale and her thin lips quivered with the mortification and regret attendant upon unwelcome discovery.

She never said a single word in reply, but she turned her good hunter sharply away with a quick jerk of her powerful wrist and set his head straight for home, although at that very moment the hounds were giving tongue in covert, and a fox had just been viewed away over the nearest field. Her revenge had been but of brief duration, and now exposure had overtaken and disgraced her.

As she moved through the crowd not a soul gave a nod of recognition. Even Mrs Paget pretended not to see her as she passed, and if ever a woman were punished Miss Palliser was at that moment. Bitterly indeed did she regret the angry folly, amounting to madness, which had caused her to copy out many of those rounded periods from certain old society papers she happened to have by her, and which had led her into so terrible a quandary.

CHAPTER XXIV.

JACK CLINKER EXPLAINS HIS FINANCIAL DIFFICULTIES.

IF pleasant moments pass away on this earth all too quickly, there remains at least a counterbalancing advantage in the steady passage of unpleasant ones. Oft-abused time possesses the virtue of strict impartiality. His inexorable hand moves on, alike indifferent to pleasure and to pain, equalising all in turn as it sweeps over them. Were it not so, the human mind must give way under the strain far oftener than it does, for if our sufferings always retained their acuteness, if with the lapse of days and months and years their fresh edge did not gradually become blunted, then life indeed would be unendurable. But a merciful Providence has ordained other-wise, in the majority of cases, and time soothes our wounds as he dulls our joys. So by degrees the incidents recorded in the last chapter faded gently from men's minds, until at length they ceased to occupy any prominent position therein, and harmony was once more restored. New topics of con-versation arose to banish the old, for oftentimes the more eagerly a subject is discussed, the more liable is it to become exhausted.

The month of December was ushered in with cold, white sea-fogs, which wreathed all the country in sullen mists, moistening the naked branches of the stripped trees and the pointed spikes of the blackthorn in the hedgerows. Rain also descended in torrents, and once or twice the hounds had to be taken home in the middle of the day, owing to the impossibility of following them through the heavy fog. The sodden leaves lay in heaps upon the saturated ground, while ditches began to open out and to reveal hitherto unseen

though not altogether unsuspected depths. The roads were
ankle-deep in rich brown mud, and the brooks and rivers in
the neighbourhood came swirling down charged with all sorts
of refuse in such rapid torrents that in many cases they broke
through their banks and flooded all the meadows and low-
lying ground, so that acres upon acres of water met the eye
in every direction. Hunting people grumbled, left all considerations of personal appearance at home, arrayed themselves in covert-coats, comforters, pot hats, and nondescript
waterproof garments of every shape and size, prior to splashing through the treacherous moisture and resisting a further
downfall; while many of the less enthusiastic, or more luxurious, either hurried up to the Metropolis under pretence of
witnessing the last new piece at the Gaiety, or stayed at home
reading French novels of a spicy nature and smoking long
cherry-wood pipes, declaring hunting under such circumstances
was not " good enough," and reiterating with more force than
originality the well-known saying about the folly of making
" a toil of your pleasures." Farmers shook their heads dolefully—all outdoor labour having come to a standstill—talked
in a dismally prophetic strain of the weather and their future
prospects, declaring, with customory and annual forebodings,
"times were shocking bad, and the country was going fast to
the dogs "—though with all due respect to these worthy agricultural authorities, it certainly looked more like being given
over to the fishes than to any dry-footed animal.

The declining days of the old year were speeding away in
damp and in misery. It seemed as if the sky wept out of
sympathy for the loss of an ancient friend, and the sun hid
his bright face among the lowering clouds, refusing to give
forth a single ray of sunshine by way of comfort. Nothing
more dreary could possibly have been imagined. Yet through
it all hunting struggled on, and horses also, while the wet
state of the ground apparently gave rise to a marvellous scent,
and such runs were recorded as but very few of the whole
large field ever managed to see the end of, for the steeds
sobbed and laboured through the deluged pastures, sending
the water squelching up each time it rose above their fetlock-

joints, and none but the very stoutest, strongest animals, a
stone or two beyond their rider's weight, could hope to live
through many hours of such work.   Some broke down hopelessly, some banged their joints and hit their legs, whilst
others again lost flesh, refused to eat, and looked like living
scarecrows.   To those who owned cattle not quite up to the
mark, it was doubly provoking to witness from a distance
becoming with each mile more and more enforced, many a
truly first-class run.   The wise sportsman was he who dis-
sembled and shielded the failing powers of his horse from
universal discovery.   An excuse was easily found—a lost shoe
a train to catch, or telegram to send off, were sufficient to
cover a timely retreat.   But this wet weather, greatly as it
was disliked by the majority, suited the Duckling exactly.
Hounds were unable to travel quite so fast as on the top of
the ground, and he could stay all day.   He literally revelled
in dirt, and galloped through it like a steam-engine.   After
an unusually fine run, in which he had covered himself
with glory, Kate Browser, wet to the skin but greatly elated
in spirit, found herself riding in the direction of Foxington,
with Colonel Clinker as her companion.

They now usually rode home together, and it had become
quite a recognised thing that they should do so, while during
the many miles they had covered side by side they had
attained a very confidential and intimate footing.   These two
young people suited each other, and found in many respects
their tastes, ideas, and inclinations were very similar.   Kate
was fond of her theories, and had all a girl's enthusiasm for
high and noble aims in life; and although he invariably
laughed at her remarks at the time, vowing they were too
highly pitched, he often ultimately adopted her views; whilst
she learnt daily to recognise more and more the inherent
goodness and kindliness of his disposition, and to look to it
with a perfect trust, which far greater talents might possibly
have failed to inspire.

"I'm always asking favours of you, Miss Brewser," said
Colonel Clinker, as they subsided into a walk, after a long,
steady jog, during which neither of them had uttered more

than an occasional fragmentary exclamation; "I want you to do me one now."

"I should say it was the other way about," returned Kato, ducking her head so as to allow a small stream of water to escape from the brim of her pot hat. "What is it? Nothing very terrible I hope?"

"Oh no, not at all. But I want you to come to Sandown next week. The races are on Thursday and Friday. You told me once 'that one good turn deserves another.' Well, I helped you through *your* steeplechase in a sort of way—at least, you were kind enough to say so—and now I want you to help me through mine."

"How do you mean through yours? You never mentioned it before?"

"No, because I feel ashamed of bothering you with all my little private affairs. Good-natured as you are in listening to them, I can't believe they possess any special interest," looking at her curiously.

"Are *you* going to ride?" she asked, a deeper flush mounting to her fresh, damp cheeks, than even their long trot could have accounted for.

"Yes."

"And you want *me* to come and look on?" She put the question in a subdued voice, for her heart was beating fast at the very thought.

"Would you think it very conceited if I said that I did?" She turned her head away without answering.

"Will you come?" he said persuasively, not realising that anything in her power to grant she would concede to him, for true love renders people curiously modest and distrustful of their own power to please.

"Yes, if I can." She spoke very softly, but something in the manner of uttering the words seemed to please him, for his face brightened instantaneously.

"That's all right," he said heartily. "So now I'll tell you all about it. You must know I expect to have a pretty busy time at Sandown, for I have promised to ride horses belonging to at least half-a-dozen different fellows, besides which I

intend running dear old Snowflake in the United Hunters'
Steeplechase. The entries this year are decidedly poor, but
the race itself is worth close upon five hundred, so that I have
pretty well made up my mind to have a shy at it. Snowflake
too, was never better in his life, and the heavy going is all in
his favour. It suits him. He and the Duckling are just a
pair in that respect. Snowflake is an awfully sound-winded
horse, exactly the sort to make light of a hill to finish against,
and I can't help thinking he possesses an uncommonly fair
chance of winning. You won't grudge giving up a couple of
days' hunting for once in a way, in order to see Snowflake
distinguish himself, will you?"

"Yes, I shall, tremendously," she said with a smile which
effectually succeeded in contradicting the assertion. "If I
hear when I come back that they have had a good run I shall
be as savage as a bear."

"Well, so shall I for the matter of that, though it's always
one's luck. . However," speaking in tones of confident cheeri-
ness, "we will have an awfully jolly time of it. We will all
run up to town together on Wednesday evening after
hunting"—

"Who's all?" interrupted she mischievously.

"Oh! you and I—and—and Miss Whitbread, I suppose, Mr. Grahame, and Terry. By-the-bye, has it ever
struck you that those two young people rather fancy each
other?"

"Which two young people?" feigning complete ignorance

"Why, Miss Whitbread and the Chirper, of course."

"Dear me! Fancy your having only just found that out!
Men *are* dull."

"Then you admit to having noticed a flirtation in that
direction?"

"I don't know. Mary never flirts in the true acceptation
of the term; she is romantic, and fancies herself in love
instead."

"And you—what do you do? Is your nature a similar
one?"

"Don't be so silly," giving the Duckling's rotund sides a

little impatient kick with the heel. "How else are we to amuse ourselves when we go up to town?"

"Why, we'll go to a theatre together on the first night, races again the following day, and catch the eight o'clock special back, which will land us safe and sound at Foxington somewhere about ten thirty p.m. What do you say to the programme? Does it please your majesty?"

"Very much indeed, if only it can be carried out."

"Why do you say '*if?*' There are no insuperable difficulties to be overcome?"

"Insuperable, no—difficulties, yes. To begin with, nice things never *do* come off according to our anticipations; and secondly, I doubt very much if Mary, who is so strong on the proprieties, will consider you and Mr. McGrath sufficient chaperones for two young ladies at a public theatre."

"Oh, bother the chaperone! Can't you raise a placid old woman somewhere?"

"What a disrespectful way of talking!" exclaimed Kate with a laugh.

"Do you mean to say the whole thing is to be knocked on the head for such nonsense?"

"I didn't say that; anyhow, I promise to talk the matter over with Mary when I get home, and see how best the outing can be managed. You know," playfully, "I don't dare do anything without consulting Mary Whitbread. She prevents my tumbling into no end of scrapes."

"Tell Miss Whitbread from me that Mr. Grahame says *he* will go if *she* does."

"Now that's nasty of you, trying to gain a mean advantage, and I shan't tell her any such thing."

"'Pon my soul, I believe the Chirper's most awfully spooney. I do indeed, Miss Browser, and it would be only charitable to give the young people a chance. The Chirper is not half a bad fellow."

"Since when, may I ask, have you developed these match-making propensities?"

"Oh, I don't know; not very long. This winter I think."

"Then if the habit be so recently acquired as all that, you

will not probably find much difficulty in discontinuing it,"
said Kate, with a mischievous spirit upon her. "I *hate* match-
making. No good ever comes of it." She was thinking of
that melancholy attempt at match-making of her Uncle Campbell's. Presently she added after a slight pause, "If Mr.
Grahame *really* cares for Mary, as you say, he is free to speak
to her of his own accord, and interference from a third party
is as unnecessary as it is injudicious."

Now when a man makes a suggestion, even in fun, and
finds that suggestion accepted with serious disfavour, he is
apt to draw in his horns like a sensitive snail, and feel rather
small. Colonel Clinker cleared his throat once or twice, and
said testily—

"I beg your pardon, Miss Brewser. I'm sorry I spoke.
I presume you will give up all idea of going to Sandown,
then?"

He sat quite straight up in the saddle, and looked steadily
out before him at the driving rain. It was clear to his mind
she had no wish to go, and therefore she should not see that
he cared one way or the other. It had been a silly fancy on
his part, not wholly free from vanity, desiring she should
witness Snowflake's success. His victory was a matter of
indifference to Miss Brewser. After all it was but natural,
and least said soonest mended. So Jack Clinker argued to
himself in his quickly aroused pride. But Kate, half guess
ing what caused his annoyance, said airily—

"You are very ready in your surmises, Colonel Clinker; in
fact, almost amusingly so, but for once they are not distinguished by their usual accuracy. I have *not* given up the
idea of going to Sandown at all; on the contrary, directly I get
home I mean to ask Mary to write to an aunt of hers living
in town, a Mrs. Tryon, and beg her to put us up for a couple
of nights, so there!"

She uttered the last words in a little mocking tone, which
nevertheless restored him to complete good humour. He could
not feel angry with her for long, though she had a malicious
way of taking up his speeches, and turning and twisting them,
which was decidedly irritating at times, especially to a man

grown over sensitive from a love he had not yet dared to avow. But now all was right again between them.

"I see you are bent on the chaperone," he said gaily. "You won't believe what a capital hand I am at looking after young ladies."

"I can quite believe that if you are not it is from no lack of experience," retorted Kate vivaciously. "Nevertheless, without wishing to place any slur upon your capacity, I think I shall feel more secure under the wing of a fat, good-natured, middle-aged lady like Mrs. Tryon."

"Oh! if she's fat and good-natured I'll forgive her for being a duenna. It's the lean, energetic ones I dislike, who are like parched peas in a tin pot, and whose restless, piercing eyes seem to look you through and through."

"If you were an immaculate young man, you ought not to object to the process."

"But I'm *not* an *immaculate young man*, and therefore I do. A constant espionage over one is enough to make the best-conducted individual in this world break loose now and again."

"And yet," said Kate sympathetically, "one can't help feeling sorry for the poor things. All the odium falls to their share, and but little of the enjoyment. It must be wearisome work sitting all night long and never dancing a step, with only supper, like a single oasis in the desert, to support and cheer the fainting spirit. But tell me, how long is it since you decided on running Snowflake?"

"Only since I've seen the entries."

"I wonder you have never raced him before."

"I have in out of the way country places; the fact of the matter is, however, he is such a magnificent hunter I never could bring myself to lose his services for so long a period."

"And if it is not an impertinent question, what has reconciled you to doing so now?"

"Don't you remember my telling you the race was worth a monkey? That sum, Miss Brewser," looking unusually grave, "is not to be despised, especially when a fellow is so awfully hard up as I am. I don't mind owning to you that it will be a very serious matter indeed for me if the old horse does not pull through next week, for I shall scarcely know which way to turn for that valuable commodity, R.M.D. I've got ten to one against Snowflake, and I've backed him altogether to win close upon two thousand pounds. If the coup only comes off I shall be in clover, but if it don't—well, I really hardly know what on earth possesses me to give you this detailed account of my financial difficulties—I shall in all probability have to make a bolt of it."

"A bolt of it?" echoed Kate, failing to understand his meaning.

"Yes, go away somewhere for a bit to give one's creditors the slip. Disappear from society, and reside for a space in a retired French watering town." He spoke with an assumed levity which but badly hid the underlying current of anxiety he found it impossible wholly to conceal.

"Oh, how dreadful!" exclaimed Kate, thoroughly distressed at this prospect.

"Do you think so?" he said with a forced smile. "Plenty of people make occasional Continental tours, and return after a lengthened period thoroughly whitewashed. Perhaps the operation might do me good, and wipe away the stains of accumulated years."

"I wish you would not talk like that, even in fun. I can't bear it."

"I wish it was fun," he answered moodily, "but it's sober earnest, Miss Brewser," with a sudden fit of candour, feeling he should like her to learn the worst; "you do not know what a bad fellow I am, a regular spendthrift."

"You may be a spendthrift, but you are not bad. I won't allow you to call yourself by such hard names in my presence."

"I'm awfully worried," continued he, finding once he had commenced, confession seemed easier than he had expected. "Only this very morning the forage-dealer sent in a bill for three hundred pounds, and actually had the impertinence to declare he must be paid within a week."

"You should not call it impertinence," said she in tones of grave reprimand. "The man has a right to claim his own, and I daresay has already displayed considerable forbearance."

"But what am I to do? I *can't* pay him. It's utterly impossible, till something turns up. He ought to have sense enough to know that."

"You can sell one or two of your horses surely. Opal would fetch a lot of money, perhaps enough to pay the whole debt."

"Opal!" opening his eyes indignantly. "Why, I would not sell her if I were as poor as a church mouse and had not fifty pounds at the bank."

"You are wrong; you ought to," she said decidedly.

In her innocence and inexperience she could not imagine a man, and a gentleman, leading a luxurious life and satisfying every want, yet unable to meet his legitimate engagements. Her notions about such things were exceedingly strict, for she had derived most of them from her Uncle Campbell. Colonel Clinker was pulling viciously at the ends of his fair moustache.

"Do you object to my plain speaking?" she asked gently. "Of course I know I have no right to advise or interfere."

It was on the tip of his tongue to say, "I wish to God you had," but he refrained, and contented himself with a simple, but somewhat moody, "No."

"People should not incur debts they cannot afford to defray," continued the girl. "It's almost as bad as cheating. Don't you see how mean an action it is to make some poor man, who probably cannot afford to lose half so well as you can, pay for enjoyments which common honesty would forego? I am sure you would think so too if you would only consider the matter a little."

There was a simplicity, a freshness, an earnestness about her reproof which touched him to the quick.

"I told you I was a bad fellow," he repeated in depreciatory abasement.

"And I," said she, with decision, "tell you you are *not* bad, only careless, and perhaps a little too much given to self-indulgence. Your heart is good, and so are your abilities."

"The former profits me nothing, the latter I have never turned to better account than a professional jockey," he replied bitterly. "Under such circumstances what would you have me do?"

"Do?" echoed she with flashing eyes and slightly raised voice. "I would *work*—go out into the world, give up all the little petty luxuries which enslave and deteriorate, put my shoulder to the wheel, and earn my bread by honest toil, until such time, as Longfellow says, I could 'look the whole world in the face, and owe not any man.' Anything rather than defraud my neighbours."

"That is easier said than done. Practically, if one turns oneself into a working man, and gains say a pound a week by the sweat of one's brow, life would not be long enough to pay off arrears."

"I would rather be the working man on a pound a week with an honourable ambition, than he who lives in idleness and corruption."

His brow darkened as he listened to her words. In his heart he knew she was right; he honoured her sentiments, and yet he did his very best to combat and reduce them into insignificance.

"Talking is easy enough," he said impatiently, "but in my position you have no idea how great the temptations are to spend money. It flows like water on every side, often without any power on my part to hinder it. The regimental expenses mount up enormously to begin with; no one would believe to what an extent who was not behind the scenes. Then we guardsmen are always knocking about town, and expected to entertain our friends, dispense hospitality, and put our hands in our pockets on every occasion."

"You might exchange into a cavalry regiment."

"Yes, and be ordered off to India. I've often thought of doing so, but the old governor objects to the plan. · It's very easy for rich fellows with several thousands a year to keep clear of debt. If I had lots of tin to-morrow I'd never owe a sixpence, but do you know what my income is?"

She fancied he might think she wanted to acquaint herself with the state of his finances, and a shrinking delicacy from any such thought made her say hastily, "Not in the least, but please don't tell me. It can make no difference one way or the other."

Perhaps she herself hardly knew that she loved him so well money could never come between them, that were he a Crœsus or a pauper it was equally indifferent to her; but he, as usual, put a totally different construction on her meaning.

"I'm not such a big fool as to fancy for one moment it *could* make any difference to you," he said irritably, "nevertheless, for my own satisfaction, I should like you to be informed of the fact that I possess but eight hundred a year. Now," narrowly scanning her features, "can you wonder if, upon so paltry a sum, I find it next door to impossible to make both ends meet? is it matter for surprise if debts accumulate in an alarming fashion and payment becomes a mockery? or do you still blame me as much as ever?"

"Yes," she said steadily, raising her clear eyes to his with a fearless gaze, "I do. To use your own words, I blame you just as much as ever. Instead of cutting your coat according to your cloth, ever since you first entered the army you have apparently been living beyond your means—spending money, in fact, which is not yours to spend. I have already expressed my views on that subject. What you ought to do is to exercise a certain amount of self-denial, give up some of your pleasures—even, if needs be, reduce your stud."

"What, and go away from Foxington in the middle of the hunting season?"

Her lip trembled, but she steadied her voice bravely and said "Yes."

"Well, you *are* a Job's comforter," he said with an audible sigh.

"Am I? Won't you acknowledge me to be in the right?" she replied, trying to speak cheerily. "I mean all for the best."

He hesitated. There was a struggle going on within him. Then suddenly his better nature gained the upper hand over self, long habit, and acquired inclinations. "I know you do," he said frankly, "and I know also that you are right and that I am a regular brute; but if Sno flake wins I promise to turn over a new leaf and become a reformed character. Kate," and his voice softened, and the grey-blue eyes shot out an electric dart which thrilled her very being, "Kate, will you be my mentor and help me in my good resolutions?' I almost think that if you would I might improve in earnest. Nobody has ever talked to me like this, or acquired such influence over me since my dear mother died."

Her tears were rising fast, but she could not bear that he should see them, or that she, who was usually so self-possessed and cool, should be caught thus deeply moved. Woman-like, she sought refuge in a counter-interrogation.

"And supposing Snowflake does not win? Will you—will you—really—make a b—b—bolt of it?"

The full lips quivered pitifully in spite of their owner's vaunted courage and determination, but they were turned away, and Jack Clinker could not see their tremulous twitchings.

"Yes," he said firmly. "In that case India will most likely be my destination. If I exchange I shall get double pay, and probably earn more than if I were to turn myself into an *honest* "—he emphasized the word—" but homely agriculturist. I would sell all the gees—all, perhaps, except dear old Snowflake and Opal, whom I should like to keep, if only for the sake of ' auld lang syne '—and live the life of a regular miser until fortune once more began to smile."

She did not answer. Her heart was too full for speech, and the possibility of his going far away wrung it strangely. Neither seemed disposed for further conversation, and they rode on in silence, with the rain trickling down their moist faces and the dark, shiny coats of their respective horses.

Presently she said in an almost inaudible voice, as if she had at length arrived at some conclusion to her thoughts, "I hope to goodness Snowflake will win."

Her words broke the spell that was fast falling over them.

"Yes," he said gravely, " it will be a bad look out for me if we are beaten. But come "—making an effort to throw off the feeling of depression that seemed creeping upon them both—"it's foolish anticipating misfortunes which may never occur. It was just like my selfishness to tell you anything about these worries. Why could I not have kept them to myself? Anyhow, we will try and look on the bright side of affairs. After all, it's not the first mess I've been in by a good many, and somehow or other I have always managed to pull through. So let's cheer up."

But Kate shook her head, refusing to be comforted, for a vague presentiment of evil had cast its oppressive influence round her.

"Come, come," he said once more, seeing how grave she looked, and trying very hard to appear cheerful, "we have talked ourselves into a regular fit of the blues instead of remembering that we are all going up to town together and mean to have a jolly time of it. That's right," as a faint smile began to illumine the corners of her mouth, "you look more like yourself again. I hardly know you with that serious face and without your usual cheery laugh."

So he rattled on, endeavouring to restore her to her customary gaiety, though all the time there was an uncomfortable choking sort of a sensation in his own throat which rendered speech difficult, and finally brought about another silence.

The short December day was drawing to a close; the dusk was fast gathering round them, the soft rain pattered noiselessly to the ground in a continuous stream; lowering grey clouds filled the sky, unbroken by any streak of light, and close at hand shone the wet pavements of Foxington, under the tall, dull, flickering gas-lamps, which struggled bravely to relieve the general gloom.

Where the cross-roads divided, just below the market-place, Jack and Kate came to a standstill.

"We part here," she said, holding out her small, dripping hand to wish him good-night; "thanks for having escorted me home so carefully."

"Good-night," he echoed, holding it firmly in his own. "You promise to come, don't you? It's something to look forward to if the worst comes to the worst."

She bowed her head in token of assent, for she could not trust herself to speak.   Two big tears had welled up into her eyes and overflowed, where they mingled with the raindrops, chasing each other down her cheeks as she rode away.   His horse was tired and impatient to return to its warm stable, but he stood watching her retreating form until it was lost in the darkness of evening.

"Oh, my darling!" he murmured passionately, "if only I were worthy of you!   If only I had not so cruelly misspent and misused my life, then perhaps I might have gained you; but as it is I feel ashamed to ask that you should link your destiny with mine.   Ah! if we could but foresee the future, how differently we would act!"

Then he gathered up his reins and rode down the deserted street, on either side of which the gutters were filled with yellow racing water, and the dreary shops, down whose panes the rain trickled incessantly, looked dismal and forlorn, while M'liss shook her head with an angry protest, which seemed to say as clearly as human speech, "Come, come, don't dawdle any longer.   It's terribly wet.   For goodness sake make haste and go home."

CHAPTER XXV.

SANDOWN RACES.

ON Wednesday afternoon, by the five o'clock express, an outwardly merry party (although two at least of their number bore anxious hearts), consisting of Kate, Mary, Colonel Clinker, Messrs. Grahame and McGrath, travelled up together to the Metropolis. Conversation was general, and time passed so quickly and so pleasantly that all were surprised to find their destination arrived at, and St. Pancras, with its huge iron girders wreathed in fog and blackened by smoke, looming overhead. Cabs were hailed, boxes sorted and put on their top, and then the quintet reluctantly separated, after engaging to meet a few minutes before twelve on the Sandown platform the following morning. The two girls were handed into a four-wheeler and rattled off to South Kensington, in which district Mary's aunt, Mrs. Tryon, resided. The kind-hearted old lady greeted them both with great warmth and cordiality, and displayed an old-fashioned hospitality by forcing all sorts of different viands upon them during the meal which promptly ensued, while shortly afterwards Kate beat a retreat, declaring she felt uncommonly tired, having been out hunting all the forenoon. But when the morrow came she appeared fresh as a sweet-pea, clad from head to foot in a dark green cloth costume which fitted her like a glove. Change of scene had enabled her to partly throw off her forebodings, and she determined to thoroughly enjoy the next few days.

They found the three gentlemen already on the look-out for them, and all got into an empty carriage together. The cards for the day were then eagerly scanned and as eagerly discussed, with sundry references to *Ruff's Guide* and the *Sporting Times*, while dear Mrs. Tryon, a benevolent smile dimpling her kind old face, nodded placidly over a copy of the *Daily Telegraph*, until at last her head subsided with a spasmodic jerk on to the shoulder of her nearest neighbour, who happened to be Mr. McGrath, where it contentedly reposed, giving rise to much laughter and good-natured comment.

Esher was reached before long, when, after recalling Mrs. Tryon to a sense of the situation, they all got out and walked two and two along the yellow gravel path leading straight up to the enclosure. There had been a very severe frost the night before, which still covered the grass with a white rime, and Colonel Clinker, digging the point of his stick into the earth, exclaimed—

"Humph! I don't half like the look of things. It must have frozen like the deuce, for the ground is just as hard as iron. Awful bad luck! Exactly when I'm running Snowflake, too!"

"Will it interfere with his chance?" said Kate in an undertone.

"I think not; he's so uncommonly fit and well, but his poor old legs, I fear, may suffer. You see aged horses are different to three and four-year-olds."

When Mrs. Tryon had been comfortably installed in a remote corner of the gallery, from which she could not possibly see any of the racing, but which she chose as being free from draught, Jack turned to Kate and said—

"What do you say, Miss Brewser; will you come and take a turn in the paddock? We're rather early, but if you don't mind I should like to go round to the boxes and see if Snowflake was none the worse for his journey up to town, and has fed all right since he came."

She assented without any hesitation, and they departed accordingly, leaving the remainder of the party to follow at leisure. They made straight for the boxes, in one of which they shortly found Snowflake comfortably located. The groom's report turned out to be a most satisfactory one, and everything promised well. As his master approached the horse, and fondly felt his firm, swelling chest, he gave a loud whinny of delighted recognition, thrusting his soft muzzle forwards as if in search of the carrot he was wont to regale himself with.

Kate stood by watching attentively. From the close way in which Colonel Clinker had crossquestioned his man concerning the state of Snowflake's health, she realised the gravity of the situation, and the importance of a successful issue to the day's proceedings. She began to feel nervous and excited."

" *Our* race," said Colonel Clinker, addressing her, " does not come off till after luncheon, being third on the programme, but I've got to ride for a brother officer almost immediately. It's young Rassington's horse. He's a good lad, so I did not like to refuse, but I know nothing about his gee. It's one he picked up quite lately."

" It's a hurdle-race, isn't it? "

" Yes, two miles over eight flights of hurdles."

" Nasty dangerous things," said Kate viciously, " I detest them."

" And why, may I ask ? "

" I don't know, but I wish you were not going to ride a strange horse."

He looked at her for a second in amazement. Then a sudden light seemed to break in upon his mind, and lit up his face with a radiant smile.

" Do you mean to say that *you* are afraid, by any chance? "

A conscious flush rose to her brow.

"I'm a goose," she said brusquely, without condescending to enter into further particulars.

" Ah ! So even you admit possessing some nerves at last," he retorted, evidently enjoying the fact. " I declare there goes the saddling-bell, and I must be off. Directly the race is over I shall come and look you up, and we will all go and have lunch together. Our fellows have got a tent over the way, just behind the coaches. Ah ! here's Terry, just in the very nick of time. I say, old

man," as Mr. McGrath lounged carelessly by, "take care
of Miss Brewser, will you, while I go and adorn, else I shall
be late?"

Whereupon he ran off in a great hurry to don Mr. Rassington's racing colours.

"Mr. McGrath," said Kate confidentially, as soon as they
found themselves alone, "what is your opinion of hurdle-
racing?"

"Faith! upon my soul!" exclaimed he, feeling slightly at
a loss, when so directly requested to express his sentiments,
"I've never thought much about it."

"It's dangerous, I suppose?" with a slight tremor in her
voice.

"Oh yes, of course, awfully dangerous," assented he,
quite unsuspicious as to the drift of the question. "Fellows
tumble about like ninepins."

"I wonder you approve of your friend riding in them,
then?"

"What, Jack do you mean? Gad! but my friend, as you
call him, does a good many things I disapprove of and that I
can't put a stop to."

"He ought not to be *allowed* to risk his neck unnecessarily,
and ride all sorts of strange horses he knows nothing about
simply because he's asked to."

"Jack's such an awfully good-natured chap. He'd do anything for anyone."

"That's all very well; but"—

The conversation was here put an end to by the reappearance
of no less a person than Jack himself, attired in a primrose
satin jacket and cap, boots, and long spurs.

"Hulloa!" he exclaimed, with a laugh, seeing Kate give
a little start of surprise. "Don't you recognise me in my
racing toggery? Do I look so very different?"

"Yes, rather," said she critically. "I should know you,
however, anywhere by your voice."

As explained before, it had a peculiarly sympathetic timbre.
But she did not tell him how among hundreds and thousands
of voices it would always be *the one* voice to her. She thought

so, however, none the less, as he stood there before her, looking so bright and thoroughly manly that few could have suspected the anxiety that consumed him.

And now the jockeys mounted their horses. and, emerging by the iron gates, walked slowly down the gravel drive under the bare trees in Indian file on to the racecourse, which by this time a cold wintry sun had somewhat succeeded in thawing. Kate and Mr. McGrath hurried back to the enclosure only just in time to witness the preliminary canter. Some little delay occurred before the half-dozen starters were sent on their way to an excellent start, and came galloping past the stand all together, though the very first flight of hurdles brought one of their number to grief, the rider escaping with an ugly shaking. When, however, the remaining five began the ascent for home, young Rassington's horse shot out like an arrow from a bow, and spread-eagling his field in a style not often seen, cantered in, hard held, an easy winner, while his popular jockey was greeted on all sides by loud cheers and hearty applause. With the exception of that memorable occasion when she had steered King Olaf to victory, Kate had never felt so proud in her life. She loved hearing him praised. And when he rode back into the paddock once more along the drive, sitting with careless ease in the saddle, his right hand resting on his thigh, and his face all flushed by success, she thought it more than good of him, while others were offering all sorts of varied congratulations, to look for her among the crowd and send her a bright little nod of recognition. Such trifles touch a woman's heart by their spontaniety.

Lunch was now the order of the day, and Mrs. Tryon did excellent justice to the meal, apparently enjoying it immensely. The best part of an hour glided quickly by before she could be persuaded to recross the course; but the all-important event was close at hand, and Colonel Clinker, before retiring to weigh in, made Kate promise to meet him in the paddock directly the race was over.

"Good-bye," he said, half in play, half in earnest. "If I don't pull it off either India or the parish workhouse will have to offer me a refuge. In the meantime common prudence dictates the advisability of looking after what loose cash I possess. Would you mind taking care of it for me, Miss Brewser?" pulling out a handful of coins.

When he was gone she counted them all most carefully, arranging the gold in a little heap, so that on his return their rightful owner should find none wanting; but among the silver she noticed a small, insignificant, much worn threepenny bit with a hole pierced in it. She turned it over in the palm of her hand, and a curious fancy stole over her to possess some little thing, no matter how trifling, belonging to him. The desire became so intense that honesty went to the wall, and she decided on committing what she regarded as a theft though she carefully put a bran new piece in the place of the one she proposed taking, which latter she dexterously tied up in the corner of her pocket-handkerchief. By the time this manœuvre had been successfully executed the horses appeared on the scene of action, Colonel Clinker wearing his own colours; and as he settled himself in the saddle with an ease born of long practice, she could not help thinking how superior he looked to any of the other competitors. But now they were actually off, starting a little way below the stand, and her attention was rivetted on the nine horses as they came boldly on to the gorsed hurdles. The majority cleared them brilliantly, but others got over in a very clumsy manner, while one timorous creature stopped dead short, and another, after smashing a couple of hurdles all to pieces, bolted out of the course in spite of every endeavour on the part of his rider to keep him straight. Needless to say that Snowflake acquitted himself satisfactorily. After the Huntingshire fences these artificial Sandown ones seemed to him mere child's play. The numbers were now reduced to seven horses, who kept pegging steadily on, no accident occurring to thin their ranks. When they descended the hill on the far side, they improved the pace somewhat, Snowflake lying last but one, but going well within himself, and tearing at his bridle as if indignant at being thus forced to keep in the rear. By-and-by they put on a spurt, and came thundering past the stand the second time. The going was evidently greasy and bad, for the sun

had only slightly thawed the outer crust of the earth, leaving
the ground beneath quite hard, and the sound of the animals'
hoofs echoed in the dry atmosphere with sharp, distinct thuds
as they galloped by. Only half the distance had yet been
accomplished; nevertheless, when the horses emerged from
behind the hill on the left, one or two had evidently had
enough already, and pecked badly at their fences. Four competitors only were still left in the front, and among these
Snowflake's white coat was clearly discernible, striding along
smoothly and evenly. They flew over the water-jump without
a mistake, also the succeeding fences, and beginning to gallop
in downright earnest, rounded the bend for home. Colonel
Clinker managed to get an inside place, and hugged the rails
with professional temerity. The excitement now became
intense. Hilarion, Daphne, and Snowflake ran locked together, with the Shaker only a length in their rear; but
Hilarion's rider was calling vigorously upon his horse, and
Daphne cut up soft directly she felt the whip, and laying back
her ears refused to try. Jack Clinker, on Snowflake, sat well-
nigh motionless. The gallant old hunter breasted the hill
like a lion and seemed to have the race in hand, though Hilarion, with a game effort, had contrived to shoot ahead for a
moment. But at that instant Jack gave his horse a slight
touch of the spurs, and, responding in a manner beautiful to
behold, Snowflake with each stride reduced Hilarion's lead.
It was a magnificent race, but cries of "Snowflake wins!
Snowflake wins for a monkey!" filled the air, as first his nose
and then his neck crept past Hilarion's girths. It seemed as
if Colonel Clinker would win by one of those artistic finishes
when nobody could tell exactly how much he had in hand.
The race was virtually over, and the faces of the Foxington
division beamed with legitimate triumph. But at the very
moment when victory appeared well-nigh assured, what mysterious mishap was it that caused the good horse to suddenly
falter in his stride, and stop as if pierced in a vital part by a
bullet? What had occurred, though he still struggled desperately on with that courage so oft conspicuous in. the hunting-field, to make him let Hilarion get his head once more in

front, and catching him on the post, win the Great Sandown
United Hunters' Steeplechase by a short neck? Alas!
the back sinews of his near foreleg had given way badly,
and poor Snowflake, to use a common racing expression, had
broken down. In a minute Jack pulled him up and was off
his back, but even with the weight removed he could not do
much more than hobble painfully on three legs. His owner
bit his lip and shook his head with a gesture of absolute
despair, for he loved the old horse dearly, and was not one to
bear the loss of such a favourite with callous equanimity. A
host of confused and painful thoughts surged up in his brain
as he sadly led the gallant grey, now shorn of his glory, back
to the paddock away from the curious, bustling, unsympathetic crowd to the quiet and comparatively remote corner
where he had begged Kate Brewser to wait his arrival. Ah!
what a different arrival to the one he had anticipated and
confidently looked forward to! His hopes had all been so
suddenly dashed to the ground that as yet he could hardly
realize the disastrous results of their overthrow. Snowflake's
hurt occupied the foremost position in his thoughts.

"I'm afraid he's done for," were his first sorrowfully
uttered words to Kate, who advanced to meet him with a downcast countenance. "Poor dear old Snowflake," patting the
drooping outstretched neck, "his bolt is shot, and never again
will he carry me to hounds. Hang it all! I would give
half a year's income for this not to have happened." As he
bent down and felt Snowflake's injured limb she could see
from his face how deeply he took the catastrophe to heart.
Light as was his touch the horse shrank from under it, and
was evidently in great pain. "D—n that hard ground,"
cried Jack wrathfully, and when he stood upright again Kate
saw that there were *tears*, actually *tears*, in his eyes.

"You will think me a most infernal fool," he said apolo·
getically, brushing his sleeve across his brow with a hasty
shamefaced gesture; "but I can't help it. I was as fond of
the dear old horse as if he'd been a human being"

All her heart went out towards him in loving sympathy.

"Fool!" she said reproachfully, laying her little hand on

his arm with a soft, lingering pressure, "how can you wrong yourself by saying such a thing? I at least can feel for y u in your misfortunes, and respect a man who shows so much honest affection for a valued friend."

Her own eyes were glistening as she spoke, but her words comforted him greatly.

"God bless you, Kate," he whispered in a thick, husky voice. "You are one in a thousand. Very few women *can* enter so thoroughly into a fellow's feelings; but you—you understand without my telling you, that it's not the money I care for half so much, serious as it is, as the loss of my dear old horse."

"I know. If anything happened to King Olaf I should be just as cut up as you are now. It's horrible, the idea of dumb animals suffering, and all through their courageous desire to serve us. I often think we are not half sufficiently grateful to them."

Poor Snowflake! Well was it for him that now, in his hour of need, he owned a master who scorned to forsake him lightly, and cast him off as a man casts off an old shoe—one who for the sake of a few paltry sovereigns would not sell a faithful servant to end his miserable days between the shafts of a cab, writhing under the perpetual lash of a cruel whip, bowed down by neglect, crushed by starvation. Pleasant days were in store for his old age, far away up in the beautiful wild northern country, where the purple heather bloomed on the rugged mountain-sides, and the rushing burns came tearing down like silver streaks through the granite boulders. There some peaceful and sheltered spot would offer him an asylum. Perhaps some verdant, golden-starred field, hemmed in by shady trees, 'neath whose green branches his worn-out limbs could repose at will, and where nothing but the cackle of the old cock grouse, calling to his mate high up over head, would disturb the surrounding silence; where he could sniff the sweet fresh air through his distended nostrils, inhale all sorts of fragrant hedgerow odours, and roll backwards and forwards on the soft sward, crushing in careless disregard the pink-tipped daisies and golden-hearted buttercups to the ground, and then rising with a struggle, a shake, and a snort, recall the triumph of bygone days, the deep bay of the familiar hounds, the cheery sound of the huntsman's horn, the whip's shrill "Forrard, awa—a—y!" Perhaps, too, now and again, that well-known master, who in many an oft-remembered run had guided him so fearlessly, might come to the meadow and hold converse with the good hunter, whose memory others could never efface. That shaggy mane and rough white head, those full blue eyes and slender ears, will conjure up visions of a happy and triumphant past.

Ah, Snowflake! broken down as thou art, it is well for thee that thou ownest such a master—one who loves thee well and truly, and who will cherish thee until death ; a master who looks upon thy kind not as mere machines, but as valued friends, and whose warm heart sympathises with every living thing endowed with that mysterious pain-subjected vitality called life.

That evening at the theatre, Kate's thoughts were far away. The actors and actresses conveyed no impression whatever to her mind. She looked at them and listened to them mechanically, all the time feeling as if in a dream. She could do nothing but wonder whether Colonel Clinker would really execute his intention of going abroad. Three hundred pounds for the forage bill, and two hundred to make good Snowflake's defeat. These she knew of already, and knew that payment was difficult, if not impossible. Then the idea suddenly struck her if only she could find means to do so anonymously, why should *she* not make good the deficiency? Money was nothing to her ; she had more than she knew what to do with, and would never miss it, while it might possibly prevent his leaving. And then like a flash of lightning she realised what she had hitherto studiously endeavoured to ignore, namely, that though she had been warned against him as a flirt, a spendthrift, and an adventurer, she had fallen head over ears in love, exactly as Mrs. Forrester had foretold.

The music sounded strangely dead and weird, the lights glared with a hateful brilliancy, a curious numb sensation stole over her senses.

"Is anything the matter?" whispered Colonel Clinker, seeing how pale she looked.

"Only a headache," she answered with a struggling smile, though a heartache would have been nearer the truth.

"Can I do anything for you?" he asked. "Will you have an ice, or a glass of water?"

"No, nothing, thanks. I dare say it will pass off by-and-by."

She sat through the whole performance, though at the end she could not have told what were the leading incidents of the piece. Her mind was occupied with but one thought, the thought of Jack's going away. Everything else sank into insignificance, and was subservient to it.

Poor Kate! She had lived twenty-two years of her life without ever having felt Cupid's torturing dart, but now at last, love which steals upon mortals in so many different ways, gradually, swiftly, fiercely, gently, unconsciously, had overtaken her. She was in its toils, and felt its pangs as well as its pleasures. Life began for the first time to unfold like a panorama, and she was new to the emotions it revealed; new to the poignant joys and still more poignant griefs, to the large capacity for good or for evil she felt growing up within her bosom. So new, and perhaps so foolish, that when she retired to rest that night, and could enjoy the luxury of solitude, she took from her pocket-handkerchief, where it still lay concealed, that little coin, *his* threepenny bit, and pressed it to her lips. Then she passed a silken thread through the hole, and hung it like a charm round her neck, where the small, worn, blackened object lay in striking contrast to her white skin.

Oh, youth! Oh, love! Such are thy follies! if indeed can be called follies those sentiments of unselfish affection which soften and chasten the heart, rendering men and women more lenient to each other, more sympathetic, more unselfish, more discerning, and yet more tolerant of human failings. Surely in the words of a great poet—

> "'Tis better to have loved and lost,
> Than never to have loved at all."

CHAPTER XXVI.

A FATAL FENCE.

The following day it came on to snow so hard, and Mrs. Tryon declared herself to be so reluctant to face the inclement atmosphere, that after many consultations the two girls at length unwillingly decided on not going to the races. Then as the weather grew steadily worse, and town looked extremely dreary, after making Mrs. Tryon promise to pay them a return visit at Sport Lodge, they took leave oft hat lady and departed for Foxington by an afternoon train, instead of by the later one they had originally intended to patronise. The homeward journey was accomplished without adventure of any kind, but when they reached Foxington Kate was delighted to find that a most welcome change had set in, for although the fields and hedges were still covered with snow, the air felt several degrees warmer, and there appeared every prospect of a thaw. Neither were these hopes delusive, for early next day, on looking out at the surrounding landscape, she perceived the green grass to be once more visible and the snow melting rapidly, although it still lay about in discoloured streaks, and in many places, having drifted from the force of the wind overnight, formed tolerably thick heaps under the hedgerows.

Kate's first act on rising was to send a message out to Stirrup, asking his opinion whether the hounds would go out or not, whereupon the satisfactory answer returned that "They were pretty sure to do so later on in the day, though Miss Kate must be careful, as the going was very bad and slippery in places, and far from safe." Such a reply was not sufficient to deter Kate from equipping herself for the hunting-field particularly as the meet happened to be within easy distance, and not further than three or four miles from Foxington. So though the sky looked overcast, as if there might be another downfall, she put on her covert coat and started a trifle later than usual, deciding to ride King Olaf out herself instead of sending him on beforehand. On her way to the meet she was overtaken by Colonel Clinker and Mr. McGrath, who had arrived the previous evening in order to hunt next day.

"Hulloa!" exclaimed the latter jocularly after salutations had been exchanged on either side. "You're a nice young lady, you are! What did you mean by deserting us so un-handsomely in our misfortunes? Why, we nearly lost our train fiddling about the platform hoping you and Miss Whit-bread would turn up. Jack grew quite melancholy at last, and predicted that the dissipations of the Metropolis had proved so ensnaring you would not return to Sport Lodge for an indefinite period, and yet the very first person we meet is your ladyship calmly going out to covert. Faith! but you should have seen the Chirper's face when Miss Whitbread did not put in an appearance! It was as good as a play, and the very model of a lovesick swain. Ha, ha, ha!" laughing heartily at the recollection.

"But all this time you have not told me one single word about Snowflake. How is *he* getting on?"

"As well as can be expected, thank you," said Colonel Clinker, to whom she had addressed the question; "but the back ligament is hopelessly sprung, and he'll never be fit to hunt any more. I've never known a sinew really broken down to stand hard work, and at the first long day the horse comes home just as lame as ever. I hate all this beastly snow and frost like poison, don't you? They play old Harry with the quads. By-the-bye, I trust you intend riding cau-tiously to-day, Miss Browser, and won't try and break your neck. I've got a superstitious fit on just now, and misfor-tunes never come singly. The fields are tolerably good going, but pray remember that the shady side of each fence is awfully hard and slippery; besides most of the ditches are chock full of snow. The less everybody goes in for jumping the better."

"I must not follow *you*, then, I suppose," said Kate archly.

"It matters little what happens to such an unlucky dog as I," he returned despondently. "If I were to be killed out hunting to-morrow even my best friends could only look upon it in the light of a good riddance. No, Miss Brewser, don't follow me. I feel in a reckless mood to-day, and should only lead you into danger."

"And is not that danger the same for you as for me? Why should you say such things? You can't possibly mean them seriously?" opening her big grey eyes wide with a pained expression of reproach.

"By Jove! don't I though. I don't believe, with the exception of my old governor, that there is a soul who would mind what really became of me. I am useful to fellows because I ride their horses, but beyond that nobody cares twopence. It is the way of the world; therefore it's useless reviling at it."

"What's the matter with you to-day?" looking at him wonderingly.

"Nothing. I'm in a bad temper, I suppose—ready to fly out at everything and everybody."

"And yet you expect *me* to follow advice you refuse to act up to yourself?"

"Yes. There can be no comparison between a fresh young girl with all the world at her feet and a desperate fellow like myself, almost at his wits' ends."

"You are unkind," she said, giving King Olaf a job in the mouth which sent him dancing on his hind legs, "and—and" —in a tremulous voice—"you don't understand."

That he certainly did not, for since Snowflake's misfortune he had been in that dissatisfied mood when all things seem to go wrong, and when one looks at the whole world with jaundiced eyes. There had been times when he fancied he detected some answering chord of affection in Kate Brewser's manner, but now he was disposed to look upon any such idea as a delusion and a fallacy, and to rail against himself as a madman.

"Come, come," interrupted Mr. McGrath with good humoured concern, "you two are always sparring at each other about something or other. Bedad! I believe you both love an argument, and therefore never lose the opportunity of plunging into one. But on this occasion, sorry as I am to side against the lady, Jack is perfectly right. The going really is *not* safe, Miss Brewser, so do please be careful."

She gave a little shrug of contempt, but in spite of it, when later on the hounds found in a belt of thin plantations, and ran very fairly through them out into the open, she stuck to the road, with a host of other reasonable sportsmen and women, whose bump of caution taught discretion in view of the uncertain state of the ground. So long as the hounds kept pretty well within sight Kate felt tolerably happy, but when they took a sudden bend to the right and could no longer be seen then she could bear the situation no more. King Olaf apparently shared the same opinion, for he was cocking his ears and prancing about in a perfect agony of impatience.

"Where are they? Where have they gone to? Can you see anything of them?" she asked with anxious insistence of those around. Then, when none but vague replies were forthcoming, she exclaimed, "Oh! it is dreadful to lose the hounds like this! Can't we find them again?"

"They be a-turning towards us now, miss," said a good-natured farmer, amused at her evident excitement. "They're making for 'Orniblow Spinney, just over the brow of yon hill. If we jog on we shall cut 'em off beautiful."

And so they did, only when one by one the hounds leapt over the fence into the road, or struggling through the gateway put their noses to the ground and took up the scent with a joyous chorus of sound before dashing out of it again, Kate, remembering what she had recently endured, found the temptation to follow in their wake quite irresistible. A fair proportion of the crowd seemed attacked by a simultaneous impulse, and shoved through the open gate close at hand with a show of valour and a complacency not a little irritating to the daring few who had ridden close up to hounds from the first.

The sun now began to shine so brightly that the melted snow lay in shallow, fast-thawing pools in the furrows, just allowing the green points of the grass to peep here and there through their midst, and splashing up in showery sprays as the horses gallopped by. That scent, too, was improving soon became evident from the increasing pace. Up to this point a line of friendly hand-gates had inspired even the most timid with courage to proceed, and the field forged merrily ahead, for it really seemed as if the fun were likely to become fast and furious. But although the hounds did not check, a check was shortly destined to be placed on the ardour of the pursuers in the shape of an unavoidable obstacle, and this heroic multitude found a disagreeable problem staring them uncompromisingly in the face. To jump or not to jump, that was the question : on the one side to place life and limb in jeopardy, a state of things always rather trying, but rendered doubly dangerous by the snow ; on the other, to beat an ignominious retreat, probably lose the hounds for the remainder of the day, and afterwards experience the disagreeable sensation of cowardice.

Now the man who has the courage boldly to turn away at the first sign of danger escapes all the discomfort awaiting those who, unable to decide promptly, dare neither advance nor recede. Fearing their neighbours' opinions, but fearing the formidable fence in front still more, they remain hesitating, until finally carried backwards or forwards, as the case may be, following the movements of the majority. To do the field justice, most of them did not hesitate for long, but executed a masterly retreat to the rear, and from thence into the road ; for the fence which had baffled them, though not large, was essentially nasty, the snow in front of it having drifted to a depth of several inches, and so completely filled up the shallow ditch on the taking off side that it appeared almost impossible for horses to distinguish it. The fence itself was not very formidable, being little over three feet in height, but it had been lately trimmed, and the smooth

pointed ends of the cut growers stuck up in its midst like an
ugly phalanx of dangerous bristles. Luckily, about a hundred yards to the right there was a gap across which a sheep-
hurdle had been placed, and it did not take long for the foremost horseman or two to descend from their horses and lift it
away, upon which it proved a comparatively simple matter to
walk or crawl down into the ditch, scramble through the
broken-down twigs of the hedge, and so into the next field.
But the passage of a large and impatient body of equestrians through a single small opening was not to be effected
without considerable delay, despite the fact that the sterns of
the leading hounds were already disappearing in the distance.
The men could push, and shove, and jostle to their hearts'
content, but Kate, as a lady, found herself at a considerable
disadvantage, for the manners of the shires were not so
chivalrous as to yield precedence to the fair sex on an occasion like the present, the accepted creed amongst the masculine members being that women who hunted ought to count
as " good fellows," and be able to shift for themselves. But
King Olaf was too thorough a gentleman to fall in with these
views, and understood no reason for delay. Several times he
endeavoured to rush at the gap, and was only restrained by
an unusually firm hand, upon which he bounded up into the
air with a half rear and impatient lunge at the bridle. In
fact he grew so irritable, his blood being thoroughly roused
by the short gallop previously indulged in, that Kate, seeing
an individual whose horse was probably equally troublesome,
emerge from the crowd, charge the fence, and got over with
a bit of a peck and a flounder, saw no reason why she should
not follow suit. What had been possible for him was surely
possible for her, and King Olaf's eyesight was so remarkably
good he was safe to see the ditch, filled with snow as it was,
and take off rightly. Perhaps in her youth and inexperience she failed to realize the full danger of those treacherous
stakes. Anyhow, she charged the fence. But whether King
Olaf got too close to it, or whether the snow balled in his feet
and impeded his true action, was impossible to determine.
Anyhow he slipped, and floundered through the low fence

"That was a near thing," thought Kate; "I've never known King Olaf so nearly down before."

Page 314.

with an ominous crash into the next field, where he pitched right on to his head, sending Kate flying almost out of the saddle. A moment of excitement and suspense ensued; then, from where she was clinging to his mane, quick as a cat— for like a true thoroughbred horse King Olaf had always a leg to spare—she saw him throw out his two forelegs, and with a powerful effort to right himself, and a backward toss of the head which caught Kate on the chest and helped her back into a proper position, the gallant little horse recovered, and managed once more to regain his footing.

"That *was* a near thing," thought Kate. "I've never known King Olaf so nearly down before; but no matter, we're over, and all's well that ends well."

But *had* it ended well? For when she set King Olaf going again, all at once it seemed as though he could scarcely move. She felt sure he must have hurt himself, and fancied that in the struggle to rise from the ground he had somehow or other sprained his shoulder. So she looked down anxiously, but failed to detect any outward sign of injury, and tried to comfort herself by thinking the horse might be suffering from some temporary blow, the effects of which would probably pass away in a little while. By heel and by voice she urged King Olaf on, and the courageous animal, though something evidently was amiss, did his best to respond to his mistress's desires, trying hard to keep pace with those who were now passing him by the score. The brave spirit was willing enough, but the flesh weak. He cantered feebly and slowly across the heavy grass field in which they found themselves, stumbled out of it into the plough, over a tiny bank, and then relapsed into a laborious trot.

Kate was rapidly becoming more and more alarmed, for she knew his gallant disposition so well she felt sure something very serious must be the matter. Times out of number that she had ridden her favourite chestnut she had never known him to lag like this, or display such a dull and drooping spirit. She made up her mind on the spot to go straight home, and see if she and Stirrup between them could not discover what ailed him.

"Misfortunes never come singly," Colonel Clinker had said to her only that morning, and now all at once the words recurred to her ears with an ugly significance, and made the very blood in her veins curdle with dread forebodings. What could be the matter? What could have happened to King Olaf to have wrought so swift and terrible a change?

She had already begun to retrace her steps, intent on putting her purpose into execution, when a sonorous voice from behind said—

"Beg pardon, miss; I hope you will forgive my making so free, but if you don't get off 'is back dirckly I'm afraid that there 'oss of yours will bleed to death. I've trucked 'im all across the snow for the last two fields."

CHAPTER XXVII

MRS. FORRESTER PROVES HER VETERINARY SKILL.

KATE turned hastily round and saw her friend the farmer, who had soothed her anxiety when on the road she fancied she had lost the hounds a short time before. His words made her heart give a great bound and then stand still with fright.

"Oh, how dreadful!" she cried in an agony of terror, "and I have been trying to force the poor thing on all this time. Oh dear! oh dear! what shall I do?"

And she leapt from the saddle to the ground in desperate haste, tearing both elastics of her skirt as she did so. But grave as were her fears she was totally unprepared for the sight which now met her eyes—a sight that turned her perfectly sick with horror, for close under the girths, spreading from them almost to the springing of poor King Olaf's thigh, hitherto hidden by the habit skirt, which accounted for her not having discovered the injury sooner, gaped a frightfully jagged and ghastly wound, at least eight inches in length, though it was impossible to see how deep it had gone. Already, in those few seconds while the horse had remained standing in one spot, the blood had dripped into a great red pool, where it lay in awful contrast to the white snow. The horror of the thing was so great that for the time Kate lost all presence of mind.

"Oh, how dreadful, how dreadful!" she exclaimed shudderingly. "Can nothing be done to stop it? He will die if this goes on."

Then, in an ecstasy of self-reproach, she put her arms round the horse's drooping head, and crying as if her heart would break, said—

"Oh, King Olaf! my darling, my poor wounded darling. *I* am to blame for this. It was my fault. I took advantage of your being so good, and put you at a place that was not fair. Oh! if I live to be a hundred I shall never, *never*, NEVER forgive myself."

She might have remained in this condition indefinitely had not the farmer, with a rough and ready sympathy, recalled her to a sense of the urgency of the situation.

"Come, come, Miss," he said kindly, "this will never do. Accidents happen now and then without its being in our power to help them, so dry your eyes. I don't like to see you take it so much to heart, besides which we ought to be a-thinking of the 'oss, and what's best for 'im."

This latter reasoning was all-sufficient. Kate controlled her tears with a brave effort, and said in a voice choked with emotion—

"Oh yes, most certainly. Don't let us lose a minute. Every moment may be of importance."

"Well, then," continued the farmer, "we had better try to get the horse into the nearest stable without waste of time. Poor thing, he's faint through a-losing so much blood, and no wonder; but there's no good to be gained by standing here, so let's be moving."

"I—I—I suppose there's *no* hope?" she asked faintly, dreading to find her worst fears confirmed. "He's sure to die?" with a little hysterical sob.

"Nobody can be sure of anything in this world, Miss. It's impossible to say at present whether he'll pull through or not. I've known animals as 'ad a good sound constitooshun make wonderful recoveries 'afore now; there's never no saying how these things may turn out from one day to the other. It's a terr'ble wound, I admit; indeed, I never seed a wusser, but while there life there's hope."

A platitude from which Kate derived but small consolation.

"It must have been them there sharp sticks," continued the farmer musingly. "I know that fence back yonder well. A nasty, trappy place as ever there was, and the growers just like so many spears since they've been cut. They have reg'lar gored the poor creature's stomach, like the 'orns of a bull, but it may only be a bad flesh-wound after all. I hope to good ness 'is vitals is safe, for if so be as 'ow they are touched nothing can save the 'oss—not all the doctoring in this world, and it would be kinder to put a bullet through 'is 'ead at once; but, as I said 'afore, there's never any telling; we must hope for the best."

"It seems difficult to hope under the circumstances," said Kate dejectedly, looking at the frightful injury with inward misgivings. "Do you know if we are near any village, or how far we are from Foxington?"

"You won't get 'im that length *this* afternoon, Miss. Fox-ington's good four miles from here, as the crow flies. There's no use thinking of 'is reaching 'ome."

"No use thinking of his reaching home! Good heavens What am I to do, then? Where am I to take him? I can't leave the horse to die out in the cold," and she wrung her hands in a state of frantic despair.

"Certainly not, Miss; but if you don't mind letting him stand at my farm for a day or two, just till we see how matters is likely to turn, I think we could make the 'oss com-furble. My place ain't above half a mile from this, and I've got a good warm loose-box a-standing empty."

"Oh, thank you! I'm so much obliged. Let's make haste and get him there. I wonder," struck by sudden thought, "whether I could induce anyone to ride into Foxington for me and tell the veterinary surgeon to come out immediately?"

They had been outstripped by their companions. The majority of the field, when they came to the fence which caused the accident, had returned to the road, and not a soul was within hail. The farmer considered a moment; at last, touched by Kate's distress, he said—

"I don't mind, Miss, if I goes myself. It won't hurt my mare to canter into Foxington and back, more partic'lar as she aint done nothing of a day's work. But I don't like leaving you all by yourself. Would you be afraid to lead the horse back to my farm quite alone?"

There seemed much reason for the question, for King

Olaf was so fearfully injured it really appeared doubtful whether he would ever succeed in reaching any homestead, and might not tumble down and die on the way. But Kate, even in her dire distress, was not " made of such slight elements."

" Afraid! no, certainly not," she answered promptly. " Tell me the way, so that I may start at once. But how are we ever to get on to the road? That's the difficulty. The horse can't possibly jump, it's out of the question; yet, if my eyes," looking round, " don't deceive me, I can't see a gate out of this plough anywhere. Do you happen to know if there is one ? "

" Seeing as 'ow I have farmed the very land on which we are standing for nigh upon twenty years, and it belonged to my father, and '*is* father 'afore that," responded the farmer with dignity, "I consider as 'ow I *ought* to know better nor most people. There ain't no gate, Miss, sure enough, but there's a bit of a gap in yonder corner which my red cow with the crooked horn made only the day before yesterday, and me as 'ad intended building it up this very morning. It really looks like the hand of Providence, don't it now? Well, we must manage to get the 'oss over it somehow, and then the road lies in a straight line. There be no mistaking it." So saying he put his mare into a walk, and rode on in advance, followed by Kate, who led King Olaf slowly through the sticky plough, her feet sinking in up to the ankles at every step, coming forth literally covered with clods of damp mud, which soon wetted her thin riding-boots through and through. Fifty yards or so, to her great relief, brought them close to the fence, a hairy bullfinch, which, however, as her companion had truly stated, was broken down, and presented a very feasible gap; nevertheless, on the far side there remained a tolerably wide and boggy ditch to be jumped, which filled Kate with great dismay.

" What *are* we to do? " she cried in despair. " The horse will never get over this. In his present condition it's simply impossible."

" We never know what we can do till we try, Miss,"

answered the farmer hopefully. " Besides," with a graver inflection of voice, " we *must* get over it. Here, give me the chestnut's bridle while you see if you can manage to cross yourself. Hooray! That's capital!" as Kate, taking a determined run at the ditch, succeeded in landing with a scramble and a flounder, hands and knees, into the mud on the opposite side, and by the aid of an overhanging branch pulled herself up into an upright position. "None the worse, I hope, only a bit dirty. Well, never mind, that can't be helped, and now," throwing her King Olaf's bridle, "if you catch hold of that and cheer the 'oss on he'll go all right. I'll be bound he knows the sound of your voice." Upon which the farmer, on his big brown mare, went behind King Olaf and began energetically cracking his hunting-crop, while Kate, in every tone of imploring endearment, encouraged the horse to proceed, until at length, after standing uncertainly poised on the brink of the ditch for several seconds, changing his feet, and moving his forelegs uneasily, the courageous animal, game as a bantam-cock, gave a spring, and by dint of much effort got safely over, though the increased motion made the blood from his wound spurt forth afresh."

"First-rate! couldn't be better! Well done you!" ejaculated the farmer admiringly, at the same time giving vent to an audible sigh of relief at the success attendant on this ticklish job. "And now, by your leave, and if you be quite certain as 'ow you don't mind, I'd best be off and make sure of the vet. You cannot go wrong if you was to try. Keep to your left on the track close to the hedge for a couple of 'underd yards, at the end of which you will see a five-barred gate leading straight into the high road. Then turn sharp to your right, and follow your nose till you come to Silverstone village. It aint above half a mile, if so much, and when you get there anyone will tell you where I live. Farmer Hammond be my name," preparing to depart.

"Very well," said Kate. "I am so *very, very* much obliged to you."

"Pray don't mention it, Miss. We all of us stands in need of a helping 'and now and again. By-the-bye, is there any message I can leave for you at Foxington, or give to any gentleman out 'unting in case I *should* happen to come across the 'ounds on my way?"

She caught eagerly at the suggestion. "Oh, yes," she said; "I am so glad you thought of it. If by chance you meet Colonel Clinker—you know Colonel Clinker, don't you? a tall, good-looking gentleman, with fair hair and blue eyes, riding a young roan mare with a bang tail—tell him that I, Miss Brewser, have met with a most dreadful accident, and shall be so thankful if he could come to me. That is to say," hesitating through fear of spoiling his enjoyment, "if hounds are not running well. You understand? Don't bother him if they are having good sport." She could not help it. Her first impulse was to seek assistance from him, to long for his presence, for the sense of protection and comfort it never failed to bring. Now that she was in trouble it seemed so natural to turn to him, to shift the responsibility of action from off her shoulders on to his.

"All right, Miss," said Farmer Hammond cheerily. "I'll do my best to find the gentleman. I knows 'im well by sight, and a thorough gentleman he is, too, as everybody in these parts agrees. Is there no message 'afore I start?"

"Oh, Mr. Hammond, if you are really so good as to ride into Foxington, perhaps you would not mind trotting just half a mile farther, and telling my groom, whose name is Stirrup, to put some things together at once—the horse's clothing and anything else he can think of—and setting off in the trap *directly*. It won't do to leave King Olaf alone all through the night. Somebody will have to sit up with him, so I hope you won't mind my sending for my own man? You see the horse is sure to require a deal of care and attention, and Stirrup is a very decent old fellow, not likely to give much trouble."

"Don't mention the trouble, Miss. It aint of no account. But I think as 'ow it will be a very good plan for your own groom to come over. He's used to the 'oss and the 'oss to him, and they understands one another's ways; besides which, you'll feel happier in your mind yourself." With

After twice stopping to inquire the way.

which parting words Farmer Hammond rode off at a good round trot, astonishing his old mare to some tune by the unusual but vigorous application of a pair of rowelless spurs, leaving poor Kate to trudge all by herself on the solitary country road, leading, with sorely anxious and heavy heart, the wounded creature who had carried her so often and so brilliantly to hounds. "Shall I ever ride him again? Will that back ever bear my weight in the future?" were the questions that forced themselves upon her as she gazed at the empty saddle and loosely swaying reins. And the thought that she might never do so, that she had for the last time felt beneath her the arch of that yielding neck, the spring of that elastic gallop, filled her eyes with tears and her heart with a bitter sorrow.

"Oh, King Olaf, King Olaf!" she repeated. "It was al my fault; the fault of your ignorant, stupid, *cruel* mistress!"

No half-mile had ever appeared so interminably long, for the horse could now only move very slowly, and with each step a great red drop oozed out from the wound, and fell with a splash on the muddy road, while each drop was like a drop of her own life-blood flowing, from the agony it inflicted on her sensitive nature. The sight of the blood and the sickening fear of his death made her feel quite faint and ill, but she would not give in. Everything depended, or seemed to depend just then, on her getting him as quickly as possible into a comfortable stable. King Olaf was growing stiff and cold; he hung his head with unmistakable symptoms of pain, and his eye looked dull and heavy. An end, however, comes to all things, and at last a turn in the road revealed the village of Silverstone close at hand. After twice stopping to inquire the way of gaping labourers, Kate finally succeeded in finding Mr. Hammond's house, and brought up before the farmyard door. Here she discovered a stableman lounging in comparative idleness, and after a brief explanation impressed the gravity of King Olaf's case so far upon him as to induce him, without further parley, to lead the horse into a clean and cheerful loose-box. When he saw the wound the man shook his head in an ominous fashion, and immediately made haste to loosen the girths, remove the saddle, and throw a warm rug over King Olaf's quarters, for what between the cold and pain, the poor animal was quivering like an aspen leaf.   But having performed these kindly offices, neither he nor Kate seemed quite to know what steps to take next for the best.   The case was one outside their limited experience, and demanding more skill and science than they either of them possessed.   After a bit, however, the man, struck by a brilliant idea, suggested a warm mash, and went off to see to its preparation, leaving Kate leaning up against the wall of the box in a state of feverish inaction, and resolving to study Youatt and Fitz Wygram on the earliest occasion.   She fully realised the lamentable ignorance she displayed when an emergency arose, and determined if possible to amend it.   The sound of hoofs rattling on the stone flags in the yard outside came as an immense relief, and going out she found Mrs. Forrester arriving in hot haste.

"Ah! there you are," exclaimed the old lady, with a friendly nod.   "I heard that you had met with a bad accident, so left the hounds immediately to see if I could be of any good.   I was told that you had staked your beautiful chestnut horse very badly, but hope the report is untrue?"

"Alas! no," replied Kate.   "I wish it were.   I'm in despair.   But how kind of you to come my assistance. You've no idea how deserted and forlorn I began to feel." Indeed she was grateful for any society to divert the utter misery of her thoughts.

"Were you at all hurt yourself?" asked Mrs. Forrester kindly.

"No.   I wish to goodness I had been if it could have spared him in any way, but he recovered himself marvellously.   I fear, however," and the ready tears once more welled up into her eyes, "that he is most terribly injured.   I never saw such a place as it is."

"Let me have a look at him."   And then Kate led the way into the box, and Mrs. Forrester, leaning forward, gently lifted up King Olaf's rug, and with the practised eye of a professional surgeon carefully inspected the wound.   "You're right," she said, in her deep matter-of-fact voice. "This is a bad business, a *very* bad business. Still, we must try what we can do to relieve the horse and make him more comfortable. He seems in great pain, but I think we can ease that a little, any way, for the present. How long has he been standing here like this?"

"I really can't say exactly. About twenty minutes, or half an hour."

"You've sent for a vet., of course?"

"Yes; Mr. Hammond has gone to fetch him, and also to tell my groom to come out as quickly as possible."

"Ah! that's right. This is a case of stitching, and the sooner the vet. arrives the better. In the meantime, the first thing to be done is to endeavour to prevent the air from getting into the wound. Have you got a chemist's shop in this village of yours?" turning to the man, who had re-entered the stable.

"Yes, marm," he replied. "There be one close by, just at the end of the street."

"So much the better. Now I want you to get me a bottle of carbolic acid, and from three quarters to an ounce of laudanum, that is to say, if such articles are sold here."

"Let *me* go," said Kate eagerly, feeling any useful employment to be a positive relief after her enforced inaction. "I will run all the way."

"All right, then," said Mrs. Forrester, "the man can be of use to me while you are gone, but be as quick as you can, for I want to bandage the wound up without a minute's further delay, and don't forget to bring back a sheet of lint. We shall want that first and foremost."

Kate needed no urging to dispatch. She flew down the road as fast as her feet could carry her, and in an incredibly short time returned, flushed and panting, with the requisite necessaries, which she had been fortunate enough to procure.

"Ah! that's capital," said Mrs. Forrester in tones of satisfaction, when she perceived the success of her mission. "And

now we can set to work in earnest. You must know, Miss
Brewser, that carbolic acid is an invaluable agency in the
dressing of wounds, possessing highly antiseptic properties,
which destroy the formation of putrefactive germs. I am a
firm believer in the Listerian theory."

Once again Kate chafed at her ignorance. She had only
heard of it vaguely.

"How clever you are!" she said with a spontaneous
admiration by no means lost upon its object. "I wish I knew
a tenth part of what you do. The truth is, although I have
hunted a good bit off and on, I am as inexperienced as a baby
in all matters connected with horseflesh requiring more than
the most ordinary knowledge. Such a state of things is positively disgraceful!"

"Not at all, since you have the wish to learn, my dear,"
returned the old lady graciously. "Besides, you are very
young, and there is plenty of time before you. Remember I
have had a considerable start in regard to years, which makes
all the difference. And now I am going to dilute the carbolic
acid with water, one part acid to forty water being the
correct proportions; but first we must make use of hot
fomentations, to wash away the congealed blood and any irritating foreign matter that may possibly remain lodged in the
wound."

So saying, Mrs. Forrester, having directed the man to fetch
a bucket full of warm water, herself proceeded, with a light
yet firm hand, to sluice the injured part with a sponge. Poor
King Olaf winced at the slightest touch, especially when,
dexterously bringing the two lips of the wound as nearly
together as they permitted, this accomplished amateur applied
a large piece of lint, thoroughly soaked in the solution she
had recommended to Kate. She displayed no hesitation, no
feminine shrinking at the ugly job. Mrs. Forrester evidently
knew what she was about, and set to work in a cool business-
like fashion, which in some measure restored Kate to confidence and hope.

"Now," she said, holding the lint in its place with her
hand, "quick, bring me a roller, or a piece of coarse linen,

with which to make everything fast. There," as she accomplished the affair successfully, "that's done, at any rate, and
may be the means of preventing the horse catching cold until
Mr. Bryan arrives. The next thing for us to do is to give him
a drink that will deaden the pain. You got some laudanum,
did you not, Miss Brewser?"

"Yes," said Kate, feeling more and more amazed by the
profundity of her companion's knowledge. "Here it is.
What use are you going to make of it?"

"I like people who ask questions," said Mrs. Forrester
approvingly. "And if folks wish to enlarge their minds they
should never be ashamed of confessing their own ignorance.
Well, you see, my dear, the principal danger we have to contend against in a case of this sort is of peritonitis setting in.
The laudanum not only numbs pain, but also exercises a
wonderfully soothing influence over the action of the intestines,
a matter just now of great importance. A small dose often
works wonders, and anyhow can do no harm. There now,
poor fellow!" she added, having administered the drug, and
patted King Olaf's neck, "we can do nothing more for you
until Mr. Bryan turns up with his sewing apparatus, which
we must hope may be soon."

Kate thanked Mrs. Forrester most warmly for her kindness.
"It is awfully good of you," she said, "taking so much
trouble on my behalf. I feel as if I could not thank you
sufficiently."

"I hate thanks," was the brusque reply. "All my life I
never could bear to see animals in pain. If I can relieve
them I must, that's just the truth; and what's more my dear,"
with more emotion than one could have given her credit
for, "I feel for you also. I know what it is to lose a good
hunter. I had one once I was exceedingly fond of. He ran a
stake into the fleshy part of his thigh, out hunting with the
Critchley, over a mere nothing of a fence, and though all was
done that human experience could devise, he died from mortification, exactly a week after the injury had been inflicted."

"Dear me, that was very sad, and makes me tremble for
King Olaf. Do you think, Mrs. Forrester, that there is any

chance, however small, of his ultimate recovery? If only I might hope "—

" That is a question neither I nor yet anyone else can answer. Very much will depend on how he goes on in the course of the next day or two. If he gets over them fairly well, and no unfavourable symptoms set in, we may begin to gain confidence. His strength should be kept up in every way. Hardboiled eggs beaten up in milk, or even strong beef tea, are both excellent for that purpose. A good bottle of port wine when a horse is weak and below par, and the inflamation has subsided, may also be of service. But Mr. Bryan, no doubt, will prescribe properly, for he's reckoned very clever among the profession, and passed no end of stiff examinations—not that they always go for much."

As she finished speaking Colonel Clinker came galloping into the yard, having evidently not delayed an instant after the reception of Kate's message, for Opal was covered with foam, and he himself splashed all over from head to foot.

" Thank goodness ! " he exclaimed in tones of relief when he saw Kate standing safe and sound, talking to Mrs. Forrester. " I have been in such an awful fright, thinking you had had another cropper, and hurt yourself again."

" No, it's not me this time," she said. " It's worse—it's King Olaf."

" I can't agree with you there. But what's the matter? Nothing very serious, I hope ? "

" Yes, something too dreadfully serious. King Olaf is frightfully staked. It makes me shudder even to think of."

Whereupon both ladies proceeded to give Colonel Clinker an account of what had happened. After hearing it he looked at the horse, but did not attempt to remove the bandages, which had been effectual in checking the loss of blood. He thought that Mrs. Forrester had acted with admirable wisdom, and done everything that, under the circumstances, lay in her power. " In fact," said he, " it's really a pity you should stay any longer and give up your day's hunting. I will look after Miss Brewser and see her safely home. I left the hounds quite close to this, and if you go at once you will have no difficulty in finding them."

Mrs. Forrester's first decision was not to lose sight of so grave and interesting a case, but second thoughts appeared best, for she suddenly began winking at Jack, and said—

"Sly dog! Ah yes, of course! Never mind, I understand all about it, and don't want to spoil sport."

He bit his lip and frowned. These allusions irritated him sorely.

"There's no sport to spoil," he said gloomily.

"You can't expect me to believe that in a hurry."

"I don't care what you believe. It's a fact, nevertheless."

"Well!" said Mrs. Forrester, turning to Kate, "I don't like leaving you in the lurch, but I can't be of any more use at present, so I may as well catch up the hounds again. Besides, I leave you in good hands. Colonel Clinker says he will see you home."

"It seems my fate to be a perpetual nuisance to my friends," said poor Kate. "I wish I could do something to show my gratitude in return."

"Tut, tut! don't talk nonsense; anybody to hear you would think I had done something wonderful instead of performing a most ordinary action of humanity," replied the old lady quite testily.

To give her her due, underneath all that outwardly hard manner beat an unusually warm heart, which sympathised on most occasions with her fellow-creatures, in spite of that sympathy being not unfrequently displayed in an original fashion. She remounted her horse, and after making Kate promise to write and tell her the result of Mr. Bryan's visit, rode off at a steady jog-trot to re-find the hounds and finish her day's hunting like the kind old lady she really was, sacrificing her natural inclinations and desire of gaining fresh experience in the veterinary science to the Machiavellian policy of leaving the young couple together.

CHAPTER XXVIII.

SUSPENSE.

WHEN they found themselves alone, Jack Clinker said to Kate—

"Do you believe in presentiments, Miss Brewser?"

"I hardly know," she replied. "It is so easy, once a thing has happened, to persuade yourself into the idea you had always foretold it."

"You don't remember, then, the remark I made this morning about misfortunes never coming singly? It certainly was not a very original one; nevertheless all through the morning I have had an uneasy feeling that something was going to happen. There's a fatality about these things. Just fancy, Snowflake breaking down badly and King Olaf half killing himself! One grows quite jumpy over such misfortunes. I wonder what will be the next to overtake us?"

"Don't talk of any more, for goodness sake! We have had enough and to spare as it is, without predicting others. I had no idea you were so superstitious. Do you know," dropping her voice to an uneasy whisper, "I feel so shaky and demoralised that if King Olaf d—d—dies I do not really think I shall ever care to go hunting again. When all goes well it's delightful, and following hounds the greatest physical pleasure that exists, but when accidents like this occur a revulsion of feeling sets in, and one doubts whether the game is worth the candle—we stand to lose too much and gain too little."

"Come, come," he said, endeavouring to comfort her, seeing also how thoroughly upset she was by what had taken place; "I will not have you give way to such gloomy views.

Like everything else in this world, hunting presents its bright and its dark side, but of the two the former decidedly predominates. I always pity those poor devils who kick their heels about town all through the long months of winter fog, and have no better resource than to toddle down to their clubs and play a rubber of whist or game of picquet. No, no, depend upon it, in spite of occasional accidents, we hunting people have out and out the best of it, and lead far cheerier lives."

He had such a pleasant way of talking, and of looking at things in general, she could not feel very downhearted when he was near. Her fits of depression only recurred in his absence.

"And what about India?" she summoned up courage to ask in a subdued voice. "Are you really going?"

"We will discuss that some other time. It's too long a question to enter into just now, and one that will require a good deal of consideration. I can't be here to-day and gone to-morrow, however, if you mean that."

She did not enter into any explanations, though she derived considerable consolation from this assurance, having dreaded, since Snowflake's disaster, that he might pack up his things any day and depart without giving her premonitory warning.

"You intend finishing the season, then?"

"I don't know; it depends on what turns up, but very probably"—

At that moment Stirrup arrived in the phaeton, looking terribly agitated, accompanied by Mr. Bryan. After some conversation and a preliminary inspection of King Olaf, Colonel Clinker took Kate aside, and said to her very gently, yet with a certain authority in his manner—

"I think, Miss Brewser, you had better go and wait inside the house for a little, while the operation of sewing up the wound is performed. Witnessing it will only give you unnecessary pain, and you have borne quite enough already. The sight is not pleasant for a lady's eyes, besides which you have now been on your legs for some hours, and what between the excitement and the worry will only knock yourself up if

you don't take care. You ought, too, by rights to change
those boots," noticing how wet they were when Kate began
to walk. "You'll catch your death of cold if you don't. I
daresay one of the women-folks will lend you a pair of dry
shoes."

"I can't think about myself," she said impatiently.

"All the more reason for others to do so, then. I can be
very stern and very tyrannical when I choose. I shall order
some tea to be got ready, and tell Mrs. Hammond to make
you take off those wet boots and stockings."

"I don't feel as if I *could* sit still while everybody else is
working and doing some good; it is so hard to remain useless.
Inaction always falls to the lot of us poor, wretched women."

"Never mind about that. What are we men here for
except to take care of you when we get the chance, and help
to carry some of the burden oppressing the weaker shoulders?
You are brave enough in all conscience; don't give in now.
Imagine yourself a child and I your schoolmaster. Well! I
beg you to go in, take a rest, and have something to eat and
to drink; then if you are an obedient pupil, I promise to look
in every few minutes and report progress. Besides, I'm
selfish, and want some tea myself. Won't you give me a cup,
just to show there's no ill-feeling between us?"

There were possibly times when Kate Brewser was wilful
and wayward, but Colonel Clinker's kindness, his soft entreat-
ing voice, and persuasive manners, conquered her altogether.
She could no more have opposed him, when he talked to her
like this, than have opposed her dead uncle had he risen from
his grave.

"Very well," she said, without offering another word of
remonstrance. I will do what you wish, only mind you come
soon. It will be awful, staying there all alone."

"Oh yes, I'll come," he promised, thinking that in many
ways she still possessed a sweet childishness of manner.
"There's the tea, you know, as an inducement." And then
with a smile and a nod he went outside, and left her to her
own resources. Perhaps the hardest trial that Kate endured
that day was having to sit in a little close parlour, furnished

in horsehair, crochet antimacassars, and wool mats, and respond to the well-meaning, but evidently forced conversation of Mrs. Hammond, a most excellent and worthy woman, though the history of her birth, parentage, fortune, marriage, and internal ailments failed, after a while, to either interest or amuse her listener. Kate's thoughts all the time were busy with King Olaf, and she longed at least to be left alone. But Mrs. Hammond's small talk was ceaseless and persevering, and there was nothing for it but to sit and smile, and endeavour to respond in a fitting manner when a response was clearly imperatively demanded. The situation grew unendurable. Kate framed all kinds of stern speeches, such as "Woman, don't you see I'm in trouble; can't you leave me alone?" or "My good soul, please don't mind me if you are busy," but although she mentally arranged such speeches, directly an opportunity arose of using them her heart failed her in the most ignominious manner, and she continued to smile, and to nod, and to ejaculate, until Mrs. Hammond was quite charmed with her guest's affability.

It is often inconceivable how the minutes fly when we are enjoying ourselves, yet at other times Old Time seems to require a good jog to bustle him up. Had Colonel Clinker not been endowed with a strong natural modesty, he could not have helped feeling flattered by the expression of pleased animation and joyous relief which overspread Kate's countenance on his reappearance.

"Oh!" she cried artlessly, "I am so thankful you have come!"

"Well, it is all over at last," he said, "and Mr. Bryan has bid me fetch you to pronounce on the results of his labours."

She went out to the stables immediately, overcome with delight at escaping from the parlour, and arriving there was greatly comforted by the different appearance the wound now presented. Mr. Bryan had made a very good job of it, and stood by looking at his handiwork with no little pride.

"I am in hopes no vital part has been touched, after all," he said to Kate reassuringly; "there's only this one little

z

spot," pointing to a certain place as he spoke, "that looks suspicious, and as if the stake might have penetrated. However, we shall know more about it in forty-eight hours' time. I have given the horse a drink, and told your groom exactly what I wish done, and will look in again to-morrow morning before ten o'clock. I shall hope to hear then he has passed a tolerably comfortable night, and is going on favourably. And now we had better leave him alone. He has gone through a good bit, and the quieter he is kept the more advisable it will be."

"Will you drive Mr. Bryan back in the pony phaeton, Miss Kate?" suggested Stirrup respectfully. "The Colonel 'ee has 'is 'oss, and I promised Mr. Bryan we would convey 'im back to Foxington."

"With pleasure," she said, settling herself on her seat and taking up the reins. "Come in, Mr. Bryan, please." Then she put out her hand to wish Colonel Clinker good-bye. "I don't dare express my thanks," she said, with a half-apologetic smile.

"That's right," he said with an answering one. "Between friends they are quite superfluous, but if you wish really to show your gratitude, be a good Samaritan, and let me fill Mr. Bryan's place to-morrow morning when you come here to meet him. I feel the greatest interest in poor King Olaf."

Was it possible that just a tiny portion of it might be assumed?

"Are you not going to hunt?" she asked guilelessly.

"Oh yes, later on. But there will be lots of time. And these double misfortunes have destroyed my nerve. Somehow I don't feel a bit keen."

Kate gave the desired promise and then drove off, extracting all the information she could, with reference to King Olaf's case, on the way home.

* * * *

By ten o'clock the following morning the party reassembled at Silverstone, and were met by old Stirrup, wearing a most anxious and unhappy countenance.

"How's the horse?" asked Jack Clinker apart, in order

that, should the reply prove unfavourable, it might not immediately reach Kate Brewser's ears.

"Bad, sir, wery bad indeed," answered he huskily. "It goes to my 'eart to see 'im. 'Ees never touched a morsel of corn, and 'im with such a appetite in a ordinary way. 'Ee seems to be suffering a deal of pain, too, hinards, breathes heavily, and changes 'is feet uneasily."

"That's a bad symptom," said Colonel Clinker, looking very grave. "I had hoped things might have improved, but I don't like the report at all."

"No more does I, sir. I would give 'arf a year's wages, and gladly into the bargain, to put King Holaf right again, and make 'im as 'ee was this time yesterday morning. Lord, Colonel, 'ee was full of life then, and as playful as a kitten, and now to see 'im, its downright 'eartrending." Stirrup turned away abruptly as he concluded the sentence, overcome by the exceeding bitterness of the recollection.

"Whatever you do, don't talk to your mistress in this way," said Colonel Clinker hurriedly. "She's so dreadfully cut up over the whole business. Try and make the best of things, and let her hope as long as she can. We don't want to make her more miserable than she is already; besides, it is just possible that things may take a turn for the better. There's never any telling." So saying he entered the box, where Kate had gone on their first arrival. Poor King Olaf was standing up in it, with his head drooping listlessly, and his bright eyes dimmed with suffering. At the sound of Kate's voice he slowly turned his neck, her presence seeming to cheer him somewhat. She had brought some sugar, and offered him a dainty morsel in the palm of her hand. He looked at it with dumb longing, as much as to say he would if he could, and turned it over several times with his soft nose. Then, as if the recollections it conjured up were too sweet to withstand, he sucked it in between his flexible lips. Kate was delighted. But alas! the taste no longer possessed any power to please, for after feebly champing at it once or twice, he let the lump fall uncrushed to the ground. The ready tears sprang to Kate's eyes at the sight. "He won't even

eat his sugar!" she exclaimed in distress, "he who loves it
so, and would follow me anywhere for a piece. Oh!" almost
angrily, as they tried to console her, "nobody need deceive
me about his condition. It's only false kindness. I know
quite well, without being told, that he is very, *very* bad
indeed." She buried her face in the horse's soft silky mane,
and cried gently to herself. There was no denying the fact
that, in his mistress's own words, King Olaf *was* very, *very*
bad, wounded even unto death. Every now and again he
would turn his head round, and gaze mournfully at his poor
injured side with a hopeless, resigned, and infinitely touching
expression, which went to the hearts of all those present.
Mr. Bryan now undid the bandages, dressed the wound, said
it bore every appearance of going on well, but shook his head
when told of the horse's total loss of appetite.

"If only he would begin to peck a bit, no matter how
little, I should be more hopeful," he declared. "Try him,"
turning to Stirrup, "with everything you can possibly think
of." Then he gave King Olaf another reviving drink, and
went his way, significantly stating that he would call in again
during the course of the afternoon.

CHAPTER XXIX

KING OLAF'S DEATH.

THE following day a perfect tempest of wind and rain prevailed, so that Kate found it impossible to go over to Silverstone, and had to content herself with sending a stable lad to enquire after King Olaf's condition. The answer brought back was not encouraging, being to the effect that the horse showed no improvement, persistently refused to feed, and was growing weaker and weaker in spite of all endeavours to maintain his strength. Next morning, fortunately, the sun shone out brightly, and although the severity of the gale had been such as to uproot several large trees, whose branches lay about in all directions, the wind had subsided, and the air after the storm felt fresh and pleasant. Kate determined she would bring poor King Olaf something nice, something that would really tempt him to eat, so directly after breakfast she went on to the lawn in front of the house, and with a pair of scissors snipped all the sweetest, greenest grass she could find, which she put into a basket, and carried over to Silverstone in triumph. But when she got there she was shocked by the terrible change for the worse which had taken place in King Olaf's appearance. The horse hung his head listlessly, as if the slender neck was quite unequal to bearing its weight aloft; his small ears felt cold as ice to the touch; his eyes—those beautiful blue eyes, which used to be so bright and full of life—were covered with a glazy film; his coat looked dull and staring; his breathing came and went in quick, flurried, feeble gasps, and already the pink flesh lining his mouth had turned a dark and unnatural colour.

"Oh, Stirrup!" cried Kate, while the hot tears coursed

freely down her cheeks, "what shall I do? He is dying, dying as plainly as can be. Nothing on this earth will save him now, and I am so, *so* wretched."

Tears were also trickling down old Stirrup's own rugged weatherbeaten cheeks, for in his heart he knew she only spoke the truth, and it was impossible to contradict the statement. He tried to reply, but broke down hopelessly.

"King Olaf, my darling, my own beautiful and courageous darling!" sobbed Kate, who, alone with Stirrup, was not ashamed to give full utterance to her grief; "I do not even dare beg you to forgive me my worse than folly, for if it had not been for me, this w—would never have happened—I ought never to have asked you to jump such a place. It was m—m—madness, downright cruelty on my part. I see it now—that it is too—too l—late. And yet," with a fresh burst of sorrow, "I shall live on, very likely for years, and years, and years, and ne—ne—never see you again, or talk to you—or—or love you. Oh, King Olaf, I *cannot* bear it! I wish I was going to die too, and we might both lie under the ground together. We have been such good friends, and understood each other's ways so well—and then—to think—that it is I, I—your mistress—who have killed you! If I had only known—if I could put things back again as they were—I would willingly lose my right had. But th—things never c—can be put back again, and you—you are dying. Oh, what a brute I feel, to be sure!"

Her self-condemnation quite overcame old Stirrup, who forgot his own grief for the time while trying to comfort her.

"Don't 'ee take on so, now don't 'ee, Miss Kate, dear!" he said in much agitation, with a kindly but somewhat clumsy attempt at consolation. "It be terr'ble to hear you a-blaming of yourself for what, after all, is a accident, and might 'ave 'appened to the most cautious of riders. Cheer up, there's a dear young lady, and try and remember there be as good fish left in the sea has ever come out of it."

"Stirrup!" was the indignant reply, as she turned a pair of flashing eyes full upon him, "I wonder how you *can* talk to **me** in such a way—you, who ought to know by this time how dearly I love King Olaf. Do you really suppose, now, for one second, that I shall ever forget him? that I should ever either *find* or *allow* another to fill his place in my affections? No; the ocean may be vast, and its inmates plentiful, but such a treasure as King Olaf is only met with once in a lifetime. I shall never meet with his like again, and even if I did he could never be to me as King Olaf has been."

Poor old Stirrup! He had wished to comfort her in some small degree, and now her words seemed to rebuke his want of heart, as if *her* love put *his* to shame, and *her* constancy scoffed at *his*. He forgot that at twenty-two misfortunes seemed more cruel, harder to bear, and more unendurable than they do at sixty-five, and that age, in spite of many drawbacks, acquires at least an increased capacity of suffering with patience.

"If 'ee would only eat 'is victuals!" faltered Stirrup, blubbering like a baby. His words inspired Kate with feverish hope.

"Ah!" she cried, "I was nearly forgetting. King Olaf, my beauty!" lifting the basket from the ground; "see, dear old man, I have brought you some grass, some newly-cut grass! You will like that, surely, for it is fresh from the field. I picked it myself only this very morning." And she held him out the most enticing looking bit she could find. King Olaf turned his weary eyes upon the dainty morsel. It smelt so sweet and so nice that it recalled the bygone days when he used to play by the side of his dam and sniff at such grass as this in youthful disdain. He took the slender green blades in his mouth, and with an effort contrived to swallow a few. The last food that should pass his lips he would take from the hand of her he knew and loved so well. Kate felt encouraged to empty the contents of the basket into the manger, but alas! King Olaf's fleeting appetite was already appeased; the grass had apparently lost all charm he turned it over fancifully, and then dropped his heavy head as heretofore. It seemed to Kate as if she were bidding her gallant favourite a last farewell, and she could not tear herself away from his side. She stayed over an hour, talking to the horse, rubbing his poor cold ears, and lavishing endearing epithets upon him. At last, however, she was forced to depart.

"Good-bye, King Olaf," she said sadly. "Good-bye, I will come to see you again to-morrow."

To-morrow! Even as she uttered the word she felt it to be a mockery, felt that there might never exist one for him; that he might not live to see the rising sun streak the morning horizon with gleams of growing light, to hear the sweet note of the cuckoo in the distant coppice, the bay of the hounds, the rustle of the falling leaves, or free fresh air playing on his forehead. Her heart felt sore within her. It ached at the prospect of losing this dearly loved friend and tried companion. And if souls be denied dumb animals, may it not safely be asserted that their affinity to human beings is great, that their instincts and affections are identical, prompted by the same desires, the same longings, the same passions? Now as Kate lingered at the door, feeling curiously reluctant to shut him out from her eyes, King Olaf, as if conscious this would be good-bye for ever, turned in his box, and with feeble, faltering steps, essayed to totter towards her. She gave him one passionate kiss, lifted his beautiful muzzle to her lips, then hurried away, overcome with despairing grief and regret, feeling this loss to be almost heavier than she could bear.

*   *   *   *   *

The clock had struck ten. Mary Whitbread was sitting in an arm-chair by the drawing-room fire, placidly knitting a pair of socks, while Kate was playing one of Beethoven's mournful minor symphonies on the piano. The notes, under her pliant touch, sent forth a plaintive music, which rose and fell in irregular cadence, sounding almost like the wail of a human voice. Presently she shut the lid of the instrument with a bang, and began pacing restlessly up and down the room.

"I don't know what is the matter with me to-night," she said. "I don't feel as if I could settle to anything."

"You're fretting about poor King Olaf, Kate, and no wonder!" replied Mary sympathetically. "You've been

"Good-bye, King Dick."

making that piano cry for the last half-hour, but you really ought to be going to bed. It's high time for both of us to retire."

"What's the use of going to bed when you can't sleep?" sighed Kate. "I know nothing more horrible than lying awake hour after hour, tormented by thoughts you can't get rid of. You go, Mary, and I'll come by-and-by."

"By-and-by, Kate? How long does that mean?"

"Only a few minutes. I promise not to be long."

Mary folded up her knitting, stuck the needles carefully into her ball of wool, gave Kate a kiss, and departed. The latter drew up the blind, pressed her burning forehead against the cool window-sill, and looked out on the still night. Everything seemed so quiet and peaceful, everything except herself, and she was filled with a bitter and rebellious sorrow, impossible to conquer. Was it true that animals had no future life? Would she never meet King Olaf again? Would his beautiful body simply lie under the earth for ever? She shuddered at the thought. It was so utterly repugnant to her youthful spirit. At that moment she envied the Red Indian, who, when the shades of death were gathering round him, looked forward to an indefinite existence in a happy hunting-ground, with his favourite war-horse by his side. Her meditations were suddenly brought to an abrupt conclusion by the unusual sound of footsteps crunching the gravel outside. A swift and certain instinct told her King Olaf's end had come. She flew to open the hall-door, and hear Stirrup's account of the horse's last moments.

"Stirrup!" she cried in a tremulous voice, "are you there?"

"It is not Stirrup, it is I." And then, by the flickering light, she saw Colonel Clinker standing before her in riding apparel.

"I hope I have not frightened you," he said, as she gave a little start of surprise. "Stirrup could not get away quite so soon. I must apologise for disturbing you at this hour of the night, but after dinner I took it into my head to ride over to Silverstone and bring you the latest news."

" And you," she said, overcome by this last proof of his kindness, " have been out hunting all day long, and must be very tired."

" Tired? I am never tired ; but I want to tell you about "—
He hesitated, hardly knowing, now it had come to the point, how to convey the sad intelligence. But she knew it already, realised fully what had happened, and for what purpose he was there.

" I know," she said drearily. " He is dead, and I have been his murderer."

There was a hopeless, cold tone in her voice that touched him to the quick.

" Why should you accuse yourself so harshly? It is not right. No one can prevent accidents happening. You might just as well blame me for having broken down poor Snowflake. These things can't be helped, much as we may grieve at them when they occur."

" But then Snowflake is alive; he did not die. That makes all the difference."

" Do you think so? For my part I would sooner a quick, even though painful death, than a life of lingering misery. King Olaf died this evening at eight o'clock. He passed away without a struggle, quietly and peacefully. Stirrup said he grew gradually weaker, until his legs could no longer support the weight of his body; then he lay gently down on the straw, stretched himself out full length, and when Stirrup went to look at him he thought at first the horse had gone to sleep."

" A long, long sleep," she murmured, " with never an awakening."

Then all at once the flood-gates of her sorrow broke loose, and she burst into a fit of passionate weeping.

Jack Clinker had braved a good many dangers in his day, but the sight of a woman's tears he never could stand.

" Hush ! " he said tenderly. " Do not cry so. I cannot bear to see you suffer. Try and think that it is well with King Olaf, and that his physical pains are at an end. He was a noble fellow, but he met his death honourably, like some brave soldier in the field of battle. You should not grieve too much. In a few years' time he might have grown old and decrepit, and to outlive affection and regret is infinitely worse than death."

"I know, I know," she said, hastily drying her eyes. "I try and tell myself the same things, but I can't reason or theorise at present. It may be horribly selfish, but I can only think of my loss and my grief."

"Not selfish, but loving and true as a woman thould be," he answered reverently. "I have brought you these." Then after a pause, "See," he said, "they are King Olaf's hoofs. I thought you would like to have them."

She did not even look at them. She could not trust herself to do so. It was so dreadful to know that never again in this life would those four trusty, willing feet carry her over hill and dale, or bound across the breezy pastures.

"Oh!" she cried wildly, "what shall I do, what shall I do without him!"

"Kate," he said, with soft persuasion, "listen to me. It is difficult for the new ever to replace the old, but Opal is a good mare; none better was ever foaled. Will you take her instead of King Olaf—take her as a free gift from me, and in course of time learn to value her as she deserves?"

"What! Rob you of your dearest possession, of the animal you declared you never would part with, not even if you went abroad?"

"I would not do so lightly, but in giving her to you I know she will find a mistress worthy of her."

"And what should you think of *me* if I accepted such a sacrifice?"

"I should think you were conferring a very great favour, and that, so far as I am concerned, there was no sacrifice whatever. Giving to a person one lo—I mean whom one likes," hastily correcting the expression, "is exactly the same thing as giving to one's self."

The clear, dark-blue sky, lit up by hundreds and thousands of radiant stars, spread like a vast canopy over their heads;

the big, soft moon shone down upon them, turning all the fields into silver, while the trees stood out in delicate silhouette against the transparent clouds, and the frosty night-air kissed their brows as they stood together under the red-brick porch. The heart of the man beat fast. He longed so to comfort her, to take her in his arms and speak of a love which would endeavour to soften every grief, to chase away dull care. Perhaps he was not altogether like most of his sex, for a naturally chivalric instinct forbade his taking any mean advantage of her distress, or profiting by it to urge his own suit, but rather prompted him to postpone telling his love to some later day, when she might better listen to the tale, and when it could cause no fresh agitation or renewed grief. Her heart, too, was stirred to its very depths, stirred by King Olaf's death, but still more by his generous offer. Our opportunities come, but, alack! we fail to recognise them, and they pass away. Had he only spoken then she surely would have yielded, would have confessed that his love was returned, that she cared for him more than for anyone in this world. But the golden moment slipped by, and once more with a powerful effort he controlled any expression of his feelings. She stood nervously plucking at the broad, shining ivy-leaves growing up the porch, pulling them to pieces beneath the hasty twitching of her trembling fingers. A crisis in her life had come, and she at last realised the fact.

"How good you are to me!" she said after a silence, during which on either side "thought had leapt out to wed itself with thought." "You will not even let me thank you."

For one moment he allowed his eyes to rest on the sweet downcast face, with its soft contour and dark long lashes; then with a passionate longing he seized and wrung her hand.

"I would do anything in the world for you," he said in a hoarse whisper. "There is nothing in this wide world that you can ask of me that I would not try and do for your sake."

Without another word, or giving her time to make any reply, he turned swiftly away, and vanished down the winding drive.

She stood with parted lips and glistening eyes listening, listening until the last sound of his footsteps had ceased. She looked at the moon, and the stars, and the still night like a living statue. But the first bitterness of King Olaf's grief was softened; his sympathy had blunted the keen edge of it, and rendered her more patient in endurance. The little threepenny piece hung in its accustomed place. She looked at it and smiled, as if it were indeed some talisman of good. Then when she reached her room she knelt down on her knees and prayed as she had not prayed since her childhood —an innocent, girlish prayer, full of trust and thankfulness.

A great calm had suddenly come upon her, while all the time those few sweet words rang in her ears—

"I would do anything for you; there is nothing in this wide world I would not try and do for your sake."

She believed in him at last. He had conquered her doubts, overcome her scepticism. And in that belief, though King Olaf lay stiff and stark upon the yellow straw in Farmer Hammond's stable, she felt happier than she had done for years. So great, truly, is that power which men call love, and which already was exercising a softening and beneficial influence upon a nature rendered hard and callous by circumstances, but which in itself was womanly, compassionate, and sensitive, fitted to make the man of its choice truly happy.

CHAPTER XXX.

"THE RIFT WITHIN THE LUTE."

THE day of the Foxington Hunt Ball had arrived, and the little town was crowded to excess. Its hotels and its lodging-houses were crammed with pleasure-seekers from different parts of the country, while the usually quiet station presented a most unwonted scene of bustle and activity. Porters trundled heavy trucks, or hoisted portmanteaus on their shoulders; anxious maids stood pointing out the enormous white-initialed trunks belonging to their mistresses, while the one-horse omnibus and capacious but shabby flies did a roaring business. Those who owned country houses had filled their mansions on this auspicious occasion with smart dancing men, pretty girls, and professional beauties whose fame had preceded them, and whom the townspeople were dying to catch a glimpse of; for the Foxington ball was considered the best throughout the midland counties, and had a high reputation to sustain, which was certainly enhanced by the presence of one or two fashionable belles. Mothers, also, of marriageable daughters were wont to consider the county ball a fitting opportunity for youthful *débutantes* to make their entry into the world, prior to encountering a larger circle of acquaintances in the metropolis. Folks, in fact, assembled from far and wide, for in the memory of the most constant frequenters such a word as failure had been unknown in connection with the Foxington ball, and year after year fresh lustre was added to its reputation for success, smart frocks, and good looks. Even the most anti-terpsichorean hunting men, a class which regards such festivities, as a rule, with openly-avowed contempt,

though refusing steadily to trip the "light fantastic" in
propria personæ, graced this gathering with their presence,
condescending to fill up the doorways and every available
opening, lounging in odd corners (where they discussed the
latest hunting news as eagerly as they would have done seated
in their own easy-chairs in smoking suits and slippers), forming picturesque wall-ornaments, whose vivid scarlet coats
stood out in striking contrast against the white mural decora-
tions. Four whole weeks had passed away since that frosty
moonlight night on which Jack Clinker had ridden over and
broken the news of King Olaf's untimely death to Kate
Brewser, and by degrees she was beginning to recover from
the shock of that sad event. At first she not only obstinately
avoided the hunting field, but also everything connected with
it, steadily refusing either to drive or ride to the meets ; but
recently Stirrup had so often and so urgently implored her to
make a fresh start that at length she had yielded to his solici-
tations, and having once fairly broken the ice and enjoyed "a
real good thing," during which the Duckling had acquitted
himself brilliantly, she took to the pleasures of the chase once
more with an ardour enhanced rather than diminished by her
temporary retirement from the ranks. She could never forget
King Olaf, but the love of sport was too strong within her
ever to be quelled, even by serious misfortune.

During all this time she had not seen Colonel Clinker
once, and though this at first appeared strange, the reason
was simple enough, for he had left Foxington. On the very
morning after he had paid that nocturnal visit to Sport
Lodge he had received a telegram from the housekeeper at
Nevis, informing him of the sudden illness of his father,
and requesting his immediate presence. He had therefore
set out for the North without a minute's delay, and without
finding time to wish good-bye to Kate. In fact, she remained
ignorant of his absence for a few days, until informed of it
by Mr. McGrath, although in the interval she had secretly
wondered at his non-appearance.

"I had a letter from Jack this morning. He desires to be
remembered to you," said Mr. Mc Grath one day when he

happened to meet her walking alone in the town. "He tells me the old gentleman is quite out of danger."

"The old gentleman?" echoed she. "*What* old gentleman?"

"Faix, and don't you know? Why, Lord Nevis, of course. He had a fit of apoplexy, and they thought at first he was a 'gone coon.'"

"Is Colonel Clinker away from home, then?" She was glad to find there had been some excuse, after all, for his apparent neglect.

"Dear me, yes. Why, he left on Friday. The house-keeper telegraphed to Jack to come at once if he wished to find Lord Nevis alive; so he stuffed a few clothes in a port-manteau and went off there and then."

"And Lord Nevis, you say, is better?" she asked anxiously.

"Very much, according to Jack—become quite sensible and knows them all. Bedad! Jack won't like losing his hunting much, for there's none to be had up there, you know. It's a very wild, dreary sort of place this time of year, though pleasant enough in summer."

"Perhaps he will come back again soon?" she suggested.

"I expect he will. Jack's uncommon fond of his old governor, but a great hulking fellow hanging about in a sick-room can do no earthly good. He is only in the way. How-ever, I dare say I shall hear how things progress in the course of a day or two."

But as time went on Lord Nevis improved, and with no ostensible reason for prolonging his absence, Colonel Clinker did not return to the Retreat.

Mr. McGrath grew so uneasy that he felt he must make a confidant of Kate, whose sympathies he knew he could rely upon. "By St. Patrick, Miss Brewser," he said to her, when another week had elapsed, "it's really very odd; I can't make it out at all, and would give a pony to know what that fellow Jack is about all this while. Every time he writes he says his father is better, and yet he never talks of coming home."

'1 suppose he can't leave him," said Kate.

"Then why the deuce does he not say so?"

"Because he probably thinks you take it for granted."

"It's a shame," continued Mr. McGrath, waxing warm. "There am I, left with all those cursed bills coming pouring in, and not knowing what on earth to do with them. 'Send my letters on Terry, old man,' said Jack, 'but open all the blue ones and chuck them into the fire.' I wish to goodness I had done what I was told from the first, but some scruples of conscience prevented my doing so, and now the wretched things are piled up literally yard high. Nobody but Jack could stand such a state of affairs and still show a cheery front to the enemy. He's a most undefeated sportsman."

"Has he ever said anything to you lately, Mr. McGrath, about going away?"

"Oh, Jack's always talking of hooking it. I've grown accustomed to that threat, and it fails to disturb me any longer. Gad! Miss Brewser, but I've graver reasons for disquietude just at present. I can put two and two together as well as most people, and when Jack stays on at Nevis, with a stud of horses here eating their heads off, I say there's something behind the scenes." And Mr. McGrath pursed up his fat, flabby little lips with an exceedingly mysterious and important air.

"But, Mr. McGrath," objected Kate, "do you think anything could be more natural than a son stopping with a father who is ill? What is there suspicious about it? She was far too loyal in her affection not to defend the absent, whatever doubts she might secretly have about him; and although all sorts of far-fetched speculations filled her brain she did not choose to divulge them to her companion.

"Can you keep a secret?" asked Mr. McGrath suddenly.

"I hope so," she answered with ready curiosity. "At all events, I'll promise to try. What is it?"

"You swear not to let it go any farther? Jack would be in an awful rage if he knew I had said anything about it."

"Then perhaps you had better not tell me. I'd rather

A A

you did nothing that would vex him, especially now he
happens to be away."

"Faith, Miss Brewser! but the fact of the matter is, I
don't feel as if I *could* keep it to myself; besides, you're to be
trusted, so here goes. You must know," lowering his voice
to a confidential whisper, "that Lord Nevis is most anxious
for his son to marry "—

"Well, there's nothing so wonderful in that," interrupted
Kate.

"Yes, but listen. It must be someone with money. Jack
can't possibly commit matrimony without. Well, there's a
girl up there, a Miss Paton—ah, I see you begin to look
interested at last!"

"Yes, yes; go on."

"There's a girl up there, as I said before, who has fallen
head over ears in love with Jack. It's really quite pitiable to
watch the poor thing."

"What's the girl's name?"

"Polly Paton—Miss Polly Paton, of Poolerorie."

"And Colonel Clinker? Does he respond?"

"Ah, that's just where it is. I don't believe, between you
and me and the post, that Jack cares a bit about her."

"Then what, may I ask, do you fear? And even if Colonel
Clinker were fond of this — this Miss Paton, since she has
money, why should you object?" Her voice sounded a trifle
hard in her own ears, but Mr. McGrath's powers of observation were not sufficiently acute to notice it.

"She's a silly, foolish little thing," he said, "not worthy
of Jack in any way. You see, Miss Brewser, Jack's such an
infernal easy-going, good-hearted fellow, he wants a girl
with her head on her shoulders, who could exercise a certain
influence over him."

"And would not Miss Paton do so?"

"Never; she's not the sort of girl. All the same, I should
not be in the least surprised if she has been setting her cap at
Jack; he's very soft where women are concerned, can't bear
to give them pain, or say an unkind word, and just to please
his father he might drift into an engagement out of pity.

Don't you understand?" It was seldom Mr. McGrath spoke so seriously on any subject, but now he was evidently greatly in earnest, while it never seemed to enter his mind for one moment that it was just possible he had lacked discrimination in the choice of a *confidante.* But Kate, though every word stabbed her to the heart, was not one to allow others to guess her emotions. She was, fortunately for herself, endowed with a large share of self-control, and carried on the conversation with an outward calm which effectually deceived her companion and put him off the right scent.

" I did not give Colonel Clinker credit for being so pliable," she said. "He never struck me as one of those men whom a woman can twist round her little finger. However, of course you know him better than I do."

"Gad!" returned Terry, where there's a girl in question, and a pretty one into the bargain, it takes a very strong man to resist. It flatters a fellow's vanity to know that some girl is awfully in love with him, even if he don't care two straws about her. I'm not sure," musingly, " that I might not even get led away myself under similar circumstances."

"Oh, the girl is pretty, is she? That makes a difference, of course."

"*All* the difference. If she were ugly the danger would be reduced to a minimum; besides, Jack don't care for ugly women; never did."

" He's a sad flirt, I'm afraid, Mr. McGrath?"

" Oh! I don't know about that. All men are pretty much the same."

" Are they? Then I'm sorry for them."

" They don't require much pity, Miss Browser. They manage to jog along tolerably comfortably on the whole."

" I *detest* flirty men," said Kate, pursuing her own train of thought.

"Do you mean to say by that you detest Jack?" asked Mr. McGrath, opening his dark eyes in surprise.

" I don't feel called upon to express any opinion one way or the other about *your friend* Colonel Clinker," she replied coldly, and then for the first time it began vaguely to dawn upon Mr. McGrath's obtuse comprehension that he had somehow put his foot in it, and signally failed to advance a cause he was conscious of secretly advocating. The conversation came to an abrupt termination, neither was it revived at any future period, Kate seeming steadily to avoid all reference to Colonel Clinker, and refusing to be inveigled into any farther discussion about him.

Nevertheless, Mr. McGrath's words made a deep impression, which as each day went by became more permanent. What a fool she had been, to be sure, and what a mercy that she had been saved from committing any crowning act of folly. The scale had dropped from her eyes, and she could now see things in their true light. Colonel Clinker did not care for her, never had cared for her, or else he would not have gone away like this. Perhaps he might even be absent on purpose. Mr. McGrath had said his heart was kind, that he could not bear to give a woman pain, and he had guessed how fond she was of him, and left Foxington out of pity—pity for *her*. To a high-spirited, proud girl like Kate, the very idea was torture. She had been mistaken in fancying his attentions meant anything; they were merely the civilities of a man whose powers of flirtation were already well known; and to think that she, Kate Brewser, had fallen a victim to his fascinations. The little seed of jealousy sown by Mr. McGrath's unconscious hand grew and grew until it darkened all her mental vision, and each fresh speculation and assumption became more bitter and improbable. Perhaps at that very moment Colonel Clinker was amusing himself with Miss Polly Paton, basking in the sunshine of Miss Polly Paton's smiles, and telling Miss Polly Paton that "there was nothing in the world he would not try and do for her sweet sake." She hated her with a fierce hatred of which a week ago she could not have believed herself capable. She was glad her rival was a weak, stupid little creature; that at least was some small comfort in her cup of bitterness; but then, on the other hand, she was pretty; Mr. McGrath had distinctly said so, and men would do anything for a pretty face, while she herself could lay no claims to beauty. She looked in the glass. No! She had good eyes, good hair, and a good complexion, but her nose was awful, and her mouth like a cavern. So she told herself, trying hard to maintain a strict impartiality, to exaggerate nothing, to conceal nothing. She had no recommendations whatever, save her money and lack of relatives, and if Colonel Clinker ever by any chance should propose—if things went wrong with Miss Polly Paton, or the settlements were not so good as he expected—and he fell back upon her as a *pis aller*, a last resource, she would know how to appreciate his conduct at its proper value. Then she remembered regretfully how once or twice he had called her Kate, taken her hand in his, how she had even allowed him to detain it unnecessarily, and once—yes, once—that night when he had told her of King Olaf's death, she had actually returned its pressure. A burning blush rose to her brow. He might have thought she was running after him—to use Mr. McGrath's expression, "setting her cap at him," and here all her pride rose up in arms. If he did return to Foxington at any future period she would at least take care to make him alter *that* opinion — to let him know he was as indifferent to her as she apparently was to him. She felt herself growing harder and colder, and rejoiced at the fact, though all the time her heart ached sorely, and her spirits sank at this sudden blighting of her joy, this cruel frustration of her hopes.

Kate, perhaps, may seem silly to many, yet there are others who can sympathise with a state of feeling brought about by mingled love and jealously. A woman's nature is passionate and sensitive, but at times wholly unreasoning, and Kate fast argued herself into a hostile condition, in which she was prepared to meet Colonel Clinker as a stranger and a foe.

Would all this animosity fade away when they met, like a mirage in the desert, like snow in the sunshine, or would it lead to grave results? She never paused to consider. Each hour of his absence only formed a fresh link in the chain of undisputable facts against him.

And now the day of the Foxington Hunt Ball had arrived,

and he was coming back to be present at it, having torn him-self away from the charms of Miss Polly Paton's society, and overcome his filial anxieties for the time being. But she would greet him very coldly; she would not allow him to imagine for one second that she was glad of his return, that she had longed for a sight of his face or the sound of his voice. That folly was over and done with, kept firmly in abeyance by a strong and insulted pride. Yet with charac-teristic contradiction she appeared in a diaphanous costume of white tulle, with a single row of pearls round her neck, and her hair dressed neatly and close to the head, because once, months ago, when they first met, he had told her that he thought "women looked to better advantage so than in any other way, except, perhaps, a riding-habit." It certainly seemed odd she should remember this now, when his opinions had become a matter of complete indifference, and still more odd that she should view her reflection in the glass with a feeling of triumph, and a sudden assumption that Miss Polly Paton might not have, probably *had* not, a good figure, and that Colonel Clinker said he placed this advantage far before a pretty face. Kate's arms and neck were white and rounded like polished alabaster; perhaps Miss Polly's were red, mottled, and countrified. There was some satis-faction to be derived from the thought. And now that the time had arrived when she would see him again her heart relented a little. It was just possible that she might have judged him too hastily, that there might be some extenuat-ing circumstances. She would listen to him at any rate, hear what he had to say, and yes—if he asked her—dance with him once or twice. She would not admit even to herself that the soul-hunger of love was upon her; but so it was all the same, although she disputed the fact cleverly, under a variety of different pretexts highly creditable to her imagination.

The two girls had persuaded Mrs. Tryon to run down from town on a few days' visit, and once more fill the *rôle* of *chaperone*, Mrs. Forrester, whom they first asked, regarding all such frivolous amusements with unmitigated contempt.

"No," she declared, "had it been a good sale, a horse-show, or even a travelling circus, I would have escorted you, my dears, with pleasure, but a ball I really can't, much as I should like to oblige. Such festivities are quite out of my line."

The Sport Lodge party arrived early on the scene, determined to derive all the enjoyment possible from the evening's amusement. Mary Whitbread was in a state of absolute beatitude, for during the afternoon a magnificent bouquet, quite bridal in its virgin spotlessness and purity of colour, had arrived in a wooden box, with her name written on the cardboard label in large letters, and although the giver maintained a strict incognito, she recognised Mr. Grahame's handwriting. She carried it now, with a flush of happiness tinging her pale cheeks, and making her, in her black ball dress, look positively pretty.

The ball itself was held in a large and lofty room, specially set apart every year for the purpose, belonging to the enterprising proprietress of the Rest and be Thankful Hotel. The walls were gaily decorated with scarlet and white draperies, festoons of flowers, and a vast array of wax candles, while the red coats of the men and the bright costumes of the ladies added additional colour and cheerfulness to the scene. The room was comparatively empty as yet, and the smooth shining boards looked very inviting, while the musicians sat tuning their instruments and idly turning over the pages of the dance music about to be played. Somewhat to Kate's surprise she almost immediately stumbled upon an old friend and admirer in Captain Fitzgerald, whom she had not met since last season in town, and who, with a strawberry-cream carnation in his buttonhole, the very latest thing in collars, and an immaculate shirt-front, fully maintained his reputation as an exquisite of the first water. At the present moment he evidently regarded himself as most cruelly insulted by being dragged to a country ball at such a ridiculously early hour. He was standing lolling up against the doorway, stroking the ends of his long, silky, flaxen moustache with an air of unmistakable boredom on his vapid but well-cut features. They assumed an unwonted animation, however, on Kate's appearance, and, advancing hastily towards her with an *empressement* as complimentary as it was unusual in so *blasé* and accomplished a ladykiller, he said—

"Aw! really now, Miss Brewsaw, this *is* a pleasaw," shaking hands effusively, "though not, perhaps, altogether an unexpected one, as I thought I should most likely see you here to-night. Awfully jolly, meeting an old friend in this sort of way, ain't it?"

Captain Fitzgerald edged insinuatingly to her side as he spoke. He was a fragile-looking man, of diminutive height; but what he lacked in physical stature he apparently made up for in self-esteem.

"Yes," answered Kate, with an irrepressible smile, "awfully jolly. Quite a pleasant surprise indeed, at least so far as I am concerned."

"Aw! now, you know, Miss Brewsaw, you're too flattering. I only wish a fellar could believe what you say, but you were always up to some kind of chaff."

"Chaff, Captain Fitzgerald? I was never more serious in my life."

His vanity was not proof against this assertion. He beamed with self-satisfaction, and said sentimentally—

"I really began to think I was nevaw going to see you again. It seems such an age since we met."

"Yes," said she with brutal *sang froid*, without an atom of answering romance, "not since we used to sit under the trees last season in Rotten Row, comment upon the fashions, and arrive at the conclusion Captain Fitzgerald was the best-dressed man in London. I remember. Why, I can even recall the pattern of that dear little blue and white scarf you used to wear."

"Aw! those were indeed happy days," said he, heaving a languishing sigh. "Do you evaw think of them I wonder, Miss Brewsaw?"

"Have I not just told you so, or do you wish me to enumerate the number and colour of your coats? Let me see, there was a brown one, and a grey one, and a black one, and a rather æsthetic but very choice dark green"—

"What a memory you have got to be sure," interrupted he admiringly. "I assure you, Miss Brewsaw, I often look back to those jolly days, and wish it were possible to recall the past."

"A very pernicious practice, Captain Fitzgerald, and a most foolish and unprofitable one. It would be far better to turn your attention to the present."

This was the first opening she had given him, and he was not slow to profit by it.

"That's what I intend doing," he said blandly. "In fact that's what I came here for to-night. 'Faint heart,' you know the rest."

Kate gave a little mischievous laugh. She felt no compunction in teasing so universal an admirer.

Her mirth appeared to nettle him somewhat, for he drew himself up with an injured air and said—

"'Pon my word now, Miss Brewsaw, you are too bad; you really are. I never met anyone so unsentimental in all my days."

"What! because, luckily for my peace of mind, I can afford to look back upon our Rotten Row experiences with tolerable equanimity? You are *exigeant*, to say the least of it."

She was in a bitter, mocking humour that night.

"Just the same as evaw I see," returned Captain Fitzgerald, quite undaunted by the off-hand manner in which she received his attentions. "Practical and charming, full of life, but, alas! no heart."

"No, no heart," she answered decidedly. "Certainly not. Hearts in the nineteenth century have gone to the wall altogether. The great god, money, has usurped their place, and people find the comforts and luxuries of life a very convenient substitute."

He looked at her with rather a conscious and disturbed expression, as if her speech had been specially directed against himself.

"You have a way of saying things now and again, Miss Brewsaw, calculated to make a fellar feel awfully small," he said, twirling his moustache uneasily. "Fellars don't like it, you know."

"No," with a mocking glance. "'Fellars' never do like home truths. But tell me, Captain Fitzgerald—just between friends—do you 'evaw' feel 'awfully small'?"

He was one of those men for whom she could feel no respect whatever. She could not help saying pert things to him, they came so naturally. He coloured a little, and said, not without annoyance—

"Dash it all! That's hardly a fair question. You can't expect me to confess my own weaknesses, even to you, Miss Brewsaw."

"Have you got any?"

"Aw! now, come, you know; I really wish you'd drop it."

"Drop it? Drop what?" she asked innocently.

"Oh! all that chaff. Let's try and talk sense."

"By all means, Captain Fitzgerald. Will you begin?"

"There, now you're at it again worse than ever."

"Dear me! You're terribly hard to please to-night. I did not know you were so huffy, and had developed this new phase of character."

He began to feel irritated by the persistent levity of her responses.

"And if I am huffy," he said warmly, "are you not enough to make me so?"

"I humbly beg pardon. I was not aware you possessed so sensitive a nature."

This was too much.

"You *must* know," he answered, "how greatly I value and esteem your good opinion."

She turned her head away, opening and shutting her fan with nervous impatience. She looked back now with astonishment to a time when she had considered this empty-headed, conceited little man rather good fun than otherwise, and when his vapid speeches had caused a certain amount of amusement. Insensibly she found herself making mental comparisons between Captain Fitzgerald's small, fragile form and the sturdy, upright one of somebody else—somebody else whom she was watching for and waiting for with ever-increasing anxiety, and whose non-appearance effectually prevented her from enjoying the present situation. Where could he be? Why had he not come? Had he changed his mind at the last moment, and remained by Miss Polly Paton's side? She was hardly conscious that Captain Fitzgerald had shifted his position and was scanning her features critically.

"A penny for your thoughts," he exclaimed after a prolonged pause.

She started and blushed up to the very roots of her hair.

"They are too trivial to bear repetition," she answered lightly; then, as the music struck up, and the strains of an enlivening waltz rang through the room, she added, "let us have a dance instead. If I remember nothing else, at least I remember how beautifully you dance."

A compliment from *her* was quite sufficient to restore him to good-humour, for if he were vain he was at the same time as easy to please and to soothe as a child. In this instance he also knew Kate Brewser's praise to be sincere, for Captain Fitzgerald was one of those pampered darlings who is asked everywhere, and knows fashionable young women by the score simply on account of the adorable way in which he trips over the smooth polished boards of a ball-room.

When the waltz came to an end he said to Kate—

"Is your card quite full, Miss Brewsaw? That was perfectly divine, and I want to make sure of another waltz or two before you have given them all away."

"I am not engaged at all at present," she said honestly.

"What luck for me! Well, first come first served; I shall be awfully greedy and take advantage of the situation."

He was as good as his word, for he took her card from her and filled in his name for every single waltz throughout the evening. Kate just glanced at it when he returned it to her.

"Oh!" she said coolly, "though flattering to my vanity, this will never do. You have sacrificed yourself altogether, and I should have every young lady in the room tearing out my eyes with envy and hatred if I were to monopolise their pet dancer entirely. There," drawing her pencil through the names, " I have left you numbers seven and twelve."

" And is that to be all? No more, when I have travelled a hundred miles to catch a glimpse of you?"

" Well, we will see later on."

She had no intention of engaging herself formally throughout the evening until Colonel Clinker arrived. She would wait and take the initiative from him. If he were to ask her to dance, and she had not one left to give him, then she migh feel sorry. There was plenty of time yet, and if when he came she elected to prove to him that two could play at the game of flirtation, that her feelings were not seriously involved, and that she had borne his departure with tolerable equanimity, why, then she had only to lift up her little finger for Captain Fitzgerald to rush to her feet. She did not care twopence about him; but if Colonel Clinker behaved badly he would do as well as anybody else with whom to pass the weary hours of the evening. Thus thinking, she chatted away very civilly, so that on her return to Mrs. Tryon Captain Fitzgerald took up a position close to the doorway, from whence he devoured her with his eyes until a fresh partner came up and carried her off in triumph. She was a favourite with the men, and never sat out very long. But though she danced with the merriest, a close observer might have noticed a watchful expectancy of glance and manner which rendered her gaiety forced, her enjoyment only assumed. For as the minutes passed she kept thinking, " Oh! if he had cared for me in the very least he would have come. No doubt he hates balls, considers them a bore and a nuisance—most hunting men do—and will turn up for an hour about supper-time, just say how do you do, and go off again. I wish to goodness I had never come to this wretched place—that I had never set eyes upon him; at least I was happy and light-hearted then in a way; and now my life seems all at an end, and nothing left worth caring for." Poor Kate! she watched, and wearied, and waited till she grew sick at heart and faint with deferred hope, till number twelve came round, and Captain Fitzgerald for the third time appeared to claim her.

"What an awfully jolly ball this is to be shuaw!" he said with unusual enthusiasm. "Good floor, good music, and," squeezing her hand significantly, "good partners. What more can a fellar wish for!"

"Yes, awfully jolly," she said drearily, though her whole face belied the words, for the light had died out of the beautiful grey eyes, leaving them cold and weary, and the full lips were pressed tightly together with an expression of inward suffering, luckily lost upon Captain Fitzgerald, who, warmed by the exercise of dancing and frequent draughts of champagne, felt in that elated spirit when the small troubles of others are apt to make but a very slight impression, even if they make any at all. He and Kate twirled smoothly round together, their steps, if not their thoughts, being in perfect unison, while Captain Fitzgerald glowed and beamed under the joy of feeling the girl he imagined himself to be in love with so close to him, and meditated, directly the band left off that very charming part of Waldteufel's new waltz and relapsed into a less dance-inspiring strain, avowing for the fourth time the hopeless passion under which he laboured; and Kate, looking charming in her white dress, bowed her head every now and again in stately assent to his frivolous small talk, too utterly wretched to plunge into argument or bandy unnecessary words.

CHAPTER XXXI.

" MEN WERE DECEIVERS EVER."

SUDDENLY her heart gave a great leap, and then stood perfectly still, for there just opposite, watching her every movement with keen and somewhat discontented eyes, stood Colonel Clinker, quite alone among the panting couples pausing after their evolutions. Now was the moment to carry her proud intentions into execution, and conceal the pleasure and the relief she felt at seeing him again. She waited until Captain Fitzgerald came to a halt, and then gave Colonel Clinker a careless little nod of recognition, much the same as she would have vouchsafed to the most casual acquaintance. It was sufficient, however, to bring him to her side immediately. The honest, open countenance looked genuinely rejoiced at the meeting, but she, anticipating any salutations on his part, said coolly and with a carefully assumed indifference only too well calculated to deceive—

" How awfully late you are! Your friends began to think you were never going to turn up ; however, I suppose you despise these sort of entertainments, and only put in an appearance as a matter of duty."

It was hardly the greeting he had pictured to himself all through the long hours of the night and day, when, as he travelled rapidly towards her, his thoughts had been filled with her image—her image as it remained graven on his mind—white, sweet, tearful, and womanly, as she stood under the red-brick porch and the moonbeams played on her pale, sorrowful face. He had fancied a very different welcome to this, and such a reception filled him with pained surprise. He was not deficient in perception, and the very tone of her voice sufficed to show that during his absence some mysterious change had taken place in her feelings towards him. What had he done to offend her? And if he had offended her, how could he best apologise and set matters straight? This was the first idea that flashed across his brain. Astonishment and disappointment for a moment prevented him from replying to her question; and she, inwardly rejoicing at the effect her words had taken, repeated in a little dictatorial manner, as if she had a right to know the reason—

"Well, what made you so late? Laziness, pleasant society, or somnolence?"

She acted her part admirably, for in such an encounter the woman always fares best and hides her feelings the most successfully. Men are more honest, or perhaps more clumsy in deception, but now she was waiting, expecting some reply.

"No," he said, "you are quite wrong; neither laziness, pleasant society, nor somnolence had anything to do with it."

"What had then, may I ask?"

"A regular chapter of accidents, as provoking as they were unfortunate. To begin with, I only arrived from Scotland this afternoon instead of in the morning, for we were delayed several hours on the road by something going wrong with the engine, and were shunted into a little country station, where we had to remain kicking our heels for an indefinite time, calling to the guard, putting our heads out of the window, and, as a last resource, strutting up and down the platform."

"Hum!" said she, "rather a trying ordeal to the temper; did yours suffer much in consequence, or are you one of those placid individuals who never allow trivial incidents to ruffle the even tenor of their ways?"

"To be honest, I suppose I cursed and swore with the rest. But I have not told half my adventures yet. As ill-luck would have it, when I finally reached Foxington Station the very first person I met was our old Earl, who insisted on my going to dine at the Castle this evening. It was an awful bore; I did not want to accept, as you can imagine, but they had a large dinner-party, one of their number had thrown them over at the last moment, and Lord Huntingshire asked me in such a way that it was impossible to refuse."

"I've no doubt you enjoyed yourself immensely."

"Did I, though! It was one of the regular Huntingshire stately, ponderous, and ceremonious parties, consisting of a few swells, a bishop, a couple of scientific men, and a large sprinkling of the neighbouring clergy. I could not wish my worst enemy a greater infliction."

"Did you not manage to console yourself with Lady Anne?" she asked, displaying an irrepressible touch of womanly malice.

"After dinner," he continued, ignoring the question alto-together, "we set off for Foxington in the family omnibus. The Fates were clearly against me, and fortune's fickle face, like some one else's," looking at Kate, "refused to smile. A pair of jibbing horses were the next difficulty to be over-come; and when we got as far as Mount Hill—you know where I mean, half way between Foxington and the Castle—the brutes refused to stir one step, and came to a dead stop. Here was a pretty dilemma, as you can imagine! A carriage full of ball-goers deprived of their evening's amusement by a couple of obstinate beasts. The coachman, to give him his due, whipped, prodded, threatened, and coaxed, but all to no purpose. At last, seeing that we ran a very fair chance of stopping there all night, we men turned out and literally putting our shoulders to the wheel, and a very muddy one into the bargain, we succeeded in starting the vehicle by sheer force. I was more fortunate than most of my neigh-bours, inasmuch that, being close to home, I was able to run in and change my clothes; but all this took time, and, the long and the short of it is, I have only this minute arrived."

His explanation was certainly plausible enough, but Kate felt that there were still other and graver mat-ters which must be cleared up before she could resume her old familiar tone or their former unconstrained intercourse.

"You certainly appear to have been rather unlucky in your adventures," she said, softening a little.

"Exceedingly. All I can now do is to console myself with 'Better late than never.' Have you by any good luck still got a dance left to give away, or is my chance quite hopeless ?"

"You can have waltz number fifteen if you like," she answered, controlling her satisfaction with an effort. Then a vision of Miss Polly Paton rose to her mind, and she added proudly, "But pray do not bother yourself about dancing a duty dance with me. We have known each other too well to stand on such ceremony."

"Why do you say '*have known*' ?" he asked suspiciously. "Are our relations so much altered as all that?"

"I should think you were the best judge."

"And," he retorted, with rising anger, "do you mean to say you actually believe that I consider dancing with you a duty dance ?"

"It does not much signify *what* I believe."

"Yes it does; it signifies a great deal. It signifies so much that the only reason why I came here to-night was to claim what you are pleased to call a '*duty dance*.' Otherwise I should have remained with my father."

Her heart began to beat fast, but she said mockingly—

"I am sorry you should have given yourself so much trouble on my account."

"It's no trouble; it was a pleasure—a far greater one, perhaps, than you suspect."

"Indeed? You are most flattering. I only wish I could believe any portion of the pretty speeches you are good enough to address to me. Unfortunately I am of a sceptical disposition. By-the-bye, I hope Lord Nevis is better ?"

"Yes, thanks. The old governor's turned the corner, and is in a fair way of recovering."

"Do you know that Mr. McGrath was getting very **uneasy**

at your prolonged absence? In fact, he began to consider you had some good reason for staying away."

She looked at him inquiringly, as though she expected to hear more.

He changed colour slightly, and said abruptly—

"Terry's a downright ass. Why the deuce can't he mind his own business? What nonsense has he been telling you, pray?"

Something in his manner confirmed her suspicions. Either he *did* care for Miss Polly Paton, or else, as Mr. McGrath had said, Miss Polly Paton was desperately in love with him, and he was conscious of the fact.

"No nonsense at all," she said sharply. "And what's more, it appears to me that Mr. McGrath has a perfect right to express his opinions."

"I don't seem able to do or say anything right to-night," he answered irritably, for the coolness of her reception and this allusion to a secret that ought never to have been revealed annoyed him more than words could tell.

"Perhaps you are less unfortunate when at Nevis," she suggested sarcastically. "By-the-bye, did you enjoy the hunting up there?"

"Hunting? You *must* know perfectly well there *is* no hunting."

During this conversation Captain Fitzgerald had darted off into the crowd to speak to an elderly marchioness, covered with diamonds, whose parties he was in the habit of frequenting, but now he was returning to finish his waltz with Kate, a bland smile overspreading his insignificant features. The opportunity might never recur of shooting so keen an arrow.

"What?" she exclaimed, arching her eyebrows in mock surprise, "not even *fortune*-hunting?"

There was no mistaking the innuendo.

"No," he said angrily, turning away, "not even fortune-hunting."

And then she was sorry she had said it—sorry directly he had left her side to have wounded his feelings; but the thing was done, and Captain Fitzgerald close by impatient to recommence his dance.

"Who's that chap?" he asked, with the animosity of suspected rivalry, directly Colonel Clinker was out of earshot.

"Oh, that? That's Colonel Clinker, the great gentleman jockey," she answered, determined to uphold his proud position.

"Aw! yes, of course. I thought I knew the fellar's face. Awful cool hand, aint he?"

"Not that I am aware of. Why do you say so?"

"Aw! I don't know. Seems to think he has only to look at a girl for her to jump down his throat."

"I have been acquainted with *other* gentlemen, Captain Fitzgerald, who possessed a similar infatuation; not that I admit it in Colonel Clinker's case."

"Aw! I twig. You like the fellar, then?"

"You have no right to assume any such thing, or to speak to me like that," she said with cold dignity.

"Awfully sorry, Miss Brewsaw, to have offended you. Beg pardon."

"Yes, you have offended me very much, Captain Fitzgerald. Please in future abstain from any remarks of the kind. Colonel Clinker is a great, a very great friend of mine, and I object to hearing him criticised."

"The devil!" ejaculated Captain Fitzgerald in tones of bitter exasperation at finding himself forestalled. "That's how the land lies, is it? Pray don't expect *me* to congratulate you."

"I don't *want* your congratulations, and what's more, I don't *care* for them," she said indignantly, stung by his impertinence, "and if you ever allude to the subject again we shall quarrel once for all. There is no truth whatever in your conclusion, but even if there were people should mind their own business."

Anybody except Captain Fitzgerald would, after such a rebuff, have considered himself effectually snubbed for the rest of the evening, but reproof rolled off the heights of his self-satisfaction as water rolls from a duck's back. He coughed once or twice, twiddled his moustache assiduously, suggested another turn, and at the end of it renewed the conversation as cheerfully as if no difference of opinion had ever arisen between them, so that Kate found it impossible to quarrel with him.

Meantime Colonel Clinker had chosen Lady Anne for a partner, and was waltzing away in resolute silence, in spite of her ladyship's artless endeavours to find some subject of mutual interest. He set his brows, looked neither to the right nor to the left, and refused to meet the furtive glances that every now and again Kate Brewser could not refrain from casting in his direction.

Already she was a little afraid of her own handiwork and its results. Perhaps, after that last speech of hers, when number fifteen came he might not appear to claim it, and then she should go straight home, cry her eyes out, and think what a goose she had been, and how badly she had behaved. Numerous little acts of kindness that he had performed recurred to her mind; she remembered how he had helped her out of her difficulties the first day they had ever met, coming home from hunting; how good he had been to her when she fell; and lastly how he had offered to give up Opal when poor King Olaf died. She never could forget that. How few men placed in the same circumstances would have acted so, or shown such delicacy and consideration! She had been wrong in allowing her jealousy to overmaster her to such a degree. If he had his faults, she at least was not the fitting person to point them out, or to throw his poverty and neediness in his face. She would endeavour to behave better if only she had the chance.

The band struck up the "First Love" waltz, and her heart beat fast and furiously. Several couples were already dancing. Would he or would he not come? Ah yes, there he was, moving through the crowd, advancing straight towards her. She looked up into his face and smiled—smiled as she had not smiled that night.

"I believe this is our dance, Miss Brewser," he said quietly, offering her his arm.

She bowed her head in assent, and rose from the seat where she was sitting.

"I was very angry with you a little while ago," he said. "You said something to me that was not quite nice—something that I do not think you ought to have accused me of."

She cast down her eyes in silence, feeling horribly guilty.

"Do you know what I am referring to?" he asked, still in that calm, grave voice.

"I—I—I think so."

She was far too truthful to seek refuge in denial.

"And you really meant it?" fastening his eyes eagerly on hers.

"I—I—don't quite know. One never knows what to believe."

"Ah! I thought so," he broke out impetuously. "Somebody has been tattling to you behind my back, filling your head with all sorts of idle tales, which you—you, even against the evidence of your own senses, have chosen to accept."

"How do you mean against the evidence of my own senses?"

"Has not Terry been revealing confidences?"

"And even if he has," she retorted proudly, "have you so little trust in me as to imagine they would ever go any farther?"

"No, but they have altered your whole manner, and made you greet me as frigidly as if I were a perfect stranger."

"And are you not very nearly one? Four weeks is a long time, and many things may happen in the interval."

"Not sufficient to effect so complete a transformation," he said bitterly. "When I left, when I said good-night to you, and we stood under the porch of Sport Lodge together in the starlight, you were very different then from what you are now."

"Ah! I have grown older and wiser in the interim. I am no longer either so weak or quite so foolish as I was."

"And yet you were nicer then than now."

"Indeed! You are exceedingly complimentary, and evidently don't consider that, like good old port, I improve with age."

"No; and yet you possess one quality in common with the wine mentioned."

"And what might that be?"

"You grow more crusty, Miss Brewser, towards one who was vain enough to count himself among the number of your friends."

"Have you only come back to force a quarrel?" she asked coldly, for the conversation was becoming very unpleasant.

"No," he said, "but I confess that I felt greatly hurt by your reception. Think what a time it is since I saw you! Not since the night of poor King Olaf's death."

The mention of the horse's name—that gallant chestnut now reposing under the green sods—revived in full force all the old memories, the old sympathies and affections. Her lip quivered slightly.

"Then why did you stay away so long?" she asked, and if he had not been blind he might surely have guessed her secret at that moment.

"Why did I stay away so long? I stayed because my father has been awfully ill, and could not bear that I should leave him; because, after what you told me the other day, I thought I would try and yield my own selfish wishes to those of others; and lastly, because we had any quantity of troublesome legal business requiring our attention."

"Oh, indeed!" Settlements, and a life interest in Miss Polly Paton's fortune, she thought with a sinking heart. "Have you settled anything yet?" she asked.

He looked puzzled for a moment; then a light seemed to break in upon his mind.

"Oh! about India. Do you know, I have been seriously cogitating over the advice you gave me the other day."

"Advice? What advice?" said she feigning complete ignorance.

"Don't you remember? Not even the very forcible manner in which you expressed your disapproval when I imparted

a few of my financial difficulties to you? I see my memory
is the most tenacious of the two."

" I really forget exactly what I said. I talk so much, and
yet say so little worth remembering."

" You told me to give up my home luxuries, endeavour to
pay off a portion of my debts, discontinue living above my
income, and go out into the world and work like a man till
things came round."

" Did I ? "

" Yes. Why do you pretend to have forgotten the conversation so completely? All these four weeks that I have been
absent it has recurred to me many and many a time—so
often, indeed, that I have come to think it is rather a low
thing after all for a man like myself to be kicking his heels
about in comparative idleness, and squandering the poor old
governor's hardly-earned savings."

" A highly praiseworthy conclusion to have arrived at."

" You see, Miss Brewser," he continued very seriously,
" when you spend a good deal of your time in a sick-room a
great many curious fancies and fresh ideas begin to dawn
upon you, and when I saw my poor old governor lying on his
bed hovering between life and death my conscience smote me
sorely for having caused him so much uneasiness and thrown
his money to the dogs. I resolved if ever he got well to try
and lead a better and more profitable life, and make a thorough
change all round."

" What sort of change? " she asked uneasily, dreading
what might be coming next.

" I hardly know. I could not settle anything definitely
without consulting my good angel."

" And who is she ? "

Though why Miss Brewser jumped at the conclusion it was
a she at all was curious in the extreme.

" *She* is the only girl in my life who has ever exercised
any real influence over me—who has tried to arouse my
better nature from the selfish frivolity in which it was
steeped, and whom I would move heaven and earth to
serve."

The answer was vague, but delicious. A soft, shy light trembled in the grey eyes.

" When I am with you," he continued, " I feel as if I must tell you everything about me—all the good and all the bad. Do I bore you awfully ? "

" No, not a bit. Go on, I like listening."

" Well then," looking at her fixedly, " Shall I tell you of something extremely funny which happened to me the very day I left Foxington ? You know all about that forage bill, and how hard up I was after Snowflake's defeat. I was bound to pay some four or five hundred pounds within the week, and I did not possess a fifty-pound note. Well—and now comes the curious part of the story—I received that morning a cheque for five hundred, signed by a respectable firm of solicitors, informing me of the fact that a client, who desired to remain *incognito*, wished to present it to me."

Not a muscle of her face moved under his searching gaze.

" Well," she said carelessly, " and what did you do ? "

" I returned the cheque immediately, but only to have it promptly sent back. Did you ever know anything so queer?"

" Never. Perhaps some rich old lady has fallen violently in love with you."

" You can't offer any other solution of the mystery, Miss Brewser ? " he asked, looking a trifle disappointed.

" No, how should I ? I hope you spent the money profitably ? "

" I felt very much ashamed of doing so, but to tell the truth I was obliged to, being so infernally hard up. I paid my forage bill first and foremost, and one or two outstanding accounts ; the remainder will just enable me to keep going until the end of the hunting season, and after that "—

" Yes, and after that what ? " she interrupted eagerly. " Are you still contemplating making a bolt of it ? " A fan is a convenient plaything at times. She began swaying hers vigorously to and fro.

" That depends entirely upon circumstances. I received the other day a most tempting invitation from a friend living in India, who wants me to go out there in March and stay all through the summer. He promises me first rate tiger-shooting, besides plenty of smaller game ; and if I were really to go out I should be removed from the way of temptation, and have no inducements to spend. What do you think of the idea ? " He had taken a sudden determination. He would find out that night, at whatever hazard, whether Kate Brewser cared for him or not. It was a desperate resolve, quickly made and as quickly acted upon.

" Why should he ask me such a question," thought she on her side. " If he wants to go, let him go, but surely—surely it is unnecessary to consult *me*. It is downright cruel of him. If he can't see for himself how much I hate the project, how is it possible for me to say so ?—in other words, to tell him that I love him, when I seem to fill so small a portion of his thoughts ? Why, oh why, does he worry me for advice that I cannot give ? "

But he failed to read the troubled workings of her mind.

" Well," he said again, " what do you think of the plan ? "

Her womanly pride and dignity availed her but little in this crisis.

" I—I—I do not think anything of it," she faltered.

" What ? Do you mean to say you have no opinion one way or the other ? That's very unlike you, Miss Brewser."

" It's not a bit of good asking me about matters I know nothing of. In an affair of this kind your own people are far more calculated to give sensible advice than a stranger like myself."

" I cannot bear that you should call yourself a stranger. However, we need not discuss this point at present ; supposing I *want* your advice, and care for it and value it more than that of the whole number of friends and relations put together ? "

" Such a supposition appears so entirely outside the range of possibility that my imagination refuses to contemplate it. Your Indian expedition is a matter for yourself and father, and perhaps one other person," meaning Polly Paton, " to decide A multitude of counsellors cannot be desirable."

"If I understand you rightly, you refuse to give an opinion ? "

"Since you press the point, Colonel Clinker, I do. My opinion can benefit no one, certainly not you."

"And yet you were the person who first advocated my going abroad ! "

"Very likely," she retorted. "I advocate it still, as an admirable means of improving the mind and removing petty insular prejudice."

He shrugged his shoulders with a gesture of impatience.

"You are utterly incomprehensible," he said, in tones of growing annoyance.

"Possibly," she replied, "though it strikes me the incomprehensibility is not entirely on my side. Other people beside myself are enigmatical.

"Well, anyhow," he said, adopting fresh tactics, "I suppose you will admit India to be as good a place as any other to pitch one's tent in ?"

"Quite as good, I should say, if not better than most."

"And there's pretty fair sport to be got out there, at least, if report is to be believed."

"Yes," she said dryly, "and snakes abound, and cholera is not uncommon, neither is sunstroke, while jungle-fever strikes down victims by the score."

"I will run my risk of those terrible evils," he answered, with a broad smile; "besides, I'm pretty good at standing heat."

"You'll be lucky if you do stand it, and don't have to *lie* in bed instead."

"Why, what a Job's comforter you are, to be sure, Miss Browser! However, I flatter myself I'm tough enough and hardy enough to withstand the climate."

"You are by no means the first man who has so imagined, and discovered his error too late."

"I declare," he laughed. "I do believe you are trying to frighten me. However, I see you set your face against my Indian trip altogether."

"Did I say so ? "

"Not exactly, perhaps, in words, but you certainly succeeded in conveying that impression to my mind.   So far you have not received my confidences in a very encouraging manner and I feel almost too shy to communicate yet another alternative which, perhaps, might meet with greater approval."

" Am I such a very formidable person ? "

" I'm not quite sure.   Sometimes I think that you are and sometimes I think that you are not.   Somehow I don't feel very certain of your sympathy to-night."

" You always have it," she said hurriedly.   " Go on."

" May I ?   Well, then, you must know that while up at Nevis my father and I have had several very serious business talks.   In fact, it was chiefly owing to some bothering deed requiring my signature, and which had to be altered and re-altered by a set of procrastinating lawyers, that I was kept such a deuce of a time."

" I suppose you did not mind it very much," she said, thinking of her rival.

" Yes I did.   I minded it awfully, and longed to get back to Foxington.   I had a real bad time of it, I can tell you, especially as the governor took it into his head to preach me daily lectures on the subject of matrimony, which worried my life out, and drove me very nearly mad."

" Why should they ?   Such a subject was a very natural one on your father's part."

" Yes, but not on mine, unless," he added significantly, " I marry the right person, and the right person will condescend to give me a little hope."

She turned her face away, so that he might not see the colour crimsoning her cheeks.   " I gather then, that the lady your father has selected does not altogether please your fastidious taste ? " she said, with renewed hope quickening the pulsations of her heart.   " Since you have told me so much, is it fair to ask if her name is Miss Polly Paton ? "

" Ah ! I knew Terry had been betraying secrets.   Yes, that is the lady's name."

" And is she—is she—*very* pretty and agreeable ? " (tremulously).

" Oh, hang it all ! I hardly know."

" And what does Miss Polly say to this proposed alliance ? Does she give her consent ? " asked Kate gravely, for it was impossible to joke on so serious a matter, and for once she felt no inclination to indulge in chaff.

" I've never asked her," he said, looking somewhat confused.

" And what sort of a girl is she ? "

" Oh, a nice, unaffected little countrified thing. Just the sort of girl to make a man an excellent wife."

" Indeed!" And her voice once more resumed an icy tone. " A highly satisfactory arrangement all round. It is not often one hears of these *mariages de convenances* fulfilling so many requirements, but in your case we have not only the parental blessing but also an unlimited fortune, and sincere affection on both sides. Allow me to congratulate you. Have you fixed the day ? "

" No," he said angrily, " and what's more I never shall. Why do you persist in distorting everything I say in this way ? I never alluded to any affection in the matter. Polly Paton and I have known each other since we were boy and girl together, and are more like brother and sister than anything else. Can't you understand that you may be very fond of a person, after a calm equable fashion, without being at all in love ? "

" Oh! You intend marrying on calmness and equability ? Well, perhaps they answer best in the long run."

" How aggravating you are, Miss Brewser. I shall never marry Polly, for I do not love her as a man should love the girl he wishes to make his wife, and under such circumstances it would only be doing Polly a wrong."

" You seem very considerate where Miss Polly Paton's feelings are concerned," she said, still actuated by a blind unreasoning jealousy which surely his words ought to have set at rest. " I suppose she is desperately in love with you then ? "

She had tried his patience very severely all through the evening. She had over-strained it at last.

"Miss Brewser," he said, with a dignity that suited him well, "forgive me if I remind you that that is a question you have no right to ask, and that I, as an honourable man, with any spark of chivalry in my composition, should be a beast to answer. Since we do not appear able to discuss Miss Paton in a kindly spirit, let us refrain from discussing her at all."

She coloured painfully at this well-merited reproof, but she knew that he was right. She loved and respected him for uttering the words, though they made her extremely miserable. But he had made two great mistakes that night. He had consulted her with reference to his going to India and also about marrying another woman, and the last error was infinitely worse than the first. Her long dark lashes lay like a fringe on the soft cheeks as she kept her eyes resolutely veiled, unconscious of his steady gaze.

"Come," he said gently, after a lengthened pause, "let us have a turn together. I have never danced with you in my life."

His arm stole round her waist; she laid one little hand in his, leant the other on his strong shoulder, and glided round the room with him. He, too, could dance, if not perhaps with the same light, elastic step as Captain Fitzgerald, with a far sturdier, manlier one, which Kate infinitely preferred. He held her tightly clasped, one little stray lock of hair brushed against his face every now and again, the music rang in his ears and intoxicated his senses.

"Oh, Kate! my darling," he whispered suddenly in her ear, with low, passionate accents. "Have you never guessed that it is you who I love? *you*, who I would move heaven and earth to call my wife? you, beside whom every other woman becomes an object of indifference? Oh, Kate! speak to me, look at me! I have waited so long, controlled my feelings so often, fearing I had no chance. Darling, give me some little hope at last!"

All at once heaven itself seemed opening to her. The lights danced in her dazed eyes, her breath came and went in quick flurried pantings.

"Kate, my own brave, generous Kate, lift those sweet eyes to mine. Tell me with those lips, whose changing expressions I have watched so often, that you *do* care for me a little, that you are not wholly indifferent to me!"

She turned her face to his, a tender light resembling the breaking of the rosy dawn illumining its every feature, but at that very moment, close behind, like some omen of evil, she heard a voice, the voice of Captain Fuller, speaking to Mr. McGrath, say—

"Hulloa! Just look at Jack! He's going it like a house on fire, taking the heiress by storm, and I land my bet an easy winner. I declare that fellow has the cheek of the Old Gentleman himself. They tell me he is as good as engaged already to a girl up in the north, and yet here he is flirting like the devil with Miss Brewser! Well, there's nothing like having two strings to one's bow in this world, for if one snaps the other is close at hand to fall back upon."

All the joy, the glad faith and trust, died out of her face immediately. Every word fell like a bitter stab on her heart. This, then, was how people talked, what people thought and said. Another second, and she would have yielded, but now all her nature seemed turned to stone. Colonel Clinker in his excitement had apparently not caught his friend's remark.

"Have you nothing to say to me, Kate," he asked imploringly.

"No!" she said, drawing herself up to her full height. "Nothing!"

A cold, pitiless light shone in her big grey eyes; even the face itself had changed so swiftly from the sweet, happy, girlish one of a moment before, it was difficult to believe it could be the same. She was experiencing one of those sudden revulsions of feeling which occur to us all at rare intervals, and which, when we think them over afterwards, make us tremble at our own sensations and the bitterness of the language we have used.

"Nothing?" he exclaimed, for his hopes had been cruelly excited by that brief silence. "Do you mean me to take that for an answer?"

"Most certainly!" she replied decidedly, hardening herself more and more against him.

"Oh, Kate! dear Kate!" he cried, beside himself. "Don't take away all hope. It is possible I may have spoken too soon, but I will wait for months, nay years, if only you will let me—if only you will tell me that perhaps some day I may be rewarded. I have been an idle fellow, but I will alter that, alter anything to please you and to win your love and affection."

"It is useless," she said scornfully. "You plead well, being probably versed in the art, and display wisdom in wishing to secure 'two strings to your bow.' A little while ago you asked me for advice, and complained because I refused to give it. I do so now. Go to Miss Polly Paton, and even although you profess not to love her, try and secure her fortune. She may be more easily won than I."

. It was cruel of her to speak like this. She knew it, but she did it purposely. A shadow of pain overcast his countenance. She had scoffed at his holiest, tenderest feelings, and trampled them in the dust.

"Miss Brewser," he said in a voice which struggled hard to conceal its emotion, "once already to-night you have accused me of being a fortune-hunter. I may be poor and I may be in debt, but I am, I hope, at least a gentleman, and I should never ask a girl to become my wife solely on account of her fortune. I have loved you, yes, and shall love you, in spite of what has passed between us to-night, quite independently of such considerations. Had you been a poor girl I should have spoken out long ago. You, however, have chosen to believe differently, and nothing that I can say at present appears likely to alter your belief. I can only give my word of honour that it is so, and that apparently carries but little weight."

"Oh!" she cried bitterly, "don't talk to me of honour. It is a mockery. What honour has the man who, before he even sets eyes on a girl, backs himself to marry her because she happens to be rich?"

"To what are you alluding?"

"I am alluding to that bet you made with Captain Fuller at the beginning of this winter."

"I have forgotten all about it even."

"*You* may, *I* have not. If you wish confirmation of my words, ask Captain Fuller to show you his betting-book."

"Captain Fuller! What has he got to do with it! Surely such a miserable trifle as an after-dinner bet, made before I even knew you, is not to part us for ever."

"Pray don't make any apologies," she said, sweeping him a mocking curtsey, "but when next you meet *your friend* Captain Fuller perhaps you will be good enough to tell him that he was mistaken after all, and that the heiress was not quite so easily caught as he imagined."

He stood and stared at her incredulously, as if even now he refused to believe the evidence of his senses.

"Kate!" he said wildly, "do you wish to drive me mad? Is there nothing I can say or do to make you believe in me?"

"No nothing.

> "Sigh no more ladies, sigh no more,
>   Men were deceivers ever ;
> One foot in sea and one on shore,
> To one thing constant never,

she answered flippantly. "Ah!" looking round with a air which intimated the conversation was ended, "I see Captain Fitzgerald seeking for me. Perhaps you will kindly tell him I am here."

"And are we to part thus? Have you no kind word to bestow?"

"Kind words," she retorted, "are wasted upon people one despises."

And then she left him with that parting speech ringing in his ears ; a sorry recompense indeed for the devotion that had brought him all the way from Scotland just to catch a sight of her face, to hear the sound of that cheery laugh he loved so well. And she felt like a demon. She was conscious of not being herself, of being in one of those moods when people are not responsible for their actions, but an evil spirit upheld her throughout, and now she was left to enjoy as best she might the results of her own handiwork. For the second time in her life the anchors of faith had been torn rudely asunder, leaving her to rock helplessly to and fro on the dark billows of unbelief.

"Nicest ball I ever was at in my life!" exclaimed Captain Fitzgerald as he gave her his arm. "Never saw such a number of pretty women in one room before. Hardly a plain-headed one among the lot."

His small talk had been wearisome enough and empty enough before, but now Kate found it simply intolerable.

"Let me sit down," she said abruptly. "I'm very tired, and want to go home."

"Shall I go and look for your carriage, Miss Brewsaw?"

"Thanks, Captain Fitzgerald. It will be the greatest service you can possibly do me. My head aches so dreadfully."

"Kate," said Mary Whitbread an hour later, when returning from the ball happy and radiant she stole softly into her friend's room, "forgive me for disturbing you, but I could not go to bed without telling you something—something which occurred to-night."

Kate was in her dressing-gown and slippers, crooning over the fire. "I think I can guess," she said, putting her two arms round the other's neck. "Mr. Grahame has proposed to you, has he not?"

"Yes, Kate, at the ball."

"Are you very happy, dear?" she said gently.

"Happier than I have ever been in my life; and you? Have things gone well with you?"

She hid her face in her hands, and began to sob hysterically.

"Kate, what is the matter? You can trust me, surely."

"Oh, Mary! I am so miserable I don't know what to do with myself. I don't feel as if I ever could be happy and light-hearted again."

"Is it as bad as all that, dearest?"

"Yes it is, and worse. Mary, do you remember telling me how one day I should wreck my whole life and refuse the love of an honest man whom I loved dearly in return? Well, I have done so to-night."

"But we can put matters right, Kate. They *must* be put right," said Mary with unwonted determination.

"No," she said drearily. "They can never be put right. It has all been my own fault from beginning to end, and I have said things to him this evening which no man with a particle of spirit could ever forgive."

"Oh, Kate! what made you do it?"

She lifted up her tear-stained face and said solemnly. "You may well ask that. I cannot tell you why. I felt like the people in the Bible, when the devil entered into them and they became perfectly unreasonable beings. I am sane now, and probably shall remain so till the end of my days, but life is done for me, and I shall never know real happiness any more. I would give everything I possess in the world to live the last two hours over again."

Alas! even as she uttered the words she knew too well that no amount of wishing could avail her, and that the past. be it good **or be it bad, can never** be recalled!

CHAPTER XXXII.

AFTER THE BALL.

Hounds met the following day at twelve o'clock, people being too drowsy and languid, after the dissipation of the previous night to turn out at an earlier hour. The meet was at a village named Stoppington, situated within a couple of miles of Foxington Ever since the time when the Hunt Ball had grown a recognised institution of vast importance, Stoppington Covert had always been the draw on the next morning, although, owing to the close proximity of a railway line, it was not always a certain find. In fact, the interests of sport were in some measure sacrificed to the convenience and pleasure of the general public, who profited by this act of grace on the part of the Master by flocking to Stoppington in vast numbers. Thus it happened that the meet was a monster one, representing all classes and grades of society, from the regular *habitués* on their finished performers to the urchins with grinning faces and tattered coats bestriding long-tailed, shaggy-heeled and hairy-coated cart-horses, some of whom were minus a saddle and bridle, a bit of old sacking and a twist of rope filling their respective places. Big men on small ponies, timorous but ardent; superior tradesmen with uneasy seats and still more uneasy hands; farmers' daughters in blue habits and gold earrings; benevolent agriculturists on stout, lazy cobs; a lean newspaper reporter fancifully attired but full of pride, and a couple of huntsmen from neighbouring packs, all helped to swell the list of equestrians; while labouring men, publicans, smiths, runners, shoemakers, tramps, smart nursemaids trundling perambulators, heedless of their sleeping charges, and giggling girls, still further added to the goodly multitude—a multitude whose activity, energy, and keen determination to witness the slaughter of a fox not only, as minute after minute elapsed, rendered the prospect of any real sport exceedingly remote, but also drove Will Steadall to the very verge of despair. Meantime hounds were whimpering in covert with plaintive, irregular notes, now rising to a hopeful chorus, anon dying away into a provoking silence, while ever and again the fox peeped distrustfully out. On one occasion, indeed, irritated by the disagreeable proximity of Gaylad, he actually endeavoured to thread his way unobserved through the eager throng, but his presence was immediately detected by the foot people, who set up such a demoniacal yell as quickly drove him once again to seek the comparative quiet of the covert. To make matters worse, a biting north-east wind prevailed, which chilled the marrow in the bones and set toes and fingers aching with pain. Horsemen lost patience, sought shelter in a friendly shed, or galloped briskly up and down, while others again stood still, resolutely striking their chests with extended arms in the endeavour to restore circulation to their shivering frames, and their steeds, animated by the cold currents of air blowing over them, put down their heads, rounded their backs, and lifted their heels in a highly disconcerting fashion. Everyone was growing out of heart and out of spirits, so that the joy became general when at length the hounds succeeded in chopping the bewildered fox in covert, thus ending his suspense and anxieties for ever. The dead body was dragged forth, the delighted crowd pressed round, giving vent to many naive and original observations, while Will Steadall stood in the midst of the pack and swung it on high, as his darlings leapt frantically after their prey, until at last it was thrown in their midst, and they fought and quarrelled over the meal. Then and not till then, did the crowd in some small measure begin to disperse, while the slip was given to the remaining foot people by the legitimate hunt setting off at a good smart trot for Horniblow Wood, some three miles distant, from which place the Master still hoped to be able to show the host of strangers out some pretty fair sport, worthy of his well-known country. The laggards had scarcely reached their destination, many of them indeed being left behind altogether, when, as if to reward the huntsman's patience that had been so long and so admirably exercised, a dog-fox broke covert immediately, and went off straight as a die for Crow's Hill, between which point of refuge and Horniblow Wood lay a stretch of the finest grass-country in the whole of the Critchley Hunt. Will Steadall came galloping down the centre ride, flung open the hand-gate at its end, stood up in his stirrups, looked round, and blew his horn ; then, when he had gathered the leading hounds together, leaving his first whip to bring on the others, he dashed forward in pursuit. " Gone away ! hark forrard awa-a-y ! " shouted the delighted field as they pressed after him. And now ensued such a galloping and chattering, such a pushing and shoving, bustling, urging, fussing, throwing away of half-finished cigars, and thrusting on of ill-fitting hats, as only those who have experienced the difficulty and importance of securing a good start in the crowded shires can fully realise. Fortunately, Horniblow Wood was a covert which accommodated itself to the necessities of all, being approached by no narrow bridle-gates or tortuous lanes, but surrounded on all sides by gently undulating grass-fields, whose verdant hue did the eye good to rest upon. Kate Brewser, after having spent a sleepless night, was out riding Sir Richard, but she looked a trifle paler than usual, and did not appear in her customary spirits; while Mrs. Forrester, mounted on her celebrated steeplechaser, Singing Bird, was also present, the very incarnation of business, impelled into stirring action by the watchful eye of a wealthy and intending purchaser. The hounds were now tearing across the big pastures at a terrific pace, "heads up and sterns down," noiseless but deadly, evidently meaning slaughter. A sheet would have covered them, they lay so close together, while Will Steadall was doing his " level best " to keep up with the beauties.

" Come along, Miss Brewser," cried Mrs. Forrester enthusiastically, urging Singing Bird to full speed. " We're in for a run at last I *do* believe, and half the field are left behind. I've known hounds run like storm before now, with just such a biting easterly wind as this, and what's more, between Maddington and Crow's Hill there is not a drain nor a patch of gorse for a fox to fall back upon. If he only keeps on as he is going now, we have a good five-mile point before us, and when Pug takes this direction he nearly always proves himself an uncommonly dashing customer. So come on. Don't lose your place on any account."

Kate, to tell the truth, had been feeling up till now a little what the sex call "out of sorts," but Mrs. Forrester's words put her on her mettle, and, giving Sir Richard his head, she let him sweep along at will. Besides, Opal's roan quarters were immediately ahead, and she did not wish to disgrace herself in the eyes of Opal's rider, however much she might affect to despise his good opinion. Giving a hasty glance backward, she perceived strings of horsemen all hurrying in the same direction as herself and Mrs. Forrester. The sweet subtle ecstasy of the chase began to glow in her veins, and dissipate sorrows, real or imaginary. Come what might, she would not lightly suffer defeat or lose her pride of place. So she answered with a smile—

"All right, Mrs. Forrester, you give me a lead and I'll do my very best to keep up."

Colonel Clinker had never spoken a word to her that morning, but perhaps, if she rode very, very well, or even if she got another bad fall, he might unbend a little and give her an opportunity—of what? Of asking his forgiveness, of telling him his love was returned, and that she was miserable at having offended him? She hardly knew; she was only conscious, as side by side she and Mrs. Forrester galloped on, of a feverish hope that something might turn up to alter the situation. The ladies never spoke to each other again, but settled down to work in real earnest; indeed the pace was so great only the most fragmentary ejaculations were at first possible. They were now in a huge hundred-acre field, with the white hounds stealing mutely away in the distance. The going, in part, was very swampy and heavy, so that it became desirable to steady the horses in order to prevent their taking too much out of themselves so early in the day.

Mrs. Forrester profited by the opportunity to say in a hurried voice—

"You follow me, Miss Browser; there's a very nasty bottom, requiring a deal of doing, running all along the end of this field, as I know to my cost, having once remained in its mud for half an hour, since which I have taken the precaution of inspecting the available spots at my leisure. The other day I was walking round this way looking at some beasts shortly to be put up for sale, when I saw a capital place, where there was a bit of a gap in the hedge on the take-off side, and a fairly sound landing. Hounds are bending a trifle to the right; but never mind, you stick to me, and depend upon it we shall gain a good bit in the long run. There will be some dirty coats soon, I'll wager anything."

So saying, Mrs. Forrester, who, thanks to her remarkable bump of locality, knew every inch of the country in which she hunted, made straight for a given point where the big, straggly, overgrown fence in front of them looked somewhat more yielding than it did on either side.

"Now," she said, "let me go first, and when I am over take your horse by the head and send him at it. It's a widish place, even here, but nothing to a free jumping animal who takes off well." She gave Singing Bird a reminder from her spurred heel, and without the smallest hesitation or any of the undecided wavering which so often proves fatal to the nervous, flew the bottom in gallant style, sitting meanwhile firm as a rock in the saddle. Kate waited till she was well in the next field, and then, having watched exactly how Mrs. Forrester had ridden Singing Bird, endeavoured to follow her example as closely as possible, with the result that a moment later she found herself also on the right side.

"Well done!" exclaimed Mrs. Forrester in tones of honest satisfaction, for she was too excellent a sportswoman ever to ride jealous. "You did that capitally. Ha, ha!" looking round with a chuckle, and seeing no one in their immediate wake, "we've given some of them the slip this time, and higher up there's no getting over the bottom at all; it widens out into a regular gully. Hulloa!" as a riderless horse, his forehead plastered with mud, galloped by, "there's somebody come to grief already. Captain Fuller, I do believe, for it looks like his black mare."

The hounds were now directly in front of them, having once more inclined to the left, and the two ladies found themselves riding close behind the huntsman and Colonel Clinker, while only half a dozen were with them in all.

"You see," ejaculated Mrs. Forrester triumphantly, "how right I was. We have pounded nearly the whole field. Woa! Singing Bird, old man, take it easy now," for they were toiling up a sticky furrow. The hounds had slightly relaxed their speed, the scent becoming colder on the heavy arable land. "There's no knowing how long this is going to last." So saying she caught hold of a lock of Singing Bird's mane, hoisted herself up in the stirrups, and leant far over the animal's neck, endeavouring to ease his hind-quarters up the ascent. The sterns of the rearmost hounds just quivered a second or two, but directly they got on to the grass again, down went their noses once more, and away they sped as fast as ever. It was a grand scenting day evidently. Will Steadall's sober face glowed with excitement, as every now and again he flung a word of approbation after his favourites.

"Bee-utiful, Colonel, aint it?" he remarked to that gentleman enthusiastically. "Did you ever see a pack hunt better in your life? Lord bless you, they *can* go, and no mistake. They'll take some of the shine and bounce out of a few of these 'ere strangers to-day, I'll lay a sovereign."

They were now sweeping over lovely flying fences, in the very cream of the country, taking them in regular steeple-chase form, without time to be too fastidious in the choice of a place, or to take much of a pull at their horses. It was glorious fun striding along over the huge grass-fields and ignoring gates with profound contempt. Horses began to lather and their coats to shine, but their blood was up, and they seemed to enjoy the chase as much as their riders. Down Scapley Hill, through Merivale Dale, past Shepstone Village, straight for Crow's Hill they flew, the company growing more and more select, with Will Steadall on his famous chestnut and Colonel Clinker on Opal cutting out the work alternately; while Mrs. Forrester and Kate lay only a few lengths behind. The countenances of this little band flushed warmly with that mingled look of elation and determination which each fresh fence safely negotiated, each fresh comrade left behind, increases. For however selfish under such circumstances, the disappearance of a neighbour is borne with surprising equanimity, scarcely, indeed, in nine cases out of ten, causing any regret. Mrs. Forrester glanced hastily at her watch. They had been galloping exactly five-and-twenty minutes, at a pace that had already told on the horses, and made their riders begin to think a short check, just sufficient to enable them to recover their wind, would be desirable. Crow's Hill was straight in front, standing up tall and dark, with its naked black trees sharply outlined against the uniform light-grey sky. Surely Reynard would seek refuge here among its friendly undergrowth, and persuade some fresh fox to take his place while he stretched his wearied limbs full length, or hid himself snugly away under the ground. He made a bold bid, but alas! for his sake, just as he began to scale the grassy heights before him, a flock of huddling sheep checked his onward career. Then he gave one or two uneasy twists, trying to still dodge his pursuers, till, finding himself too hard pressed, he took a sudden fresh resolution, and set his brave face straight for Manford Hall, good three miles further on.

"He's a grand old dog-fox, with a white tag to his brush," said Colonel Clinker to Will Steadall, as after a momentary hesitation hounds took up the scent in concert, and dashed forward in pursuit. "I caught a glimpse of him just now stealing down the hedgerow. He's not done yet."

"Ay, Colonel!" responded he. "I do believe 'ee's the very self-same fox as give us that grand run we had last year from Maddington. Do you remember?"

"I should rather think I did! Why, it was the best run of the season."

"It was so," said Will Steadall; "but I believe this 'ere one is going to beat it. Forrard, my beauties! forrard on!"

and Will Steadall once more set the grand chestnut he bestrode galloping full speed, for there was work in store for them both still, and Reynard had proved himself far stouter than either could have anticipated at the outset. But Royal's courageous spirit was destined to be severely tested, for as they tore down the green incline, leaving Crow's Hill with its snug earths on the left, right ahead could be seen that dark fringe of pollarded willows bordering the treacherous banks of the nastiest brook in the county, and one at which many a gallant steed and daring rider had come to grief ere now.

"Is Sir Richard a good water-jumper?" asked Mrs. Forrester significantly, as the thin silvery streak flashed in their eyes, "because if not you had better lose no time, but hook it off at once to the nearest bridge."

"I don't know," answered Kate, with a resolute look, "but," with an emphasis which clearly showed the bridge to be quite out of the question, "I shall very soon find out."

"Bravo!" cried Mrs. Forrester, approving of this daring spirit, so entirely in unison with her own. "We won't be beaten now, will we?"

"No, I should think not. Not if we can help it, that is to say."

For a brief space fictitious hopes were raised in the breasts of the pursuers that the hounds after all might not cross this dreaded obstacle, but they were speedily dashed to the ground. Gaylad feathered and whimpered a little, then he plunged boldly into the stream, followed by the rest of the pack, who half leapt half swam across, and clambered up the opposite bank, emerging with dripping coats, heaving flanks, and moist, red tongues.

Will Steadall gave a cheer when he saw his darlings safely over and racing on with an ever-forward scent. He clapped his spurs in Royal's noble sides, the first time they had felt their prick that day, and, putting on the pace, rode gallantly to meet the danger. But it failed to prove one for him and Royal. Rider and horse apparently possessed but one mind, were animated but by one impulse, namely, wherever hounds went, there too must they. So Royal cocked his slender ears, glanced contemptuously at the dark gurgling waters beneath him, and, springing from his powerful hind legs, cleared the whole thing without an effort, though from bank to bank could not have measured less than sixteen feet.

"Well done, Royal, old man!" cried Will Steadall heartily, as he gave the grand hunter's firm crest a friendly pat of commendation. "Water, timber, banks, everything comes alike to you. You *are* a game 'un, if ever there was one, and there be mighty few as can jump in that style at the end of the fastest thirty minutes ever I seed in my life!"

There might not be many, but there was one, and that one only a novice in the art, for almost immediately Colonel Clinker, on his beautiful roan thoroughbred mare raced up alongside with a "Hullo, Bill! we did that tolerably well, I take it."

"Aye, sir," was the response, "I thought Royal one in a hundred, but for the weight I'm not sure that nag you're riding ain't almost as good."

"She's a clipper, and no mistake," said Opal's well-pleased owner.

Meantime Mrs. Forrester had slackened her pace for a moment in order to make quite sure the hounds were not likely to retrace their footsteps; but when she saw the now lessening pack racing away in the distance she said to Kate—

"There's no help for it, Miss Browser, we must do or die. After beating nearly all the field, with a very few exceptions, we cannot show the white feather now for fear of a wet jacket."

"All right," assented Kate. "Will you go first or shall I?"

"I've got the run in. Let me."

So saying she shortened Singing Bird's bridle, and drove the horse with wonderful pluck at the brook. He was beginning to get done, and did not respond to her call with much alacrity; besides which, Singing Bird, like many another good hunter, entertained a decided aversion to the sight and sound of rippling water, more especially when perfectly open, as in the present case. Now when he perceived the swift current

rushing many feet beneath him, and looked down into the
cavity his heart suddenly failed him, and for one fatal second
he stood hesitating on the brink. Mrs. Forrester was thoroughly roused. Over or in, she did not care which, but
she was determined not to put up with denial. Singing Bird
tried hard to cut it, but there was no avoiding that resolute
hand and sharp-rowelled heel; therefore, trembling, but
obedient, he gave a huge spasmodic bound, and jumped high
into the air—too high and not wide enough, for he lacked
the necessary impetus, and fell short with both hind legs.
There was a scramble and a breaking away of loosened earth
as Mrs. Forrester half rolled, half threw herself off, and by so
doing avoided immersion; but she never lost hold of the bridle,
and Singing Bird, finding the weight removed from his hind-
quarters, succeeded in struggling up the bank without injury.

"Humph! not a very grand performance," reflected the old
lady, quite unmoved by the catastrophe, preparing promptly
to remount. "It's just as well Mr. Baker was not anywhere
near at the time, and if he gives me the hundred and eighty
I'm asking, why, I'll say good-bye to you, my friend," addressing Singing Bird, "with pleasure."

As she was soliloquising, a hard-riding farmer on a grey
horse came pounding down at the brook and immediately
disappeared headlong, which spectacle did not prove altogether
encouraging to Kate; nevertheless, the idea of turning away
never entered her head for an instant.

"Come on," cried Mrs. Forrester; and then, doing as she
was bid, Kate set Sir Richard at a place rather more to the
right, where the banks had not been broken down by the passage of other horses. A rush through the air, a sudden ces-
sation of the beatings of her heart, followed by a quite
inordinate sense of elation, and the next minute she found
herself in the same field with the hounds, Sir Richard having
cleared the brook like a bird. She passed Mrs. Forrester and
sailed away triumphantly after the two leading horsemen,
never once pausing to look back. For a good ten minutes
longer on they raced, over ridge and furrow, and the wide-
ditched fences, but at last the hounds were beginning to

Kate set Sir Richard at a place rather more to the right.

Page 386.

slacken their pace and throw up their noses. Will Steadall left them alone to puzzle it out, and then hunting beautifully they led the field over sundry small enclosures, from thence to a road into which a very uncompromising piece of timber barred the way. Will Steadall, being a powerful man on a powerful horse, managed to crash through the fence, while Colonel Clinker, perceiving haste just then to be unnecessary, pulled Opal back into a trot, and waited to see what turn things were likely to take; but Kate, intoxicated with the success hitherto achieved, and conscious of his eye being upon her, charged the timber. There are limits even to the very best horse's powers of endurance, and Sir Richard, after five-and-thirty minutes' terrific going, was undeniably a wee bit pumped, Still he rose gallantly at the stiff ash palings, and managed to get over somehow, though he rapped them hard all round, and landed well on to his head. Truth compels the statement that Kate nearly cut a voluntary—nearly, but not quite; she struggled back into the saddle and saw Colonel Clinker looking at her from where he stood.

"Don't ride over the hounds, *please*, Miss Brewser. Hold hard one second," he cried, his sportsmanlike instincts overcoming every other consideration.

"I'm not going to," she said shortly, blushing crimson with mortification, conscious that she had only taken this hazardous leap in order to gain favour in his eyes, and feeling greatly disappointed at the result. "I wouldn't spoil sport for anything."

Just then the hounds began feathering down the road, and one by one, as they picked up the scent, giving tongue streamed ahead. The end of this grand run must be surely near at hand.

"Have you seen our hunted fox, missis?" inquired Will Steadall of an old woman marching along with a bundle of sticks on her bowed back.

"Ay, sir," came the mumbling reply "He be just in front of you."

"How long gone, my good woman?"

"Not a couple of minutes, if as much."

With renewed ardour the small company of pursuers clattered on till, as they rounded the turn for Pinckney village, the whole pack burst out into a chorus of sound. They were close on their fox evidently, when suddenly Will Steadall's sharp eyes spied a poor stiff, weary, and bedraggled object, crawling stealthily along the narrow ditch bordering the roadside.

"Tally-ho! Tally-ho!" he yelled in delight, with all the bloodthirstiness of a professional huntsman. "Yonder he goes. Forrard on! forrard on, my beauties!"

The hounds bayed eagerly in response, and then in another second they closed round the bold, stout-hearted fox, and rolled him over and over in the dust. He had made a gallant bid for his life, and deserved to escape, but the Critchley beauties were renowned for their deadly slaying powers, and had earned some reward after the most brilliant run of the season. Forty minutes in the open, and never a check to speak of, does not fall to the lot either of men or hounds every day of their lives.

Mrs. Forrester and three or four men came trotting up just at this period, and they, with Kate Brewser, Colonel Clinker, and Will Steadall, were the only representatives remaining out of all that huge field of horsemen and women who had started in the morning, intent upon doughty deeds. Their ardour had apparently failed under so crucial a test of prowess. No wonder, then, that these successful pursuers of the chase were on uncommonly good terms with themselves, and chatted away while the obsequies were being performed in a state of high self-satisfaction, all except Colonel Clinker, who stood apart from the little circle and busied himself with his mare, whose feet he carefully examined, and whose girths he promptly unloosed, while she, standing with outstretched neck and quivering tail and dripping flanks, gave evidence of the severity of the pace, despite the stainless pedigree which had upheld her throughout.

"I've been rather rough on you to-day, Opal," said her owner regretfully, "but it could not be helped, and I think and hope you will be none the worse by this time next week."

He put out his broad-palmed hand and the mare began licking it like that of an old friend, while Kate, standing near, thought no man could possibly be really bad who possessed the power of endearing himself so to dumb animals, and who showed so much sympathy with and consideration towards them. Her animosity was fading away entirely, and she longed to ask forgiveness for her conduct of the previous night, only she scarcely knew how; she, who as a rule was but little addicted to shyness, now felt almost too nervous to utter a single word of apology or explanation. If only he would give her an opening, then perhaps it might come more easily; but apparently he had not the slightest intention of doing so, and studiously kept aloof. And yet, all the while, as he stood there fondling Opal she longed to go up to him and say—

"Jack, it was all a mistake; I love you dearly, better than anyone in the whole wide world, and I feel perfectly miserable now that you are angry with me and won't speak to me."

CHAPTER XXXIII.

GOOD-BYE FOR ALL ETERNITY.

MEANWHILE people continued to straggle in, arriving with desperate haste, and each and all vowing the run to be the most brilliant thing they had ever seen, though how much they had actually witnessed remained matter for conjecture; nevertheless, so bountiful are the dispensations of Providence that their self-satisfaction appeared utterly unassailable. For full ten minutes the hounds scrambled over poor defunct Reynard's remains, while ever and anon some fierce quarrel arose, ending in a regular tug of war among the ravenous candidates, while Will Steadall stood triumphantly in their midst, his weatherbeaten face beaming with delight, cracking his whip and encouraging each hound in turn.

"Leu leu, pull him! leu leu, pull him!" he cried in mysterious and incomprehensible dog language.

Then when the repast was well-nigh concluded the beauties stretched themselves out on the grass and lay there panting after the exertions of the afternoon, with their parched tongues protruding, and their eyes looking fierce and red as they rested wearied heads on still more wearied paws.

"I suppose you won't draw again, sir?" said Will Steadall to the Master, touching his black velvet cap with respectful interrogation.

"No, certainly not," was the reply. "Hounds and horses have had quite enough for one day, and it is now close upon four o'clock. Daylight will have gone by the time we get them back to kennels and stables."

"Home, sweet home," was now the order of the day, the

air growing chilly, and nothing much to be gained by longer delay.

"We ought to give our horses a drop of gruel," remarked Mrs. Forrester to Kate, when both of them had once more remounted. "People are far too apt to forget that their animals' stomachs are about twice as small as their own, and consequently much less able to resist the effects of a long fast. Horses, indeed, often feel faint and distressed after a hard day through sheer want of food; therefore I always make it a rule to give mine something or other when I get the chance, even a bucket full of chilled water answering the purpose when no oatmeal is forthcoming. After such a run as we have had to-day the poor things feel frightfully thirsty."

"I expect they must," answered Kate. "Have we a long jog before us?"

"Foxington is a matter of ten miles or so from here, even going by the short cut across the fields. However, Pinckney is quite close, and there we can halt at the public—a very decent sort of little place—put up for a few minutes, have the horses attended to, and indulge in a cup of tea or glass of beer, as the case may be. Come, Jack," turning to Colonel Clinker, who having ascertained that Opal's precious limbs had escaped unscathed was now devoting his attention to Sir Richard's, who moved his near fore leg rather tenderly, "will you escort us?"

Thus directly appealed to, a negative reply became impossible, so he bowed his head in grave assent, and the trio proceeded in the direction of the village. They had not gone many yards, however, before he said to Kate in a courteous but distinctly frigid voice—

"Are you aware, Miss Brewser, that your horse has lost a shoe? His hoof is a bit broken as it is, and I am afraid he will go lame if you don't have one put on at once."

"Thank you," she said with a shy and furtive glance, for somehow her heart began to sink when she perceived his cold, impenetrable expression. "Is there a smith in the village? Poor Sir Richard!" patting the horse's smooth neck, "he has behaved so well to-day, I should be sorry to bring him home a cripple through any want of attention on my part."

"He'll be right enough directly he is reshod, and if you will permit me, Miss Brewser" (it seemed so strange to hear him call her Miss Brewser after the low, passionate, imploring Kate of the night before), "I'll take the horse to the smithy myself, while you and Mrs. Forrester go inside the inn and order tea to be got ready. You must be tired," for the first time displaying a slight interest in her condition.

She crimsoned suddenly under the brim of her neat pot hat.

"No, I'm not," she said ; "not a bit," though the lassitude of physical fatigue and mental trouble had already begun to steal over her. "I'm horribly strong; always was since my childhood."

He made no reply, but when they arrived at their destination helped her to dismount, still with that grave unsmiling courtesy which awed her more than any words could do, for it made her feel that they were indeed far apart, and that she had offended him even more deeply and more seriously than she had imagined. Meanwhile, he left Opal, with Singing Bird, in the ostler's hands, saying he would return in a few minutes, and throwing Sir Richard's bridle over his arm led him through the village to the smithy.

"Oh, Kate, Kate!" he sighed, looking at the empty saddle where the girl so recently had sat, as if the sight of it had conjured up all sorts of visions, "you have treated me cruelly, nobody knows except myself how cruelly; but I love you still, and shall think of you always in the future."

While Colonel Clinker stood by during the fitting on and reshoeing of Sir Richard, Mrs. Forrester superintended the preparation of the gruel at the inn, and not till she had seen the two animals under her charge plunge their thirsty muzzles into the pail and bid against each other for another draught of the welcome beverage did she return to the little clean parlour, with its stiff horsehair chairs, cheap prints, artificial wax flowers, and many-coloured wool antimacassars. Here she found Kate intent upon pouring out tea from a huge earthenware teapot, whose cracked spout made the opera tion somewhat difficult. Presently Colonel Clinker came in, and the trio enjoyed a simple but refreshing meal, after which they immediately set out on the homeward journey. The horses had revived a little, but showed unmistakable signs of the great exertions they had made, and could only proceed at a slow jog. Conversation between their riders was also extremely slack, in fact, had it not been for Mrs. Forrester's occasional observations, would have remained at a standstill altogether. The party had not gone above a mile when they were overtaken by Mr. McGrath, who cantered up on old Juniper, both man and horse looking suspiciously fresh in face of so good and so protracted a run.

"Why, Terry, old man!" exclaimed Colonel Clinker negligently, "where the dickens do you spring from? I've never seen you all the afternoon, and made sure you must be lost."

"Lost! no, not I," returned Mr. McGrath somewhat indignantly. "It ain't my habit to go out hunting and get *lost*," with a contemptuous patronage that was very amusing. "I leave that part of the business to my neighbours."

"And they succeed in doing so most effectually at times," put in Mrs. Forrester. "The field to-day were scattered all over the place."

Whereupon she and Mr. McGrath promptly entered into a lively argument on its achievements, during which Kate and Colonel Clinker insensibly fell to the rear.

"May I say a few words to you, Miss Brewser?" he asked in a low voice directly they were alone together.

She was startled at the suddenness of the request, but said "Yes," with great humility.

"I will not detain you long, only a minute or two."

"It's no matter, I'm not in any hurry," she replied, and then an awkward silence prevailed for a second. Colonel Clinker seemed to be brooding over recent events, for he apparently fell into a brown study, which lasted so long that at length Kate ventured to say timidly--

"Yes; what is it?"

He started and looked straight at her.

" Miss Brewser," he said, " I wished to bid you good-bye, that was all."

" Good-bye?" she echoed faintly, turning deadly pale.

" Yes, good-bye, perhaps for ever, certainly for many months, if not years. I am going to sail for India in the spring."

" In the spring?" she repeated, while all hope seemed to die within her breast. " So soon? Why, that is quite close at hand."

" The closer the better," he said gloomily. " I am leaving Foxington by this evening's train. I have no time to spare as it is," looking at his watch.

" And—and—you are really going? Giving up hunting" —she hesitated, then added softly—" and—and—all?"

" Yes, giving up everything—father, country, home, hope, happiness, all for the sake of a girl whom I was fool enough now and again to imagine cared for me ever so little. Listen, Miss Brewser," he continued, while his brows grew dark and stern, " yesterday you told me, or as good as told me, when I spoke of my love, that all you had to give in return was contempt. How that speech wounded me it is needless to discuss at present. Well, in this world we are all of us, perhaps, too prone to overrate our own capabilities, and possibly you were right. I may be the despicable creature you more forcibly than politely intimated—"

" Oh no," she interrupted in ever-increasing distress, " please don't say that."

" It is too late now to retract your spoken words, but," and his face assumed a look of manly determination, " I intend to remain despicable no longer. Man is man, and master of his fate. I will wrestle with mine; go far away, and either overcome my unfortunate passion for you, or else prove myself worthy of a love I have hitherto aspired to in vain. I dare say I have been presumptuous in my hopes, but they are over and done with for the present. As you have frequently told me, I can work and put an end to this idle frittering of precious days. You don't know, Miss Brewser, how strong your influence is, or perhaps you might have exercised it in a less open and unfeeling manner; still I have no wish to reproach you, no wish to say a single harsh word, or part from you with any unkind thought in my mind; nevertheless, the time may come when I shall prove to you that your judgment of my character has been erroneous, and that I am not quite so mean, so mercenary, and so utterly devoid of every feeling of honour as you imagine."

He spoke very low and hurriedly, but in those tones of deep emotion which only too clearly indicate a crisis in a man's existence. She had never loved him so well as at this moment, when he was parting from her perhaps for ever; and yet some curious, fatal power kept her silent, paralysed, and tongue-tied, when one little word would have sufficed to put all right between them. She was not even insensible of this fact; she recognised it fully, but she could not bring herself to speak, and the eventful moment slipped by, as it does with so many of us.

He paused a second as if half hoping to provoke some reply, then continued hastily, " In all this business one thing alone rejoices me, namely, that if I have never done any particular good in the world, I can at least not accuse myself of having done any particular harm. Nobody will be any the worse for my going away—nobody, that is to say, except my creditors, and I intend to pay them at the earliest day possible. Fox-hunting and horse-racing up till now have satisfied my aspirations, without the perpetration of any worse follies. That thought may perhaps give me some comfort during all the long years of my voluntary exile. It is only quite lately I have begun to realise the fact that pleasure is not the sole god to be worshipped through life, and that profitable occupation may be found elsewhere than on the racecourse. I have to thank you, Miss Brewser, for my mental enlightenment."

She could endure the situation no longer. She felt she must say something, however trivial, to lessen the ever-increasing tension.

" And when—when do you go?" she faltered, though she knew perfectly well it was in the spring.

" Next March to India," he replied, " to-night from here."

"Why n-n-need you leave?"

"It is a little late in the day to ask that question now," he retorted sarcastically. "I thought you were fully aware of my reasons, Miss Brewsor, but if you are not it would take too long to recapitulate them. I should have gone sooner only, as bad luck would have it, I promised to ride a certain horse in the Liverpool, and can't possibly get out of the engagement, so must wait until the races are over."

Poor Kate! she had made her little effort, or intended to make it, and failed utterly. Her timid overtures of peace had been repulsed with scorn. He no longer asked her to marry him, never even besought her to alter her decision of the previous night, but, taking his dismissal as fixed and irrevocable, acted in such a manner that it was now perfectly impossible for her to endeavour to explain.

"Oh, dear! oh, dear!" she said to herself, "what a terrible muddle I have made of my life to be sure. I am miserable, so is Jack, and all for what?" But that question she found it impossible to answer.

Suddenly Colonel Clinker put out his hand with a farewell gesture, and took the passive, unresisting little fingers in his.

"Good-bye, Kate," he said hoarsely, squeezing them in one long, parting, lingering clasp. "Good-bye; I shall never forget you so long as I live. It is folly, I know, but I cannot help loving you better than anybody in the world, and your image will always remain graven on my heart. Don't forget me altogether in return; think of me now and again, and remember if ever you want a friend, if ever you are in trouble, you may count upon me until death. Good-bye, my darling. God bless you and protect you, and grant that every happiness may fall to your share."

He raised the small gloved hand to his lips, and pressed one passionate kiss upon it; then, though Opal was faint and weary, and her head drooped and her slender limbs lagged, he dug the spurs into her sides as she had seldom felt them before, and galloped off at full speed. So fast and so furiously indeed, that he never heard Kate Brewser's bitter cry of, "Oh, Jack! dear, *dear* Jack! Take me with you, take me with you; my heart is breaking!" or saw the out-stretched arms, which seemed to implore heaven for his return.

The gusty, freshening winds blunted the echoes of her voice, losing them among the sadly-swaying trees and low-drooping clouds of evening; while Opal's hoofs clattered on the moist shiny road, bearing her gallant rider swiftly away, and the unheeded tears of bitter self-reproach rolled down Kate Brewser's face as rain shaken from the petals of a fragrant rose. Her opportunity of forgiveness was gone, and she remained behind, charged with the deadly burden of a life-long regret.

So, by a cruel fate which rules our destinies, are men's lives made and marred.

CHAPTER XXXIV.

WHAT'S DONE CAN'T BE UNDONE.

THE prompt resolution which rendered Jack Clinker so daring and so successful a rider stood him in good stead now, and enabled him to contend bravely against this, the first great sorrow of his life. His decision, though swiftly taken, was unalterable; and of one thing he felt perfectly certain, namely, that under the circumstances the very wisest and best course he could possibly adopt was to go away, to some place where he should not have the daily intermingled pain and pleasure of seeing Kate Brewser, of watching her ride to hounds, and hearing her converse; and where, perhaps, in course of time, he might grow to review the past with tolerable calm. He had accordingly telegraphed early that morning to Bob Prendergast, a particular "pal," intimating his intention of paying him a lengthened visit, and with that object in view despatched all his horses, with the exception of Opal, to the less-distinguished hunting-grounds of Cheshire. Needless to say that this hasty action on Colonel Clinker's part gave rise to no little surprise, and disturbed poor Terry McGrath's equanimity most violently.

"What the devil's up, Jack?" he said, endeavouring to argue his friend into a more reasonable frame of mind. "Begorreh, my boy! here you are in a first-class hunting country, enjoying nailing good sport, and you suddenly take it into your head to bundle off, stud and baggage, and go into Cheshire of all places in the world. What the deuce is the matter?"

"Cheshire's a very good hunting country also, Terry," returned the other carelessly, "and you ought not to talk of it in that deprecating manner. I can assure you, Terry, that the Cheshire people themselves think no end of it."

"So they may, and welcome," returned Mr. McGrath discontentedly, "if only they would leave us our crack jockey."

"Terry, don't be a fool, old man. It's far better I should go away."

"Faix, Jack!" and Mr. McGrath laid his hand anxiously on his friend's shoulder, "something is amiss with you, I can see. Come, make a clean breast of it. Has that minx of a girl been doing anything to vex you?"

"I don't know who you mean," he replied haughtily, refusing to allow Kate—his Kate—to be called by such a name.

"Oh! Miss Brewser, of course. I like her awfully, as you know; but if she is playing the fool, why—why"—looking uncommonly fierce—"I'll tell her a piece of my mind—that's all."

"There is not the slightest occasion for your doing anything of the sort," retaliated Jack coolly. "And if you don't mind, Terry, I'd rather not hear Miss Brewser abused. She's the nicest girl I ever met in my life,"

Terry glanced at his friend compassionately.

"Hulloa, Jack!" he exclaimed. "Has it come to this already?"

Colonel Clinker coloured under the other's inquisitorial gaze.

"Never mind what it has come to," he said evasively.

"You're awful close, Jack, and at least you might tell an old friend like me. Why, if I had proposed to a girl, gad! you should be the very first person to hear of it. There would be no secrets between us."

"Different people have different ways you see, Terry. You must not quarrel with me on that account.

Mr. McGrath wrung his friend's hand warmly. "Quarrel with you?" he said. "No I should think not. All the Miss Brewsers and the rich young women in the world would never make me quarrel with my best and kindest pal. Dash 'em! I wish to goodness all these infernal women were at the bottom of the sea instead of coming and upsetting two peaceable people like you and me, who are perfectly happy without them."

"What's done can't be undone, Terry, old man," said Jack

with a faint smile. "The only thing is to cry as little as possible over spilt milk."

And then the two friends drove off in a fly to the station together, and after Jack had taken his ticket, ensconced himself in a first-class carriage, and been treated by the guard and porters with as much respect as if he were a royalty, Mr. McGrath went up to the window of the compartment to wish him a final farewell.

"Good-bye Jack," said he in a very subdued and forlorn little voice, "I suppose you don't mean to stay away for ever, and you'll let me hear from you now and again, won't you?"

"Of course I will, old chap," said the other, trying to speak cheerily, and then as the train gave a whistle and began to move slowly off, he added hastily, "I say, Terry, just tell me how Miss Brewser is going on when you write—if she's quite well, you know, seems in pretty good spirits, and all that sort of thing."

"Damn Miss Brewser," growled Terry irritably, but luckily the remark was lost upon Colonel Clinker, who was now being whirled at increased speed past the platform, leaving his friend to return to a solitary home and inveigh disconsolately against women in general and the heiress of Sport Lodge in particular. Perhaps his wrath might have been somewhat mollified if he could have seen Kate at that moment down on her knees before a photograph of his absent friend, gazing at it with loving streaming eyes, and a woe-begone expression that surely must have appealed to any man's pity.

*   *   *   *   *

Next morning Kate received through the post a letter and a small parcel. She opened the former with feverish haste, for she recognised at a glance the bold round characters of a handwriting that had grown familiar to her. The note contained but a few short lines. "Dear Miss Brewser," it said, "For the sake of old times, those dear and happy times that may never come again, I hope you will not refuse to accept the accompanying trifle which I had made up, thinking you might like some small souvenir of poor King Olaf. That it may occasionally prove a means of recalling the donor to your

mind is more almost than he dare hope." There was no
signature, but that did not matter in the least; she knew
perfectly well whose hand had penned the letter. She read
it twice, nay thrice, as if committing the brief contents to
memory, and then with trembling fingers undid the parcel.
It contained a hair bracelet, beautifully mounted, clasped
with a true-lovers' knot, and fashioned out of her dead favourite's soft, silky chestnut mane. The kind thought which had
prompted the gift, more than its actual worth, touched her to
the quick. How good he was, how kind and considerate, and
how different to any other man she had ever known! But it
was no use thinking of all that now, after she had sent him
away, and told him that she despised him. She, indeed! who
was not fit to hold a candle to him in any respect! So she
mused bitterly. But there was still another and greater surprise in store, for when she entered the stable a couple of
hours later, there, to her astonishment, stood Opal, placidly
tearing down the sweet-smelling hay from the rack overhead.

"Stirrup," she exclaimed, "what is the meaning of this?"

"It be Colonel Clinker's horders, Miss Kate," answered
the good old man respectfully. "The mare come up at six
ho'clock this morning, with a message to say as 'ow Colonel
Clinker was gone away, and 'ee 'oped you would take care of
Hopal and ride 'er till 'ee come back. 'Owsomdever, Miss, if
I 'ave done wrong in taking the mare in, she can go 'ome
at once."

Kate looked at the sleek roan quarters she knew so well
with fast-filling eyes. "No," she said in a husky voice, "no,
Stirrup, let her remain. Since Colonel Clinker wished it I
will take care of Opal till—till he comes back." She left the
stable hurriedly, went into the drawing-room, which happened
to be empty, and buried her face in her two hands. What an
inestimable treasure had she not thrown away in refusing this
man's love! Sob after sob rent her frame; she sat weeping
there all alone, taking no count of the passage of time, until
the door suddenly opened and Mary Whitbread entered.

"Kate," she said, "what is the matter with you?"

She raised herself with a guilty start from the prostrate

position into which she had fallen, and hastily wiping away her tears, answered "Nothing."

"Nothing? Oh, Kate! what is the use of trying to deceive me? Has anything fresh happened? Ever since yesterday evening you have looked perfectly miserable, and yet you tell me nothing is the matter. Will you not trust me, dearest? Troubles are doubly hard **to** bear when kept to one's self, and you know how gladly I would help you if I could."

Mary's sympathy touched her heart.

"Do not pity me," she cried. "I cannot bear it. He—he has gone away for ever, and I shall never s-s-see him again," relapsing into passionate weeping.

Mary looked serious at this piece of intelligence.

"And I suppose you have driven him away, Kate? Is that it?"

"Yes," she sobbed, "I—I fear so."

"Kate, you deserve to be whipped."

"I—I know I do, Mary," she said very penitently; "I only wish I *could* be whipped, if it would mend matters."

"You are a perfect fool."

"I have nothing to say in self-defence. I feel that I am."

"And this misunderstanding is entirely your own doing?"

"Entirely. But that only makes it ten thousand times worse."

"Not altogether. Colonel Clinker must be brought back. If no **one** takes any steps to do so, why, I will, that's all." Mary's fair face wore an air of resolution seldom depicted thereon, but Kate rose from her seat and began pacing impetuously up and down the room.

"I forbid you, Mary," she cried with great vehemence. "Once for all I positively forbid you. It shall never be said of me that I ran after any man, however much I might care for him; besides," she added reluctantly, speaking as if the words were dragged forth one by one, "after what has happened—between—us, he—will—not—ask—me—to—become—his—wife. I—know—that—quite—quite—well."

"Then what is to be done? Are things to remain as they are?"

"They must. No interference can be of any avail."

Mary threw her arms round her friend's neck, and pressed the tear-stained face to her own.

"Oh, Kate!" she cried compassionately, "poor darling Kate! Wont you let me try and help you if I can?"

Kate shook her head weariedly. "No, Mary," she said. "It will do no good."

"But, Kate, you love Colonel Clinker, and Colonel Clinker, by your own confession, loves you. Why on earth should you keep apart?"

This was an interrogation impossible to answer.

"I—I don't exactly—know," mumbled poor Kate dolefully."

"I should think you didn't. No more does any one else in their senses. The whole thing is childishly ridiculous, and I shall sit down and write to Colonel Clinker at once. A few words of explanation will suffice to clear up all this foolish business and set it on a sensible footing. Eh! What's wrong now?" for Kate was facing her like a wounded tigress, the big grey eyes all aglow with painful excitement and ill-suppressed passion.

"Unless you wish to make me sink into the ground with shame," she cried, "you must not do any such thing. Colonel Clinker has GONE of his own free will, and must *return* of his own free will. I will not hold out my little finger to bid him come. It would be unmaidenly, indelicate, and immodest, and any interference on your part will only succeed in driving us still farther apart than we are already,"

"But, Kate, I thought you cared for him?" protested Mary in astonishment.

"So I do," she answered vehemently. "I care for him more than I could have believed it possible I should ever care for anyone; but that is neither here nor there—oh, Mary!" she continued, suddenly dropping her voice into a plaintive minor key, "can't you understand? Since he has been so blind, so utterly dense and stupid as not to find out that fact for himself, how can I allow you or any third person to point it out to him? I would rather die first. He may be proud, but so also am I, and no nice girl cares to fling herself at a man's head in that sort of way."

"But it wouldn't be flinging yourself at his head, Kate. He has asked you once already to be his wife."

"Yes, but he won't do so again in a hurry. Oh, Mary!" passing her hand wearily across her contracted brow, "if you were in my place I am certain you would feel just as I do. It is so hard to explain things, to put one's meaning clearly. We have had a desperate quarrel. He was not to blame in any way; it was my fault throughout."

"Then you ought to ask his pardon, Kate," said Mary decidedly.

"I wish to goodness I could. I tried to do so, but somehow the words would not come, and then everything went wrong."

"And in the meantime you are thoroughly wretched?"

"Yes, I am; but there's no help for it."

"There's a great help for it," retorted Mary vivaciously. "Nothing can be more foolish than for two people who love each other to go on as you are doing. Kate, dear, do be sensible. I promise not to write to Colonel Clinker, since you dislike the idea so much, but sit down and write him a line yourself. Pretend you wish to thank him for the bracelet."

"No," she said doggedly. "He would not come. He will never propose again."

"Then take the bull by the horns and propose to *him*," answered Mary cheerfully, for at length she fancied she could detect symptoms of yielding. "Remember this is leap-year, and you would only be fashionable."

But Kate refused to vouchsafe any answering smile.

"It cannot be," she said sorrowfully, and then without another word she walked out of the room, and Mary knew she had proved unsuccessful in her endeavours to bring about a reconciliation, and that the breach between the pair was wider and deeper than she had imagined.

"I must see what I can do yet," she said to herself; nevertheless she felt somewhat defeated, as a person naturally does when his or her friendly offices have been peremptorily and

conclusively rejected.   She determined, however, on making
one last effort, and with that object in view followed Kate up
into her bedroom.

"Kate, dear," she said regretfully, "I can't tell you how
sorry I am about all this sad affair.   I hoped so much that
everything might come right, and thought how nice it would
be for you and me to be married together, on the same day,
and in the same church."

"That's a foolish fancy, destined never to be realised," said
Kate sadly.   "But tell me, Mary, about yourself.   Are you
in earnest or only joking?"

"Very much in earnest," replied Mary, the colour mantling
in her pallid cheeks.   "I did tell you, if you remember, on
the night of the ball, but since then, seeing you so unhappy,
I have not liked to trouble you with my small affairs."

"What a selfish wretch I am to be sure!" exclaimed Kate
in a fit of sudden penitence, for her conscience smote her as
she remembered how completely her own individual concerns
had absorbed her attention lately.   "Tell me about everything now, Mary dear, just by way of showing how kind and
forgiving you can be."

"Well, then, you know that Mr. Grahame has asked me to
be his wife," said Mary with a blush and a smile.   "Very
foolish of him, is it not?"

"I don't agree with you at all.   I consider Mr. Grahame
displays very sound judgment and most excellent taste in his
choice.   So you two are actually engaged?"

"You are not angry I hope, Kate?   It seems so ungrateful
of me to think of leaving you, especially now, when you are
in trouble."

"Mary," she said gravely, "I'm not so bad as all that,
quite, and whatever my own feelings may be, I cannot help
being glad for your sake."

"If you would rather, Kate," said Mary timidly, "I will
give him up even now."

"And a nice sort of creature you would think me if I
accepted such a sacrifice.   No, no; if I cannot be happy myself
I can at least try and make others so.   Besides, you are not

going to get rid of me so easily as all that. I propose paying you and Mr. Grahame most unconscionably long visits."

She was struggling hard to bear up, and not let Mary guess how terribly the prospect of this second parting affected her.

"You might live with us altogether," suggested Mary eagerly.

"It is impossible to make definite plans at present, dear," she answered gently. "I contemplate a solitary future as an elderly spinster, with no other companion save a pampered and indulged cat."

"It goes to my heart, Kate, to hear you talk like that. Why should you not allow yourself to be happy, too?"

She strode a pace or two up and down the room, then went to the window and looked out drearily on the still grey sky and pale green fields.

"Do not let us discuss the matter any more," she pleaded with a great unconscious sigh. "I do not want to bother people with my troubles if I can help it."

Poor Kate! Short as her life had been, she had already learnt how the outside world only appreciates what is bright and cheerful, and turns its face away from the dark, sorrowful side of the picture.

Time went by very, very, slowly; at least so it appeared to Kate, hanging terribly heavy on her hands, while even hunting seemed shorn of its chief enjoyment since Colonel Clinker's departure. The zest of a good run was in a great measure lacking now that he was no longer present to cheer, encourage, and show her the way. People, to her mind, had suddenly grown more stupid and uninteresting than formerly, horses more troublesome and unsatisfactory, hounds less swift, foxes more twisty than at the commencement of the season; the whole world, in fact, out of gear. And all because one particular person, who, waking and sleeping, filled her thoughts, happened to be absent.

By degrees, as the weeks wore away, Kate grew fitful and uncertain in her moods, at times feverishly talkative, at others abstractedly silent, while at covert-side, after the first

greetings were over, instead of laughing and jesting with
every fresh comer as formerly, she now preferred slipping
away by herself into some quiet corner, from which she only
emerged when imperatively necessary. She liked to stand
there lost in a brown study, alone and unobserved, till hounds
found, and then she crammed her hat on her head and rode
in a reckless, desperate, devil-may-care way which alarmed
the hard-riding men for her safety and filled her own
sex with envy, hatred, and malice. She never would hunt
Opal, though she hacked her several times out to covert,
feeling she was only keeping the mare in trust for her
owner, and fearful of injuring her in any way. Curiously
enough, also, she seemed in these days to bear a charmed life,
for now when she went harder than she had ever done
before her horses scarcely put a foot wrong, and covered
themselves with glory. She courted danger in vain, as the
brave so often do. All invitations to dinner, except with
Mrs. Forrester, whose friendship she valued, she steadily
refused. People—especially extraneous people—bored her;
and though she tried hard to be civil to them, she shunned
their society whenever it was possible. She, who formerly
was so bright and lively, so easily amused by trifles, now took
but slight interest in passing events. She lived a purely
passive existence, just as if all the mainsprings of her
soul had been stricken down. The Foxington doctor, a
kindly old man, meeting her one day in the streets, declared
she looked pale and thin, and strongly recommended change
of air. She shook her head with a quiet protesting smile. It
was nonsense to talk of change of air. What good could it
possibly do *her?* It was not *that* she pined for by day and
by night. She kept her sorrow bravely and resolutely to
herself, never mentioning it again even to Mary Whitbread,
though the latter, seriously alarmed at her altered habits and
condition, would often say—

"Kate, dear, don't grieve any longer. Do try and forget
the past."

"I *am* trying," she answered wearily, "God only knows
how hard, but I can't forget so soon. Only a few weeks have

gone by. Give me time, Mary, give me time, and above everything take no notice. I don't want to spoil anybody's pleasure if I can help it—and—I would rather be left alone."

And whenever the subject was bought forward that was the constant burden of her reply, "Leave me alone; let me be by myself."

She was like some noble, wounded beast, who, when he feels he has received his death-wound, separates himself from the herd, and lies down in solitary agony to bear his cruel hurt apart, untended, and alone.

So time passed till March, the roystering, blustering month of March, was ushered in with clear skies, dry, pitiless winds, and hurricanes of dust, which whitened all the trees and hedgerows as they were whirled along by the violent blasts of chilly air. Meantime the sporting papers were full of the forthcoming Liverpool, and the odds against the favourites. Among these latter Figaro's name appeared frequently. He, Kate knew, was to be Colonel Clinker's mount, and she followed Figaro's alternations in the market with the deepest interest. The *Field* became her constant study, for among its pages she occasionally came across the name of the man she loved.

And as March set in, Mr. Grahame not unnaturally began to press his marriage, and to urge that some day might be definitely fixed.

"Waiting can do no good, Miss Brewser," he said; "I have somewhere about eight thousand a year, and the sooner we are married the better."

Kate would not hear of standing in the young couple's way, so she gave her assent immediately, knowing procrastination could only delay, and not avert, the evil day when she should lose Mary.

"You will look upon our house as your home, of course," said Mr. Grahame, who entertained a profound respect and admiration for Kate. "That is to say until you marry, I suppose."

"Thanks," she replied gently, grateful for the kind offer, "but I am not thinking of matrimony at present."

In consequence of this conversation she took Mary up to town, and insisted on ordering a most handsome trousseau, with gowns suitable to every conceivable and inconceivable occasion, the expenses of which she defrayed, in spite of Mary's repeated remonstrances.

"You are going to be a dreadfully rich lady soon, Mary," she said playfully, "and I may never have the chance of giving you any more presents. Let me do so while I can. It pleases me, dear." She never once let Mary guess at the true state of her feelings; only in the solitude of her own room at night, when the bustle and confusion of the day were over—for what with trying on dresses and shopping they had been terribly busy since their arrival in town—she would break down, and think despondently of the future. How desolate and forlorn her life appeared as it stretched away in all the long, long years to come. Nothing to live for, nothing to look forward to. True she had wealth, but wealth could not give her what she wanted, could not fill the aching, desolate void in her heart. Sometimes she thought she would turn hospital nurse or sister of charity, and try and merge her own sufferings in those of others, but the vitality within her was too young and too strong not to rebel against such a consecration of her youth. She would wait—wait, at all events, until after the Liverpool; perhaps something might happen, some unforeseen event, which might alter the present aspect of affairs. A faint, unconscious hope fluttered in her heart. At twenty-two to go on living day after day, month after month, year after year, perhaps till she was seventy or eighty, without any change taking place, was a prospect altogether too dreadful for her imagination to realise. A heavy, lowering cloud darkened her brain, making her feel unlike herself, and seeming as if it must burst before the clearness of her mental vision could be restored. Perhaps it was well for her in these days that the constant bustling from place to place, the hurrying from shop to shop, proved some distraction. But in the midst of all the business she had to attend to she went about dreamlike, as though in a trance. Her imagination, fired by Colonel Clinker's project of going

abroad, was picturing foreign lands and far-off countries. The
Scotch blood coursing in her veins rendered novelty, enterprise, and adventure eminently attractive.   The spirit of the
old Highland Brewsers had descended upon her, and she
wearied of the strict conventionalities and petty meannesses
of everyday life.   She longed to go away, far from all
hackneyed and frequented resorts, to distant continents,
where the foot of man was but rarely implanted on the virgin
soil, and where life was beautiful in its primitive simplicity;
where huge forests, rolling prairies, lofty mountains, and
boundless plains filled the mind with silent adoration of
nature, and a sense of the insignificance of each tiny atom
called a human being.   When accompanying Mary to that
eminent *modiste*, Madame Sophie, and listening mechanically
to the voluble foreigner's explanations as to how *ruches* were
better worn this year than kiltings, and how bodices *à la
vierge* would be all the "mode," her thoughts invariably wandered off in this direction.   She pictured herself living all
alone with Jack (or perhaps just old Maggie to do the dirty
work) in a cosy wooden hut, situated in a picturesque valley
surrounded by tall purple peaks, with a clear and rippling
stream meandering through the dale, on whose verdant
banks the shaggy-haired, meek-eyed cattle clustered—for
they would own a ranche—and in the morning quite early,
while the sun was still struggling with the hazy clouds of
dawn, Jack would go out on horseback, lasso in hand, attired
in light shooting clothes, palm-hat, puggery, and yellow boots,
and capture the stragglers or count the calves; while she,
also up with the lark, would clear away the breakfast, make
the beds, mend the linen, do a little gardening, feed the
chickens, churn the butter, polish the furniture, and then,
when Jack was expected, put on a pretty clean print frock,
such as he liked, all ready to receive him, and give him his
dinner.   After that they would talk over the events of the
morning, and perhaps go out fishing together in the burn
and catch some trout for their evening meal, or else have
a scamper on horseback over the prairies, or employ themselves usefully in carpentering.   Anyhow, they would never

remain idle. And then in the evening, when the day was done, when the round moon rose silvery clear from behind the tall outlines of the misty hills, when the bright stars twinkled and shone like myriads of sparkling gems, when the sky overhead resembled a pure blue-green vault, and the night air, soft and balmy, whispered sweet lullabies of rest, then Jack would light one of his long cigars, the red end gleaming like a glow-worm in semi-darkness, and they would sit side by side in their little garden, glorious with all sorts of beautiful many-tinted flowers, thousands of miles away from the old world, and talk of times gone by, of Snowflake, of Opal, of poor King Olaf, of Foxington, Nevis, and familiar friends and places. Talk till the peaceful twilight grew drowsy and dark, till the tops of the tall trees in the neighbouring forest began to rock gently to and fro, sighing and moaning like living creatures, till Kate's heart melted and throbbed under the sweet delicious spell, and suddenly Madame Sophie's shrill voice rang out—

"Mais oui, certainement, n'est-ce pas, Mademoiselle Brewser, il faut absolument que le corsage de Mees Whitbread soit coupé en cœur, surtout pour une fiancée? Cela va sans dire, et ce sera bien, bien mal autrement."

With a hasty conscious start, Kate, thus appealed to, returned from dreamland to the exigencies of the present, as represented by Mary Whitbread, struggling manfully but vainly to impress upon Madame Sophie the fact that she detested gowns cut with only an inch or two of waist, sleeveless, and all but bodiless.

"Ce ne fait rien, Mees Whitbread, je vous assure. C'est la mode, et lorsqu'on dit ça, on dit tout, n'est-ce pas, Mademoiselle Brewser."

The pleasant visionary castles in the air tumbled with a crash, all the more forcible from the exalted altitudes to which they had been raised.

"I place every confidence in your good taste, Madame Sophie," answered Kate with a sigh, "only you must be sure and please Miss Whitbread. Remember it is she, not you, who will have to wear the garment when finished."

"Thank goodness," she reflected wearily, "*corsages en cœur* will not be *de rigueur* in my castle. We can leave all those frivolities behind, all those senseless and idiotic fashions of which we poor fools of women are the slaves."

"Allons donc!" exclaimed Madame Sophie, with a significant and despairing shrug of the shoulders, as the two girls took their relieved departure, "cette Mademoiselle Brewser, elle est jolie personne certainement, mais mon Dieu! bizarre comme tout!"

Poor Kate! she might be foolish and in love, but even at the best of times she and Madame Sophie could have but little in common. That, however, is seldom any reason for one's fellow creatures to stay their judgments or withhold their hastily formed opinions. On the contrary, the less we are acquainted with each other the more apt are many of us to jump at unfavourable conclusions, charity, in most cases, being a quality acquired rather than inherent in the human species.

CHAPTER XXXV.

AN EVENTFUL GRAND NATIONAL.

THE great Liverpool steeplechase was over and past. Kate Brewser would have given all she possessed in the world to have been present at it, but a curious and utterly novel feeling of shyness had prevented her suggesting such an idea, even to Mary Whitbread. She remained quietly at Sport Lodge, inwardly consumed by a burning curiosity to know how matters had prospered on the course, and whether Figaro and his rider had distinguished themselves. She had intended asking Mr. McGrath, who left Foxington for the occasion, to send her a telegram directly after the race, but her heart failed her at the last moment, and he took his departure quite unconscious of her wish. It was customary at Sport Lodge for one of the stablemen to ride down to the station immediately after breakfast and bring up the morning papers. Kate was eagerly awaiting their arrival now in order to gain the desired intelligence, and stood at the hall-door watching for the first sign of the man's return. Presently she distinctly heard the slow tramp—tramp—tramp of a horse's hoofs coming up the drive, and rushing out obtained the newspaper without loss of time. She never paused to look at the daily telegrams or leading articles, but made straight for the sporting column. Figaro, Figaro, Figaro. No, his name was not even among the first three placed! Then she returned to the drawing-room, sat down on a chair, and prepared more calmly to read the details and learn the reason of his non-success. It appeared interesting, for she sat quite still, with her great eyes fixed on the paper she held in her hands ; but suddenly, with a quick, sharp cry of pain, she let it fall to the ground. She had been deep in an account of the Grand National, and was perfectly unprepared for the appearance of any such alarming and startling paragraph as the following :—

" Figaro now seemed to have the race at his mercy, for he landed on the racecourse ahead of everything else. but Captain Moonlight's rider, making his effort, somehow struck into the heels of the leader, and the pair rolled over together. Mr. Cockerstone escaped with a severe shaking, but we regret to say that Colonel Clinker was most seriously injured, and conveyed from the course to the Adelphi Hotel, Liverpool, where he now lies insensible."

She seemed completely stunned by this intelligence, and for many minutes sat there, to all intents and purposes paralysed with horror. Sounds fell unheeded on her deafened ears, external objects failed to create any impression. The cloud which had been hovering over her so long had burst, and produced a state of semi-unconsciousness; but gradually a resolution began to shape itself in her mind. At first it was dim, hazy, and undefined; but it grew and grew, until at last it reached such a pitch of intensity that she determined to act upon it at once. She would go to him and nurse him. Every consideration of propriety and circumstance went to the wall before the one great overpowering longing to see him again and be by his side. For aught she knew he might be dying—dying at that very moment, while she sat lazily at home, with those false, cruel, wicked words of hers still ringing in his ears and embittering his last moments. The thought was terrible. He probably no longer cared for her—might, indeed, have grown to hate her in the interval; but she felt she could never rest until she had seen him and implored his pardon. No matter what he thought of her, what anybody thought; she knew such a course of action to be right, since her conscience unsparingly told her so. Her pride had brought her to this pass, and now her pride must stoop to the very dregs of self-abasement before she could hope and expect forgiveness. But she would keep her intention to herself, she would tell no one of

it, not even Mary Whitbread ; she was very kind and very
good, only in moments of such agonising sorrow as the
present the sympathy of others failed to bring any comfort ;
they could not enter into her grief or realise what she felt ;
and besides, Mary would either oppose the project or else offer
her company, both of which Kate felt to be undesirable.
No, she would go to him, and go by herself, all alone. No
one should help her, give her good advice she did not want
and should refuse to follow, or put any other idea in her head.
Now and again occasions arose in one's life when the first
swift, unreasoning impulses were the best, the impulses that
came straight from the heart, untrammelled by petty, conven-
tional, prudential considerations. So she said to herself,
and then went hastily up-stairs, put on her hat and jacket,
hurriedly stuffed a few necessaries into a bag—for it was just
possible she might be detained, or miss the evening train—
wrote a short note of explanation to Mary, accounting for her
sudden departure, and then slipped down-stairs, stole noiselessly out by the back-door, and so into the drive, where the
tall laurels growing on either side of the winding drive soon
effectually hid her from sight. Once fairly on the high-road
she shouldered her bag and set to work running as fast as
she could. The station was quite close, only about three-
quarters of a mile from the house, and she arrived there
shortly afterwards in a panting and breathless condition.

"I want a first-class ticket for Liverpool," she gasped
through the pigeon-hole. "Can you tell me when the next
train goes ? "

"Almost immediately, miss. You're just in the nick of
time," replied the man in charge. "There's a special running
from town due here in a couple of minutes, which will reach
Liverpool soon after the first race."

"Oh, I don't care twopence about the races," she exclaimed
impatiently ; "I hate them."

The man looked up in astonishment as he handed her her
change, but refrained from any further remark. Her cheeks
were scarlet, and her whole frame trembling with excitement.

"Is that the train coming now?" she asked, as a distant rumble that increased every second made itself heard.

"Yes, miss, and you'd best look alive, for she don't wait a minute."

In a moment more the huge locomotive dashed into the station, making the very earth tremble as it passed along. Kate remembered being hoisted up by a porter, hearing the door banged violently to, and the sound of a shrill whistle in her ears; then she found herself whirling onwards through the flat green fields that were familiar to her, over the brows, and past the villages and the revolving landscape. Not till some time afterwards did she notice the carriage to be occupied by a lady and two gentlemen, evidently sporting characters, who discussed the previous day's racing eagerly.

"They tell me," said one, "that poor Jack Clinker is awfully hurt."

Kate pricked up her ears and listened in agony.

"Really?" said his companion. "I'm sorry to hear it"

"Yes, they do say, indeed, that he will never be able to ride again."

She leant forward and said in a polite but trembling voice—

"Can you tell me, please, what is the matter?"

The gentlemen both stared at her. Then seeing she was a good-looking, well-dressed girl, and evidently a lady, replied politely in the negative, whereupon she relapsed once more into silence, and flattened her nose against the somewhat dirty window panes.

How interminable the time seemed, to be sure! Jack, Jack, Jack was the one idea, the one engrossing and overpowering thought which filled her mind, and before which all others were utterly subservient. Faster, if only they could go faster; every minute was a lifetime, every stoppage an eternity. So terrible did her impatience become that she could scarcely sit still in her seat, and had it not been for the restraining influence of her companions she would have paced to and fro the compartment like a wild beast in a den. Already they evidently viewed her with that distrustful suspicion characteristic of the British nation abroad on its travels, and hid themselves behind their respective newspapers, taking furtive peeps at her when they imagined she was not looking, which she as invariably detected, to their joint discomfiture.

What a relief it was when at length the train steamed into Liverpool Station, and its human freight quickly dispersed amongst the expectant host of porters, omnibuses, and cabs. The crowd, indeed, was so great that Kate was forced to wait some little time before, thanks to the activity of a friendly official, she succeeded in obtaining a vehicle.

She had never been to Liverpool before, and everything was new and strange to her. She began to feel nervous, but the excitement of the moment bore her up until they arrived at the Adelphi. Hitherto her sole idea had been to reach Jack, to get to him as quickly as possible; but now, when she had paid the cabman and found herself in the midst of bustling waiters who appeared to have no idea of attending to anybody's business except their own, suddenly her heart failed her, and she felt a horrible sense of shyness and isolation stealing over her, while all sorts of disagreeable speculations and possibilities, which she had never contemplated before, presented themselves to her mind. What if Jack were in a room full of people? She should die with shame, especially if he treated her coolly and appeared surprised at the visit; or he might have some of his female relations already in attendance, and that would be worse than anything, for they would stare at her and question her, and laugh at her, and pull her to pieces, and perhaps even take her character away. She began to wish she had taken Mary or even old Maggie with her—anybody to lend a little countenance and support. But it was too late to go back now; and besides, though she counted the costs of her enterprise, the desire to see Jack, and seek his forgiveness, remained as strong as ever. If only he were pleased, then everything would be right, and she felt she could defy the world. But supposing he was not, supposing he looked upon her coming as a bore and an intrusion; supposing, though he had loved her once, he loved her no longer, and, like most of his sex, proved fickle and changeable; supposing he thought she was making a fool of herself, and supposing he greeted her as an utter stranger? Why, then, she declared she would never face any of her old friends again, but hide away in some remote corner where she must try and bear her disgrace as best she might.

Poor Kate! as she stood in the lobby, racked with doubts and hesitations, her most inveterate enemy could have devised no greater torture than she was enduring at that moment. Love battled against pride, decorum, and propriety; but love weighed down the scale, love gained the day and made her finally stop a hurrying waiter laden with hot dishes and ask him the number of Colonel Clinker's room.

"He is here, is he not?" she added, summoning all her courage to her assistance.

"Yes, Miss," answered the waiter, pausing for a second in his onward career; "but I am sorry to say as 'ow he met with a ugly accident yesterday a-riding that brute Figaro. I know Colonel Clinker well, and a real nice gentleman he be, to be sure."

"Do you think I could see him for a minute? I have come a very long way on purpose, and don't want to go back disappointed."

The man looked at her critically, as if the entry or non-entry to Colonel Clinker's apartment were entirely dependent upon his approbation.

"Some relation, I suppose?" he said curiously.

Kate blushed scarlet at the question.

"Yes," she stammered, scarce knowing what explanation to give. "I—I—am—his—sister."

The waiter honoured her with an incredulous stare.

"Humph!" he muttered *sotto voce*. "Sisters don't go all of a tremble like that, even when their brothers *do* meet with a haccident. Sweetheart would be a deal nearer the mark."

Fortunately, however, for Kate, the little waiter was at that moment deeply in love himself with a fair kitchenmaid who employed her time in peeling potatoes and scraping vegetables, and he therefore sympathised heartily with the romance of others.

"Come this way, Miss," he said, "and I'll show you Colonel Clinker's room."

So saying he deposited the silver dishes he was carrying on a side table and ascended a flight of steps, after which he deftly wended his way through a series of labyrinthian passages and finally brought up before a light deal painted door, on which number thirty-four was legibly written in white characters.

"There, that's it, Miss," he said, immediately disappearing, and leaving Kate standing on the threshold, a prey once more to anxious doubts and self-torturing scruples. "You've nothing to do but turn the 'andle and walk in."

But she found it was easier said than done, for to turn the handle and walk in was exactly what she could *not* bring herself to do, at least, not all in a hurry and without due preparation. She might have remained there, indeed, indefinitely had not the door suddenly opened from the inside and a gentleman—evidently a doctor—stumbled right up against her, to their mutual surprise.

"I beg pardon," exclaimed he, as soon as he had recovered from the shock of meeting. "Are you waiting to go in? if so, please do not let me remain in your way."

He made her a low bow, and, almost before she knew what she was about she found herself in Colonel Clinker's sitting-room. It was a tolerably large and tolerably cleanly apartment, furnished with the usual red carpet, green fustian chairs and curtains, artificial flowers, and wax ornaments, but on the hearth burnt a bright, cheery-looking fire; and before it, with his back to the door, full length on a sofa lay Colonel Clinker. Kate took all this in at a glance. He did not see her, neither had he heard her entry. He looked very pale, and his brow was so evidently contracted by suffering that all her woman's heart went out towards him. She advanced softly and timorously till she was within a few paces, then she stretched out her two arms with a sweet suppliant gesture, and whispered rather than said, "Jack, oh, Jack! I am here!"

CHAPTER XXXVL.

KATZ'S CONFESSION.

AT the sound of her voice he started and looked round hastily. He was no longer insensible. She thanked God for that. The rest seemed easier to bear in comparison.

"You!" he exclaimed, opening the clouded blue-grey eyes with astonishment. What has brought *you* here?"

She had hoped for some other, some warmer greeting than this. The blood mounted to her cheeks, her neck, her brow.

"Are you so much astonished?" she asked.

"Yes. May I inquire to what I am indebted for the honour of this visit, Miss Brewser? It is a great condescension on your part."

"It is no condescension at all. It's only right."

"I fail to see in what way."

She was cruelly disappointed at his reception. This cold categorical manner checked her eloquence, as biting frost checks the rising sap in a young tree.

"I—I—think I'd better go; I am sorry I came," she faltered.

He raised himself on his elbow and looked at her attentively. Some subtle change in her countenance seemed to strike him.

"Don't say that," he answered, struggling hard to retain his self-command. "Tell me instead what you really came for."

All the barriers of constraint that were closing round her broke down suddenly at the question.

"Jack!" she said, in tones of such beseeching humility that he would not have been mortal could he have remained

insensible to them, "you are ill. I came to be—with you."
Her voice died away as she finished speaking, and a soft shy
light trembled in her eyes.

He could not believe his ears.

"Good God!" he cried. "Are you mad?"

"No," she retorted with gathering courage. "I am *not*
mad; I was mad once when I said that I despised you and
that I did not care for you; but I am perfectly sane now. I
know quite well what I am about. Oh, Jack!" throwing
herself down on her knees by his side, "you have been blind
from the first, but surely now—now that I have stolen away
all by myself, without consulting Mary or taking anyone with
me—you *must* guess what has brought me. Does not your
own heart tell you the reason, or shall I go on? Well, I have
come to you to say that ever since your departure from
Foxington my life has been utterly wretched; I have been
tormented with self-reproach and the desire to beg your
pardon for my wicked words. I will conceal nothing. Jack,
till I knew you I cared for nobody and believed in nobody.
I was hard and sceptical. You taught me to believe once
more in human nature, to believe in man. I had been badly
treated once, and I imagined all men alike. You showed me
differently. You showed me that honest, true, good men, incap-
able of a mean thought or action, men who believe in the purity
of women, who are chivalrous and upright and honourable,
still exist. And I—I, what return did I make? I—because my
pride was wounded by some foolish bet, the explanation of
which was simple enough if only my incredulity had not been
so great—I, who am your inferior, who ought to learn of you,
look up to and respect you as a superior being—said in a
moment of insanity that I despised you. Jack, my darling,
my darling! You don't know how I have suffered for my sin.
Oh, Jack!" and the big eyes grew liquid and the long lashes
moist with tears, "have you ever felt what it is to get up
morning after morning, day after day, look out drearily on
the cold pitiless sky and naked trees, and say to yourself,
'There is no chance of my seeing the one being I long to see,
of hearing his voice, or watching his movements?' To feel

as the weeks go by that there is no hope, no prospect of any
break or change, and that your life is hateful, devoid of all
interest and attraction? Do *you* know, Jack, what it is to
rise without joy or spirit, and drag through the long, long
weary hours, struggling all the while to do your duty, to
appear happy and contented, and not trouble other people
with your grievances, and then to lay your aching head
on the pillow at night and wish yourself dead? Wish
that instead of a temporary and fleeting rest it might be
for ever? Do *you* know what it is to try and drown
sorrow in amusements that yield no pleasure, in occupations
that fatigue and drudgery that sickens, only to find whenever you are alone all the old thoughts come crowding
back with such renewed intensity, that it is impossible ever
to forget? Jack, dear Jack, speak to me, look at me, for
I have realised such suffering to the full." Passion trembled in the low pleading voice, in the sweet upturned face,
and in the dark glistening eyes passion and entreaty combined.

"I too have suffered," he replied, "and know what it is that
you describe."

A light illuminated all her countenance.

"You? Oh, Jack! Tell me, then, what it is?"

He clasped her hand in his with solemn fervour.

"It is love, Kate," he answered. "Unsatisfied love longing and craving for the presence of its object. Do you
remember how we stood and said good-bye to each other at
the four cross-roads ; leading to Sport Lodge the first day
you went out hunting? We little knew then, Kate, what
dear friends we were destined to become? Well, from that
moment I have never ceased loving you. You are the only
woman who has ever satisfied my aspirations and appealed to
my better nature. Kate, dearest," putting his hand to his
brow with a gesture of pain, "It does seem hard, doesn't it,
that now at length, when we understand each other, things
should all be so terribly changed? When last I asked you
to be my wife, though it might have been considered a piece
of presumptuous folly on my part, I had at least health and

strength in my favour, now they have gone from me, perhaps for ever."

"Jack, what *do* you mean? For heaven's sake explain yourself."

"You know I have had a bad fall, Kate. Well, this time they have pretty well done for me."

"But you will get over it, Jack. You will get quite well after a time."

"That's just the question. The doctor says not. Do you know, Kate, that I have lost all power in my lower limbs, and cannot even move a foot?"

"Oh, Jack! you don't say so! How dreadful!"

"Dreadful? Yes it *is* dreadful. You think it dreadful, don't you, Kate? It would be dreadful for your young life to be tied to a confirmed invalid, and all your days spent in nursing him."

"I did not mean that, Jack, a bit. I meant it was dreadful for you, who are so active and so energetic and so fond of riding. If it comes to a question of nursing, why, who should nurse you and look after you better than your own wife?"

"Yes, if I had one."

"But you *will* have one, Jack. You are going to have *me*."

He looked at her fondly, with a tender, loving, admiring smile illuminating his countenance.

"And do you suppose," he said, "that in my present condition I should be such a brute as to allow any woman to link her fate with mine? If I have to suffer, there is no reason why *you* should too."

"But if I like it, Jack, dear? If my selfishness is so great I cannot get on without you?" she pleaded.

"You think so now, Kate. You would not think so a dozen years hence."

"Yes I would," she said stoutly. "I should think so all my life. But tell me, Jack, are you in much pain? Perhaps I ought not to stop."

"No, no, Kate, don't go away. Why, it is over two months since I have seen you, and I can't let you run off so soon.

Besides," with an attempt at playfulness, "the doctor strongly recommended cheerful society"

"Did he, Jack?" reseating herself by his side. "What else did he say?"

"Oh! I don't know. He's an old fool. He does not much like the feeling of numbness; says it comes from the spine, and is the worse symptom of all."

"He's a donkey to say such things," said Kate angrily. "And I dare say he knows no more about it than a twaddling old woman."

"He happens to be the first surgeon in the place, and very highly spoken of."

"I don't care; that's nothing to me. Besides, the cleverest folks make mistakes. Why over and over again medical men declare a case to be perfectly incurable, and the patient ends by laughing all their professional knowledge and fine long Latin names to scorn. *We* mean to do so, don't we, Jack, dear. You and I between us will spite the doctors."

She was trying hard to cheer him up and induce him to take a more hopeful view of the situation, but even she, smiling as she was through her tears, with her sweet face close to his own, could not succeed in making him deceive himself altogether.

"Kate!" he cried, with a shuddering self-pity cruel to witness in so strong and gallant a man, "fancy if I shall *never* be able to walk about again, never move without crutches, or feel the spring of a good horse under me. It will be little short of living death."

The tears rushed to her eyes, but she brushed them hastily away.

"Nonsense, Jack," she said, "you must not talk in that gloomy fashion."

"I can't help it, Kate, dear. Every now and then, when I think of what I *was* and what I *am*, the present seems harder than I can bear."

With an infinitely tender and womanly gesture of compassion she twined her two arms round his neck and pillowed her head on his shoulder.

"Jack, dear," she whispered, "it *is* hard. I know it is hard. But you will let me help to bear it, won't you? I will try and be so good, and make up in every way that I can for this cruel trial, and will be hands and feet, and comforter and consolor all in one, if only you say you will let me be your wife? Things might seem a little easier to bear if we two were always together. Don't you think so, Jack, dear?"

To feel her there close to him, to look down into the loving upturned face and the sweet mournful pleading eyes, was such a trial as wrings a man's soul when he knows that of his own free will he must renounce the proffered treasure, that he must stifle his own passions, and think only of the ultimate good of the woman he loves.

He put her from him gently but resolutely. "Kate, my darling," he said, "you don't know what you ask. It cannot be. It would be wickedness on my part. You are young, and can't picture to yourself the future. I *will not* accept this sacrifice—I, who in the long long years to come shall settle down into a peevish, fractious invalid, dragged about from place to place in a Bath chair. People are apt to lose their tempers under such circumstances; all the vinegar comes out and the honey dries up when one feels one's self to be reduced to nothing but a useless, helpless burden to all. I love you far too dearly to permit your innocent girlhood to be sacrificed at such a shrine, and, as I said before, it would be unnatural and cruel."

" Sacrifice!" she echoed scornfully, with the light of a great and holy love shining in her clear eyes. "It is my turn now to appeal to your memory. Don't you remember telling me once that no sacrifice counted where I was concerned? Well, I answer you back in your own words. Do you think *my* love is so slight, so egotistical and surface-deep as to be deterred by any thought of sacrifice? Why, Jack, I tell you frankly, I would rather tie your shoe-strings, black your boots, be your body-servant or your slave, than marry the finest lord in the land. Jack, since it has come to this I lay aside all reserve, and I ask you, nay implore of you—I, Kate Brewser—to grant my request. All I want and wish is to be

with *you*, to live with *you*, and not to leave you alone to your
sufferings, both mental and physical."

The words came easily enough now. Perhaps if he had
been well and strong matters might have turned out differently; perhaps he then might have been the wooer and she
the wooed. As it was, never was man on this earth more
sorely tempted. If his love had not been as pure and great
as her own he never could have resisted so long. He desired
to act in a way that would prove best for her, not best for
him, but her last speech weakened his good resolutions—if
indeed good they could be called—to their very foundations.

"Kate," he said, "they will say, perhaps, that I married
you for money."

She laughed. An airy joyous laugh which rang through
the room, for at last she knew she had prevailed.

"Let them say what they like," she cried. "Who cares?
Certainly not you and I, Jack. We know better, and can
afford to smile at the world's criticisms. 'Wealth and rank,'
can't you hear them saying so? only it so happens in our
case they forget the love. And I say, Jack, if Captain Fuller
makes himself disagreeable, just you tell him from me that
it is quite true the heiress *was* bowled over, and will be most
happy to settle his bet on her wedding-day."

"I wish you were not so horribly rich, Kate."

"Now Jack, hold your tongue this minute, unless you
mean quarrelling. What are riches given us for except to
enjoy life with and relieve other people's necessities when we
get the chance?"

"But a man ought not to be indebted to his wife for his
fortune."

"Dear me!" she said playfully, "some people are most
terribly proud. Nevertheless, so long as between us we have
a sufficiency of means, I see no wisdom in going into the
vexed question of proprietorship. 'What is mine is thine,
and what is thine is mine.' I shall take that pearl pin of
yours and wear it when we go hunting together, Jack, and
you can have my little coral horseshoe instead."

"All right, little woman. You shall do exactly what you

please. But I say, Kate, I wish you'd tell me one thing. Did you send me that cheque for £500?"

"Never you mind, sir. It's no business of yours," she said, rubbing her soft round cheek against his like a young kitten.

He had never kissed her all this time, but now he folded her in his arms, and their lips met in one long, loving kiss.

"My darling, my guardian angel, my little wife that is to be," he murmured passionately, closing his eyes in the intoxication of the moment. Heart beat against heart in perfect sympathy and unison. Past and future merged themselves in the glorious present. Such happiness as Kate's and Jack's was too deep, too firmly rooted, for mere superficial words. Love, honour, respect, and esteem all combined to render its foundations secure.

* * * * *

The big ormolu clock on the chimney-piece swung its heavy pendulum to and fro with stately, measured solemnity as it doled out the time, and nothing but its gentle tick-tack, tick-tack disturbed the peaceful silence, while the wintry sun, struggling from behind the grey clouds, gleamed fitfully through the window-panes and shed a golden halo round the lovers' heads, as if auguring a life of joyous sympathy and true companionship, such as now and again falls to the lot of a well-mated couple. . . . Time? There was no time for them. The minutes counted for nothing. They were content to remain together, speechless but united.

* * * * *

They never heard the door open or saw Mrs. Forrester enter the room. It took a great deal to startle that lady, but when she perceived Kate Brewser in such close proximity to the gentleman she had come to condole with, she fairly drew back in unfeigned astonishment.

"What is this?" she asked severely, at the first glimpse somewhat distrusting the propriety of the situation.

"Nothing very terrible, Mrs. Forrester," answered Jack cheerfully, while Kate hid her blushing face behind her seal-skin muff.

"Humph! I'm afraid I am intruding."

"Not in the least. Pray don't mention it."

"When I heard of your accident," said the old lady with unusual dignity, "I left Foxington immediately to look after you and nurse you, Jack. There's no comfort to be got in an hotel, especially during the race week, and I was hoping I could have been of some use, but I perceive my mistake, though I must say I feel greatly astonished at finding Miss Brewser here already." She evidently laboured under some delusion, and eyed Kate suspiciously.

That Kate was well aware of the fact was shown by the telltale colour which dyed her cheeks.

"Yes, Mrs. Forrester," she said stoutly, and before Jack could offer any explanations, for she felt no fears and no doubts now, "but Miss Brewser is now the proper person to be at his side. I am quite aware," she continued mischievously, "that you find me here in a somewhat equivocal position. Girls, as a rule, are not supposed to take journeys in order to visit invalid friends. Nevertheless, I travelled here for the express purpose of nursing Colonel Clinker and asking him to allow me to be his wife."

She could not help laughing at the effect this latter statement produced. Mrs. Forrester held up her hands in amazement. It certainly sounded a little peculiar, that any young lady should have acted in such an indelicate fashion; yet she had heard the fact from Kate's own lips—Kate, who scorning all superfluous forms of speech, had gone straight to the point at once, and divulged the plain, unvarnished truth.

Mrs. Forrester looked from one to the other incredulously.

"Is this true, Jack? What am I to believe?"

"Exactly what Miss Brewser tells you," answered he. "But now listen to my version of the story. I have loved Miss Brewser ever since I first had the pleasure of making her acquaintance, but she chose—perhaps not unnaturally—to imagine that it was her fortune, and not her own sweet self, I coveted."

"Jack, don't be foolish!" interrupted Kate.

"I'm *not* foolish," he replied sturdily. "Well, Mrs. Forrester, she refused me, and I determined on leaving Foxington and going abroad. I thought I should never see her again, that she did not care two straws about me, and that I should remain a miserable, love-forsaken bachelor all my days. But directly she saw the account of my accident in the newspaper, she came straight here of her own accord; and now, although the doctor gives me little hopes of being able to walk or to get about in the future, this dear, brave, noble girl declares she loves me better than anyone, and will stick to me through thick and thin, cripple or no cripple."

Many a long year had passed since tears had fallen from Mrs. Forrester's eyes; but now, all of a sudden, they began to twinkle and glisten, till at last, though she winked the lids most vigorously, two great drops rolled silently down her wrinkled, weatherbeaten cheeks. She went up to where Kate was standing, and putting her hands on the girl's shoulders, with genuine emotion said in a thick, husky voice—

"God bless you, my dear! You are one of the real right sort, and they are very few and far between in this world, but a good heart goes before everything, and that you have got." Then turning to Jack she added solemnly, "As for you, learn to appreciate her as she deserves, for a true and pure woman is the greatest treasure a man can win, though many of your sex are not capable of understanding that fact." Mrs. Forrester was apparently ashamed of the unusual feeling she had displayed, and at the end of this speech retired behind a huge bird's-eye pocket handkerchief, from whence she several times blew her nose with great frequency and determination. Common sense, however, soon resumed its usual power over her.

"What do you two precious young people intend doing?" she asked after a somewhat prolonged pause. "You can't stay here billing and cooing for ever."

"I wish we could," returned Jack.

"Oh no you wouldn't. You'd find when the dinner-hour arrived that the pangs of hunger would make themselves felt in spite of all your love. But seriously, you must not be

allowed to remain in this hotel longer than can be helped.
What you chiefly require, Master Jack, is rest, absolute quiet,
good nursing, and perhaps," glancing at Kate with a pleasant
smile, " every now and again, just to keep your spirits up to
the mark, a little congenial society. Now all these conditions
can be much more easily fulfilled at Foxington than they
would be here ; therefore what I propose is this. Kate and
I—you must let me call you Kate in future," turning to the
girl—" will get a bed somewhere for to-night, and to-morrow
I shall order an invalid carriage, pop you into it, and march
you off to my own house. There I can nurse you, and Kate
can come and see you just as often as she pleases, and without any fear of that dear, circumspect Mrs. Grundy's long
tongue, while between us I hope we shall set you on your
legs again very soon. Eh, Jack, what say you?"

" Why, that, thanks to two such excellent friends and comforters, I feel half cured already, and quite a different creature
to what I did this morning. It almost makes one become
reconciled to having a smash, finding out how kind everybody is."

Then, after some further conversation, the two ladies took
their departure, in order to arrange about their sleeping
quarters, promising to return directly they had succeeded in
finding them, the hotel being already quite full.

" Don't be long," Colonel Clinker called out after them,
almost in his own old cheery voice, as they disappeared
behind the doorway ; and neither were they. They returned
in an incredibly short time, and then they rang the bell,
drew up the table, and ordered such a nice, cosy little
dinner that by the time Mr. McGrath arrived he was
astonished to find how wonderfully Jack seemed to have
improved since the morning, and in what excellent spirits
he appeared.

" Why, Jack, dear old man," he exclaimed, his rotund and
good-natured countenance beaming over with satisfaction,
" this is astonishing. Gad ! but I never expected to find you
entertaining ladies in my absence. Sly dog ! "

Whereupon Jack had to explain to Mr. McGrath the events

that had taken place, and the relation in which he and Miss Brewser now stood towards each other. Terry shook Kate warmly by the hand.

"Pray accept my congratulations," he said. "I have known Jack ever since I was a big boy and he a small one, at Eton, and a better, kinder, truer-hearted fellow never walked the face of this earth. Gad! but when you refused him, Miss Brewser, I *was* angry. I vowed I never should be civil to you again; but bygones are bygones, and here we are, all of us, I hope, greater friends than ever.

"I hope so, Mr. McGrath," said she smiling. "It will not do for you and I to fall out in the future, else we shall vex Jack, and Jack must be humoured and cared for in every way till he gets quite, quite strong again."

Alas! there seemed but little prospect of that at present, for even as they were speaking, Jack, who had been doing far too much, and was worn out by the excitement he had so recently gone through, fell back on his sofa in a dead faint; so that Mrs. Forrester, who immediately constituted herself head nurse, insisted on clearing the room, sending them all—even Kate—away, and with the help of the doctor, who called in the nick of time, putting the invalid to bed. Neither did she leave him until he fell asleep, calling on Kate in his dreams, and with a placid, happy smile on his face that told of a contented spirit. Then she put the night-light within reach and stole softly out of the room

CHAPTER XXXVII.

CONCLUSION.

AFTER all, Mary Whitbread's wish was fulfilled.

Towards the end of April, when the young leaves burst through their husky sheaths and uncurled themselves in the genial sunshine and gentle dropping showers—when the grass put forth vigorous shoots, which changed the bare fields into one vast silver and gold-starred carpet—when the lambs were bleating and the birds singing, the white clouds scudding along in the azure sky, and nature itself rejoicing at the coming of spring, she and Kate Brewser were married in the grey-walled ivy-covered church of Foxington. The double wedding took place very quietly, none but the immediate friends and relations of the contracting parties being present, while Captain Fuller and Mr. McGrath acted respectively as best men. Colonel Clinker's health unfortunately still gave rise to grave anxiety. During the weeks preceding his marriage he had consulted several eminent London physicians without deriving any marked benefit from their advice, and now on his wedding-day it was sad to see him come limping painfully into the church on crutches. He showed a brave face to the world, but both Kate and Mrs. Forrester knew how deeply he fretted at his continued inability to move about with any freedom.

But directly they were married Kate assumed the reins of authority.

"Jack," she said one day to him, "it's not a bit of good going on like this. You don't improve at all. I shall take you to see Wharton Hood."

He protested a little at first, but gave in directly he perceived her heart was set upon the project. And they went. The eminent surgeon, after a careful examination, pronounced one of the smaller vertebræ of the dorsal column to be slightly dislocated, and with some severe manipulation wrenched it into its proper position again, and bade Jack get up and walk.

He laughed in his face, but nevertheless, to his astonishment, found himself able to obey. It appeared little short of a miracle.

"Now," said this apparent conjuror, "go your way. Begin by taking gentle exercise, then gradually increase it."

"And shall I be able to ride again?" asked Jack hopefully.

"Ride? Yes, of course you will. Still, if I were you, I should give myself a rest this winter; go abroad, or amuse yourself as best you can," and so saying he bowed the happy, grateful patient politely out of the room.

"Oh, Jack!" cried Kate, with the tears starting to her eyes as they hailed a hansom passing by, "I am so, so happy! I nave nothing left to wish for now."

His heart was too full for speech, a great joy and relief being almost as difficult to realise in their first intensity as a great sorrow.

"Jack," she continued softly, "I've got such a splendid plan in my head—a really perfectly glorious idea!"

"What is it, little woman?" he asked, smiling at her enthusiasm.

"Why, *we*," with a saucy, loving look, "will make a bolt of it now."

"A bolt of it, Kate? I don't quite understand."

"Don't you, Jack? I'll soon explain. The doctor said you were not to hunt this winter, so we'll go to India instead."

"Oh! so that's your glorious idea, is it, little woman? Why, I thought you did not approve of India—were afraid of jungle-fever, sunstrokes, snakes, spiders, and all the rest of it."

" So I was, Jack, but I'm not now."

" And what has inspired you with so much valour, eh ? "

" You, Jack," she said, nestling close up to him. " I could not bear the idea of your going so far away all by yourself, but now it is quite different."

" Oh, indeed, is it ? "

" Yes, altogether ; I don't seem to mind it in the least now. I suppose, Jack," she added archly, " that I should not be very, *very* much in your way ? "

" Awfully, you audacious little compliment-seeker. I've half a mind, if you say any more, to leave you behind."

But terrible as the threat sounded, it failed to produce the slighest effect. She continued her own train of thought quite serenely.

" Jack," she inquired, " how many rupees a week do you think I should be worth as maid-of-all-work—button-sewer, stocking-darner, breeches-patcher, tea-maker, and general tease to the establishment, eh ? "

" Why, just your weight in gold," he answered, putting a stop to any more such pertinent queries by a kiss, which shocked a virtuous old lady, who, walking down Bond street, was horrified at the depravity and questionable morals of the couple passing by in a hansom.

They remained in town till Ascot races were over, where, by-the-bye, now that money was no longer of paramount importance, Jack had a real good time, and then went to Nevis. There Kate made the acquaintance of Miss Polly Paton, and was surprised to find, directly she heard that that young lady had fallen back on a tall, raw-boned, red-headed youth of her own nationality, how any animosity she might have entertained towards her faded away, and she could view Miss Polly Paton's charms with complete complacency, and even banter Jack on the subject. As for Lord Nevis, he fell in love with his daughter-in-law from the first, and they remained fast allies ever after.

And on the still, fine August nights, when the purple hills, melted into a dim, soft haze, and the air was pure and calm, Jack and Kate would stroll out after dinner on the terraced walk in front of the Castle, where, in the field beneath them, they could see Snowflake's white quarters gleaming in the moonlight as he cropped the sweet, crisp grass. Ever and anon he caught a sound of the well-known master's voice as it rose and fell; then he paused, lifted up his noble, shaggy head and gave a low whinny of recognition. The brave hunter's old age is spent peacefully in comfortable and well-earned repose.

*　　　*　　　*　　　*　　　*

The stars shine out like countless jewels, vying with each other in point of brilliancy. The big moon, in the pale, pure sky, sheds her gentle lustre on the broad ocean, silvering each tiny wavelet as the phosphorescent waters, charged with their burden of minute insect life, glide from the keel of the P. and O. Company's good ship, "Sea King." All day the thermometer has stood at eighty-two degrees, but now the subtle charm of a tropical evening is upon Jack Clinker and his wife as they pace up and down the deck together, enjoying the comparatively cool night-air.

"What a jolly world it is to be sure," says Jack with a sigh of satisfaction, knocking away the ash from his half-finished cigar. And though the reflection may not be couched in terms of great originality, it exactly expresses at that moment the sentiments of husband and wife.

"Yes, Jack," Kate answered seriously, "we ought to be very grateful for all the blessings we have received."

They are fairly started now on their long-talked-of, much-contemplated cruise, and with perfect love and sympathy, hope, youth, faith, and health, seem, indeed, as if they had little left to wish for.

"Are you glad you came, Kate?" asks Jack after a while, during which they gaze at the beautiful scene before them in silence.

"Oh, Jack! how can you ask such a foolish question? I am always happy and content with you."

The shining stars and pale moon, the soft wind and rippling waters, all seem to murmur good luck, as the husband and wife stand side by side on deck at the commencement of their

Indian cruise. Dangers are no longer dangers to Kate, now that she and Jack are together, and her theories about man have vanished.

> And on her lover's arm she leant,
>   And round her waist she felt it fold,
> And far across the hills they went
>   In that new world which is the old.

HIGH-CLASS BOOKS OF REFERENCE.

Price	
10/6	**HOUSEHOLD MEDICINE:** A Guide to Good Health, Long Life, and the Proper Treatment of all Diseases and Ailments. Edited by GEORGE BLACK, M.B. Edin. Accurately Illustrated with 450 Engravings. Royal 8vo, cloth gilt, price 10s. 6d. ; half-calf, 16s. "Considerable is the care which Dr. Black has bestowed upon his work on Household Medicine. He has gone carefully and ably into all the subjects that can be included in such a volume. . . . *The work is worthy of study and attention, and likely to produce real good.*"—ATHENÆUM.

THE BOOK FOR AMATEURS IN CARPENTRY, &c.

7/6 — **EVERY MAN HIS OWN MECHANIC.** Being a Complete Guide for Amateurs in HOUSEHOLD CARPENTRY AND JOINERY, ORNAMENTAL AND CONSTRUCTIONAL CARPENTRY AND JOINERY, and HOUSEHOLD BUILDING, ART AND PRACTICE. With about 750 Illustrations of Tools, Processes, Buildings, &c. Demy 8vo, cloth gilt, price 7s. 6d. ; half-calf, 12s.

"There is a fund of solid information of every kind in the work before us, which entitles it to the proud distinction of being *a complete ' vade-mecum' of the subjects upon which it treats.*"—THE DAILY TELEGRAPH.

BEETON'S ILLUSTRATED,

7/6 — **DICTIONARY OF THE PHYSICAL SCIENCES.** With explanatory Engravings. Royal 8vo, cloth gilt, 7s. 6d.

The care and labour bestowed on this new work has rendered it a complete and trustworthy Encyclopædia on the subjects which it includes. The latest discoveries, improvements and changes have been noticed and duly chronicled in the various articles, and no pains have been spared to attain at once completeness, clearness, and accuracy in every part of the book.

BEETON'S ILLUSTRATED

7/6 — **DICTIONARY OF RELIGION, PHILOSOPHY, POLITICS, AND LAW.** With explanatory Woodcuts. Royal 8vo, cloth gilt, 7s. 6d.

The object in the preparation of this work has been to give a complete compendium of the essential points in the various subjects of which it treats. Each article is complete in itself, and the general scheme has been so arranged that information in any of the departments can be readily found.

TECHNICAL EDUCATION FOR THE PEOPLE.
The FIRST VOLUME OF WARD & LOCK'S

7/6 — **INDUSTRIAL SELF-INSTRUCTOR** in the leading branches of TECHNICAL SCIENCE and INDUSTRIAL ARTS and PROCESSES. With Coloured Plate, and about 650 Working Drawings, Designs, and Diagrams. Demy 4to, cloth gilt, 7s. 6d.

This New Work, devoted to the spread of Technical Education, appeals to all who take an interest in Manufactures and Construction, and in the progress and operation of practical Science. As a useful and interesting book for youths and those engaged in self-education, it cannot fail to recommend itself, while it will be found a book of useful reference to the general reader.

"Promises to be *one of the most useful books ever issued* from the British press."—FREEMAN'S JOURNAL.

WARD, LOCK & CO., London, Melbourne and New York.

THE
STANDARD GARDENING BOOKS.

Price	

Gardening, properly managed, is a source of income to thousands, and of healthful recreation to other thousands. Besides the gratification it affords, the inexhaustible field it opens up for observation and experiment commends its interesting practice to everyone possessed of a real English home.

7/6   **BEETON'S BOOK OF GARDEN MANAGEMENT.** Embracing all kinds of Information connected with Fruit, Flower, and Kitchen Garden Cultivation, Orchid Houses, &c., &c. Illustrated with Coloured Plates and numerous Engravings. Post 8vo, cloth gilt, price *7s. 6d.* ; or in half-calf, *10s. 6d.*

The directions in BEETON'S GARDEN MANAGEMENT *are conceived in a practical manner, and are, throughout the work, so simply given that none can fail to understand them. The numerous Illustrations show a large number of different kinds of Plants and Flowers, and assist in the identification of any doubtful specimen.*

3/6   **BEETON'S DICTIONARY OF EVERY-DAY GARDENING.** Constituting a Popular Cyclopædia of the Theory and Practice of Horticulture. Illustrated with Coloured Plates, made after Original Water Colour Drawings, and Woodcuts in the Text. Crown 8vo, cloth gilt, price *3s. 6d.*

2/6   **ALL ABOUT GARDENING.** Being a Popular Dictionary of Gardening, containing full and practical Instructions in the different Branches of Horticultural Science. Specially adapted to the capabilities and requirements of the Kitchen and Flower Garden at the Present Day. With Illustrations. Crown 8vo, cloth gilt, price *2s. 6d.*

1/—
1/6   **BEETON'S GARDENING BOOK.** Containing full and practical Instructions concerning general Gardening Operations, the Flower Garden, the Fruit Garden, the Kitchen Garden, Pests of the Garden, with a Monthly Calendar of Work to be done in the Garden throughout the Year. With Illustrations. Post 8vo, cloth, price *1s.* ; or cloth gilt, with Coloured Plates, price *1s. 6d.*

1/—   **KITCHEN AND FLOWER GARDENING FOR PLEASURE AND PROFIT.** An entirely New and Practical Guide to the Cultivation of Vegetables, Fruits, and Flowers. With upwards of 500 Engravings. Crown 8vo, boards, *1s.*

1/—   **GLENNY'S ILLUSTRATED GARDEN ALMANAC AND FLORISTS' DIRECTORY.** Published Annually, with Engravings of the Year's New Fruits, Flowers, and Vegetables, List of Novelties, Special Tables for Gardeners, Wrinkles for Gardeners, Alphabetical Lists of Florists, &c., &c. Demy 8vo, price *1s.*

1d.   **BEETON'S PENNY GARDENING BOOK.** Being a Calendar of Work to be done in the Flower, Fruit, and Kitchen Garden, together with Plain Directions for Growing all Useful Vegetables and most Flowers suited to adorn the Gardens and Homes of Cottagers. Price *1d.* ; post free, *1½d.*

WARD, LOCK & CO., London, Melbourne, and New York.

www.ingramcontent.com/pod-product-compliance
Lightning Source LLC
Chambersburg PA
CBHW052343110726
47901CB00005B/1345